INNOCENCE TAKEN

PRAY HE KILLS YOU QUICKLY

Victoria M. Patton

Dark Force Press – www.darkforcepress.com

Dark Force Press
www.darkforcepress.com

Publisher's Note: This is a work of fiction. Names, characters, places, and incidents are a product of the author's imagination. Locales and public names are sometimes used for atmospheric purposes. Any resemblance to actual people, living or dead, or to businesses, companies, events, institutions, or locales is completely coincidental.

Book Layout © 2015 BookDesignTemplates.com

Innocence Taken/ Victoria M. Patton. -- 1st ed.
ISBN 13: 978-1-946934-01-7
ISBN10: 1-946934-01-1

Library of Congress Control Number
2017936600

Cover Photo: Credit/Copyright Attribution: Lario Tus/Shutterstock
Editor: Mari Farthing, Oklahoma City, OK www.marifarthing.com

Dedication

I'm sitting here trying to write this heartfelt incredibly thoughtful dedication. Thanking all those people who helped with the completion of this book. I can hear my kids screaming at the top of their lungs and banging against the walls of their rooms. And I realize—this book would've been done six months ago if I could only get some damn peace and quiet.

To my husband; thanks for still sleeping with me even though you know what floats around in my head.

To my editor, Mari; you totally rock. I can't imagine going down this crazy road with anyone else by my side. Thank you.

AUTHOR'S NOTE

I know this is a work of fiction. But I want to extend my heartfelt sympathy to any parent that has lost a child to an act of senseless violence. At the time I wrote this book my daughter was thirteen and my son was twelve. I couldn't imagine the loss and heartbreak I would feel if something like this happened to one of them.

CONTENTS

CHAPTER ONE

He straddled her chest—for leverage. His hands tingled as his fingers curled tight. He had to apply just the right amount of pressure. Her jerky movements increased as he squeezed her neck. The girl's chest hardened under his weight, holding on to the last bit of air in her lungs. The beautiful smoky brown color of her eyes faded, replaced with a dull gray cloud that crept from one side to the other. A gleeful smile tugged at his mouth when red dots popped on the sclera. Her bladder released, announcing the end. His fingers uncurled from her neck, and a heavy sigh escaped his lips. He stared down at her as the stillness and quiet of the room engulfed him.

The corners of his mouth twitched as his trip down memory lane was interrupted. He heard the begging from the far side of the room. He stared at the girl he held captive. He'd chosen this one because she resembled HER, but she didn't live up to his expectations. None did anymore. He wondered if he would ever find another like HER. The one thing all these girls had in common, they all begged—eventually. He turned away and finished the preparations.

***

The thin mattress offered Becca little comfort. Leather straps bound her ankles and wrists to the bed. The slow melodic tune he whistled bounced off the cold concrete walls and pierced her eardrums like a hundred tiny pinpricks. Becca flinched at the sound of the chain hitting the floor as he hooked it to a ring in the ceiling. She closed her eyes. The man didn't care about her pleas. He had no plans to let her go.

She thought about how she got here. Becca's parents had given her a reprieve from her month-long grounding and allowed her to go to the mall with her two best friends. They chortled and bounced from store to store as they flirted with all the cute boys. The smell of freshly baked cookies and pretzels wafted through the air. Becca and her friends stopped for a snack and to chat with the boy behind the counter. That's where she met him, outside Cookie Crumbs. She bumped into him and then spent a few hours walking around the mall with him. Her stomach fluttered when he asked her to leave with him. What seemed like the best way to spend the remainder of her one day of freedom turned into the start of her worst nightmare.

Becca rocked back and forth muttering to herself. She watched him and prayed that he planned a quick death for her. As if he knew she stared at him, he glanced over his shoulder and winked at her. Becca shook uncontrollably, gasping for air as she clawed at the straps around her wrists.

Her eagerness to push her parents and their rules aside landed her here, in a cold, damp basement. Becca spent the last few months pushing as hard as she could to get away from her life. A life that seemed filled with endless chores and babysitting her little brother. As bad as she thought her life had been, these last few days were nothing short of Hell. She wanted that life back.

She cried out. "Oh God, please help me—please help me. Please, please help me." The sobs that choked her now burst out as her begging erupted into broken wails. The man turned and glowered at her, but she no longer cared. He planned to kill her. What did she care if he beat her before he did it? Becca leaned forward and wrapped her arms around her thighs. "I'm so sorry Mom, I'm so sorry." She hiccupped between the sobs. "I love you, Mom—Dad, I love you..." She repeated the mantra until her throat ached.

Becca saw the man turn and walk across the basement towards her. Her eyes widened; her prayers and pleas stopped. The man leered at her. She noticed the light as it bounced off the blade. Becca screamed.

CHAPTER TWO

Division Central Chicago, IL

Detective Damien Kaine dragged himself into the Vicious Crimes Unit. He plopped down at his desk, letting his arms hang limply. His athletic body sagged in his chair as he closed his eyes and leaned back. The air in the VCU hung thick and stale with the odor of burnt coffee and smelly socks. The stench made Damien's stomach roll. He blocked out the noise of the squad room and contemplated using his weapon on himself, the relief it might bring from the pounding in his head. Whiskey from the night before still coursed through his veins; flowing to the same beat that thumped inside his skull.

The morning had started off crappy when he threw his alarm clock against the wall. That made three this month. He could kick his own ass for letting Joe, his best friend and partner, talk him into going out last night. Damien had drunk too much, and today he paid the price. Hell, he'd been paying the price for several months now. Damien hadn't been a big drinker until the night he found Camilla in that hotel room. Since his canceled engagement, he and a bottle of whiskey spent a lot of time together.

He couldn't lay all the blame on Camilla, unfortunately. The job had taken its toll. The nightmares were never-ending. The dead never stayed dead. They liked to hang around in his dreams and bug the living shit out of him. Damien had considered turning in his resignation when Captain Mackey asked him to take the lieutenant's exam. Against his better judgment, he did. He passed. Now he felt stuck.

Damien opened one eye and checked his surroundings. VCU shared the seventh floor with the Electronics and Cyber Division. His eyes widened as he stared at the detectives behind the glass wall of the ECD enclosure. They never sat down. They danced and shimmied to an unheard rhythm. Damien imagined that beat came from the constant tapping of their fingers on computer keyboards. *Why do they move around so damn much?* His body shook at the disturbing sight.

Damien spun around in his chair. He ran a hand through his jet black hair, causing it to stand in a wavy mess. Detective Jenkins sat across from him. Jenkins' shaggy brown hair hung over the collar of his shirt. It swayed a little every time he tossed that damn tennis ball into the air, which he did whenever he got stuck in a case. Usually, it didn't bother Damien, but today it added an echo to the thumping in his head. Jenkins was with them last night. He drank just as much as Damien did, and yet he looked like he hadn't touched one drop.

Detective Jenkins smiled at Damien who glowered back through bloodshot eyes. "Kaine, you sure don't seem as happy as you did last night at Mulligan's." Reclining in his chair, he stretched his long legs to the far side of his desk. "This morning you resemble dead dog shit warmed over. Nice hair—Lieutenant."

Damien pressed his lips tight to keep from smiling. "Fuck you, Jenkins."

"Ouch," Jenkins said. "Not very nice."

Detective Joe Hagan entered the VCU looking upbeat and well-rested. "Yo, Kaine, how do you feel this morning? Did we keep you out past your bedtime last night?"

Damien watched as Joe's muscular legs carried his linebacker body with the stealth of a panther, his dark red hair still wet from his morning shower. Damien hung his head in his hands. "You're a detective, you figure it out."

Joe's eyes narrowed as a broad grin pushed his cheeks up high. "Shit man, you're a wuss. A few drinks and you think you're going to die. Not to mention you're a cranky fucker, Lieutenant."

If Joe only knew it wasn't just a hangover from last night. There haven't been too many nights he hasn't used the bottle to help him sleep. Damien ransacked his desk looking for something to quiet the drum core in his head. "*Stai zitto!*" He snapped at Joe as he rubbed his temples.

"Yeah, yeah. Shut the hell up. Like I don't hear that every day." Joe reached into his desk drawer. "Hey cranky pants, here you go." Joe smiled as he threw a bottle at him.

Damien glanced up as the bottle smacked him in the chest. "Seriously you stupid fuck, can't you throw?"

Joe roared with laughter. "Can't you catch?"

"Whatever." Damien popped four aspirin into his mouth and washed them down with a gulp of the liquid this place tried to pass off as coffee. Hell, most of the time it didn't even resemble liquid. He peered into his coffee mug. "What the hell is this? It can't be coffee."

"Nope, it's Chicago Sludge," Joe said.

"Well, that explains why it smells and tastes like shit." Damien laid his head back against the chair. "How the hell can you be so fucking chipper? You drank more than I did."

"Aye, well, we Irish know how to hold our liquor. Plus, Melanie helped me sweat out any extra alcohol. You should've considered taking her friend home with you. I bet you'd be in a much better mood."

After he had called off his engagement, Damien decided there would be no more women. Well, no more relationships with women. A few one-night stands here or there was all Damien cared to indulge in. And he never spent the entire night with a woman—that meant some kind of commitment. Damien shook his head. "Who the hell is Melanie, and why the hell would I want to take her friend home?"

Joe sat on the corner of Damien's desk. "Melanie is a new waitress at Mulligan's. You would know this if you went out with me more often. Her friend wanted to make sure you got home okay and help tuck you into bed." Joe winked as he took a sip of his soda. "Anyway, turns out Melanie has quite the talent for sucking alcohol right out of your system. Her talents don't end there either. Did I mention she was a gymnast in high school? Damn, the positions that girl can get into, un-fucking-believable."

Detective Jenkins threw his head back and howled. "Dang, Joe. Have you slept with the entire female staff at Mulligan's?"

Joe smiled. "No, only a select few."

"Kaine, Hagan—you two in my office now!" The captain's booming voice reverberated off the walls.

Damien jolted upright. He rubbed his eyes hoping the Visine had worked. That morning, his dark blue eyes were almost indigo due to the red ring that surrounded them. He looked like a demon. Which seemed appropriate since he felt like he was in Hell anyway. His headache had receded, but his stomach churned and not because of the whiskey. As a former Marine and the director of VCU, Captain Mackey's anger could be a dangerous weapon. His six foot four frame carried nothing but muscle, and his head held a lightning fast brain.

Damien and Joe entered Mackey's office. The captain loomed behind a massive gunmetal gray desk he had brought with him to the VCU. His square face and wide, strong jaw rose above broad shoulders. Even sitting down, the captain commanded respect.

Damien scowled at Joe as he took a handful of jellybeans from the captain's candy jar.

Joe frowned at Damien. "What? He wouldn't have the damn jar if he didn't want us to eat them." Joe popped a handful of the colorful beans into his mouth.

Captain Mackey halfway snarled at Joe. "You might find yourself a few digits shy of a full hand one of these days Hagan."

Joe managed a sheepish grin as he sat.

Damien settled into a chair. His stomach had soured, and the knot that formed now tightened like a coil.

Captain Mackey clasped his hands together on his chest. "First, before we get started," he stared at Damien, "good job on passing the lieutenant's exam. Your ceremony will take place when you return. Starting immediately, you get the benefits of your rank, its privileges, and pay. We also need to discuss your new assignment."

Damien shifted in his seat searching for relief that wouldn't come from moving his ass around. His mouth tightened, and his face became taut and rigid. *When he returns? New assignment? What the hell did that mean?* He studied Mackey, looking for reassurances.

The captain's lip twitched. "Quit worrying, you're staying here, and you and Joe will remain partners." Captain Mackey shook his head. "Even though you two are my best detectives, you both are pains in my ass. Try to pay attention to what I'm about to say.

"I have been toying with the idea of putting a Lieutenant in charge of this Division. These bureaucratic fuckwads finally got their act together and put this damn Unit in place. When I first took this position as head of the VCU, I wanted to get this Unit set up and operating right.

"Now that the Unit is working the way it should, I have more responsibilities that need to be handled. Chief Rosenthal expects certain things from the captains here at Division Central, but as with any other government bureaucracy, shit always rolls downhill. I need someone who can take over the daily responsibilities of this Unit but who can also carry his own caseload.

"I need to put someone in place to handle this group and the Detectives in it. I want someone I can trust. That's you, Damien." Captain

Mackey sat back and opened his desk drawer. "You'll report directly to me." Captain Mackey held a shield out for Damien. "Congratulations. You deserve this. You'd normally get your new shield at the ceremony, but since I must send you off on an assignment, I can't very well have you introduce yourself as a Lieutenant without a Lieutenant's shield."

Damien's mouth hung open as he stared at it. He never considered the possibility of being put in charge of the VCU. His hand shook when he reached for the shield with a sinking feeling in his gut—he wasn't sure if it was the whiskey remnants or that he didn't think he wanted the job.

The overhead light bounced off its shiny new surface. He ran his thumb across the front of the badge. Damien almost gave it back. It seemed to sizzle in his hand as if it knew he didn't deserve to hold it. His actions that night in the hotel should have put him behind bars.

He'd taken the exam thinking if he passed and made rank it would ignite his passion for the job again. He knew from early on he wanted to be a Homicide Detective. Damien felt responsible for helping these victims; they called out to him even in the silence of their death. What he saw daily made him question his own faith. Faith in God. Faith in the Catholic Church. Faith in his ability to uphold the very law he protected.

Damien glanced at Joe. One of the main things keeping him in this job, his friendship with Joe. He no longer knew if that was enough anymore. He forced a faint smile as he focused on the captain. "Wait, you're telling me I still have to be this knucklehead's partner?" He nodded towards Joe. "What happened to the perks of rank? This sounds more like punishment."

Joe punched him in the arm, the equivalent of a congratulatory hug. "Lieutenant or not, I'm the best damn partner you've ever had. Who else can put up with your Guinea ass?"

"Boys," Mackey growled. "You two are worse than my kids," he said as he pinched the bridge of his nose.

Damien started to say something smartass but saw that Captain Mackey's pleasant demeanor had changed. He opted to keep his mouth shut.

The captain sat up and placed his elbows on his desk. "A case has come in, and I want you guys to cover it." He opened the folder in front of him. "Locals who keep a strip of highway clean just outside Springfield, near Astoria, discovered the remains of a young girl."

Mackey's face flushed and his nostrils flared as he continued. "Crime

Scene Techs have been dispatched, and they'll deliver everything collected to the Forensic Lab in Springfield. You two need to get down there. You'll work out of the lab. Director Jones will provide you with whatever you need. Kaine, you need to keep me updated on what you find every step of the investigation. Shoot me a daily report. I don't want any surprises on this. As of now, this hasn't been picked up by the media. Let's keep it that way if possible." He leaned back in his chair and raised an eyebrow. His gaze locked on Joe like a laser. "Stay out of trouble."

"What?" Joe shrugged. He grabbed another handful of jellybeans. "We never get in trouble, Captain."

"Sure you don't." Captain Mackey said. "Now go! Get the hell out of here." He waved them out the door.

***

"Fuck me running," Joe whispered. He hated cases like this. He had a younger sister, and these cases always hit a little too close to home.

Damien cocked his head towards Joe. "This day is just getting better."

Detective Jenkins stopped working on his computer as Damien and Joe walked back into the pen. "The expressions on your faces tell me that wasn't a friendly sit down with the captain."

Joe slammed his desk drawer shut. "Fucking—A on that. A cleanup crew discovered a murdered girl on the side of the road."

Jenkins winced. "Oh shit, where?"

"Outside Springfield," Joe said.

"What about Coach, Kaine? I mean Lieutenant." Jenkins asked with a wild grin. "You need someone to watch him?"

Damien clipped his new shield to his belt. "Jenkins, you hate cats. Why do you want to take care of mine? Wait, I know why—it's the only pussy you'll be able to get."

Jenkins' lips twitched. "Man, did that sense of humor come with your shiny new badge?"

Damien's smile filled his face as he tapped the shield. "Sure did. Maybe they'll put one of these in a Cracker Jack box because we all know that's the only way your sorry ass is gonna get one." Damien grabbed his jacket and nodded at Jenkins. "Thanks for your offer, Jenks. My neighbor Mrs. C. will watch after him. She takes him to her place and spoils him rotten. He loves it."

"Well, anytime you need me to take him I will," Jenkins said.

Damien shrugged. Coach showed up one day at his condominium and never left. With his rotund belly, Coach lorded over the condo as if it were his personal kingdom. Oddly enough, Coach had never liked Camilla.

CHAPTER THREE

Damien threw his keys on the table near his front door and headed to the kitchen. He wanted to clean up his place before he packed and picked up Joe. He opened the fridge door, and within minutes, Coach strolled in. No matter where the cat hid in the condo when that refrigerator door opened, Coach magically appeared. Like a fat gargoyle, the cat perched himself next to Damien and beamed disappointment as he watched him clean it out.

"What?" He asked the cat as he scratched Coach's head. "I will be gone for a while, and this will stink by the time I come home. I'm damn sure your fat ass won't clean it out." *What the hell, I'm now talking to the cat like he can understand me.* Damien sighed. He scratched the cat's head. Coach head-butted Damien's thigh, then waddled back out on his beefy legs, no doubt in search of something soft and warm.

Forty minutes later, Damien finished cleaning and packing. He found Coach sprawled out on the sofa. The butterball opened one accusatory eye, questioning the interruption. "Mrs. C. will be by later to check on you. Try to lay off the kibbles, fat ass." Damien rubbed his belly and scratched under his chin. Coach stretched, yawned, and went back to sleep.

***

Joe had finished packing his bags and sat in the quiet of his large apartment, glancing around. On the top floor of a two-family home, the high ceilings gave it an open and airy feeling. The couple who owned the house lived on the first floor and traveled extensively. In the summer he enjoyed the back deck. It overlooked a park and a wooded area. He had furnished the space with oversized furniture that invited visitors to stay awhile. He'd dated this interior designer for a few months, and she tired of his bachelor pad décor and decorated it for him.

Joe smiled at the memory. The woman's talents didn't just stop at interior decorating. She had a very adventurous streak in bed. *Damn, I should call her when I get back.* He frowned. Joe remembered why he'd quit seeing her—she assumed that because they were intimate, they were on the verge of getting married. He'd come close to that once with a horrible ending. *Yeah, not gonna happen.* Plus, he had witnessed firsthand all the crap Damien had gone through with Camilla, no way. Joe didn't want that kind of relationship. Not for a long time. If ever. He wasn't the settling down type. He enjoyed dating a variety of women.

Joe looked at his watch. He leaned back in his chair closing his eyes. He tried to shove everything out of his mind, just relax and enjoy the silence. But he couldn't. His thoughts circled back to Damien.

Over the past few months, he'd watched his friend and partner transform into a different person. Ever since he broke it off with Camilla. Truth be known, Joe couldn't stand her. Joe knew from the start Damien shouldn't have been with her, but he kept his mouth shut. His friend had to figure it out on his own.

Damien never explained what caused their break up, and Joe never pressed for information. He figured Damien would tell him when he felt ready. Now with this case and a three-hour ride ahead of them, Joe might broach the subject. He knew his friend well enough to know a break up wouldn't make him act this way. There had to be something else.

Joe jumped at the sound of Damien's horn. "Showtime," he said with one last look around his place. Joe bounded down the stairs and heaved his two bags into the back of the SUV, climbed into the passenger seat, and moved it back as far as he could.

Joe stretched out his long legs. "You ready for this?"

"No, but what choice do we have?"

A broad grin formed across Joe's face. "How's your headache?"

Damien smirked. "Ha ha. You're such a friggin hoot. I doubt you'd have been laughing if my head had exploded and you'd had to clean my brain matter off the walls of VCU."

Van Halen's *Jump* rang out from Damien's phone. The dash's video screen displayed a phone number of a person he had no desire to speak with, especially with Joe sitting right next to him. "Oh crap, just take my gun and shoot me." Damien dragged his hand through his hair pulling on the ends. "Yeah, Kaine here."

"Hey baby, how're you doing?"

"Camilla, I'm not your fucking baby. Why the hell do you keep calling me?"

"I wanted to know how things are going and see if you wanted to get together this week."

Her raspy voice used to sound sexy to him. Now, it made Damien want to jab a stick in his ear. Damien clenched his jaw. "Camilla, I told you, I don't want to see you again, ever. What part of that conversation did you not understand?"

"Come on Damien, I miss you. I want another chance. I'm sorry. You know I love you. Please, let's get together and talk."

Damien smacked his hand against the steering wheel. "You have a problem understanding me. I do not want to see or speak to you at all! *Capisci?*"

"Please Damien, I made a mistake. How long are you going to hold it against me? Things snowballed, and I did things I shouldn't have done. Please, give me—give us another chance."

"Are you fucking kidding me? A mistake? You call banging some suit in your office, repeatedly, a mistake? You're fucking delusional. It's been over for almost a year. It will stay that way. Hell, it had been over long before I threw your crap out of the condo. You screwed up Camilla! Now you can live with the fucking consequences!"

"Pleeease Damien, I'm sor–"

Damien disconnected the call. "Well, shit, shit, shit! What a fucking miserable day."

Joe's eyes bulged, and his jaw hung to his lap. "You didn't tell me she cheated on you."

"No, I didn't," Damien said with a little more venom than he intended. "I told no one except my Dad, and that was hard enough. She cheated several times and lied about all sorts of shit. I wanted her out of my life." Damien glanced over at Joe. "I wanted no one, you included, telling me 'I told you so.'"

Joe scowled. "Hey, I might have said she wasn't the right girl for you, but I never would have rubbed it in your face. Especially if I had known, she cheated on you. As your Italian tongue would say, she's a *stupida cagna*, and you deserve so much better."

Damien ran his hand over his face. "Yeah, she is a stupid bitch. So, now you know." He turned and stared out the window. He looked back at Joe, "Man, it never occurred to me she would do something like that. I gave her everything she wanted. Treated her like a damn queen. I loved her. Loved her more than I thought I could ever love a woman." Damien had told no one about how he found out Camilla was cheating on him, with who, or what had happened that night in the hotel room.

Joe punched him on the shoulder. "Better it happened now rather than after you'd married her." He grinned at Damien. "Next time save yourself the hassle and listen to what I say. You know I always watch out for you."

He gave Joe an easy smile. "Yeah, next time I will." The knot in Damien's stomach tightened just a little more. Joe had proven himself a damn good friend and partner, and he deserved to know the whole truth.

Joe pulled out his notepad. "So, about this case, Astoria is a small community with roughly a couple thousand in population. Seems like nothing but farm country in that area. The stretch of Highway 24 where they discovered the girl has nothing but pastures surrounding it. No buildings, no houses, no nothing. I'm leaning towards dumpsite only."

Damien took a swig of soda. He glanced at the can. Joe had gotten him hooked on this diet soda. Everyone at Central gave them hell for it too. "Since the CST's will be back at the lab before we get to town, I say we go there first. We can hit the dumpsite later if we need to."

Joe patted his stomach. "Sounds good. Now swing through someplace and let's get some food."

"You're always hungry. Didn't you eat breakfast like two hours ago?"

"Sure, key phrase—hours ago. I took an enormous dump at the house before you got there. Now I'm hungry again."

"Seriously, dude why do you tell me these things? I don't need to know about your bowel movements. You know you're going to end up being a *vacca grassa*—fat cow—if you don't watch it." Damien chuckled as Joe gave him the finger.

CHAPTER FOUR

He sat and watched her apartment. Waiting. He looked at his watch, anytime now, he thought. He had first seen her a few weeks back, at the outdoor market he sometimes delivered to. He couldn't believe it when he saw her either. She looked like she could pass as HER older sister. Her short and very curvy build was a little different than what he normally went for. God, she was beautiful, though. He had been so close to her in the parking lot, just a few feet away. He almost grabbed her then, but the timing wasn't right. However, he followed her home that day. Knowing where she lived had allowed him to follow her regularly.

He saw her again at the mall, the day he took Becca. He bumped into her and couldn't believe it was her. He'd considered pursuing her, but it had been too hard to approach her. He didn't think she would fall for the same lines he used on the others. After all, she wasn't as young as they were. He'd come close to following and taking her that day, but then he saw Becca. More his type and much easier prey.

His phone rang. "Yeah, what's wrong now?" He barked into the phone. "Well, what the hell am I paying you for? How the hell should I know? They're fucking farm animals." He laughed. "No shit. You're right about that. They are only good for cooking. Get over there and get them. Tell the old man we keep trying to keep them from getting out. I don't think he's too pissed. He has never complained formally. I'm about an hour from home. I should be there soon." He threw his phone in the passenger seat.

He reached for the ignition about to start his truck when she came out. He had a direct line of sight to her. She locked her door and headed down the walkway. She always parked in front of her apartment.

He watched as she threw her bags into her car. She wore a pink shirt and her dark brown hair contrasted nicely against it. For a moment, she paused at the driver's side before she got in. His heart raced as she looked in his direction. He sunk in his seat. He was sure she couldn't see him, but what if she did? She might remember him. He cursed himself. This was a stupid idea. He didn't do stupid. He hated stupid. But God, he wanted her.

She got into her car and drove off. He almost thought about following her, but he had to get back to the farm. That's okay, he thought. He knew where she liked to go and knew where she lived. He knew where she worked too, but that didn't scare him. He would just make sure he took her far away from her office.

CHAPTER FIVE

Forensic Lab

The Springfield Forensic Laboratory was comprised of several buildings connected by a series of underground tunnels; making it easy for employees to travel between the buildings on the large compound. Damien drove down the winding drive to the main building, which housed DNA, Trace, Autopsy, and the Administrative offices.

A stunning brunette greeted them at the front desk. Joe gave Damien a sly smile and sauntered over to her. She wore a name tag centered above one perfectly shaped breast. He leaned in close to her and lowered his voice. "Hey, there—Taylor Reese. I'm Detective Joe Hagan and this," he nodded towards his right, "is Lieutenant Damien Kaine. We're from Division Central. We need to speak with Director Jones. Is he available?" Joe smiled one of his sexiest smiles at her.

"Sure, let me call back there. One moment please." Her shaky finger punched a few numbers on the keypad. "Jamie, the two Detectives from Chicago are here to meet with the director. No, they're standing right here. Okay, I'll let them know. What? Oh yeah, no I don't know who he is. I've seen him at that track by the outdoor mall I go to. No. First I will ask Matt to look into it. Yes. I will tell the director if it keeps happening. Okay, I will. Thanks, Jamie." Taylor smiled at Joe. She could feel her cheeks burn as she stared at him. "The director will be with you in a moment," she said.

Damien and Joe stepped away from the desk. Damien hung his head to hide his smile. "Dude quit gawking at her. Can't you see you're making her nervous?"

Joe frowned at Damien. "I'm not making her nervous," Joe said.

Damien chuckled. "Right. She can't even make eye contact with you. Look at yourself, you're drooling right now. Just remember why we are here, Casanova. You need to keep your head on straight."

A wicked grin spread across Joe's face. "Jealous, huh?"

"Yeah, you got me. I'm jealous."

***

"Lieutenant Kaine and Detective Hagan," Director Jones said as he walked towards them. He shook both of their hands and guided them to the doors he had come through. Sliding a key card through the security lock, the light on the keypad flashed green.

Director Jones pushed open the heavy metal doors and led them down a corridor. "I spoke with Captain Mackey, not ten minutes ago. I'm glad to have you two here."

Damien liked the director right off. He had a lean body carried by legs with a long smooth stride. He looked as if he glided down the hallway with minimum effort. Unlike Captain Mackey, Director Jones wore his authority casually. Damien had no doubt that the director's casual demeanor left no room for his authority to be questioned, under any circumstances.

Director Jones stopped in front of an empty room. "As you can see, we set up a whiteboard and two laptops for you. If you find you need anything else, let me know or ask Taylor up front. She always knows how to reach me. Have you checked into a hotel yet?" Jones continued down the hallway.

"No. Not yet," Damien said. "We passed a couple on our way. We figured we'd get one of those after we finished up here."

"Don't worry about the arrangements. I'll tell Taylor to get you two rooms at the Holiday Inn down the street. That way you can stay here as long as you need to."

"Sounds good. Thanks," Damien said. "What do we have?"

"The CSTs got back about an hour ago. The ME is already in autopsy with the body. We're checking her fingerprints now. We're also tracking down some missing person reports. The girl seems about seventeen or eighteen. The killer didn't cut her face, but it has some hellacious bruising."

As they reached another set of metal doors, Director Jones stopped and hung his head. "I've seen some pretty nasty crap in my day, but this—it's one of the worst. He cut her into pieces and then put her body parts in a heavy-duty plastic bag."

Director Jones used his keycard to unlock the door. A hiss escaped as the door swung open. The heavy scent of disinfectant wafted out. Classic soul music emanated from a room at the end of the corridor. They walked down the long dimly lit hallway. With every two or three steps, an overhead fluorescent bulb clicked on, creating eerie shadows on the walls. Damien sensed those shadows were the dead that traveled through these doors.

"This is Dr. Langley, our Medical Examiner," Jones said.

Damien stepped forward. Doctor Langley's blond hair glistened under the glare of the lights. A bright blue lab coat draped his broad shoulders. He had to be in his fifties with the body of a much younger man.

Hunched over a steel slab, Doctor Langley smiled at the two Detectives. "Music off. Sorry, I play my music a little too loud. Detectives, pleased to meet you. I wish we were meeting under better circumstances." His gaze shifted to the table in front of him.

"Same here Doc. Do you have anything yet?" Damien asked, moving up to the table. All the air in his lungs hissed out.

Joe followed Damien and took two steps closer to the table. "Fucking bloody hell!" His Irish lilt heavier than usual.

The remains of a once beautiful young girl lay before them. The girl's hair, a matted mess of tangles and dried blood. Her head clung to her torso by a few tethers of tendons, ligaments, and skin. It laid on its side, and her dull cloudy eyes glared at Damien and Joe. Her head couldn't even rest in the U-shaped headrest most of the dead had the privilege of using.

Dr. Langley rested a hand on the top of the girl's head with the tenderness a loving father might do as he watched his daughter sleep. "Well, as you can see, we're having trouble stabilizing her head. The killer cut her arms off at the shoulders and then separated them at the elbows. He then removed her legs at the thighs and separated them at the knees."

The ME exhaled a long heavy breath. "Upon preliminary findings, it appears she suffered repeated sexual assaults, both vaginal and anal. The tearing indicates severe trauma. From the destruction of the tissue, I would say he used some kind of instrument at some point."

Joe dragged his hand down his face. "Damn."

Damien stared down at the young girl. Above one of her breasts, there appeared to be a deep indentation. "Doctor Langley, are those bite marks on her chest?"

The Doctor glanced up at Damien's stoic face. "Yes, Lieutenant. There are several bite marks on her breasts and her shoulder area. We will cast those for future identification of our suspect. Bite marks are as individual as fingerprints. They can be tricky to cast, but when done properly it will stand up in court. However, something that isn't tricky to do is figure out what she ate last." Dr. Langley held a small container filled with a cloudy liquid. "Once I analyze this, her stomach contents— or lack thereof. It seems he gave her limited food and fluids while he held her."

Dr. Langley rolled his shoulders and twisted his head from side to side, causing Joe to wince at the cracking sound. "We took samples for DNA. We could get a hit if her parents put her in the system. Last year during Abduction Awareness Week, we made DNA/Fingerprint kits available to every school-age child's parents. We had widespread participation in the program. There is a good chance we can identify her quickly."

Damien clutched the St. Michael medal he wore around his neck. His chest constricted. The trauma this innocent girl suffered sickened him. He swallowed the lump in his throat and pushed down the bile trying to work its way out.

***

Just outside the conference room door, Damien stood with Joe and the director. Jones' jaw clenched. "One hell of a way to start the week. I want this bastard. I have a fourteen-year-old daughter. This hits too close to home."

Damien spun around at the sound of footsteps jogging towards them. A young man who looked barely twenty-one came down the hall. "Sir, we have the identity of the young girl. Rebecca 'Becca' Martin through her fingerprints. The parents registered both their kids last year with those DNA/Fingerprint kits. She went missing from a mall in Decatur last Saturday afternoon. Her family lives in Blue Mound, thirty-five miles up Interstate 72."

Jones nodded. "Good job Matt. Let DNA know she's in the system." Jones glanced at Joe and Damien. "We placed those cards and samples in a different catalog for easy indexing. When we have a missing child, time is of the essence." Jones watched the young man as he headed back to his work area. "Well, I don't envy your next stop, family notifications suck." He handed them several of his business cards. "You met Matt Dillard, one of our lab techs. He'll assist you here in the lab. If you need him to gather information on the computer or get anything for you, just contact him."

Director Jones handed one of Matt's cards to Damien. "You two, don't forget to get your ID badges at the desk. It'll allow you twenty-four-hour access to the lab while you're here. Give me your cards; I'll pass them on to Matt." He took the cards from Damien and Joe and headed down the hallway.

Damien studied his watch as if it gave him instructions. "It's now four p.m. What do you say we go over to the hotel, drop our stuff off and then head up to Blue Mound? I could use a few minutes before we tell the parents about their daughter. Let's also call the local Sheriff's office and make sure we can stop by and speak with him before we head out to the parent's house. I'm hoping he has something that will help us in this case."

"Sounds good. I wouldn't mind a few minutes to clear my head, and maybe throw up my lunch." Joe said.

CHAPTER SIX

Just outside Springfield

He finished his last delivery and stopped off at a little diner on his way back home. Two booths down from him a girl sat with a few of her friends. Her eyes darted quickly between him and the kids at her table. He smiled at her every time he caught her stare.

He thought of Becca. He hadn't planned on getting rid of her so hastily, but he had become bored with her. Every once in a while, a girl doesn't live up to his expectations. He'd also tired of burying them on his property. A few of the previous girls he'd dumped far away, scattered in various areas. Now dumping them was not only easier, but it made the game more fun. More exciting.

He also hadn't planned to take another girl this close to Becca. However, eating his dinner, his attention kept coming back to this new girl. She looked like a younger version of HER. The girl sitting across from him had the same color hair and eyes.

She couldn't keep eye contact. He liked the way she blushed. She snuck glances his way while she played with her hair. Sometimes twirling it around her finger, sometimes she pushed a loose strand behind her ear. Just the kind of girl he liked.

He needed to separate her from her friends like a lion might separate his prey from the pack. Catching her eyes one last time he winked at her. Leaving his booth, he headed towards the restrooms. As much as he wanted her, he figured he would have to let this one go. He couldn't risk her friends seeing and recognizing him.

He exited the restroom and stopped. "Excuse me. I didn't expect anyone to be here." He said to the young girl.

She bit her lip as she looked down at her feet. "Hey," she said. "I'm Tiffany." She pushed a strand of hair out of her face and dropped one of her books.

He watched her fumble around, her jerky movements oddly cute. He leaned in to smell her fruity perfume. "Hello, Tiffany, nice to meet you. Are you hanging out with your friends?"

"Yeah, we met to study for a test tomorrow in math. I'm getting ready to leave now, but I wanted to say hi."

He reached out and stroked her upper arm. "Well—Tiffany, I hope you do well on your test." He headed for the door. He tucked his head towards his chest and pulled the bill of his baseball cap down.

"Have a good night." Betty, the waitress, called out to him.

He waved to her and continued out the door. He glanced back over his shoulder and noticed Tiffany moved towards a vehicle parked on the passenger side of his truck. A thin sneer crept across his face. He strolled around his vehicle. Pretending to inspect one of his tires, he bent down right as a large delivery truck drove by on its way out of the parking lot.

He watched over his shoulder as the young girl unlocked her car door. She placed her schoolbooks on the back seat, and when she closed the car door, they were face to face.

Tiffany gasped as she shuffled back, bumping into her vehicle. "Hey, what are you doing here?"

"I needed to check my tires before I got on the road. So where do you live?" He leaned against her car keeping his head low.

She gave him a sweet smile. "Chatham. Not too far from here."

He pushed a piece of her hair out of her face. "I need to do one last delivery just up the road. I can come back past here. Would you like to take a ride with me? We can talk more and maybe make plans to get together. I can return you back here. I promise." He smiled, then pretended to pout as he crossed his heart.

She blushed and giggled. She glanced around, "sure, but I need to be back in an hour—okay?"

His smile filled his entire face. He reached over, opened the passenger door to his truck, and helped her climb up. "Absolutely." He got into the driver's seat, pulled out of the parking lot, and turned in the opposite direction.

***

Something seemed off, but Tiffany's revelation came too late. She clutched her purse in a death grip. Her body trembled. "You said you had a delivery. Where are we going? I have to get back to my car."

He gave her a stony glare. "Tiffany, Tiffany, Tiffany. Didn't your mother ever tell you not to get into cars with strangers?"

Terror slammed into her. Her throat burned as the snack she had earlier *made its way back up. Tiffany yanked on the door handle pushing against it with all her weight. It didn't budge. She fumbled in her purse and tried to get her phone out. It fell to the floor. She yanked on her seatbelt trying to reach her phone. It locked her into place. "Why are you doing this? Please just let me out—I won't say anything. I want to go home! Please let me go!"*

He cocked his head to one side. "Well—I can't do that Tiff."

Tiffany panted. "Please let me go, please! I want to go home." Tears streamed down her face. She begged and pleaded as she continued to yank on the seatbelt and the door.

He gave her a mocking frown. His fist collided with the side of her head. The force of the blow knocked her into the window. Tiffany slumped to the side. He pulled over to the edge of the road and grabbed her phone off the floor. He turned it off and removed the battery. He whistled the rest of the way home.

CHAPTER SEVEN

Blue Mound, IL

Damien and Joe shook the chief's hand. "Chief Reynolds, thanks for seeing us so late in the day."

The chief laid a hand on his heart then gestured to the two men. "Hey, it's my pleasure. Anything I can do to help you guys while you're working this case. I don't have the resources or the manpower to do a proper investigation. My men and I will provide you with any help you need while you're here in this area." The chief handed Damien a flat file. "I made a copy of the file for you. Sorry, there isn't much in there to go on. It's all over the scanners that the CSTs recovered a body out by Astoria, is it Rebecca?"

Damien nodded. "Yes sir, it is. Thanks for the file, but I want to ask you a few more questions."

The chief's shoulder's sagged. "Shit!" With a somber look on his face, he let out a heavy sigh. "Sure, anything I can do to help."

"Do you have any reports of stalking or girls who reported being followed or called, anything at all like that?" Damien asked.

"No. Nothing of that nature. I went through our records after Rebecca disappeared. In our area, we haven't had any other girls go missing. We haven't had a murder in these parts for some time. I'm sorry I don't have anything to help you out with your investigation."

"Do you know anything about the young girl? Did she get into any trouble, hang around with a rough crowd? Anything at all that may point to someone?" Damien asked.

The chief placed his elbows on the desk. "I've known the Martins for a long time. Becca didn't get into any real trouble. She stayed out past curfew a few times and didn't always want to do her homework. Show me a teenager who does. She started to show a rebellious streak now and then. That's really about it." The chief rubbed his face. His eyes were wet. "This will hit Abigail and Jeff hard. It's the thought of what this will do to Tommy, Rebecca's little brother that has kept me up at night since she went missing. That boy idolized his sister."

***

Damien drove through a neighborhood lined with tall trees wrapped in pink ribbons. Any other time the stark contrast between the dark wood and pale pink color would be charming. Now it represented a nightmare unfolding for these parents. "Damn, will you look at all these trees?" Damien glanced from one side of the street to the other. "How long do you think it took them to put these ribbons up? Did you notice all the missing person fliers? Shit Joe, telling them their daughter isn't coming home when they are living on a few fliers of hope sucks. *Cristo ci aiuterà.*" Damien whispered as he made the sign of the cross.

Joe read over the file from the chief. "Christ is going to have to do a lot of helping because according to the file we don't have jack shit to go on. The Martins blanketed the surrounding area with missing person posters and searched for any sign of Becca since the day she didn't come home from the mall. No one had any solid information, even the two girls who were with her."

Damien pulled alongside the curb in front of a quaint two-story house. Randomly scattered patches of green littered the surrounding lawns.

Joe reached for the door. "Let's get this over with."

"I hate this part of the job. What do you say to a parent who lost their teenage daughter? And how the hell do we to tell them the details of what their daughter endured before this asshole killed her?" Damien's phone pinged as they headed up the walkway. "It's Matt, the DNA matched," he said. *No chance of a mistake,* he thought. Rebecca Martin lay in pieces at the Springfield lab.

***

A lovely young woman answered the door. "Yes, may I help you?"

Damien noticed the resemblance as he stared at the attractive woman. The eyes. Even in death, Rebecca's eyes were intense, and her mother's held the same intensity. He and Joe held out their badges as they introduced themselves. Within an instant, her gaze went from welcoming to fearful. "Mrs. Martin, I'm Lieutenant Damien Kaine, and this is Detective Joe Hagan, we're with the VCU out of Division Central. We're here to speak to you about your daughter Rebecca, may we come in?"

The color drained from her tense face. She yelled for her husband. "Jeff, Jeff hurry it's the police, they're here about Rebecca." She stepped back and gestured for them to enter.

A young boy about ten years old rushed down the stairs. Skipping several at a time. "Mom, who's at the door?"

Mrs. Martin spun around. Her face softened. "Tommy, go to your room, honey. Close your door and don't come down until I call you, okay sweetie?" Her voice trembled and tears floated near the surface of her eyes. As Tommy turned to leave, Mrs. Martin reached out and pulled him to her chest. She hugged him tight and kissed the top of his head. Then pushed him towards the stairs. "Go now, Tommy." She faced the Detectives. "Please, have a seat."

Mr. Martin entered the room. At some point, he tried to tuck in his rumpled shirt but gave up halfway through the process. He extended his hand. "I'm Jeff Martin, and you've met my wife, Abigail. Do you have any news for us about our daughter Rebecca? We put up fliers, we called everyone we know to pass out fliers, and we ran a notice in the local paper out of Decatur. Are you here for more information? Whatever you need, we want her home. Please." Mr. Martin dragged his hand through his short cropped hair as he sucked in air. His last word carried the weight of his sorrow.

Their fear hit Damien like a heat wave from a blast furnace. The acid in his stomach burned its way up. He swallowed and glanced from one parent to the other. "Mr. and Mrs. Martin, I'm so sorry to inform you that we recovered your daughter's remains early this morning."

A sound like that of an injured animal bellowed out of Mrs. Martin. White-knuckled hands clung to her husband's arm. "No, no, no, no, no, you made a mistake." She stared at her husband. "Tell them, Jeff, tell them they're wrong!" She glared at the Detectives. "She has run off with friends, and she doesn't want to get into trouble. No, you're wrong! You're mistaken!"

Mr. Martin squeezed his wife's hand. Tears swam in his eyes. His lips trembled. "Are you sure it's our Becca? Could there be a mistake? Maybe you found someone else's daughter."

Damien pursed his lips together and shook his head. "No, sir. There hasn't been a mistake. We confirmed her identity from DNA and finger-prints. Last year you filed DNA/Fingerprint kits on both your children."

Mrs. Martin covered her mouth with her hand. "No, no, no," she whispered.

"I can't even begin to understand how horrible this news must be, but if you think you're up to it, we need to ask you a few questions. Every bit of information we can gather will help us find who did this to Rebecca. Do you think you can answer a few questions for us?" Damien asked.

Mrs. Martin rocked back and forth on the sofa and wept. She babbled incoherently. Mr. Martin took a deep breath. The tears that swam near the surface spilled over and ran down his cheeks. "I'll try to answer what I can."

"First," Damien said, "we know Becca went to the mall with two friends. Can you tell me Becca's movements that day?" Damien had this information, but he wanted to hear it from the parents. Sometimes recounting events helped bring more information to light.

Damien waited for Mr. Martin to answer his question. The man's eyes held a pain Damien had yet to experience.

Mr. Martin sucked in a breath and hissed it out. "She went to the mall in Decatur with Melissa Lewis and Jamie Watkins this past Saturday afternoon. They both live down the street. Umm, one of the girls drove. They had been at the mall for a few hours before Melissa and Jamie noticed Becca talking to a guy. The girls couldn't tell for sure but the impression they got—he seemed to be in his early twenties—maybe. They figured he attended the local university. A lot of college kids go and hang out at the mall, especially after football games."

Jeff Martin took a few deep breaths and pinched the bridge of his nose. It didn't stymy the tears. His voice trembled as he spoke. "Melissa and Jamie wanted to go check out a sale, and Becca didn't want to leave the guy. She told them she would meet up with them in a few minutes. Becca never showed up."

Martin's breath hiccupped. "The girls searched everywhere. They had to leave and assumed she would get home." He rubbed the back of his neck. "In the past, Becca had lied about where she would be. She'd come home late, well past curfew. That's why we grounded her in the first place. She had finished her punishment on Saturday. She hadn't been to the mall for about a month."

Abigail Martin continued to rock back and forth, her arms wrapped tightly around her chest. She sobbed, making it hard for her to catch her breath. Jeff Martin put his arm around his wife.

Joe spoke softly. "Mr. Martin, did your daughter get any phone calls which might have led you to think she had a particular friend, a boyfriend maybe?"

Mr. Martin tilted his head down and stared at his lap. "No. She didn't have a boyfriend. We didn't allow her to date. I don't know if she had known the boy at the mall or not."

Damien glanced up from his notepad. "Does she have an email account or use social media sites?"

"No," the father said flatly. "We didn't allow either. Last year a friend sent out an invite on one of the social media sites for a party. Half the town showed up as well as a bunch of kids from Decatur. It was a mess." He sobbed now. Unable to control it.

Abigail Martin clasped her hands in her lap. Her voice scarcely above a whisper. "We did our best to keep her protected. She said the house felt like a prison and we had become the wardens. We tried to explain to her if she got her chores done, did her homework, and didn't lie to us about her whereabouts, we would give her more privileges." Abigail Martin's jaw clenched. "All those arguments. All that time wasted. Now she's gone, my baby girl, she's gone! My God, what am I supposed to do now?" She grabbed her husband and buried her face in his chest.

Damien's throat tightened. He had to get out. He handed Mr. Martin a card for Director Jones. "Mr. Martin, call the Forensic Lab, and they can tell you when the funeral home can pick up Rebecca."

On the way out the door, Damien glanced over his shoulder and noticed that the ten-year-old brother sat at the top of the stairs. Tears streamed down his face and in his arms, he clutched a stuffed pink teddy bear.

***

The sadness that surrounded the Martin's followed Damien and Joe like a thick fog as they continued on to Melissa Lewis and Jamie Watkins' houses. According to both girls, their suspect had been a gorgeous guy who seemed into Becca. The girls described the suspect as average height, but they weren't sure. He wore blue jeans and work boots of some kind, nothing fancy though. A generic jacket that may have had a logo on it, but again, they weren't sure. He wore a baseball hat, possible logo but they couldn't remember.

The only description they were sure of—his eyes. He had ice blue eyes that were dreamy. *Whatever the hell dreamy meant.* Damien had thought. They mentioned that he seemed familiar to them, but they couldn't place it. Damien left cards with the parents and explained to them if the girls had anything else to add to call him, no matter how small the detail might seem.

At the vehicle, Joe looked up at the cloudless night sky and inhaled the fresh, crisp air. For mid-September, the temperatures were perfect. "How many families have we notified over the years, hundreds?"

"Too damn many," Damien said as he unlocked the SUV. "Both those girls feel responsible. I don't think they'll be able to get through the guilt without extensive counseling. They'll carry this with them for a long time."

Joe slammed the door. He took a few deep breaths trying to calm the anger and frustration that burned in his gut. "Well, crap," he hissed out. "We got nothing to go on. A dead girl and two traumatized friends who blame themselves. They can't tell us diddly squat. They remember a handsome lad, with generic clothes and dreamy fucking eyes. Wow! Let's put out the APB now. Good-looking young mate, watch for blood on his hands, and he'll stink because he's a bloody piece of shit."

CHAPTER EIGHT

He carried Tiffany down the stairs with little resistance. He secured her hands and legs to the bed. He grabbed a sharp pair of shears from a table at the far end of the room.

Tiffany's eyes widened her lip and chin trembled. "What—what are you doing? Stop—please, please—stop," she pleaded.

"We have to get these clothes off. They're in my way." Methodically he cut away her clothes. She lay there in her panties and bra. Her breath burst in and out of her chest. The front of her bra had a tiny piece of fabric holding it together. He slid the shears under the thin material and snipped it in half.

"Pop." He chuckled at his own sound effect. He swallowed several times and licked his lips at the sight of her breasts. He reached down and squeezed one. It was soft and yet firm, like an overfilled water balloon.

The girl recoiled at his touch. Her futile attempts at escape made him snort. He offered a bemused smile as he grabbed her hands and pulled her arms over her head. He adjusted the strap, taking out the slack. His pulse increased as he tightened each of the straps on her ankles. He positioned himself on the bed. "Listen, you can scream all you want. No one will hear you."

A shrill scream filled the basement.

***

Tiffany clamped her eyes shut and let a home movie play in her mind. She saw her Mom and Dad as they stood on the deck in her backyard. Her little brother and sister chased her dog Trudy. The surrounding air swirled with the odor of hamburgers and hot dogs on the grill.

When he finished, Tiffany snapped back from the drift. Her brain scrambled to understand what had just happened. She blinked, unable to comprehend what he said to her. His voice sounded muffled and far away. The restraints around her wrists and ankles loosened a little, and the scratchy fabric of a blanket rubbed against her skin. His heavy boots echoed off the concrete as he clomped up the stairs. Tiffany's body stiffened when the door to the basement slammed shut. Sobs trapped in her throat made their way out as tears flowed down her cheeks. He had taken her innocence. She would not allow him to take her faith. She prayed the Lord's Prayer, seeking comfort in the only thing she had left.

CHAPTER NINE

Holiday Inn, Springfield IL

Joe set the pizza and the diet soda on the table in Damien's sitting area of his hotel room. "Oh man, what a long, shitty day. Right now, we don't know shit about this killer. We know he's handsome with dark hair and he's of average height. We know—*rud ar bith*—nothing. Not just nothing but fucking nothing!"

Damien sank down in one of the oversized chairs and closed his eyes. "I keep thinking of little Tommy Martin. Did you see him sitting at the top of the stairs? He held a pink teddy bear. Damn. I'm so glad we didn't tell the parents any of the details. Tommy would've heard all of it, and it would have given him nightmares."

Damien guzzled his diet soda. "Hey," he motioned to Joe, "make sure the door between our rooms is open. That way if we get a call I don't have to bang on the door."

Joe gave him a cheeky grin. "You just want to sneak a peek at me, don't you? You can admit it."

Damien waved his hand in the air. "Seriously? You with the SID— Small Irish Dick. What exactly do I want to peek at? Your fat ass?"

Joe barked out a laugh. "Well you're a bit of a *gobshite,* and I happened to be the only one willing to be your partner. We drew straws, you know. Long ago. I obviously got the short one."

Damien smiled as he filled his plate with pizza. Taking a bite, he tried to relax.

Joe checked his watch. "Well, at least, it's early. If you call nine early. Hopefully, we can get one good night of sleep." Joe cocked an eyebrow at the sound of Damien's phone. *What news could a late evening text carry?* He thought.

Damien rubbed his face. "Son of a bitch. The Martins plan to be at the lab tomorrow afternoon. They want to see their daughter. Shit. They were so distraught today they didn't ask about her or any of the details about her death. I guess I hoped they wouldn't want to come to the lab." He rested his elbows on his knees. "I know they are going to ask what happened to her. Fuck me, Joe. What are we going to tell them? The truth? They aren't even near ready to hear the truth."

"Listen, we have to inform them. We can't tell them much, but what we can, they need to hear it from us. You can't hold anything back. If they don't hear it from us, they may hear it from the wrong person. I agree; they aren't ready for all the details. Nevertheless, what do you hold back? It's not our decision. You have to tell them everything."

Damien threw his empty can across the room. "Bullshit! It is our decision. It's my decision. If I don't think they should hear something, I'm damn well not going to tell them! I'll deal with the aftermath if they find out later. I'm not going to put them through unnecessary pain if I can help it."

"Hey, *relax the cacks*, for fuck's sake, and pull that stick out of your arse, you *knacker*. I'm not telling you what to do. Just what I think. What the bloody hell is wrong with you, anyway?" Joe asked.

"What do you mean what the hell is wrong with me? I don't want to put the family through any more than I have to."

"You know damn well what I mean, and I'm not talking about the Martins. I noticed when you found out you made Lieutenant you weren't that excited. When we were all out at the bar Monday night, everyone else may have thought you seemed happy, but I know something else is going on.

"In the captain's office, this morning, you looked like someone kicked your cat instead of promoting you. These last few months you've kept your distance, no hanging out with me or any of the other guys. Not to mention I don't know the last time you got laid. Which I'm telling you goes against the fucking laws of nature." Joe took a bite of pizza. "What gives? And do not lie to me."

Damien sighed as he ran a hand over his face. He didn't want to tell Joe anything, but maybe he needed to tell him part of it. But which part? "I don't know if I even want to be the lieutenant over the VCU. Hell Joe, I'm not even sure I want to stay on the force."

Joe gawked at Damien. He dropped his piece of pizza on the table. "Are you fucking kidding me? You must be bloody fucking nuts! You made rank, and now you don't know if you even want the job. Why? Why, Damien? What in all that's holy would make you walk away from the one thing you've wanted more than anything else?"

Damien placed his head in his hands. *He shouldn't have said anything.*

Damn, he should have kept his mouth shut. "Listen, I don't want to get into things right now. I promise I won't make any decisions without discussing it with you, but I just don't care to get into it, okay? This case is hard enough as it is. I don't want to have to deal with personal shit. Let's just let it go for now. Please."

Joe gaped at him and lifted his hands. "Fine. I know there is more to this than you're telling me. I hope you will feel comfortable telling me everything. But for now, I'll let it go. However, Damien, I'm not going to let you just walk away from this without a damn good reason. As for this case, I trust your judgment, and I'll back you. Concerning Becca's parents, if I were the parent, I'd want to know everything—but hey, that's me." Joe shrugged and went back to eating his pizza.

Damien's head fell back against the chair. "Fuck! I guess we will see what happens tomorrow." He wanted to tell Joe, tell him everything. But what if Joe turned him in? Or hell, he might not want to be his partner or his friend. And he wouldn't be able to blame him.

An hour later, six empty cans of soda pop and two empty pizza boxes lay in a mess on the little table. Joe stood on his long legs and did a series of stretches. He headed for his room. Stopping mid-stride, he turned back to Damien. "How many do you think he'll kill before we stop him?"

Damien stared at his friend and partner. "Too fucking many. This is the first that we know of. I sure as hell don't think it will be his last."

"As much as I hate to say it—I think you are one hundred percent right. If I thought for one minute, I could tuck my tail and run, I might consider it. But as long as my arse is pointing downwards that will never happen. I sure as hell don't think this will end with roses coming out our butts." Joe disappeared into his room.

A slight smile tugged at the corners of Damien's mouth. He shouldn't have taken his nasty attitude out on his friend. Joe had been correct. From the moment he got the news he had passed the lieutenant's exam, Damien had a gnawing feeling that maybe he should just walk away. Money wasn't a concern; his father had made sure of that. He could become a PI or work for his Dad at his security company. Lord knows his Dad has wanted him to come work for him for years.

Camilla's phone call had reinforced his desire for a change. To this day, she did not understand how close she came to losing her life. The rage that Damien felt that evening, months ago, flooded back as he remembered the events of that day.

***

Damien had been searching for something in his home office when he came across some of Camilla's business receipts. She had been over the night before doing paperwork and must have left them behind when she left. As he read the receipts, Damien noticed the dates matched up to days she had said she had out of town business meetings. All the receipts, however, were from a Chicago area hotel.

He took personal hours for the rest of the day and figured out just what Camilla had been up to the last few months. During the next few hours and a few illegal computer searches, he tracked down her movements and found out she had cheated and lied for most of their two-year relationship. By the time Camilla came to his home from work that night, Damien had uncovered all her dirty secrets.

Camilla gasped and stared incredulously at him as he sat on the sofa when she entered his house. She hadn't expected him to be there. She spent a few moments gathering a few items; explaining she had an unexpected overnight trip and needed a few things she had left at his place. She told him she would be back the next day by the time his shift ended at work. Damien kissed her, told her he had to dash out and take care of something, and he would see her the next day. He waited in his truck for her to leave, then he followed her—right to the Ritz.

Having a badge can get quite a bit in Chicago. Damien had strolled up to the hotel's front desk and used his charm to get what he needed. "Hey, I'm looking for my sister, Camilla Rogers? She has a room here." He smiled at the young girl behind the counter. "I'm supposed to surprise her, but I can't remember her room number." He flashed his badge. "She has no idea I'm coming, and I'm hoping to keep it a surprise."

As he rode the elevator up to her suite, the rage boiled in his gut. He posed as room service. The asshole opened the door smiling and laughing. Damien shoved him aside and walked into the suite. The guy started to protest, but the anger on Damien's face shut him up. That and he held his Glock in his hand.

The guy reached for the phone to call for security when Damien advised him it wouldn't be in his best interest. The man made a move to push him out of the room when Damien punched him in the stomach, then pointed his gun at him. "Listen, George Dunlap. I'm pretty sure your wife, Margaret, wouldn't be too happy finding out how you're spending your evenings. Or learning that you seem to have a couple of million tucked away in hidden accounts. Do you?

"Plus, I'm wondering how your law firm would fare once your clients found out one of their senior VPs is having an illicit affair with one of his employees. And the money—can't really forget that now, can we? I think it would cost you a few million in revenue. So, unless you want the whole fucking city knowing where you like to stick your dick, I suggest you have a seat."

Camilla, who'd been reclining on the lounge in an open robe when Damien entered the suite, jumped up and tried to cover up her naked body. She attempted to explain it wasn't what he thought.

He glowered at her. "Do you think I'm that fucking stupid? You're naked in a robe and drinking champagne. Some business meeting." He gestured towards the asshole she had just fucked. "Is this how you conduct most of your business meetings, George?" Damien glanced around the suite. "Pretty good set up if you can get it."

Damien's hand tightened on his weapon. One shot. Diminished capacity, the heat of the moment. But who should get the bullet? Camilla's eyes met his. The hand that held his weapon shook. Damien took two steps towards her and reached for her hand. He ripped the engagement ring from her finger and put it in his pocket. "You don't get to keep this."

She didn't protest the removal of the ring. Damien glared at her but spoke to the man. "She's a great fuck, isn't she? Did she do that thing with her tongue? Yeah, she's definitely talented." Damien glanced at the asshole. "Oh, just so you know, you aren't the only douche bag she's been fucking. Seems our girl here has quite the long list of business associates."

Damien's gaze focused back on Camilla, who stood in stunned silence. Her lower lip quivered, and her eyes glistened. "Save your tears for someone who gives a shit. Don't bother coming to the condo, you won't be able to get in. Might as well enjoy the rest of your business meeting." Damien holstered his gun and walked away.

Within hours of getting back to his home, he'd had her shit packed, sitting on the front porch and the locks changed.

CHAPTER TEN

Joe woke from a nasty nightmare. He looked at the clock on his nightstand, four o'clock. "Bloody hell," he groaned. Tangled in the sheets, a sheen of sweat covered his body. He glanced timidly around the room. He half expected to see Becca. In his dream, she had been sitting right there on the bed.

He unraveled his sheets and laid back against the pillow. He closed his eyes, visions of Becca trying to hold her head up filled his mind. She tried speaking to him, but due to the whole head thing not being attached, that was next to impossible to do. Her lips moved in a silent scream.

"Jesus, what a fucking creepy dream," he said. He turned on the TV trying to get rid of the eerie glow that had settled in the room. He closed his eyes hoping sleep would come. It didn't. "You would think that after so many years in this kind of job, you would get used to the nightmares," he said out loud. He glanced over at the clock, four twenty. He knew sleep wouldn't come. Might as well work out. He got up and threw on some shorts and a t-shirt. Grabbed his phone and some earbuds and headed towards the hotel gym.

He entered a small, dark empty room. *Nice, all to myself.* He headed straight for the treadmill. Just what he wanted. He plugged in his earbuds and hit play. Classic rock mixed with some hard rock, and just the right amount of heavy metal. He started the jog off slow until he got his rubbery legs under him. Ten minutes in, he hit his stride.

He would much rather be jogging through the streets of Dublin or Chicago, but this would do. His family moved him here sometime around the eighth grade. He didn't like it at first. He had a heavy Irish accent, and his body hadn't filled out yet. Shortly after the move, he tried out for the football team. Although puny would be the word to describe his body, he sure as hell could move. He made the team, and he got bigger, stronger, and better. At everything.

As he ran, his breathing evened out. Becca drifted further and further away. AC/DC played in his ears. The thumping base drove his steps. Once he got into homicide, jogging became a way to deal with the evil he saw. Humans were nasty creatures. They did things to each other he didn't understand. Joe wanted to help the victims get justice. To help the families of the dead move forward knowing their loved one's killer wouldn't get away with the cowardly act of murder.

Every step on the treadmill thudded in his head. Joe's chest tightened. His body wanted him to quit, but he pushed through it. Thirty minutes just wasn't long enough. He wiped the sweat from his face. His pace kept cadence with the beat of Metallica's base.

He thought about Damien. They had come into the same squad together. Placed as partners, they had clicked just as fast. Their families became close, and now they spent most holidays together. His parents and Damien's parents hung out regularly and took a trip together once a year.

Joe couldn't imagine having someone else for a partner. They shared the same Catholic beliefs and family values. And they both loved women. Although Damien was more of a hopeless romantic when it came to relationships.

He wanted to smack Damien when he said he didn't know if he wanted to stay on the force. Who the fuck was he kidding? Joe knew damn well that Damien had wanted to do this job more than any other. If he didn't, he would have quit long ago. No one with the amount of money Damien and his family had would stay in a job like this. No, they both stayed in this job because they were meant to do it.

Joe's family didn't have the wealth Damien's did, but they weren't hurting for money. His father owned one of the best construction companies in the state. He could work side by side with his father and brother, but Joe had no desire to do that.

He ran faster. The music's steady beat leading his pace. Joe had concerns about his partner. No way in hell Joe would let this man walk away without a fight. Plus, it would suck having to break in a new partner and the VCU would end up with an asshole for a Lieutenant.

Forty-five minutes later Joe slowed his pace, bringing his heart rate down. His thoughts came back to why they were in Springfield. He knew better than to think this case would end with one dead girl. Joe also knew his partner would shoulder the dead, no matter how many, and carry them until they solved this case. He glanced at the clock on the wall, five twenty. A long hot shower and a quick power nap and he'd be good to go.

CHAPTER ELEVEN

Forensics Lab

Joe stopped dead in his tracks, causing Damien to smack into him. "What the hell, Joe? Running into you is like smacking into a brick wall. You mind moving your fat butt out of the way?" Damien had to squeeze by to get into the conference room.

Joe said nothing, and he didn't move. Taylor leaned over as she placed assorted muffins and bagels on a tray, and a pot of coffee in the middle of the large table. The sight of her doing a domesticated task scrambled his brain. *Damn, she is sexy.* Yesterday she wore a pink top, today she had on a light blue one that hugged her curves.

Taylor's eyes lit up, and a smile spread across her face. "Hi, boys. I figured you two might like some stuff to nibble on while you're going through the evidence. I know Jones, the ME, and Matt will be in here as well. Let me know if I can do anything for you." She winked at Joe and strolled down the corridor.

Joe grinned at Damien. "You know; I think this might not be such a bad trip after all." His eyes sparkled as he watched Taylor leave the room. "Damn, she has a perfect ass." He leaned in close to Damien. "What I wouldn't give to see that ass naked in my bed. I just might be falling in love." Joe placed a hand over his heart.

Damien rolled his eyes. "Taylor's perfect ass is going to get you in a lot of trouble."

Joe smacked Damien in the chest. "Dude, you're turning green before my eyes. The least I can do is give you something to dream about. I'll tell you all the salacious details. I promise."

Matt walked through the door. "What details?"

Damien scowled at Joe. "Nothing about this case, that's for sure."

Matt shrugged. "Director Jones decided to have me help you two. Being in the lab has its perks, but helping with fieldwork has always been something I've wanted to do. This will be awesome." Matt pumped his fist in the air.

"Did you just do that?" Damien asked.

Matt grinned. "Yeah, I did. I couldn't help myself."

Joe poured a mug of coffee. "Well trust us, we will use and abuse you, Matt."

"Who are we waiting on—Jones and the ME, is that it? Anyone else?" Damien asked.

Matt poured a cup of coffee. "I think that's it. We have a few things to go over. I've..."

Director Jones and the ME walked into the room. "Good morning." Director Jones filled a mug with coffee. "Before we start, Lieutenant Kaine, how did the family notification go with the Martins? I tried to talk them out of coming in today when they contacted me yesterday evening. I suggested they take a few days and give themselves a chance to deal with the shock, but they insisted. If I had said to meet me here at one a.m., I have no doubt they would've shown up."

Damien ran his hand through his hair. "Joe and I have done tons of family notifications, but for some reason, this one had to be the worst. Maybe it's the circumstances of the case, I'm not really sure." He leaned back in his chair. "You learn to compartmentalize this part of the job. The Martins have a ten-year-old son Tommy. He idolized his sister. When we left the house, he sat at the top of the stairs clutching what I assume had been his sister's stuffed bear. I haven't been able to get that picture out of my head."

Joe crossed his arms. "I have two sisters. If someone did to my sisters what was done to Becca, I would hunt him down, and no one would ever find his body."

Director Jones glanced around the table. "In this job, Dr. Langley and I have had some harrowing notifications. Matt, this will be the first case where you'll have a more hands-on approach. You're used to the protection the lab offers. This may not be the right case for you to get your feet wet as an investigator. It's going to get much harder from here."

Matt nodded but remained silent.

Jones shifted in his chair and grimaced. "As a father of a teenage girl, this case has already proven itself to be one of the hardest I've ever had. I see that girl on the table and it's hard not to see my own daughter." He gestured towards Dr. Langley. "I trust you came up with something that will keep the Martins from seeing their daughter's head roll off the table."

Dr. Langley's lips pursed into a tight thin smile. "I sure did. I positioned a sheet at the base of her chin and pinned it, so there won't be any chance of it falling away and revealing her body. Had a hell of time rigging a way to hold her head facing up. Thank God for my assistant. He figured out a way, and the parents won't be able to see the damage at all."

The ME put a muffin and a bagel on his plate and poured a cup of coffee. Once settled he continued the conversation. "I've been doing this job for a long time. I've seen some nasty stuff done to people. But this—what this guy did to this young girl, it beats all I've ever seen."

Matt stared at the photos of Becca Martin. "This guy is a monster. I can't help but wonder how he convinced Becca to leave the mall with him. He must be a hell of a charmer. Why else would a young girl want to leave with someone she didn't know?"

Joe placed his coffee mug on the table. "We may have the answer to that. We got the impression the parents kept Becca on a tight leash. She'd been on restriction for a month. The parents kept her off social media and didn't let her date. Between babysitting her younger brother and school, she didn't have much free time. Her mother made the comment that Rebecca said her home reminded her of a prison and her parents were the wardens."

Director Jones glanced at the photos of Becca. "At that age, girls are nothing but a ball of hormones. Throw a cute boy into the mix and all their reasoning goes out the window." He leaned back in his chair. "Dr. Langley, what new information did you gather from the autopsy?"

The ME watched as Joe placed the pictures of young Becca Martin on the whiteboard. "Her last meal seemed to be some kind of muffin or bread and corn chips, which I don't get at all. The blood samples taken from under her nails came back as her. I'm thinking she clawed at her restraints. Which would account for the fiber or pulp-like substance I took from under the nails as well. Especially if our killer used leather restraints. Trace has those samples now."

Dr. Langley took a sip of coffee. "A very sharp blade cut her throat. No evidence of hesitation marks. One clean, smooth, very deep cut. I found an extreme amount of swelling and blood vessel eruptions present around the head area." Dr. Langley dragged a hand down his face. "I believe he hung her upside down before killing her. Then he slit her throat and let her bleed out."

Joe grunted. "Son of a bitch. That tells me he hung her upside down for a while. He kept her like that to cause her severe pain. Sadistic torture."

"You are right about the pain. Pressure builds in the chest, throat, and head causing the pain to become intense. It wouldn't take more than ten or fifteen minutes for it to become—unbearable." Doctor Langley's voice had gone flat and monotone as his shoulders drooped. "The amount of damage done to the surrounding tissue suggests that he held her in that position for at least thirty minutes. He dismembered her with the same knife he used to slit her throat. It cut through both skin and muscle like paper. The dismemberment happened after she died. Becca Martin had suffered so much by that point. At least he had the decency to kill her before he cut her into pieces."

A rumbling noise came out of Joe. "This fucker is a sick bastard. Maybe instead of a cell we should hang his ass upside down and let the Chicago rats eat him." He glanced around the table. "Hey, it's just a suggestion."

Director Jones drew in a long breath. "Matt, what else do we have in the way of evidence?"

Matt opened a folder. "The bag came from Caldare Farm Equipment and Supplies. They provide all kinds of things for the agriculture industry. Caldare stamps the bags along the seam with the lot and bin numbers assigned during manufacturing. I'm working with the manufacturer to get a list of buyers from this state."

Damien glanced around the table. "I believe this killer won't venture too far from his own area. A radius of one hundred to no more than two hundred miles. The killer had to be familiar with Highway 24 and the times it would have the least amount of traffic on it. I think he planned for Becca's discovery, but I don't think he planned on how fast it happened. Leading me to think he didn't know about the cleanup crew that works that stretch of highway." Damien looked at Matt. "Have any witnesses reported suspicious or unusual activity in the hours around the body dump?"

"No, none," Matt said. "There are three farms in the heart of this radius. Macomb has a huge hog farm. I think it's the largest in the state." Matt closed his eyes and licked his lips. "Just a side note, their products are delicious."

Joe laughed. "A boy after my own heart."

"Seriously?" Damien stared at Matt and Joe. "You two are idiots."

Matt waved off Damien's comments. "Back to the farms. Findlay has a soybean farm, and Waverly has the best cheese and dairy farm. If we get lucky, maybe one of these will be on Caldare's list. Also, Blue Mound happens to be about a hundred and six miles from Astoria and fourteen miles from Decatur. This fits into your theory, Damien."

Damien had a large state map up on a board and put pins in each of the farms locations. "Okay, let's start with these. If we don't get anything, we can expand our search. Matt, did the CSTs find any other fingerprints, hairs, anything on or in the bag that held Becca?"

"Two trace substances. The lab has been working on identifying them. So far tests reveal that the samples are degraded. Once identified, I'll find out what role they play in farming if anything at all. For all we know, they may have come from something unrelated. Unfortunately, there were no fingerprints found," Matt said.

Damien finished writing on the whiteboard. "Without much in the way of physical evidence, we need to use everything we can find on the victim or victims to identify our killer. Matt, call the mall, see if they have any surveillance from last Saturday. Maybe we can track Becca's movements. Get the two girls with Becca that day to give you a timeline of where they were at in the mall. That may help narrow down the search of the tapes. Then check for any other reported missing girls from this area."

"You got it." Matt typed away on a laptop.

"Go back ten years on the missing girls. Stay within the age range of fifteen to eighteen." Damien added.

"This guy..." Joe said when Matt's phone beeped and he excused himself from the meeting. "I'll start again. This guy must have a place..." before Joe could finish the phone in the conference room rang. "Are you kidding me?" He threw his hands in the air and rocked back and forth in his chair.

Damien's lip twitched. He tilted his head down to hide a smile. The smile vanished once he found out what the caller on the other end wanted. "I'll let him know." His gaze landed on Director Jones. "Becca's parents are up front."

***

Abigail Martin sat in a chair wringing her hands while her husband paced back and forth across the lobby. As soon as the door opened, Jeff

Martin spun around and hurried over to them. His shoe caught the leg of one of the chairs and sent it careening to the other side of the room with a terrible screech. Mr. Martin clenched his hands into fists, and a thin line of sweat rolled down from each temple. "I'm sorry we came early. We couldn't wait any longer to see Becca." He reached behind him, grabbed Mrs. Martin's hand, and dragged her through the door.

Director Jones laid a hand on Jeff's shoulder, steadying the man as he weaved down the hallway. "That's quite alright Mr. Martin. I'm so sorry for your loss. I'm sorry that you have to experience this."

Jones led the Martins into a viewing room with a large glass window. They couldn't risk letting the Martins be in the same room as Becca. They might reach out and touch their daughter only to have her head roll off the table.

A tech on the other side of the glass raised the curtain and Mr. and Mrs. Martin gasped at the site of their daughter on the metal table. Abigail Martin clutched her chest with one hand and covered her mouth with the other, leaving nothing to catch her as her knees buckled. Joe reached out and grabbed her, saving her from smacking the floor. He helped her into a chair by the wall and went to get her some water.

Mr. Martin stood in front of the window with his forehead and hands pressed against the glass. When Joe came back into the room, Jeff Martin spoke. "I need to know the truth." He moved from the viewing window and placed a hand on his wife's shoulder. "We need to know the truth. What did that bastard do to our girl?" He sat in the seat next to his wife and took her hand in his.

Damien pulled a chair from the wall and sat in front of the Martins. "Mr. Martin, are you sure you're ready to hear all the details? They're horrific, and I don't think you should have them in your head. It's not the way you should remember your girl."

Jeff Martin clenched his jaw so tight that the muscles in his neck resembled corded braids. "We need to know. I can't bury her in the ground and not know what she went through. Please."

"Very well," said Damien. His voice had a soft and calm tone. "During the time the killer held Becca, he sexually assaulted her."

Mrs. Martin shivered in her chair. She kept spinning her wedding band around. Tears flooded her eyes. "How did he kill her? I need to know how he killed her. Did she suffer?"

Damien caught Joe's eyes, who gave him a little nod. "He slit her throat. He then left her where a group of residents located her." Damien pulled his chair closer to the Martins he took their hands in his. "Mr. and Mrs. Martin?" He waited for them to look at him. "I can't give you too many details, this is still an ongoing investigation, but I will tell you, your daughter died quickly. However, the damage the killer did to Becca's body warrants a closed casket. When the funeral home takes her, they may suggest this. I recommend you follow their suggestion." Damien lied. He gave a quick glance to both Joe and Director Jones as if warning both not to say a word. He hoped instructions given to the funeral home would spare the parents any extra heartbreak.

The Martins collected themselves, and Jones explained they would release the body when they could for burial. After Jones had taken the funeral home information, he hugged both and again offered his condolences. Damien stood there and watched them leave the building.

Director Jones placed his hand on Damien's shoulder and gave it a squeeze. "You didn't tell them about many of the details, including the dismemberment. I wouldn't have either, son. It's a tough call. But I would have done the same thing."

"I didn't think they could handle hearing the details. Also, we can't afford for them to get out into the news, not yet anyway. When your people call the funeral home will you make sure they don't let the family see her, and that they make it a closed casket?" Damien followed Jones back down the corridor.

"Of course. I'm pretty familiar with the funeral home they use." He gave Damien a sly grin. "I know the owner. We play golf together. I even let him win occasionally."

CHAPTER TWELVE

Damien walked back into the conference room to find Joe studying the measly evidence they had to go on.

Joe looked up. "So how do you think the Martins are going to cope? I personally hope they have some other family members they can rely on," Joe said.

"Mr. Martin can barely keep it together, and Mrs. Martin isn't even present. If her husband didn't lead her by the hand, she wouldn't know where to go or what to do. I hope they don't forget about Tommy. He could get lost in all their sorrow, and he'll need them more than ever." Damien sat and rested his head on the table. "I need a minute."

Ten minutes later, Matt walked into the conference room with a few files in his hand. "Hey, I got a few missing girls from this area, one from about six months ago and four starting around eight years ago."

"Wow! Wait—what—no one made any connection?" Joe grabbed the file Matt held out to him.

Damien's head popped up. "How could no alarms go off? Seems like a small area for five girls to go missing and no one put the links together?"

"Well," Matt said, "the girls went missing from five different counties. All the girls' ages range from sixteen to eighteen. Umm, except for this one girl. When she went missing, her age at the time of her disappearance—almost twenty. Seemed a little old, but I put her in the mix anyway." Matt set the rest of the files on the desk. "These small Sheriff's departments, they don't have a lot of resources, especially for missing person cases. Come on, you two should know that."

Damien moved to the map on the board. "Fine. We get it. Unless you're doing what we're doing now, you would never connect the girls. Let's start with the most recent the one from six months ago. Where did she go missing from Matt?"

Matt read the missing person's report. "Jesse Franks—seventeen, went missing from Macon, about thirteen hundred in population. This town also feeds into the Decatur school system where Becca went to high school."

Damien placed a pin on the map. "Okay, Matt—where did the four girls go missing from?"

"Alright," Matt said. "We have a seventeen-year-old, Jill Macon, from Rockbridge. A town in Greene County. Wendy Bettis—seventeen, from Murryville that's in Morgan County. We then have Tracy Fordham—seventeen, from Palmyra, in Macoupin County. Last, we have Beth Haut from Pawnee, that's in Sangamon County. Haut seems to be the first girl we have to go missing. The oldest girl I mentioned earlier. Again, she was almost twenty at the time of her disappearance."

Once Matt finished, he saw that Damien had put a different colored pin in each of the four cities. "You like using push pins, don't you?" A wicked grin pushed Matt's cheeks up.

Joe erupted with laughter. "This boy always uses different colored push pins. Says it helps keep things orderly for him." He waved his hand around his head.

"Har—de—har—fucking—har. You two mind getting back to the job?" Damien smirked. "How about the bodies, have any been recovered?"

"No. None," Matt said.

Joe stopped reading the file containing the missing person reports. "This girl from six months ago, Jesse Franks, did the investigators find any trace evidence or anything else at the scene?"

Matt checked his notes. "Nope. All the trace evidence at the scene came from the girl and her parents since they owned the car. No one matching her description or any of the other girls has been found anywhere in the state. I could see if outside of Illinois there have been any unidentified girls found matching their descriptions."

Damien didn't entirely discount the idea Matt had. He stared at the map and the pins that represented the missing girls. Damien's gut told him the killer lived in this radius. "Do a search but narrow it down to Illinois and stay within a two-hundred-mile area. Don't get too bogged down in this. It seems like a local thing. He will stay around here. It's what he knows. If we get nothing of interest, we can always expand our search, but let's keep it tight for now."

Matt made a note on his pad of paper. "We know all the schools in this area participated in the Abduction Awareness Week last year. I searched the records, and Jesse's parents participated in the program. If we do find another girl, we will have something to compare to."

Damien opened a bottle of diet soda he had brought with him from the hotel. "Alright. I don't believe in coincidences. Let's set the first four girls aside, for now. Let's focus on Jesse, our most recent disappearance besides Becca. Matt, did the CSTs ever find anything in the debris they picked up out on Hwy 24 when they recovered Becca's body?"

"No—they are ..." Matt trailed off. All three men lifted their heads as the smell of food wafted through the door.

"Sorry to interrupt, but Director Jones asked me to order you some lunch—he had to go to a meeting in Rockford. I ordered you a variety of pies. Enjoy, boys." Taylor smiled as she set several cans of soda on the table. "Hey Matt, by chance did you get anything from that information I gave you?"

Matt looked at Taylor. He walked over to her laying a hand on her shoulder. "No, I didn't. I found nothing that looked suspicious in that area. Are you sure you weren't just spooked?"

"C'mon, Matt. You know me. I don't spook easily, but something doesn't feel right." Taylor said.

Damien noticed the frown on Joe's face as he studied Taylor. "What's going on, Taylor? Anything we can help you with?" Damien asked her.

She looked from Matt to Damien. "I don't know. I noticed an older truck following me. A few weeks back. At least I think it followed me. I came out of a shopping center near where I live." She sighed. "It's kind of like an outdoor market. First, I noticed this guy dressed in dark clothes and a baseball hat. He seemed to be following me around while I walked through the market. I think I've seen him before, just recently too. I can't remember where though.

"But to be honest with you I just thought I imagined it. I mean why would anyone want to follow me? Another time, a week or so ago, it could've been longer. I don't know. I'm sure someone was following me again around the outdoor market. Again, when I was driving home, I could swear I had the same older truck following me that followed me weeks back. This time I didn't go home. I went to a friend's house in a gated community where he couldn't follow me in. I think it's the same guy, but I have no proof. I swear I'm not crazy. Then, yesterday morning I was sure someone was watching me when I left my apartment, but I couldn't see anyone."

Joe stared at her as she told her story. She wouldn't normally be the type of woman he was attracted to. Not skinny, not super short, but she could pass for a young girl. Joe had a good eye for bullshit, and he didn't get that vibe from her. He didn't get the impression she would make something out of nothing and he sure as hell didn't think it had anything to do with her imagination. "Taylor, where do you live?" Joe asked.

She shifted her weight. "I didn't mean for this to be a big deal. I shouldn't have even said anything."

Joe stood up and walked over to her. "You did the right thing by saying something. This is serious. Now, where do you live?"

"In a neighborhood between here and Chatham." Taylor looked up at Joe. She had to lean back to see him. Rugged and manly, and so damn tall. She must look like a child next to him, she thought.

Damien glanced at the map on the board. "That's right in the area where all these girls have been taken." He turned to Taylor. "With all that is going on right now, you need to be extra cautious. Don't go anywhere at night by yourself, and don't park far away from the store."

Joe nodded. "Yeah. If you happen to see the truck again, try to remember as much information as you can. Pay attention to every detail, especially the driver. Write down anything you remember." Joe reached out and touched her shoulder. He wanted to pull her into him and hold her close.

Taylor blushed as she smiled. "Thanks, guys. Call me if you need anything else." She turned and walked out.

Joe couldn't take his gaze off the way her hips swayed as she walked away.

Matt watched Taylor leave too. He turned towards the pizza and filled his plate. "I wouldn't get any ideas about Taylor. She isn't the kind of girl to have a fling."

Joe reached for a piece of pepperoni pie. "What, I'm merely admiring those outstanding hips."

"Yeah right, you look like a lion getting ready to chow down on a gazelle."

Damien pushed away from the table and spewed soda as he burst into laughter. "Shit, Matt has you pegged." Once he stopped laughing and could breathe, he continued, "Joe doesn't know what the word relationship means. To his credit, he never leads the girls on. They know what they're getting into from the start. It must be a contributing factor as to why I haven't had to investigate his murder." Damien winked at Matt.

"Hey, I'm single. I let them know upfront that I'm not available for a serious relationship. Then we can have a good time, no strings or expectations to get in the way. Plus, what can I say? The ladies love my awesome personality." Joe wiggled his eyebrows at Damien and Matt.

"Back to your earlier question, the CSTs are going through everything collected now, but they aren't finding anything interesting. The killer left her naked and partially rinsed her off, so nothing there. Doc retrieved semen, but no matches in the system," Matt said.

"Wait a second, he goes to all that trouble to keep her clothes and leaves no other trace of himself, except for his semen." Joe reached for another slice. "Why? He doesn't strike me as a *dingwop.*"

"He thinks he won't get caught. So why use a raincoat? He thinks we won't be able to tie him to anything. Maybe his reputation or his position makes him believe that we would never suspect him. That's arrogance. It's the arrogance that will put his ass in a sling," Damien said.

"I think we should go up to Macon and talk to Jesse Frank's parents. See if we can get any more details about her disappearance. Maybe if we speak with the Sheriff, he might be able to shed some light on some stuff. Hopefully, it will give us more than we have now. Cause right now, we are up shit creek without a paddle," Joe said.

"That's a damn good idea, Joe. You know, for a *Harpie* you aren't a *dingwop.*" Damien said. "Hey Matt, continue to search for any more missing person reports and hunt down as much information on these missing girls as you can. My gut is telling me these cases are connected. I don't like coincidences; there can't be any way the abductions of these girls involved different UNSUBS." Damien ran his hand through his hair. "Check with Caldare and see if they can give you any more information on the bags." Damien grabbed a can of soda as he walked out the door, Joe followed behind loaded down with soda and a few slices of pie.

Taylor smiled at Joe and Damien as they walked past her desk on their way to the parking lot. Damien saw the pink flush on her cheeks.

"Hey?" She called out before they walked out the door. "Later tonight a bunch of us are going to be at your hotel, my friend's band has a gig to play there this evening. If you two get back in time and want to stop by, I'd love to see you there." She stared at Joe with laser-like precision. "We'll be there around seven-thirty."

Damien watched Joe and waited for him to answer. Joe's eyes were wide, and all he could manage were a few mumbled words. "Sure, sounds like fun. We should be back by eight. Keep an eye out for us and don't go anywhere alone," Damien said as he walked towards the door.

Joe smiled and winked at Taylor.

Outside the SUV, Joe shimmied back and forth pulling on the top of his jeans.

"What the hell happened in there? *Gatto ti ha liugua?*" Damien climbed into the SUV.

"No, you fucking knacker. No cat has my tongue. I just couldn't get it to work; I had a mouthful of pizza." Joe smiled and tried to play it off. He turned and stared out the window at the landscape as it went by. But he couldn't get Taylor and the fear in her eyes out of his head. She tried to play it off as nothing to worry about, but he knew better. And that's what bothered him most.

CHAPTER THIRTEEN

Macon, IL

Damien and Joe walked into the Macon Sheriff's office. The small building had a layer of thick dust on every surface. They followed the Deputy down a skinny hallway. Damien watched Joe turn sideways to get into the office and coughed to cover the giggle that bubbled out.

"Sorry for the cramped quarters." Deputy Marcum gestured to Kaine and Hagan to have a seat. "We're remodeling; you're in our overflow room."

Damien pulled out a little notebook from his pocket. "No problem, we appreciate you taking the time to speak with us. What do you remember about the missing girl Jesse Franks?"

Deputy Marcum pulled two sheets of paper from a folder. "The parents reported Jesse missing after she didn't come home from a friend's house. She went over to hang out for a few hours, and her parents expected her to return home by ten p.m. Once she didn't come home, they contacted us. We went out to the Franks' house, as well as the friend's house. The friend, Marcia Wilson, said Jesse left her house at eight thirty. Marcia stated that Jesse had planned to swing by the Piggly Wiggly grocery store. We have eyewitnesses that place her at the store. She bought a few things and then got into her car and left."

Joe read over the report while the Deputy continued.

"After she had left the parking lot, she drove about five or six miles before her tire went flat," the Deputy said.

"How far is it from the Franks' house to the Piggly Wiggly?" Damien asked.

"It's just under twenty miles from the store to the house. Jesse stopped to get her spare from the trunk. She didn't make any phone calls. The parents weren't surprised Jesse didn't call asking for help with her tire. She had changed it before, so she knew how to do it."

Joe set the report on the desk. "Did you find any evidence of another vehicle stopping on the side of the road near her car? Anyone witness her on the side of the road?"

"No. The Baptist church held their potluck dinner that night—they're located at the other end of the town. Everyone in town attends it, it's not your ordinary potluck dinner. They combine efforts with the Catholic Church. They hold this dinner every year—it's almost like a fair. Most everyone in the town either participates or attends. Even the people who you never see at church go to this thing." The Deputy took a sip of his root beer. "Jesse's friend lived on the other side of town."

"Did you guys find anything in or on the car?" Asked Damien.

Marcum shook his head. "No. We collected fingerprints from the car, but they all belonged to the family. The tire looked like she ran over something causing it to go flat." He paused dragging his hand through his hair. "I know we're a small-town Sheriff's department; we just couldn't find anything pointing to any one person or group of people. No witnesses, no evidence, Jesse just vanished. I find myself driving down the roads around here half expecting to find her one day." He interlocked his fingers above his head and leaned back in his chair. "You two are here cause of the girl located on the side of the road, right?"

"Yes, and we think Jesse's disappearance may be related but we don't have actual proof," Damien said. "Tell me this, have you had any girls or parents complain about stalking, being followed, or being watched?"

"Heck no. Maybe the impetuous sixteen-year-old boy. Nothing that warrants charges or an investigation. Usually, the threat of a father's shotgun proves to be enough to deter the boys around these parts." Marcum smiled.

Damien rose and reached out his hand. "Okay, thanks again for your time. If you come across anything you think may be helpful to our investigation, please call me." He handed Marcum a card.

***

Damien stared out the window at the Frank's house. "I don't want to have to come back in a few days and tell them we recovered their daughter. But I'm positive the same person who killed Becca took Jesse. There are too many similarities to overlook."

"Let's go in and be as honest as we can. In their heart, they have to know Jesse isn't coming back. All the background information points to her being abducted. She earned good grades and had an excellent relationship with her parents. Jesse had no reason to run away."

Damien faced Joe. "Parents hold on to hope because the minute they let go of it, they have to face the cold hard truth." Damien crossed himself.

Both Mr. and Mrs. Franks answered the door. "Please, come in. Can I get you anything to drink?" Mrs. Franks fussed over the Detectives like they were teenage boys. She ushered them into their living room.

The house seemed normal. Clean and well kept. Damien's gaze moved over every surface. He noticed the many pictures of Jesse around the house. Even though the house had heat, furniture, and two people who loved each other, it felt cold and empty as though the day Jesse disappeared; all the life left this house.

"Mr. and Mrs. Franks, we have a few questions we'd like to ask. We think it might help us find out what happened to your daughter." Damien took his notepad out of his pocket as he spoke.

"Anything you need." Mrs. Franks fidgeted with the cuffs of her sleeve.

"Had your daughter met anyone recently? Maybe an older boy?" Damien asked.

Mr. Franks shook his head. "No. We would have known. She spent time with her girlfriends, but we didn't let her date. The random group thing with kids from school, but never a one-on-one date."

"How about social media, email, anything like that? Any involvement in any of those?" Joe asked.

"No. We tried to keep that to a minimum. We let her do things online that she needed to do for school. Nevertheless, as for the social aspect, we kept her away from that. Too many predators." Mrs. Franks let out a muffled gasp. Her husband reached over and took her hand in his.

Damien smiled at Mrs. Franks. "I know how hard this must be for you, but can you tell us anything about that night she went missing? Did she complain about being followed or that she had been threatened or harassed in any way?"

Mr. and Mrs. Franks both shrugged. "No," Mr. Franks said. "Jesse came home from school that day a little late. She and Marcia had decided they didn't want to go to the Church Fair. They decided instead of going to it, they would spend some time hanging out together and then Jesse would come home. She called us before she left Marcia's house and said she was going to stop by the store on the way home. When she didn't show up, we assumed she got distracted. However, when we phoned Marcia, she said Jesse had left hours ago, we called the Sheriff."

The father stared at Damien. "We heard about that young girl found near this area. Is that why you're here?"

"Yes, sir we are. We aren't sure if your daughter's disappearance has any relation to that case or not. We don't have any new information regarding the whereabouts of your daughter. If we get anything during this investigation, we'll contact you." Damien handed him a card. "If you need to reach either of us, here are our cards. Thank you for your time."

Damien and Joe headed for the door. Joe reached for the knob when Mr. Franks asked the one question they hoped they wouldn't hear. "You think the same man who killed that girl may have taken our daughter, don't you?" Mr. Franks stood stone still waiting for an answer.

Joe made a quick glance at Damien. "Mr. Franks, we don't have any evidence that points to the same person doing both abductions. I hope when we speak to you next, we will have some solid information to give you."

Mrs. Franks' long slender fingers reached out and grabbed Damien's arm, hard. "You think our Jesse is dead, don't you? I know as parents we're supposed to have hope. However, in my heart, I know my daughter is dead." Tears streamed down Mrs. Franks' cheeks. "I know she isn't coming home no matter how much I hope and pray. Damn it! We need her body! We need to bury her. The hardest part of this is the waiting. Waiting for answers that never come."

"As my partner just said, we have no evidence..."

"Oh, screw your damn evidence! Tell me what your gut says. Tell me what years of being a detective tells you about this case." Mrs. Franks' shoulders sagged as if a heavy shawl wrapped around them. "Please. Please, I need to hear you say it." Her fingers dug into his arm. "Please, Lieutenant Kaine."

Mrs. Frank's pale blue eyes pierced through Damien, pleading with him for the truth, to say the words she needed to hear. Damien placed his hand on hers. "I believe the same man took both girls. I don't think they will be his last. I can promise you we will find and stop him. I do believe your daughter is dead—I hope and pray I'm wrong and we find her somewhere. However, I don't think it's a realistic expectation. I'm so sorry."

She threw her arms around his waist and buried her face against his chest. Her entire body shuddered in his arms. "Thank you—thank you."

She placed her hand over Damien's heart. "I know you and your partner will find out what happened to our Jesse."

Back in the SUV, Joe stared out the front windshield. "We almost made it out. So fucking close to getting out the door, weren't we?"

"No shit. In one way, I'm glad they're not pinning their hopes on their daughter returning alive. On the other, I felt like I smacked her in the face with a bat." Damien's head rested on the steering wheel.

"She point blank asked you, and she didn't want smoke blown up her ass. She wanted the truth. This gives her hope. Hope for closure. Hope she and her husband will be able to bury their daughter." Joe squeezed his partner's shoulder.

CHAPTER FOURTEEN

Tiffany brushed her fingers over the bite mark. The roughness of her cracked and dry fingertips on the swollen oozy skin of her right breast made her cringe at her own touch. Another ugly reminder of his late-night visit. He called her by another girl's name. He spoke to her as if they had known each other from long ago. Tiffany had no doubt he was insane. Every time he came to her, he spoke of things in the past, as if they were happening now.

Her weighty limbs pulled her down to the mattress. Her head bobbed from side to side as her eyelids struggled to stay open. Oblivious to the awkward angle her head rested on her arm, Tiffany drifted off. Jolted awake by the sound of his heavy boots entering the house, she yanked on the restraints. They tightened on her wrist and ankles as she cowered in the corner at the head of the bed.

Long bangs hung over Tiffany's face. She watched his lanky legs carry him down the basement stairs towards a table at the far end of the room. A metal bowl clanked against the table. A water bottle bounced out of the bowl, and he grabbed it before it rolled onto the floor. She swallowed at the sight of the water. Holding her breath as he came closer, Tiffany's body shuddered. The air she held hissed out in a hot blast. His bony fingers reached out and pushed her bangs out of her face.

"Please let me go. I won't say anything. I won't tell anyone what you look like. Please, I just want to go home." Soft sobs erupted from Tiffany.

"Oh, Tiffany. I can't do that. You and I both know you would tell them who I am," he said. "No, I'm afraid you are going to have to stay here until I no longer have a need for you. And I have a feeling that time won't come too quickly. Now, as much as I would like to stay and finish our conversation, I can't. I brought you something to eat and drink. I wouldn't want you to starve to death. Where would the fun be in that?" He walked back to the table.

Her mumbled pleas rolled into humble thanks for God's mercy that he at least wouldn't be staying. Her breath came in rapid pants, and she squeezed her eyes shut. Starbursts exploded behind her eyelids and brought a wave of nausea. Tiffany's whole body shivered as a wave of relief swamped her. She expected him to hurt her again.

She watched him with dull, lifeless eyes as he set the bottles of water and bowl of food on the floor next to the bed. He glanced over his shoulder as he headed towards the door. "I brought you your favorite snack—you need to keep up your energy." A sneer curled his lips. His heavy boots carried him out, leaving her behind in Hell.

The bile burned its way up Tiffany's throat. She tried to stop the caustic fluid from escaping. "Oh God. Why? Why is this happening to me? Please God, please help me. Don't leave me here to die at his hands." She laid there rocking back and forth for some time, begging God to save her. Her faith had carried her this far, but fear and agony tore at the foundation of that very faith. She repeated the Hail Mary prayer hoping comfort from the Blessed Mother would surround her.

When Tiffany reached for the water bottle on the floor, a bubble of laughter escaped her lips. The sight of what lay in the bowl brought her the first signs of hope. Her heart raced at escaping this living hell.

Tiffany bit her lip. Confusion and doubt clouded her thinking. Tears welled up in her eyes. At one time her Catholic faith taught this action constituted a mortal sin. But she knew he planned to kill her. She knew his identity. She realized it last night. Knowing she had admired him had shocked her. She had no idea this kind of monster lived here, in their community.

She had no doubt after all he had done to her, her death would be nothing short of acute pain and torture. Her heart ached to tell her parents she loved them. Tiffany longed to see her little brother and sister and tell them how proud they made her. She missed her dog, Trudy. She wanted to hug her one more time. To touch her soft fur and her cold nose.

If she followed her faith, she would die at his hands. For the first time in two days, she controlled her own fate. She had to take this opportunity. She cried out. Tears flowed down her cheeks. Her sobs made it hard for her to breathe. "God, I have to believe you brought me a way out of this. I want to ask Your forgiveness and ask You to help me through this." She pressed her fist to her chest and rocked back and forth. "Please help my family, they will need You. Please send Your angels to guide me. I have no other way out. Please don't let another girl go through what I have had to endure."

Tiffany confessed her sins, and she asked God for His grace. She remembered a prayer for the dead from Confirmation. "Lord grant me Your mercy that at the time of my death, Your angels would guide me to Your presence free from sin." Tiffany made the sign of the cross. Her hand shook as she *lifted the water bottle to her lips. She took several long slow breaths, savoring each one. She knew she had to do this, but that didn't make it easy. Inhaling to her chest's full capacity, knowing these breaths would be her last. She couldn't stop the tears from flowing as she ate the contents of the bowl.*

CHAPTER FIFTEEN

Holiday Inn, Springfield IL

Joe gathered the case files from the front seat while Damien drove around the parking lot in search of a spot. "Well, it's pretty crowded for a Wednesday night, what gives?"

"Taylor's friend, the one in the band, he's playing here tonight; maybe that's drawing the crowd."

"Oh man, I forgot about that. I need to go upstairs and drop this shit off. You going to come down and have a couple of drinks with me?"

Damien yanked the hotel door open. "I could go for a couple of beers. Maybe enough of them will help me sleep without seeing Becca the human jigsaw puzzle. I can't get her out of my head."

Joe pushed the elevator button for their floor. "No shit, right? This case has totally mind fucked me. Last night Becca sat on the edge of my bed asking me how long it would be before I caught this asshole. Her head kept falling to the side, and she couldn't get her arms to work right and lift it back up. I woke up covered in sweat with a horrible headache."

***

They entered the hotel bar to the band's classic rendition of *Santa Monica* by Everclear. They grabbed two beers and headed towards Matt and a few of the other lab employees.

Matt took a long sip of beer. "Hey, Damien. Joe. How did your trip to Macon turn out?"

Joe reached out and shook Matt's hand. "Not too bad. We got a lot of information. Whether it will help us catch this bloody killer or not, I'm not sure. Let's save it for tomorrow. We want a few beers, and a break from this case say for ten hours." Joe pretended to check his watch.

"That's a stellar idea. Let me get you two another round." Matt waved to the server, pointed to his beer, and held up three fingers.

Sitting at a table near the stage, Matt and Damien discussed sports. Joe listened to the intense exchange concerning this year's NFL teams. He glanced around the bar at the young crowd. Several women caught his eye, but they did nothing for him. Yet spending another night with

Becca wasn't very appealing either. Joe had a lot of women back in Chicago he could call to keep him company. Here though, he just didn't have the desire to pick up one of these women.

Damien had given Joe shit during his engagement to Camilla. Tried to suggest he too should think about settling down with one girl. At least for longer than a weekend. After watching Damien's life gets turned upside down by one woman, no thanks, Joe had thought. He had no desire to commit to one woman. He didn't want the responsibility of having to worry about someone else. Or remember to call them when he would be home late, or ask permission to go out with the boys.

As Joe continued to scan the bar, laughter carried over the loud music. He searched the dance floor and found the source of the best sound to fill his ears. Taylor. His lips parted as he watched her fantastic hips dance in perfect rhythm to the beat of the music. Joe's brain tried to tell him he had moved into the danger zone, but another part of his body insisted he ignore his brain.

Joe's legs parted, and he rubbed his hands on his jeans. Taylor's eyes met his. Her cheeks pushed up with a huge smile that filled her face. She spun around and shook her ass in his direction, laughing as she glanced over her shoulder at him. When the music ended, she strutted over to him, still swaying to the song in her head.

Her curls bounced up and down as she plopped down in a chair next to him. Her mahogany brown mane hung below her shoulders. He tightened his grip on his beer to keep his hand from reaching out. His fingers twitched itching to slide through those thick curls.

"Hey, Joe—Damien, I'm so glad you guys showed up. Let me introduce you to the band." Taylor went around the table and introduced everyone. "Did you get any useful information today?" Taylor took a swig of her beer.

Joe watched the amber fluid flow from the bottle as it traveled down her throat. He almost lost it. A small drop of condensation fell onto her chest and slid down between her breasts. Fantastic breasts, round and plump. Taylor continued to stare at him with a quizzical look on her face. She sat waiting for his reply. The problem, he paid no attention to what she had said. Joe smiled at her. "Hmm, what?"

This time, Joe paid attention—to her mouth. *Good Lord her mouth.* She had the plumpest lips he'd ever seen. Lips that begged for kissing.

He could also see those kissable lips wrapped around something else. Her lips quit moving. She cocked an eyebrow at him and tilted her head, waiting for him to respond.

"Yeah, I think we got some good information. Whether it will help us in catching him, I don't know. I want to put him in a cage before he hurts another girl." Joe took a long swallow of his beer. His throat had become gritty and parched. He could almost taste the small grains of sand as they coated his throat. Joe became hyper-aware of his body. His pulse raced in rhythm to the hammering of his heartbeat. A wave of heat washed over him, causing a trickle of sweat to bead around his hairline. *What the hell?* Joe thought. His body betrayed him. He never reacted like this to a woman. He needed to regroup and get his body under control. Joe winked at Taylor and turned towards Matt and Damien.

"No disrespect intended, Lieutenant, but you are a complete dumbass if you think the Chicago Bears can hold a candle to the Patriots," Matt said.

Damien's eyes narrowed. "Your brain has been exposed to all those lab chemicals for far too long. This year the Chicago Bears not only have the talent, but they have the toughness in the defense they've been lacking. Not to mention the protection the O-line has been offering up. Those *asini viola del pensiero* are going down." Damien winked over his beer at Joe.

Joe had to stifle a laugh at what Damien said. He didn't think Matt would find any humor in Damien calling his team a bunch of pansy asses. Joe opened his mouth to join in their discussion when he caught Taylor staring at him.

Joe held his beer next to his lips about to take a drink. "It's not polite to stare at someone." Joe grinned at her. Taylor squirmed under his gaze; her cheeks flushed a beautiful shade of pink. He had no idea blushing could be such a turn on.

"I'm sorry," Taylor said flustered. "How did you get the scar above your eye?"

Joe rubbed it. "This? Had a little argument with a suspect a few years back. Sliced me with a knife. It wasn't too deep, but it required about ten stitches. Does it make me look sexy and dangerous?"

She laughed. "Yeah, absolutely." Her eyes lingered a little more on his handsome face. "You have the most beautiful eyes."

He tilted his head towards her and fluttered his eyelashes. "Really, you like my eyes?"

She smacked his arm and giggled. "Yeah right, like you don't know the effect they have on the female species."

Before she could pull her hand away, Joe reached up and grabbed it. He held it under the table and rubbed his thumb over her knuckles. "Hmm, if you stare at them long enough, I can put you in a trance. Then I can make you do things against your will." He wiggled his eyebrows.

A half smile tugged at her lips. "Who said it would be against my will?"

Before he could respond, Taylor spoke to someone at the table. She winked at him while she continued her conversation. Joe's brain came up with various escape scenarios. *How inappropriate would it be to throw her over my shoulder and carry her out of here? I could probably get away with it.* Under the table, his grip tightened on her hand.

The conversation around the table flowed smoothly. Joe continued to watch Taylor as she engaged everyone around her. He felt the cool breeze from the bar's AC blow on his skin. He muttered to himself. What the hell was happening? His body didn't react like this to women. Joe sighed. He blamed it on the case and wanting nothing more than a mere distraction.

Taylor watched Joe as he concentrated on something. He seemed lost in his thoughts. She leaned in close to him. "What has your brain working so hard Joe?"

Joe's eyes met hers and held them. "You said it wouldn't be against your will—did you mean it?"

She leaned into him. "I never say anything I don't mean."

His eyes stayed locked on her. Joe replayed the conversation with Matt earlier. His words of warning that Taylor didn't do flings. Yet, Joe didn't want a fling. Not with Taylor. But that's not what came out of his mouth. "I can't give you a relationship. I'm not able to give you any kind of commitment." The words weren't out his mouth two seconds, and he wanted to smack himself. "Oh fuck me!" He dragged his hand through his hair. "Ahh hell Taylor, I would really like to spend time with you, preferably alone and naked."

Her eyes glossed over and softened. "I'll take whatever you can give me. No expectations, no strings."

Joe kissed the knuckles of her hand. "Would you spend the night with me in my room?"

She placed her lips close to his ear. "Yes. Can we leave now?"

CHAPTER SIXTEEN

Damien and Matt had moved to the bar, and both nodded at Joe as he and Taylor left.

"Your partner is in way over his head," Matt said.

"I know that," Damien said. "He—does not. Joe thinks this will be like all the other women. Have a little fun. Enjoy some mind-blowing sex and walk away. Maybe see her once in a while but nothing too serious. Well, not this time. This time, it's different. I'm not sure how long it will take him to realize that." Damien chuckled to himself.

Damien's phone vibrated in his pocket. One hand reached for his phone the other ran through his hair. He cursed under his breath. For a split second, his heart stopped. He reached into his back pocket and pulled out his phone. His hand had a slight tremor as he flipped it over. *Please God let it not be a dead girl.*

A shaky laugh escaped Damien's lips. No dead girl this time. Mrs. C. sent him a picture of his cat Coach. She had dressed him in a little sailor's suit complete with hat. *Thank you, Mrs. C.*

"Your girlfriend?" asked Matt.

"No! Hell no! No girlfriend for me." Damien caught the suspicious glance from Matt. "Bad break up with my fiancé. So, no girlfriends." *Ever again.* He took a drink of his beer. "My elderly neighbor watches my cat, Coach, when I travel. She likes to dress him up and send me pictures." He held his phone so Matt could see his pudgy cat dressed up like a sailor.

Laughter rumbled out of Matt. "Oh shit! That's the funniest thing I've seen in a long time." Tears threatened at the uncontrollable laughter. "Is that a smile or a grimace? I can't tell if Coach is enjoying the humiliating experience or plotting revenge."

Damien smiled at Matt's reaction. He had grown to love getting the pictures. Shortly after he moved in, Mrs. C. attached her heart to his. She had been a great help to him and his family as his Nonna became sick and eventually died of her illness. His mother and father had become close to Mrs. C. too, and now she was an integral part of their family.

Matt nibbled on pretzels. "Hey, thanks for hanging with me until my girlfriend shows up. Drinking beer alone seems so depressing."

"Not a problem. I'm not in a hurry to go back to the room." *Not true,* Damien thought. He just didn't want to go to sleep. He didn't need to see Becca's dismembered body dance around like a marionette puppet. Very disturbing.

Matt rambled on about the last major case he worked on. Damien listened suggesting he think about becoming a detective. Damien made no promises but offered to help if he could when Matt decided what he wanted to do. As Matt continued to talk about the possibilities, Damien's back straightened, and the hair on his arms stood on end.

He rubbed the palm of his hands on his jeans to get rid of the dampness. His eyes scanned from one end of the room to the other while his hand hovered near where his weapon usually rested on his hip. Half expecting to see a terrorist ready to blow the place up, Damien didn't expect what he found. A gorgeous blonde sat at the far side of the bar.

They stared at each other. She seemed very cognizant of everything going on around her, yet her eyes never left his. Damien's heart pounded against the inside of his chest. He placed his hand over it to make sure it didn't fly out across the room. A small line of sweat formed down his spine.

She had honey blonde hair that cascaded down her back. Damien couldn't see the color of her eyes, but they were big and round. High cheekbones accented her heart-shaped face. She sat at a tall table which hid her body, but from what he could see, it looked like she kept herself in great shape.

She gave him no smile or invitation to join her. When their eye contact broke, his body relaxed. *What the fuck just happened?* He thought as he shifted in his seat. This case messed with his head and screwed with his body. *What happened to just getting a hard on at the sight of a beautiful woman?* Damien shook off the encounter the same moment Matt grabbed a very attractive girl.

Matt gave his girlfriend a passionate kiss. "Hey, there you are."

"Hey, yourself," she said in a husky voice.

"Melissa, I'd like you to meet Damien. He kept me company while I waited for you."

She held out a hand. "Nice to meet you, Damien. Matt explained you and your partner are here for that nasty case."

Damien smiled at her as he shook her hand. Her fingers were long, yet her hand seemed on the small side. She had the slightest trace of Asian heritage, but the contributions of one of her parents helped soften those sharp features. She had pulled her dark hair into a high updo, with enough tendrils surrounding her face to keep her from resembling an uptight schoolteacher. "Nasty would be one way of looking at it. Nice to meet you, Melissa."

Matt grabbed Melissa's hand and headed for the door. He kissed her as he led her out. Matt nodded over his shoulder in Damien's direction. "I'll see you and Joe in the morning."

Damien tilted his beer towards him. "Sure thing." He searched for the blonde woman. She no longer sat at her table. He sulked as a pang of disappointment shot through him.

A noise to the left of the bar caught Damien's attention. He turned to see a young woman throw a drink in a man's face and storm out. He turned back to his beer, only to see the seat next to him had been taken. By the blonde.

She looked at him and smiled. "What a waste of a good drink." The woman said. She motioned for the bartender, "Could I get a Michelob Ultra and a shot of Fireball Whiskey? Thank you."

Damien cocked an eyebrow at her but said nothing. She wore little makeup. Her stunning looks didn't need the enhancements. Her honey gold hair had woven strands of blonde, gold, and browns.

He signaled to the bartender to get another beer. The blonde sat staring at the baseball game on the television across from them. "You like baseball?" He asked her.

She turned towards him. "Yeah. I prefer football, college, but any sport will do. Hell, I like watching the old eighties wrestling. You know when the empire of WWE was just starting? Actually, I'll watch anything except reality television."

Damien tilted his head to the side. He thought he heard incorrectly. A woman who liked watching sports. He didn't think such a woman existed. "Do you live here in Springfield?"

"No, just here for a meeting. Figured I'd stop in and have a beer." She lifted her shot and threw it back. "And a shot."

Damien watched as she licked her lips. He wanted to taste the whiskey on her lips and tongue. "Where do you live?"

"Near Washington DC. How about you—you from here or near

here?"

"Nope. Chicago. Just here on business."

She turned to stare at him. Damn if he wasn't gorgeous. He had an oval shaped face, perfectly symmetrical and full lips, but not awkwardly so. Kissable, they looked kissable. "What kind of business? Or is it top secret?" She peered at him over the top of her beer.

Damien noticed the dimple in one of her cheeks which made her smile slightly crooked. "Security. And you? What has brought you all the way to Springfield from DC?"

"I'm in research," she said.

Damien turned in his seat to face her and tilted his head to the side. "Okay, you got me. What kind of research?"

She chuckled. "I doubt you would be very interested in it." Grateful she left her weapon in her room, she didn't want to have to explain anything about what she really does.

He lowered his head and stared at her. "Well, that just isn't fair. Now you've piqued my curiosity. Tell me what you do."

She laughed. "Alright. It isn't that interesting. I study human behavior and how it's affected by external stimuli."

Damien laughed. "Well okay then. That sounds very—clinical. Surely there's more to it than that? By the way, what's your name?" He didn't mean to let his eyes drift. However, when she swiveled around in her chair towards him the top button of her shirt had come undone, and he could see the curve of her breasts. They weren't too big, and they didn't look fake. When his eyes met hers again, she had either not noticed, or she chose not to say anything. He smiled at her while he waited for her response.

"Dillon. Yours?"

"Damien."

Dillon cocked an eyebrow at him. "Nice to meet you—Damien."

"Back to your work. Can you explain it better? It sounds—sort of interesting." He grinned at her.

She leaned in a little closer to him. Dillon watched as his eyes were drawn towards her chest. She winked at him. "You tried to fight the urge to look at my breasts, but you couldn't quite stop yourself."

He smiled coyly at her. "Did I?" Now he looked directly at her chest. "However, they are fantastic."

She laughed. "Thank you. However, when you looked at my boobs your breathing sped up just a bit, your pupils dilated, and you bit your bottom lip."

Damien looked quizzically at her. "I did all that?"

She nodded. "Yes. External stimuli and behavioral response. That's what I do."

"Well, I'll be." He paused and looked at her. Long thick lashes surrounded her big, round eyes. "What other things happen when people are attracted to each other?"

"Did you know that the smell you give off is what actually attracts someone?" She asked him.

He frowned at her. "Huh?"

"Have you ever seen a really hot chick, one you wouldn't mind spending the night with, say—across the room? You're attracted to her looks. You talk to her, and the conversation is going well, she has a great personality, but it's almost like a switch goes off. And wham—you're no longer attracted to her. As a matter of fact, you can't wait to get away from her?"

"Yeah, I guess that may have happened before," Damien said. "What's so important about that?"

"It's her pheromones that turned you off." Dillon saw the questionable look on his face. "Her smell. We each give off a certain odor—that's what attracts us to each other." She popped a pretzel into her mouth. "It happens across the entire animal kingdom."

Damien stared at her. She seemed like a Brainiac. Which didn't go with her body. But hey—a lot of his fantasies in high school included the librarian so—it worked. He took a long pull on his beer.

She made a pouty face. "You don't believe me? You think I'm crazy, don't you?"

He shrugged. "Not at all. I just hadn't heard that before."

Dillon leaned in close to him. Her breasts brushed against his arm. She placed her nose next to his neck and inhaled deeply. Then sat back up. "You smell like wood and the outdoors—very masculine. Very nice. I bet a lot of women are attracted to your smell."

Damien swung his legs around. He placed his hands on the sides of her bar stool blocking her in. He moved his face close to hers. Just before his lips touched hers, he moved to the side of her neck. His cheek brushed up against hers. Damien felt her body go rigid. He inhaled, but he didn't move when he blew the air out. He inhaled again before he sat back down on his stool. "Mmm, you smell like—fruit and candy."

Dillon's eyes were wide. She could still feel his warm breath on her neck. She hadn't been that close to a man in a long time. Dillon swallowed and blinked at him before speaking. "Fruit and candy. I guess that's better than smelling like fish."

Damien almost spit out his beer. "Fish?" He scrunched up his nose.

Dillon moved away from Damien and turned towards the bar. "Oh yeah, if you smell a fish odor around someone, and they aren't a fisherman, that's an indicator that you're not attracted to them at all. Actually, if you smell any unpleasant smell around someone that means you aren't attracted to them."

Damien noticed her immediate withdrawal from him. He glanced at his watch.

"Do you need to leave? Early appointment?" She asked.

He sipped his beer. "Not really. I still have half a beer. I do have a meeting, but it's not until around eight."

"Client? You said you did security, right?"

He gave her a side look. "Something like that. Helping someone track some information."

Dillon got the distinct impression he hid something from her. But she hadn't been honest with him. Although she hoped her deception wasn't as obvious as his. Probably for the best anyway. She couldn't let herself get involved with him. Things were about to get messy. And it didn't feel like one night with this guy would be enough.

She finished her beer and stood next to him. "Thanks for keeping me company for a while. I'm going to head out." She brushed up against him and inhaled. "You do smell very nice."

Damien gave her a wink and smiled at her. "My pleasure. I love fruit and candy." He watched her walk away laughing. *Damn that ass.*

Two beers later Damien entered his room. Joe had closed the connecting door. Not sure whether or not Taylor might still be there, he didn't knock on it. Undressing, the image of the blonde came to mind. He imagined her lean athletic body lying on his bed waiting for him. She stirred his libido, no question about that, but something else rooted inside Damien and squeezed his chest. Something far more dangerous than mere physical attraction.

CHAPTER SEVENTEEN

"Hey," Joe said between bites of pancakes, "where we going first?"

Damien smiled at Joe, not saying anything.

"What's with the smile you *mongo sap*?"

"I can't believe how much you eat. Don't you ever get full?"

"Hey, I'm still a growing boy. Plus," Joe raised his eyebrows and gave Damien a huge grin, "Taylor used up all my energy last night. I need to replenish."

"Whatever you say, Romeo. Just remember—vacca grassa."

Joe started to say something when the young woman who takes care of the buffet came up to Damien and filled his coffee cup.

Without acknowledging Joe, she concentrated all her attention on Damien. "Can I get anything else for you?"

Damien flashed her a smile, causing the waitress to blush. "No thank you."

"You let me know if I can." She sauntered away with an extra swing in her hips.

"Isn't this the self-serve breakfast? Everyone else in here has to go fill their own coffee or orange juice." Joe arched his eyebrows. "You know you might need some extra fuel, too. Our girl over there would bring you whatever you wanted to your room."

Damien glanced at the waitress as she walked away. "Do you ever think of anything else, or just sex?"

"Hey," Joe placed his fork on his plate, "we deal with some pretty ugly shit all the time, like this crappy case. Therefore, two different ways I can keep my head from exploding is to drink Macallan Scotch Whiskey and have a little fun with a *rosspot*. That's better than letting these fuckers we chase take up residence in my head without paying any rent." Joe picked up his fork and went back to eating, with a devilish grin on his face. "Sex and food. Those are my top priorities."

Damien finished his orange juice. "What the hell, a rosspot, seriously—where do you come up with these words?"

Joe smiled at his friend. "Have you not learned any of my Irish all these years as my partner? A rosspot is a good looking young lady."

"Let's get out of here. At the lab, we'll put all our information up on the board. Hopefully, Matt has something for us. Then we'll decide where to go from there." Damien left a tip on the table. "Oh hey, I got a text from Mrs. C. last night."

"Something wrong with Coach?" Mild concern ebbed in Joe's tone.

"Well, it depends on if you're asking the cat." Damien took out his phone and showed him the picture.

"Not again." Joe's gaze flickered with amusement. "She has way too much fun dressing him up." Grinning as he handed the phone back to Damien.

"I know. I don't have the heart to tell her to stop. I'm her only family. Both her kids died young, and her husband died a few years ago. I think I'm all she has."

Joe snorted. He reached out and patted his cheek. "You're such a softy. Hey did you put your phone number or room number on one of those bills? You could get lucky tonight." Nodding towards the server Joe threw a few extra bills on the table.

"Joe, I still can't figure out how you got to be a cop. It seems your talents lie in comedy. You're so damn funny."

***

Van Halen rang out again from Damien's phone as he and Joe entered the lab.

Joe frowned. "You've got to change that ringtone. It's annoying."

He shooed Joe away as he answered it. Damien stepped off to the side. "Morning Captain." As he spoke with Captain Mackey, he watched Joe's interaction with Taylor. They were so comfortable together, almost as if they had known each other for years. Damien put his phone away and headed for the security doors. "Good morning Taylor." Damien gave her a devilish grin.

"Hi, Lieutenant Kaine," she responded.

Damien noticed the delicate shade of pink Taylor always turned when she spoke with Joe. That alone had to be a turn on for Joe, it sure as hell was for him.

Joe followed Damien through the double doors and down the hallway. "Damn it," Joe whispered.

Damien glanced over his shoulder where Joe shimmied his leg trying to adjust his pants. "Seriously? Why don't you buy some underwear that fits your fat ass?" Damien smiled.

"Oh, *scree tú*. Hey, what did the captain want?"

"Director Jones called him while he had been in Rockford. Evidently, Jones and Mackey go way back. He updated him on what we had and explained to him that an FBI profiler had been speaking at his conference, an Agent McGrath. The Agent said he could come down and help us out on the case. The captain thinks he could help us narrow in on a suspect. This profiler is one of the FBI's best. The captain needs us back at the VCU, so he wants this to get solved, or we turn it over to the FBI by the middle of next week."

"Ha," Joe said. "It's the FBI's way of keeping their hand in the cookie jar. But makes no difference to me." Joe Shrugged. "The sooner I can get home the happier I am. Plus, I play nice with everyone."

"You are severely delusional." Damien chuckled. "You playing nice means you get all the crayons, and if someone doesn't like it then fuck them."

"You know I work well with others," Joe said. "What about Johnson in records, he and I get along great. It may have started out rocky but now—we get along fine."

"Only after you scared the shit out of him for saying those nasty comments about Rose," Damien said.

"Yeah well, Rose happens to be the sweetest little old lady. Johnson said some nasty shit." Joe paused. "Okay so maybe that isn't the best example."

"You think?" Damien glanced over at Joe. "The Agent will be here sometime today and help us any way he can." Damien and Joe rounded the corner the same time Matt did. "Hey Matt, just in time."

They all three walked towards the conference room and heard more than one voice from inside. Director Jones spoke with someone. As he spun around, he stepped off to the side. "Morning boys. Let me introduce you to Special Agent Dillon McGrath."

Damien almost shit his pants. He tried not to glare, but she seemed to do the same thing. She showed no signs she recognized him, and Damien tried to keep his own face devoid of any reaction. His body had its own plans, however. His skin tingled and sweat beaded down his back. He didn't have to get close to her to smell her. The air surrounding the Agent smelled of Jasmine and Vanilla. Joe gave him a sideways glance. Damien ignored it.

Jones introduced them all. "Agent, this is Matt, our resident does-all lab tech. These two men are Detective Joe Hagan and Lieutenant Damien Kaine from Division Central, Captain Mackey's Vicious Crimes Unit."

Damien zeroed in on Agent McGrath's full pouty lips. They twitched and curved into a smile.

"I'm aware of Captain Mackey's team and the work the VCU has done. Your Division has had some cases that have been of interest to the FBI. I've wanted to meet the men in his Unit for some time." She held out her hand. "Didn't realize I had already done that."

Damien studied the Agent as she shook hands first with Matt, Joe, and then him. "Yeah, I know what you mean. Behavior and stimuli, huh?" He stared at her big saucer-shaped eyes. In the bright lights of the room, her hair shimmered with highlights. The gold and honey wheat colors brought out the amber in her eyes, which resembled a well-aged whiskey. Gold and yellow flecks surrounded the pupils giving them a starburst effect. When Damien's hand touched hers, a slight shock ran through his fingers. He pulled his hand back and rubbed his palm. He noticed the Agent flinched at the same time.

Dillon's nostrils flared. "Hell of a lot closer to what I do. Security—really?"

Damien noticed everyone in the room stared at them. He just stepped away from the group offering no explanation. His jaw rippled with tension. She lied to him. He wondered if anything she said last night had been true.

Director Jones cleared his throat. "Agent McGrath has been with the Criminal Apprehension Unit and happens to be one of their best profilers. She should be an added asset to this team to catch this son of a bitch," Director Jones said as he poured himself a cup of coffee. "I've brought her up to speed on what we have so far. I think you can start from last night regarding Jesse Franks and go from there. I have some things to attend to so I will leave you all to your work."

Director Jones nodded to the Agent. "Agent McGrath, let me know if you need anything." He focused on Damien and Joe. "You two, take advantage of her being here. Let's get this guy." Jones patted Matt on his back as he left the room.

Agent McGrath nodded in agreement with the director.

Damien eyeballed her. He had no problem working with or for a woman. His problem with Agent McGrath—she was a proven liar, and she aroused him—and scared him. He nodded at her. "If you need any clarification, jump in with questions." He didn't smile at her or pretend to be happy about her presence. But if she helped them save another girl, that's all that mattered. He turned towards the other end of the table. "Matt, please start us off."

Matt glanced between Damien and the FBI Agent. There seemed to be more going on between them. "I got the surveillance video from the mall. There are hours and hundreds of people to search through. I called the parents of the girls who went to the mall with Becca. I hope they'll have a timeline for me later today. If I can find them in the video, I can backtrack and then follow them through the mall. It'll take some time, though."

"If you find this task is too much for you to handle, let me know. If you can get a timeline from the girls, I can send this up to our Electronic Detectives in Chicago and get them to go through it. If we can get one picture with our UNSUB, that's all we need. What else do you have?" Damien asked.

Matt flipped through his notes. "The lab identified the two substances found in the bag. PPG, Propylene Glycol is one. PPG helps process all kinds of foods. It can help stimulate milk production, although that isn't a widely-used practice anymore.

"The second substance present on the bags, iodine. Actually, an iodine derivative. Not sure, what its particular application is yet, but it could be for anything from cleaning of equipment to cleaning animals. Remember that both samples were old and somewhat compromised. The amounts didn't come from the manufacturing process, transfer only. The techs said it seemed like they had either been sitting around for a long time or they weren't properly stored."

Matt took a drink of coffee and then continued. "Caldare distributes these bags to various farm and feed stores, as well as selling them in bulk to several individuals. Caldare sent this batch to a local feed store down in Raymond right off Interstate 55. It's called Tankers. It's an enormous store and tends to service many of the farms in this area. I have a call to the manager to see if they can give me any information."

Agent McGrath spun around in her chair. She stopped spinning long enough to place her coffee mug on the table. "These are great chairs. They spin so easily." She spun around one more time. "Iodine is the best cleaning solution for the teats of the dairy cows before milking. The milking machines can increase the chance for swelling and inflammation of the teats. However, you'll find the cost of iodine has skyrocketed.

"If anyone is still using it for these purposes, they'll be switching soon, if not already, to chlorine-based disinfectant. Way cheaper and more cost effective. There are several cleaning agents used on farms. Depending on what area you need to clean. Anyway, back to the iodine, it's too expensive." She spun around in the chair again. "These chairs are awesome. I want one."

Everyone stared at Agent McGrath. She looked up and saw their expressions. She let out a little snort. "My grandfather used to have a few milking cows. He didn't have a huge dairy farm operation, but he did manage to have the creamiest milk. I spent endless summers learning how to milk a cow, the old-fashioned way." She smiled at the men around the table. "These chairs really are fun." She continued to spin.

Damien glowered at the Agent. He hadn't expected her to bring anything to the discussion. She seemed more interested in how fast she could make the chair spin than in the evidence briefing. She annoyed him. "Well, thanks for the lesson in dairy farming. I appreciate any help that will catch this killer. You might want to just put in a PO for the chair with your office in Quantico. Maybe they can have it there by the time you get back."

Dillon stopped abruptly. "You're just a little hostile Lieutenant. I'm surprised. You weren't this way last night."

He turned and stared at her. "You're kidding me, right? You lied. You made it out like you were some kind of science chick."

"I am a science chick. And by the way, you said you were in security, was that the truth?"

Damien fumed. He had never been so aggravated by one female before. But as much as he hated to, he had to be honest with himself, he did the same thing she did. Neither one of them had been honest the night before. "Well, it seems we're both guilty."

Joe and Matt just sat in silence. They looked at each other then back at Damien and Dillon. Joe sighed and scooted his chair closer to them. "Umm—I get the feeling you two have met before." They both started to speak. He held up his hand shaking his head. "Nope. Don't even want to know. Whatever the problem is, you two need to figure it out. If you don't think you can table your differences, then we need to ask for another profiler." Joe let that sit for a few minutes. He then continued, "I think you two are adult enough to do that. Matt do you have anything else?"

Joe's question caught Matt off guard. "Uh—give me a second." He looked through his notes.

Dillon and Damien sat in silence. Neither looking at the other. Dillon looked at Joe. "I can work fine with anyone. We need to focus on these girls."

Joe turned to Damien but said nothing. He just lifted an eyebrow and stared.

"Yeah, yeah, I can work with her. Let's move on," Damien said. Even with his anger about to erupt Damien still wondered what waking up on Sunday mornings with that firm body wrapped around him would be like. *Whoa, where the hell did that come from?* He thought. Not good. Don't think that. Lost in his thoughts, he jumped in his chair when Taylor walked through the door.

"Lieutenant Kaine this just came in; I think you might want to see it." Taylor handed a paper to Damien then stood next to Joe. Her hand rested against his chair, her fingers barely touching his shoulder.

"Thanks, Taylor." Damien read over the report. "Hey—holy shit, this is a missing person's report, for another girl in this area," Damien said.

Matt reached for the paper. "I set up a program last night to filter through past cases and print out anything that matched up with our search criteria. Tiffany Basset went missing from a diner up on Route 104, Toni's Café, two days ago, on Tuesday." Matt stopped reading. "They found her car in the parking lot, with her books in it. No sign of her belongings or keys. Goes to school here in Springfield."

Damien read the report again. "She disappeared shortly after Becca had been found. This person is moving fast, and I don't like it." Damien nodded to Joe and Agent McGrath. "Let's go talk to the parents and then the people at Toni's." He gathered up some files. "Matt, what did you gather concerning those four other girls?"

"Oh, here." He handed him a file. "It has everything reported and what the Sheriff's found regarding each case. Also, here is information on the three farms in our radius. The bacon, the cheese, and the soy farm. I'm also conducting another search for unsolved cases in the area relating to any girls within our established age range. I should have some results before too long."

"Great. Good thinking on that. If you get anything else on the bags, let us know." Damien turned to the FBI Agent. "Agent McGrath, you want to ride with us?"

"Sure. I'm going to go to the bathroom, give me a minute." Dillon headed out the door.

Damien occupied himself so his gaze wouldn't follow her. He grabbed two diet sodas from the little fridge in the corner of the room. Restocking magically occurred every night. He looked back to see Joe had stopped to talk to Taylor in the hallway. He couldn't hear their conversation, but he didn't need to.

Taylor leaned into Joe and handed him a folded piece of paper. Damien watched Joe and could tell by his body language he wanted to touch her. He whispered in her ear but kept his hands in his pockets. Taylor blushed. Damien watched Joe smile as his gaze followed Taylor's ass down the corridor. Smiling to himself, Damien continued out the doors.

***

"What the hell are you doing?" Damien asked Joe. "You got to pee or something?" He noticed Joe shift from foot to foot while he waited for the car door to unlock.

"No, you *gowl*." His Irish accent thick with annoyance. "Every time I get near Taylor, I get all *horned up*. It's like an automatic reaction. I get all these *manky* thoughts about her. I can't control myself." Joe climbed into the SUV.

Damien stared at Joe. "What the fuck is wrong with you? You're like a sixteen-year-old who's touched a girl's boobs for the first time. What the hell do manky and gowl even mean? C'mon for crying out loud."

"Green isn't your color." Joe snorted at Damien's dirty look. He stared at the picture of the missing girl. "Our killer is sticking with what he likes, young and beautiful. She's been missing for thirty-six hours. We have maybe two days to find her alive if he keeps to his current killing schedule." He paused making sure Agent McGrath didn't walk up on them. "What's up with this McGrath? You two were ready to kill each other. Where did you meet her?"

Damien leaned back against the seat. "Damn. I met her at the bar last night. We spent an hour or two talking. She told me she studied behavior and external effects on it. She even used her boobs as an experiment. But she never once told me she was an FBI Agent."

Joe chuckled then smirked at him. "From what I heard you weren't completely honest with her either. Did you tell her you were here for a homicide investigation?"

"No."

"Then why are you so pissed?" Joe shook his head and laughed. "You wanted to sleep with her, didn't you? Now you find out you have to work with her and it's killing you." Joe slapped his thigh and laughed even harder.

Damien tilted his head and growled. "Shut up. Just shut up. Sometimes you act like an idiot."

Joe continued to chuckle.

After a moment of silence, Damien turned towards his partner. "Do you think she's any good as a profiler? She seems a little off. I mean she seemed to enjoy spinning around in the chair more than paying attention to the meeting."

Joe gazed with focus at Damien. "Hmm, those chairs do spin fast. And they rock like a rocking chair. But I do think she has a few quirks. All profilers do. They spend their time inside the heads of some very nasty people, it's what keeps them sane." He smiled at Damien. "Look how quickly she got into your head."

***

Agent McGrath splashed water on her face. She couldn't believe the man at the bar worked for Captain Mackey. The man she almost asked if he wanted to come back to her room and fuck her brains out. That never would've happened, but she wanted it to. And now she had to work with him. *Okay McGrath, get ahold of yourself.* Dillon stared at her reflection. *Damn that man was sex on a stick. Get yourself together and be professional.* She told herself.

Dillon hadn't reacted to a man like that, ever. The underlying attraction between them scared the crap out of her. She would much rather stare down the barrel of a gun than have feelings like this. When she touched his hand, she had a tingling sensation. And forget about last night. She could still smell him this morning when she had woken up. But he's a liar. He didn't even come near telling her the truth. At least she hinted at the truth of what she did.

Dillon shook her head. No, she wouldn't let herself go through that kind of heartbreak again. Her last boyfriend, a colleague no less, took her heart, ripped it out, and stomped on it. He didn't even have the decency to hand it back to her. He left it bleeding on the ground.

Dillon finished up in the bathroom. She had never let someone she worked with get to her. She took a deep breath and readied herself. Dillon buried any attraction she had for him down deep. She had to treat this like any other case with any other law enforcement agency. The only difference, Damien Kaine.

CHAPTER EIGHTEEN

He had visited Tiffany during the night only to have his plans interrupted. One of his cows found an opening in the fence and took a midnight stroll. He wanted to spend extra quality time with her today, so he lied to his workers. Tiffany had drawn him to her, the minute he saw her in the diner. It's because she looked most like HER. If he didn't know better, he would have thought it was HER. But he knew better. She just reminded him so much of that bitch. Even some of her mannerism were the same. The only other one to resemble HER so much was the woman he saw at the market. He just hadn't been able to get to her. It definitely wasn't from lack of trying.

He took the long way around to the old house. He started spending time there after his Mom had died. Over those first few years, he would just come down and sit on the porch. It had been during one of those visits he decided he wanted to expand the farm. He tried to convince his Dad, but that proved harder than he'd expected.

After dear old Dad died, he had made sure everyone on the farm understood that no one could come down to this area. No one had permission to step foot on or around the old property. He had even extended the fence across the back part of this property, and he had put up a gate down at the entry off the road. Locking it when he wasn't there.

If someone wanted in, they could get in, but everyone in this town knew he owned the property. His reputation and business bought him more respect than the average person, so he didn't worry too much about trespassers. He chuckled to himself. Everyone believed the loss of his father had made him sentimental, and that he came down here to remember his dead father and mother. Idiots. They were all idiots.

Through the years, he had kept up the old house, repairing it when necessary, keeping the electricity and the water connected. If he stayed in the old house, he could see the girls anytime he wanted. However, that would be hard to explain to his employees.

His pulse increased as he thought about HER. She had been a bitch to him, ignored him, and made him look like an ass in front of his friends. To top it all off, she had gotten him banned from the swimming hole. He had kept tabs on her after school ended. Kept track of where she was hanging out. He didn't make it obvious. Still, he hadn't seen her for some time when he had bumped into her by pure luck. There she stood, filling her car with gas, as he drove by. She had deserved everything he did to her. He had taught her a few things about humility.

As he pulled onto the long drive that led to the old house, his attention returned to the young girl in the basement. Tiffany. He had plans for her. He whistled as he entered the kitchen carrying a bag. Its contents had become an integral part of his enjoyment. He had decided Tiffany needed to be his guest for a long time. He could do some of those things he had done to HER. He frowned as he thought back. SHE didn't last as long as he had hoped. This time he would make sure not to do too much at once. His smile widened as he descended the stairs.

It took a moment for the scene to register. His nostrils flared, and his lips pulled back, baring his teeth. A guttural roar filled the room. "NO—NO—NO! You stupid bitch! How could you do this?"

He ran to the bed and grabbed Tiffany's lifeless body. "You fucking bitch!" He saw the bowl on the floor and stared at the contents. Tilting his head back, he howled. "You fucking knew the minute I set the bowl down, and you didn't say anything. How could you?" He grabbed her by her hair and yanked her head back. He flinched recoiling at her swollen face and neck. Her eyes bulged from their sockets. He released her head, and she crumpled on the mattress.

He paced back and forth pulling on his hair. "You had no right to make that kind of decision! It's not your choice to make. You had to take all the fun away from me. Fuck, Fuck, Fuck! I had plans for you."

He grabbed the bowl and flung it across the room. He unhooked the restraints and grabbed her by one of her ankles. "How dare you do this to me! You had no right." He continued to rant as he dragged her off the bed. Her head hit the concrete floor with a sickening thud. "I hope you suffered. I hope the pain and fear of what you went through made your last few minutes fucking hell."

He dragged her over to the drain near the opposite end of the basement. He glared at the far wall. He scanned the tools he had to choose from. His lips pulled back into a tight smile as his hand settled on the axe. Lifting it off its hook, he turned it over in his hand, the weight of it helped calm him. He grabbed a thick pair of work gloves. He rolled his shoulders and took a deep breath. With one last look at her, he cursed, heaved the axe above his head, and swung.

Thirty minutes later, panting, he threw the axe; it skidded across the blood-soaked floor. He gathered the chunks of flesh and threw them into several bags. He carted the bags up the stairs and tossed them into the back of his truck. They hit the flatbed with a mushy wet sound.

Washing at the sink in the kitchen, he watched the pink-tinged water swirl down the drain, carrying with it blood, tissue, and disappointment. The disappointment that Tiffany didn't suffer all that he had planned for her.

He decided as he got behind the wheel of his truck, a trip down the proverbial memory lane would be the perfect spot to dump old Tiff.

CHAPTER NINETEEN

Chatham, IL

Joe hung up the phone with the Chatham Police Department. "The chief said Betty worked Tuesday night and might have some information for us. He said she would be there until eight tonight. He sent me an email with all the information they have, which isn't much. There were no witnesses, and no one reported any screams or yelling, nothing. It's as if Tiffany just vanished, like Jesse. I forwarded the file to you, Damien. Agent McGrath, I can make sure you get a copy, too," Joe said.

She nodded. She reached into her pocket and handed him a card. "Send me everything you have to that email. I appreciate it."

"Alright." Dragging his hand through his hair, Damien cursed softly. "Maybe we will catch a break. Maybe the parents have something that will help us. Shit! Maybe we can find their daughter before he kills her." Damien kissed the medal he wore around his neck and whispered, *"Proteggici padre."*

***

Damien followed Joe and Agent McGrath up the short walkway. Although it may have been poor timing, he liked watching the Agent walk in front of him. She had a very nice ass. He may enjoy her looks, but he would not pursue the physical attraction he had to her. He had to push that and her as far away as possible.

Joe rang the doorbell of the modest two-story house. Damien glanced around the neighborhood. Perfect place to raise a family. A dog barked and whined, and a minute later a disheveled man with bloodshot eyes answered the door. He looked like he sported two black eyes. *Not sleeping for the last two nights will do that*, Damien thought.

Holding the collar of a medium-sized black and brown dog who danced around, the man's brow furrowed at the three strangers on his doorstep. "Yes, may I help you?"

All three held out their identification. "Yes sir, Mr. Basset, I'm Detective Joe Hagan, and this is Lieutenant Damien Kaine and Agent McGrath with the FBI. We're here to ask you some questions about your daughter."

Glancing at the badges, he motioned for them to enter. "Oh yes, yes please come in." He let go of the dog. She ran to them and gave each the sniff over. "Trudy won't bite. She isn't much of a watchdog. Go lay down in your bed Trudy, go on girl, go lay down." The dog sulked over to her bed and spun in a circle several times then plopped down. She let out a long whine, letting everyone know she wasn't happy.

"Trudy minds well," Damien said. His heart went out to this man. Mr. Basset seemed as if he wanted to crawl out of his skin.

"What—oh—yes. Tiffany spent a whole summer training her. We went through an endless amount of dog treats. She comes on command and follows without a leash. She's an excellent dog. Tiffany's pride and joy." His last comment rolled out of his mouth on a wave of sadness that crashed into everyone. "Hannah, Hannah, some detectives are here about Tiffany."

Mr. Basset moved from the foot of the stairs back to the center of the room. "My wife Hannah will be down in a minute. She's trying to get the twins down to nap. We're attempting to keep some kind of normalcy while we wait for answers." He waved them into the living room and gestured towards a pair of chairs and a sofa. "Can I offer you something to drink?"

"No sir we're fine. We have a few questions we would like to ask you," Joe responded.

Dozens of posters and fliers lay scattered on the table in front of them. Mr. Basset noticed the Detectives staring at all the fliers. "When we found out about the other murdered girl, we couldn't sit around and not do anything. We put up fliers all over the city as well as in Springfield. We want to find our daughter; we will do whatever we need to." He stood extended his hand out. "Here's my wife, Hannah. These are two Detectives from Springfield, and this is Agent McGrath with the FBI. They are here about Tiffany."

"Oh no sir," said Damien. "We're with the Division Central's VCU. We're here to help with this case." Damien glanced over at Joe. Damien wanted to keep the details of Becca's murder under wraps for as long as possible. He knew word had spread about the dead girl being found, but no other details had been leaked. These parents didn't need the extra heartache of knowing what Becca had gone through and wonder if Tiffany might experience the same thing.

"I see," said Mr. Basset. "Well, whatever we need to do. We want our Tiffany back."

Hannah Basset sat next to her husband on the couch with her hands clenched. Damien could see she held on to a very delicate and fragile thread.

"Could you tell us about Tiffany? How was she doing in school, did she have any problems?" Joe asked.

Mrs. Basset took a deep breath. "Tiffany loved school. She wanted to go to college next year, study math, and become a teacher. Her grades were excellent, and she got along well with the kids in her class. She didn't have a boyfriend; we didn't allow her to date." Hannah glanced at her husband who nodded in agreement.

"Has Tiffany been staying out past curfew, or has her behavior changed?" Damien asked.

"No," Mr. Basset responded. "She studied a lot because she wanted to do well on this placement test. Tiffany needed it to help her get into an advanced math class at her school this spring. That class would help her get into summer classes at the local college."

"What had her schedule been the day she went missing?" Joe asked.

"Nothing out of the ordinary." Mrs. Basset closed her eyes for a brief moment. "She went to the community center after school. Tiffany helps there two hours every Tuesday. She started volunteering there when she needed a service project for her Confirmation. She enjoyed it so much she continued to do it." Hannah Basset's breath hitched. "From there she went to meet a few friends at Toni's Café, in Auburn. She called me as soon as she got there and said she would be home by eight." Hannah Basset all but whispered. "I didn't speak to her again."

"The meeting—spur of the moment or scheduled?" Joe asked.

Mrs. Basset sucked in air and shook her head. "No, Tiffany and her friends just decided that day at school. She called me from the community center and asked if she could go. I didn't think it would be a problem." Hannah Basset could no longer hold back her sobs. She buried her face in her hands. Trudy slinked over and laid her head on Hannah's lap.

Dillon glanced around as she listened to Kaine and Hagan ask questions. The family had an orderly home, but not in an OCD way. It had a homey and inviting atmosphere. They burned some kind of religious candle on the mantle. "Mr. and Mrs. Basset, do you think your daughter would get into a car with someone she didn't know? I know you said you didn't allow her to date, but do you think Tiffany would do something like that?" Dillon asked.

"I—I don't believe so. I hope not." Mr. Basset looked down at his hands before he continued. "We've had open and honest conversations with our daughter about predators and the tactics used to gain a young girl's trust."

Damien glared at Dillon, who seemed oblivious. He asked one last question. "Can we get the names of the kids in the study group? Do you by chance know them? And could you give us Tiffany's cell number, we may be able to track her movements with it?"

Mr. Basset shifted in his seat, unsure of what to answer. Mrs. Basset lifted her head. She stroked Trudy's head and ears. "I only know one girl, Maryanne Rogers. Hang on, and I'll get her number for you." She lifted Trudy's head and bent down to kiss the top of it just before she pushed her off her lap. Trudy slid to the floor and waited for Mrs. Basset to return.

Mr. Basset rose and wrapped his arm around his wife when she came back into the room. "If there isn't anything else, I need to tend to my wife and children."

All three thanked the Bassets for their time. They left their cards with them and started towards the door when Mrs. Basset spoke up. "Agent McGrath, do you think that's what happened with our daughter? I mean, do you think she willingly got into a car with someone?"

Dillon looked between the two parents. "Mrs. Basset, I don't think anything you did or didn't do led to Tiffany's disappearance. I asked that question to try to understand your daughter's mindset at the time of her disappearance." Dillon ignored the hard stare from Damien. "You're doing the right thing here, by trying to keep your younger children on a regular routine. That will help them through this." Dillon kept all emotion out of her voice when she spoke to the Bassets.

Damien addressed Mr. Basset. "If you think of anything, please let us know." He walked out but stopped and turned back to face them. "I noticed the St. Jude candle you have burning on your mantle. I can see that your faith is strong. I can't tell you anything about the investigation, but I can tell you we will find Tiffany. *Christo proteggere il suo gregge.* Christ will protect his flock." He left the Bassets holding on to hope and faith.

CHAPTER TWENTY

Joe closed the car door. "Let's get to the restaurant and see if we can get some more answers from Betty. Maybe she has something, anything. We only need one piece of evidence that will lead us to a suspect."

Dillon touched Damien on his back. "I didn't mean to cut in on your interview."

Damien turned around and gawked at her. "Are you serious? You didn't think of us or the Bassets for one minute. You just jumped in and asked a question the parents weren't ready for. Can you tell me, Agent McGrath, what made you ask that question in the first place?"

Dillon heard the dismissive tone in his voice and the anger. "Look if you're going to keep your panties in a wad over how this working relationship started, it's going to be a long fucking week. And not that I owe you any kind of explanation of how I conduct my investigations, I will tell you that asking questions and catching someone off guard, can often reveal way more than just the answer they give." She glared at him. "That's investigation 101, surely I don't have to explain the concept to you?" Dillon understood most agencies didn't want her help, and normally it didn't bother her. But damn if she had to justify her methods to Lieutenant Kaine.

Joe's phone rang. "There's the bell kids. Go to your corners for a time out." He glared at Damien as he answered it. "Hey Matt, what's up? Sure, okay...so they don't have a lot to go on. No, get the list of who they sold the bags to. Maybe that will give us a lead. We are going to Toni's Café now, we should be back by..." he glanced at Damien and shrugged, "I think by three or four. Okay sounds good. Thanks, Matt. See ya."

Damien popped a piece of gum in his mouth. He held the package out towards Agent McGrath. She just shook her head. Damien turned to Joe, "What's up with Matt?"

"Matt went up to the feed store," Joe paused as a grin spread across his face. "I think he's been itching to go ask questions in person. He seems very interested in this case. It's got to be because this is his first major case where he is working outside the lab." Shaking his head, he continued. "Anyway, they didn't have a lot of information, but they gave what they had. The bags are expensive. The feed store orders them only when the customer pre-pays. They don't want to be stuck with a whole bunch in stock.

"The list has four farms on it. The store doesn't log batch numbers or anything, just who bought the items." Joe grabbed a piece of Damien's gum and popped it into his mouth before he continued. "He's going to meet us back at the lab and go over everything. He has a few things to check out. By the time we get back, he should have everything sorted out."

Damien hunched over the steering wheel. "We've been here three days, and we don't have shit. Nothing. We're chasing a damn ghost. He'll kill Tiffany before we get to her; I've no doubt about that. But maybe we can keep him from getting another girl." Damien let out a sigh. He pulled into the parking lot of the diner. "Hey before we leave let's get sandwiches to go. I'm starving, but I don't want to take the time to eat here. I want to get back to the lab."

Joe licked his lips. "Man, I'm starving too. A sandwich sounds perfect. Just thinking about it is making my mouth water. Ooh, I hope they have pickles, can't eat a sandwich without a pickle."

Damien furrowed his brow. "Seriously, are you five years old?" He focused his attention on the Agent in his backseat. "Agent McGrath, are you hungry?"

"I could eat something." She laughed at herself. "I tend to get caught up in what I'm working on and forget to eat, so yeah I'm hungry."

Damien pinched the bridge of his nose and let out an exasperated sigh. "How can you forget to eat?"

She frowned at him as she got out of the car. "I get busy. I guess we just can't all be as perfect as you." She slammed the door and walked to the front of Toni's Café.

Damien slammed his door and stomped towards the diner. He stood next to Joe and Dillon and studied the parking lot layout. There were no obstructions, nothing but a huge wide-open lot. The diagonal design of the parking lot allowed for the larger capacity delivery trucks and eighteen-wheelers to park and be on the edge of the lot. All other vehicles had the rest of the lot to park in. He glanced to his right and noticed that Dillon also studied the layout. "What do you see Agent?"

She stared at Damien's handsome face. Its oval shape curved into a masculine squared-off chin. *God, she wanted to kiss him.* Surprised at the lust swirling inside her, and the equal feeling of disappointment in herself for having it; she fleetly turned away. "I think this guy didn't care about being in the open, or about being seen."

Dillon paused and took a few steps off to the side, then focused on Damien and Joe. "I think it's a good possibility he could have used his own vehicle to block the view from any other patrons. He could have either planned this, or he just lucked out. He'd had to have parked near or right next to Tiffany's car. There would be no other way for him to get Tiffany into his vehicle without anyone seeing them."

"Joe, what do you think, you agree with Agent McGrath?" Damien asked with just a hint of sarcasm.

"Hell yeah. This person seems to have the luck of the Irish that's for damn sure. I don't think he planned this though. There've been no reports of stalking of any kind, no one noticed anyone watching Tiffany or following her. I think things just fell into place." Joe scanned the parking lot. "I don't think he necessarily forced her into his car either. We can explore it later back at the lab, but he may have convinced Tiffany to get in his vehicle. That's why no one heard any screams."

Dillon looked at Joe. The big Irish cop had a keen mind inside that well-toned body. "Lieutenant Kaine, you wondered why I asked that question at the Basset's—well for the very reason Joe just stated. The missing person report said there were no witnesses, and no one heard any screams. I got the impression that Tiffany had a level head on her shoulders. I think Joe is right, she got into the vehicle willingly."

Joe had a big smile on his face. "Of course, I'm right. Let's get inside and talk to Betty. I'm starving. And for God's sake don't argue in here, it'll make us all look bad."

Damien rolled his eyes. "Bite me." Damien spun and led the way into the diner. A woman behind a long counter greeted them. Damien found himself drawn to her.

The woman's button up shirt had an embroidered name tag across her left breast. Large cursive letters spelled out her name. The letters also brought more attention to her already large chest. She had a bouffant hairdo that came straight out of the seventies.

Even though she had to be in her fifties, Betty had something oddly appealing and attractive about her. She reminded Damien of Flo, from the reruns of Alice. Her bright red lipstick and the touch too much eye makeup mesmerized Damien. He smirked glimpsing Dillon out of the corner of his eye. He had no doubt his attraction had nothing to do with the way Betty smelled. "Hey Betty, I'm Lieutenant Kaine. This is Detective Hagan and FBI Agent McGrath. Could you take a few minutes to speak with us?"

"Absolutely sugar. The Sheriff called me and told me to expect you. George, take over my tables for fifteen." Betty motioned for them to go sit in an empty booth.

"You got it, Betty," George said, but his gaze never left Dillon. His crooked teeth on display for her.

"I can't believe a young girl went missing from this parking lot. We've never had any problems around here—ever."

Damien noticed Betty's face was slightly ashen and her voice quivered. "Can you tell me about that evening? Did anything that night stand out to you?"

Betty took her time answering. "Tuesday night, it happened during the dinner rush, we had a pretty good crowd. Regulars from around here, nothing unusual about them. A group of young kids had come in with their books. I guess that's the missing girl and her friends." Her lips turned down in an exaggerated frown before she continued. "The study group paid their bill. The kids seemed to say goodbye at the table." She cocked her head to the side. "That struck me as odd. I walk out with my friends, but I'm old fashioned, what the hell do I know, right? That's when I noticed the missing girl went to the bathroom while her friends went to their cars."

"Betty, did you see if anyone seemed to be overly interested in the study group? I imagine they must have generated a lot of attention." Damien asked her.

"Oh yeah, they acted like typical teenagers. There seemed to be a lot more giggling going on instead of studying. But no, I didn't notice anyone paying particular attention to the kids."

"Betty, did you see Tiffany speak with someone on her way to or from the restroom?" Damien asked her.

"Well, no I didn't see her actually talk with anyone, but I got a feeling she *might* have spoken with someone. Jim, one of my regular customers, headed out the door, and I yelled out to him to have a good night and good luck with his deliveries. A short time later I watched her walk out the front door and head towards her car. That's all I remember seeing."

Dillon cut in before Damien or Joe could ask a question. "What makes you think she spoke to someone near the restrooms?" Dillon noticed Joe elbowed Damien.

Betty shrugged. "I don't know; I guess it's an impression I got. Her friends started to head out to their cars, and the girl took longer than normal. After she'd come back from the restrooms, she was flushed and seemed a bit flustered. It's the way the girl acted that made me think she'd flirted with someone. You know when you talk to a good-looking boy or something. Maybe someone you had a crush on," Betty said as she winked at Joe.

"Betty, do you remember seeing anyone, before or after she went to the bathroom?" Dillon asked.

Betty gave it some consideration before she answered. She shook her head. "No, I really don't. Jim went to his old delivery truck, and he pulled out of the lot when the young girl walked to her car, at least, I'm pretty sure, anyway." Betty smiled at Joe.

"Can you tell me who Jim is?" Joe asked.

"Yeah, he's a driver with a massive dairy farm in Taylorville. They have to be the largest dairy farm in the state. He went to work there right out of high school. Jim's father has worked there for many years. Let me think, oh shoot, I know his last name. C'mon think—what is it?" Betty tapped her long red fingernails on the table. Closing her eyes, her head bobbed slightly. She snapped her fingers, "Jim Goshen. Yes, that's it, Jim Goshen."

"Are there any surveillance cameras?" Damien asked.

"No. We told the owner he should get some. He has one in the back office where the money is and one right above the register. It's angled to pick up the money going in and out. He doesn't have them angled to get the customers in the frame."

"We want to give you our cards, and if you think of anything else, even if you don't believe it's relevant, please call us." Damien handed his card over to Betty as did Joe and Dillon. They left Betty and headed for the takeout window to place their orders. Damien could swear Joe drooled while they waited.

In the vehicle, Damien got his container situated and started the drive back to the lab. He caught Dillon's eyes for a split second before she turned away. They rode in silence for a few moments while everyone ate their lunch. Damien noticed Dillon staring out the window. "Hey Dillon, I can smell the smoke, from the wheels spinning in your head. Do you have any ideas you want to share with us? Or is that against federal regulations?"

Joe heard the terse tone and glanced over at Damien and mouthed, "What the fuck?"

Damien simply shrugged.

Dillon glared at him in the mirror. He caught her stare and rolled his eyes at her. "Well under normal circumstances, you'd need clearance for me to divulge anything to you. But I'll make an exception." Her voice had an antagonistic edge to it. "I think our guy spoke with Tiffany. I believe Betty when she said Tiffany seemed to be blushing. I can see it playing out. Tiffany sits down with her friends. She sees him. Flirts with stares and smiles. Then when it's time to go, she goes to the bathroom. Quite possibly, she followed him. But either way, she meets him in the hallway by the restroom." Dillon paused taking a sip of her drink. "I think she left with him willingly like Joe suggested. Maybe he said something like, *hey ride with me and I'll bring you back here*—I don't know—that's how I see it playing out."

Joe gave a side look to Dillon, "I don't know how a teenage girl's brain works, but that sounds plausible." Joe closed his eye and patted his stomach. "Damn, this sandwich tastes like it came from one of our Chicago delis."

Damien shrugged. "Tiffany had to feel damn comfortable with this person to get in his vehicle. She seems like a very smart girl."

"Lieutenant Kaine, May I have that number for the girl from the study group?"

"Why?" Damien had no reason to ask. Technically she outranked him. But he couldn't help himself.

"Again, I do not owe you an explanation. I don't even need your permission. I could just take over the case and kick your ass to the curb." She smiled at him in the rearview mirror.

Damien stared her down with venom in his eyes. "Try it. I'll make your life miserable."

She laughed at him. "Trust me, you already make my life miserable." She smirked at him. "Listen, Lieutenant, I'm on your side. Even if you are too stubborn to see it. I think she will feel more comfortable speaking with me. I wanted to start with a call then if I need to do a face to face I will," Dillon said.

Damien sighed as he tore the note in half and handed the girl's number back to her. "Here." Damien's clipped response brought another annoyed glance from Joe. He handed the other number to him. "Text this number to Matt, see if he can find out if Tiffany's cell is still on or where and when it was shut off."

Joe looked between the two as he took the piece of paper. "This work environment is so nice."

Dillon shrugged as she stared at Joe. "Sorry." Her lips curved upward. "Anyway, Joe, could you tell me about Jesse Franks who went missing six months ago? What information did you and the lieutenant get from the Sheriff and the parents?" Dillon asked.

Joe swallowed his bite of sandwich. He had to smile at the way the Agent addressed him. She used his first name while calling Damien Lieutenant. She had a spine, and she enjoyed getting under Damien's skin. "I forgot we didn't get to her before we left to talk to the Bassets, hang on." He reached over and grabbed the file they had received from the Sheriff. It also had notes he had taken during the interviews. "She left her friend's house after hanging out on a Saturday night. She left there and went to the local grocery store. The store clerks all said they watched her come in, make her purchases, and then she went to her car.

"The store's location is approximately twenty miles from her house. She got a flat tire and had to pull over to change it. That's when our guy took her. No signs of a struggle, no signs of another vehicle. No one saw her parked on the side of the road. No fingerprints on the car except for family. That's all we got." Joe took another bite of his sandwich.

Dillon sat quietly for a few moments. She placed her trash in her container and shut the lid. "Becca went missing from the mall, Jesse off a highway, and Tiffany from a parking lot. I don't think our killer planned these abductions. What I mean by that, is he didn't see these girls before the day they went missing. I think they were spur of the moment."

Damien turned and glanced at Joe. "I'm betting he did something to Jesse's car while she shopped in the store. Which means he had to see her at the store that evening. Either he did a late evening delivery or he happened to just be going by and sees her go in, then does something to her tire. The killer planned it so she would be away from the store, alone. She pulled over, he shows up. He's handsome, kind, and charming. Not threatening at all. She lets her guard down, he takes her."

Joe held up his hand. "He's handsome, that's all we know for sure. The girls who were with Becca at the mall made sure we got that detail. Average height, simple dark clothes and a baseball hat, but they didn't have any other information."

Dillon nodded and waved her hand in the air. "That accounts for the lack of detail from Becca's friends. They paid attention to his face; not to any other details. The girls gave you a vague description of his clothes, but they couldn't give you much of anything else. Teenage girls are much worse when it comes to getting details than women. The randy teenage girl gets googly-eyed over a boy's handsome face, maybe his body, especially if he is in shape.

"They may notice clothes if they're designer, but they don't pay all that much attention. The girls described him as good-looking, but he isn't standing out in any other way. Betty said she didn't see anyone speaking with Tiffany, yet she seemed positive the girl spoke with someone."

Dillon tilted her head to the side. "I bet our killer visits Toni's Café often. I think this UNSUB can be invisible when he needs to be. He's like a chameleon. He can blend in, hide in plain sight." Dillon's eyebrows furrowed together. Her brain spun out of control. Something niggled at her. An important detail she missed.

Damien snickered. Dillon seemed to get lost in her thoughts a lot. He wasn't sure if she didn't want to share information or if she just plotted out her cases that way. Either way, it bugged him, she bugged him.

"Hey Dillon, what's up? I can see that look on your face," Joe said.

She turned and stared at him. "Hmm, that obvious huh?"

"Well I'm a trained professional—but yeah, that obvious," Joe responded. He glanced back at her as he finished his sandwich. "What are you thinking, Special FBI Agent?" A crooked grin plastered on his face.

She rolled her eyes at him. At least, Joe didn't seem to have any hang-ups about her assistance. "I don't know. Something has been nagging me, but I didn't get much time to go over all your evidence in detail yet. It must be something I noticed this morning when the director went over everything with me. I need to look at the other girls that went missing some years back. I feel like I have missed something. I'll figure it out."

She trailed off as the SUV pulled into the parking lot of the lab.

CHAPTER TWENTY-ONE

Forensic Lab

Dillon's eyes followed Joe as he headed straight for Taylor. She watched the interaction between them. The handsome detective leaned over the counter as Taylor pushed into him. Joe's lips hovered right next to her ear. Taylor's cheeks flushed a dazzling pink hue.

A tingling sensation swept up the back of Dillon's neck and across her face as she watched their exchange. She averted her eyes feeling like a voyeur watching a very intimate moment and turned towards Damien, who stared at her. She had an intense awareness of her pounding heart. Her body flooded with warmth and the fluttering in her chest made her breath quicken. It didn't matter anyway; Dillon didn't get the impression he liked her. Or he didn't trust her because she's a Fed. She stunned herself by hoping it was the latter. "Uh—hey—Kaine, I'm going to call Tiffany's friend from the study group. I'll meet you in the conference room." She headed down the hallway to find a quiet place.

"Sure," Damien said flatly. He and Joe headed to the conference room to begin work on the murder board.

Joe nudged Damien's shoulder. "What the hell is your problem with Agent McGrath? You really are acting hostile."

Damien grimaced. "I don't know what you're talking about. I'm just trying to muddle through this damn case."

Joe shrugged. "You know you're full of shit, right? What's the real issue?"

Damien pursed his lips together and squinted at Joe. "I don't know what the hell you are talking about. She's a fucking profiler here to help us. What should I be doing, drooling over her the way you do over Taylor every time you see her?"

Joe chuckled and shook his head. "Boy, are you screwed."

Damien went back to working on the board. "Whatever."

Both continued placing all notes and reports up next to photos of the missing girls. Damien glanced up as Matt walked into the room. "Hey, Matt we'll be ready in a minute. What did you find out about Tiffany's cell?"

"Nothing much to go on. The phone lost network connection just a few miles from Toni's. The cell service wouldn't tell me much, but they did say the phone had been shut off and it hasn't come back on since the day of Tiffany's abduction. I'm guessing our guy removed her battery, making sure it couldn't be traced or remotely accessed."

"Damn," Damien muttered as he and Joe arranged the board. The first section had the four missing girls from several years ago. The next section had Jesse Franks' picture and all the information on her abduction. They followed Jesse with information about Becca, including her autopsy photos. The last girl on the board, Tiffany Basset.

"No matter how many times you see this information, it still sucks." Matt watched the two men work.

Dillon stepped into the conference room. "I spoke to the girl." Dillon moved to the board and grabbed the marker from Damien. Her fingers brushed against his, and she felt the heat from the spark. "May I?" Dillon took it without waiting for his response.

"By all means. As if I had a choice," he muttered. He and Joe took seats at the table.

Joe smacked him on the shoulder and whispered to him, "Chill the fuck out."

Dillon sighed. "What an ass," she said softly as she rearranged the photos. She placed Beth's on one side and the other girl's photos on the other side of the board. She squared her shoulders. "Alright," Dillon said as she turned towards the men. "Tiffany's friend said there had been some guy Tiffany kept staring at. Maryanne couldn't get a clear view of him. He wore a hat, with some kind of logo on it that she didn't recognize. She said it made her think of something like a farm or something having to do with agriculture. She couldn't seem to place it. But she seemed sure she had seen it before.

"Every time she tried to see his face he would duck down, so his ball cap blocked out most of her view." She stared at the photos of all the girls. Her head tilted from side to side, and she whispered to herself as she scanned all the information on the board.

"Hello?" Joe said. "Are you done?"

"What—oh—sorry, bad habit." She rubbed her neck. "This will be preliminary, but I can give you a quick profile of our killer."

"Are you sure?" Damien asked narrowing his eyes. "Isn't it a little early on for a profile?" Damien glanced over at Joe as he made the crazy sign nodding towards Dillon.

"I have eyes, you know. *Tá mo shúile ar tú.*" Dillon winked at Joe.

"Oh fuck no. You sly wench," Joe said as he laughed.

Damien gaped at Dillon. "You know Irish?"

Matt's face contorted as he glanced between all three. "C'mon guys. What the heck does that mean? I don't know Irish. Hell, half the time I don't know what you two are even saying." He motioned between Joe and Damien.

Joe had a gleam in his eye when he looked at Matt. "She has eyes on me." Joe turned back to Dillon. "That makes me wonder what else she's not telling us. She is a Fed after all."

Amusement danced in Dillon's eyes. "That's all you're getting from me. Back to the profile. We know he's handsome. I believe the killer is between twenty-five and thirty-five. I believe he falls into this age because he can make himself appear younger. That's part of his chameleon-like personality. Lieutenant Kaine, you are correct in your assumption this area is his backyard. He lives and works near all the abduction sites. I would be willing to bet within a fifty-mile radius of here." She wrote all this on the board.

She scanned the room. Three pairs of eyes waited for more answers. "He thinks he is smarter than most, if not everybody. He'll be very successful in his line of work. That success adds to his arrogance. However, something has shifted. He is stepping up his abduction and killing times of these girls."

She moved to the board and positioned herself so everyone could see the photos. "That's it for him—for now. Next, we have the girls. The victims play as much a role in a killer's profile as the killer himself. They are, after all, what drives his desire to kill in the first place. And with no suspects to focus on, we have to use his victimology. Something has been bugging me since I got here. I had looked at the pictures of the missing girls, but I didn't see it right away. What do the pictures of these girls tell you guys?" She waited for them as they scanned the photos on the board.

Joe started first. "I see beautiful girls. Similar in their hair coloring or styling, they are all naturally beautiful."

"Okay, good. Anyone else?" She asked.

"They don't look alike," said Matt. "I guess there is something familiar about all of them, but I'm not sure what it is."

"Excellent Matt. There is something about all of them that ties them together. Actually, there are two things. Anything else?" Dillon asked.

Damien studied each picture. "They are all within the same age group or range. Except for girl number one. She's older."

"You guys aren't just a bunch of pretty faces." She winked at them and smiled. "Take the first girl out, for the moment. She is connected but let's set her aside." Dillon bounced from one foot to the other. She waited. She waved her hand in front of the photos. "You guys don't see it do you?"

"No, see what?" Joe asked.

All three men looked at each other.

Damien saw Dillon's mouth curve into a smile that lit up her whole face as her cheeks reached her eyes. She was even more beautiful when she smiled. *But she's annoying.* He felt a little relief knowing after this case she would go back to the FBI. Far away from him.

Dillon quit moving and stood still. "One common thread weaves between all the girls. C'mon you two are detectives, don't you see it?" She nodded at Damien and Joe. She waited—nothing—crickets. "INNOCENCE. They all have a fresh and virtuous appearance. Whether they are innocent or virtuous isn't in question. He perceives them to be innocent. He probably hopes they are virgins."

She pointed towards the board. "Except for the first known victim. She doesn't fit. Beth's disappearance happened before he decided on this pattern, or could quite possibly be the reason for the pattern. I believe she's the catalyst for him to begin killing. However, I don't know why. That brings me to the second thing they have in common. Her." She pointed to Beth. "All these girls are similar to Beth. They don't necessarily look exactly like her, but Matt, going back to what you said, that's what makes them familiar to you. They all slightly resemble Beth, but they are a few years younger. That's where I believe their innocence comes into play."

All three men sat with their jaws on the floor. Her forehead wrinkled as she drew her eyebrows together. "What? Is my hair on fire?"

Joe cocked his head to the side. "Did you just come up with this observation?"

Dillon's brow furrowed. "Um—yeah, I did. See the girl from Tiffany's study group mentioned that Tiffany had been clueless when it came to boys. All the boys at school liked her, and they all wanted to date her. The girl, Maryanne, said Tiffany had been one of the prettiest girls in school. Since Tiffany's parents didn't let her date, Tiffany didn't understand how to interact with the boys.

"Maryanne said that even when boys flirted with Tiffany, she was oblivious to it. That got me thinking. All the parents seemed to keep their girls secluded. Limited online presence, limited social outings with boys. I'm betting these girls were easily charmed because of their innocence. I'm also willing to bet they had particular mannerism that made them more appealing to him, like shyness, unable to maintain eye contact because they are embarrassed, things like that. Along with their resemblance to Beth."

"The girls caught his attention, and the opportunity presented itself to abduct them." Damien paused. "It's that naiveté that makes them vulnerable to his charm and good looks." Damien's heart cracked at the thought of what Becca went through and what Tiffany had already endured at the hands of this sick, sadistic bastard.

"Except girl number one," Joe said. "She may very well have been a virgin, but she doesn't fit the apparent innocent-looking stage the other girls seemed to fall in. But if all the girls resemble her in some subtle way, there must have been something special about her. Do you have any idea what that is?"

"That's the other thing I'm missing. I'm working on that. Trying to figure out what the connection is," Dillon said. "I'm working on that." She all but whispered to herself.

"If we get a person of interest, we have some great stuff. But with no one in our sights, we are still chasing a ghost," Damien said.

Matt cut in. "Here's what I got. The bag is a high-grade industrial bag. The feed store in Raymond is the only place where this particular batch went. It didn't go anywhere else. However, even though this narrows our list, it doesn't offer much help. The purchase of these bags occurred a very long time ago. Some of the sales go back over ten years."

Joe sighed. "Whoever purchased these, may have done so long before Beth went missing. Damn."

Damien used a different color pin to mark the feed store location on the map. Matt let out a small snort as he watched Damien put the pin on the map.

"Do you have something you'd like to say, Matt?" Damien asked.

"No, not at all PIN MAN," Matt said.

"Stai Zitto." Damien's mouth twitched.

Joe snorted at the expression on Matt's face. He nodded towards Damien. "His favorite saying—shut the hell up."

"Oh, good one," Matt repeated the Italian phrase. "I like that. I'm going to steal it. Anyway, as Agent McGrath pointed out earlier, iodine is used to keep cows from getting infections during the milking process, as well as a cleaning agent." Matt took a drink of soda. "However, many of the farms now use a chlorine-based disinfectant, it's cheaper, and it can be used to disinfect large areas. You were right," Matt said nodding at Dillon. "They also use other cleaning agents depending on the livestock."

Matt glanced at Damien. "That search I set up looking for any other crimes similar to ours, well I got quite a few hits. I used a few parameters to narrow in on specifics." Matt shuffled papers. "It looks like within a hundred and fifty-mile radius there were five that met our criteria. All the girls were reported as runaways. All the bodies were found naked, but not in bags. There wasn't anything in the way of forensic evidence. All the bodies were in various stages of decomposition. Two were located near the Chicago area, the other three were in smaller communities. It seems no one tied these cases together."

"Until now," Joe said. "With the lack of evidence at any of these scenes, we know he didn't kill them where they were found. We know the killer almost decapitated Becca when he slit her throat. We also know this asshole hung her upside down before he killed her, for further torture. He had to have her where he could take his time with her, then kill and dismember her with no worry of someone walking in on him.

"This place has to be secluded. I'm betting these girls weren't too quiet. We know he drives these roads regularly, so he has a familiarity with this area. Either for work or home or both. Traveling would make it easier for him to find other girls. By dumping them far away, it keeps them from being grouped together. This guy is smart." Joe guzzled his pop.

Dillon glanced around the room. She took a breath straightening up as she let it out. "There may be another scenario I know you guys aren't going to like. I was already leaning towards this, but with what Matt just told us about these five girls—I believe the gaps are from his abducting other girls. Lots of other girls. Could be girls from this area that we haven't found yet, or they could be more girls from far outside this area. Especially, like Joe pointed out, if his job includes travel." Dillon let her chin fall against her chest. "He's been doing this a long time. Since Beth, or because of Beth.

"He wouldn't necessarily have to have a secluded place," Dillon continued. "Robert Ben Rhoades was a long-haul trucker from the '80s. He became known as the Truck Stop Killer. Our guy could be using his delivery truck for some of these kills."

Everyone stared at Dillon. She frowned at their stunned faces. "What?" She asked.

Joe shook his head. "Wow, you must be a barrel of fun at the family reunion. What the hell kind of random fact is that?"

"Look, it's before our time I realize that, but it's what I do. I study these kinds of killers. I'm just letting you know there are other possibilities."

Damien went to the board. "Starting eight years ago girls began to go missing. We have established four from this area disappeared during a six-year period. Couple that with these new five girls that is still a lot of time. There seems to be no activity for extended periods of time. Then six months ago, Jesse's abduction occurred. Recently we have Becca and Tiffany, set them aside for a minute. Why the long gaps between all these girls? I don't think for one minute this guy is that patient. And while I appreciate your insight Agent McGrath, I believe even though our guy may have used his truck for the dumping of the girls, I think he has a place he takes them to."

Joe realized at that moment what his partner meant. "Ahh, shit. We don't know how long he kept the girls for. Our killer may be holding them for long periods of time."

Damien nodded. "He could be keeping them for a few days or for as much as a few months. He very well may be taking just one or two girls a year. And if that is true, I don't even want to think about what those girls went through. Although I think Agent McGrath is more than likely correct in her assumption that he is taking other girls, and lots of them."

Joe muttered something in Irish. "Oh man, that thought is so disturbing. Thinking he may be keeping these girls for an extended period, and knowing what he did to Becca in the short time he had her, I can't imagine the level of torture those other girls endured."

Damien noticed Agent McGrath had said nothing. "Agent, what else is on your mind?"

Dillon sighed. "I can't give you the reason why he didn't keep Becca as long as he might have kept the previous girls. *If* he kept them for extended periods." Dillon crossed her arms over her chest. "I believe he does this for his sexual pleasure and fun. I think when he started," she glanced over her shoulder at the picture of Beth and pointed to her. "He started for different reasons, and she will be the key. However, as the years have gone by, now he does it for sport or his own satisfaction like a game. With two daughters abducted in a weeks' time, I'd say his desires are outweighing his patience. He could very well have had some kind of psychotic break with reality causing him to speed up his abduction and kill times."

Silence draped the room. Joe leaned back in his chair and rubbed his face with his hands. "Well, bloody fucking hell." His Irish lilt thick with emotion. "We have to catch this *boggin cac dúr*. And when we do, I say we shoot the little knacker."

Dillon and Matt's eyes widened with amusement. They howled with laughter. "I don't always know what the hell you and Damien are saying, but damn it sure makes me smile," Matt said.

The rant by Joe eased the tension and heaviness in the room. Damien shook his head. "Alright, let's see if we can get any more ideas on where to find this boggin—sorry, motherfucker. Agent McGrath, what else do you have?"

"I don't have anything else to add." Dillon sat in a chair and leaned back with her eyes closed.

Damien was just about to speak when Dillon spoke up.

"The thing I keep coming back to, is why did he take Beth? Something is off. We are missing something. I'm still missing something." She spun around in her chair. Her eyes still closed as she spoke. "You guys do understand if he keeps this pace; Tiffany will be dead by the weekend, and another girl will go missing." She continued to spin in her chair.

That matter-of-fact statement sobered everyone in the room. Damien had concluded that they wouldn't get Tiffany back alive, but knowing that fact didn't prepare him to deal with the abduction and death of a third girl in a week. Damien took his phone and excused himself from the room.

Joe spun around. "Maybe he didn't plan on it, such a rapid acceleration. Maybe after he dumped Becca, he expected to wait. Then he sees Tiffany—can't resist—and the opportunity is too good to pass up." Joe drank his soda pop until he emptied it and then continued. "I have a question for you Miss Fancy Pants. Why are these girls leaving a safe place with a strange man? I still don't get what would make these girls leave with someone they don't know?"

Dillon's eyes squinted with a twinkle of mischief. "You think my pants are fancy?" She wiggled her eyebrows at Joe. She started to answer his question when Damien walked back in.

"I called Toni's Café and spoke with the manager. I wanted to find out who delivered their supplies. They have only one, an all-inclusive provider. An out of state delivery service. They can order all their stuff from one place. I hoped one of the local farms delivered to them.

"I called the Piggly Wiggly, they have several different companies that deliver to them. The manager said he'd gather a list and fax it to me. I asked them to check the day Jesse went missing, as well as the few deliveries before and after that date. It could take a day, though.

"The killer knows all these places because he delivers to them or he has some kind of business with them. He happened to be in the right spot at the right time. He sees the girls and finesses the situation to take them." Damien ran his hand through his hair pulling at the ends.

"I think you're right. I said the same thing to Miss Fancy Pants here. The killer took these last girls because the opportunity had been too good to pass up." Joe cracked open another soda.

"I believe you're right too, Lieutenant. These weren't stalking or planned abductions. His everyday life puts him at these places." She turned back to Joe. "Back to your previous question Joe, why would these girls leave a safe location with a man they don't know? You've never been a teenage girl, for obvious reasons. Unless you have something you need to share with us?" She raised her eyebrows at him.

He threw a balled-up piece of paper at her. "Funny, har—har, just get to your point."

"Yes, back to my point. At their age, I understood the stranger danger rules and not to go with anyone anywhere. But if a really cute boy paid attention to me, I tended to forget all those rules. I think that's what's happened here. He has a very smooth, non-threatening way about him. He's accessible and desirable.

"I believe that's part of the allure. All these girls are young, same age, and innocent. That's how he targets them. They are like babes in the woods, and that makes them vulnerable and easy prey."

Dillon made eye contact with everyone in the room. "I don't think he has been in trouble, either, not with the law anyway. I believe Joe hit it out of the park, Tiffany's abduction happened because of the opportunity. He saw her, he wanted her. When he finishes with her, he will want a fresh one. Make no doubt about that."

Damien and Joe cringed at the last statement. Damien stared at the board and mulled around the Agent's analysis. He pointed to the picture of Beth. "I don't know why he started with Beth. Whatever the reason that it started there, something had to have happened that made him want to abduct and kill her if it wasn't random. Then he changed his victimology and started abducting much younger girls."

Damien smacked his hand against the table. "He uses them for what he wants. Abuses them, hurts them and then discards them like fucking trash. When we find him, I'm going to put a fucking bullet in his head, forget about a trial. I really hate this bastard."

Matt pulled a sheet from a folder. "There are basically four farms on the list from the feed store. The three we already discussed, Macomb, Findley, and Waverly, and another one. A farm located in Taylorville. It, too, is a dairy farm, but it happens to be the largest in a three-state area. Taylorville is the one farm that bought several packages of the bags. They purchased their last order about three years ago—a substantial order too."

Damien pulled on the ends of his hair.

Dillon smirked at him. "You know pulling on your hair can be a sign of a deep-rooted mental illness."

He squinted at her. "Doing what? What the hell are you talking about?"

Dillon spun around in her chair. "Whenever you get really stressed or frustrated you pull at your hair. And while it does add to your overall sex appeal, the whole bed head thing, it could be the first signs of trichotillomania. Although I'm not seeing any bald spots yet, I think maybe you should consider using the counselors at Division Central."

Joe broke out in laughter. "Trichotil—whatever the hell that word is, I'm sure Damien doesn't have that, but a deep-seated mental illness I would definitely agree on that."

Damien frowned at them. "Ha ha, hilarious. Agent, it seems you and Joe have gone to the same school of comedy. Listen, we need to hit these farms and see what shakes loose. Macomb is north of here; let's go there now. The three remaining ones we can catch tomorrow since they are in the other direction. Matt, does the file you gave us earlier contain the information on the Taylorville farm?"

"No, I will gather that and have it for you by tomorrow," Matt said.

"Okay, before you leave, could you also gather information on Jim Goshen? He works at the Taylorville farm."

"Is he a suspect?" Matt wrote the name down.

"Everyone is a suspect. Whether he's guilty or not, I don't know. The farm he works at uses the bags found at the dump site. Betty said Jim walked to his truck when Tiffany left. Maybe he noticed something, maybe he's our guy. Either way that puts him high on the suspect list. I want all the information you can find on him when we hit the farm tomorrow."

"No problem. I'll get whatever information I can find," Matt said.

Damien turned to lead everyone out of the room when he noticed Joe just sitting and staring at the board. "Hey Joe, what's up?"

Damien glanced at Dillon, she offered him a slight eyebrow raise and shrug but said nothing.

Joe got up and rearranged the photos. He stopped and spun around towards Damien, eyes wide. "Matt call Taylor. Get her in here."

"Uh—sure." He picked up the phone and called her extension. "She'll be right here."

Damien saw something he rarely saw in his partner's eyes—fear.

Joe took a deep breath. "I need to wait for Taylor for you to see it."

Within a few minutes, Taylor walked into the room. "Hey, guys, what's up?"

Joe looked up. "Come here babe, I need you to stand next to the board." He guided her to where he wanted her to stand.

Damien ran his hand through his hair, stopping just short of pulling at it. "Joe, we have to get to that farm. What the hell is all this about?"

"Look at the board. Look at all the pictures of the girls. Dillon has already pointed out their resemblance to Beth," Joe said.

Everyone sat still for a moment. Taylor's eyes glistened with moisture. Matt noticed it first. "Oh shit. Shit." His head drooped. He stared at Taylor. "You look like the spitting image of Beth, only older."

Taylor let out an audible gasp and placed her hand over her mouth. "Oh my God. That's who has been stalking me. That's who I've seen at all the places." Taylor turned to Joe. "He wants to kill me because I look like her?" She pointed to Beth's picture and panted. "What if he knows where I live?" She leaned on the board. "Oh my God, he does know where I live. I told you the other day when I left for work, I felt like someone was watching me."

Joe took two steps and wrapped his arms around her. "I won't let anything happen to you. I promise you."

She wrapped her arms around his waist and cried. "All these weeks I thought I was imagining things. It's been him, all along."

Joe kissed the top of her head. He looked at Matt. "I need you to take her home, let her get some clothes then bring her to the hotel. She has a key to my room." He lifted up her chin. "You will stay with me at the hotel until this is over."

Damien mumbled something no one understood. "Matt you're going to need to fill Jones in on what is going on. He needs to be made aware of what we've discovered here today. Joe, Matt can handle things on this end. If the director thinks it warrants it, he will provide security for Taylor when we aren't around." He pinched the bridge of his nose. "Agent McGrath we will fill you in on the way to the farm."

CHAPTER TWENTY-TWO

On the road to Macomb

Dillon studied Joe as he plugged their destination into the GPS. He glanced over his shoulder and gave her the most incredible smile, highlighted by vivid green eyes. A darker green rim surrounded the iris making the color pop. The scar above his left eye only added to his rugged handsomeness.

"I guess we owe you an explanation about what just happened in there," Joe said.

He and Damien explained everything that Taylor had experienced. When they finished, Dillon let out the breath she had been holding. "I'm sorry someone you care about is in danger. I hope what I'm about to say doesn't make it worse." She paused for a moment.

Dillon scribbled on a pad of paper, a habit she formed long ago when she worked out a problem or puzzle. "I still can't figure out Beth's importance or the reason for it, but I tend to lead towards a conclusion he is trying to recreate his experience with Beth. He wants to relive everything he did to Beth. I think what he wants to repeat the most is the punishment. Beth did something, real or imagined, and he punished her then, and he wants to continue to punish her. Oh, and he is also a sexual sadist, so that is driving him too."

Joe shook his head. "I don't get it. Taylor is so much older than the other girls."

"He didn't stalk Jesse, Becca, or Tiffany. Those were spur of the moment. He saw them, sees the resemblance to Beth and abducts them. Again, it all seems to come back to Beth. He must have seen Taylor somewhere. Her resemblance to Beth is uncanny. He fantasized about her after that first encounter, enough that he has continually sought her out. We believe he travels this area, so he must have seen Taylor and fixated on her. The timing for him to abduct her hasn't seemed to work out, making Taylor a very lucky woman. She will need to be aware of her surroundings until we apprehend this guy."

Joe glared at Dillon. "You don't have to worry about Taylor. I'm not about to let anything happen to her."

They sat in silence for a while. Dillon cracked her window to let in some fresh air and let out the thick heavy air that filled the vehicle.

Joe finally spoke. "I have to tell you I don't think our guy will be from this farm. It seems too far out; my gut says our man will be more local."

Dillon snorted and shook her head. "Well, I can only imagine what your Irish gut has to say."

"You obviously have no idea how accurate my gut is." He stuck his tongue out at her.

"Oh, on the contrary, I agree with you, and your gut. I don't think this farm will have anything to do with our guy. I think your original assessment of him staying close to his area of comfort will take this place off the list," Dillon said.

The AC blew out semi-warm air and carried Damien's incredible smell. Dillon had no idea if it was soap, cologne, or both. Whatever he wore made him even more delicious. She could see his eyes in the rear-view mirror. They were a dark sapphire blue. So dark had it not been for the bright starburst of a paler blue that surrounded the pupil, they would lean towards indigo. Damien's dark as coal hair beckoned her to reach out and drag her fingers through it. Lost in her scrambled thoughts, she jumped and sucked in air when Joe asked her a question.

"How long have you been an Agent?" Joe had shifted in his seat so he could watch her as he spoke.

Dillon rubbed her hands together. "For five years. Came in right out of college. I'm about to turn twenty-eight."

Joe kept an expressionless face. He studied her for a moment as he took a drink of his soda. "What degree do you have?"

"Psychology. A dual degree in Forensic and Abnormal Psychology."

Joe cocked an eyebrow at her. "It didn't take you long to get through college, with two degrees none the less."

She smiled at him. "I skipped a couple of grades in school, so I got into college earlier than most. Then it took me about five and a half years to get the degrees."

"Smart and a smartass." He arched one eyebrow as he smiled at her. "Did you always want to be an FBI Agent, or did you fall into it?" Joe asked. As he waited for her answer, he could see Damien's jaw go rigid. Joe smiled at him but laughed inwardly at his partner.

"Yeah, I always wanted to work for the FBI. From about the age of fourteen or fifteen, I decided I wanted to hunt down the worst of the worst criminals." She shifted in her seat. Adjusted the seat belt. The FBI and her grandparents knew of all the details of her past. Occasionally a smart news reporter did their research and pieced together parts of her story. However, she didn't share it with just anyone. "I gather from the way you two silently communicate, you have been partners for a while?" Dillon asked wanting to change the subject.

Damien smirked at Joe. "We've been partners for almost five years. We ended up at the same homicide division before coming to the VCU. I'm sure my sins from the past caught up with me. This partnership must be some sort of atonement for them."

"Ha, you knacker! I'm the best thing to happen to you, you greasy Guinea. You'd be a blithering idiot without me in your life," Joe said.

"At least, I don't have a SID." Damien raised his eyebrows and smirked at Joe.

Joe doubled over with laughter.

"I guess that's slang for something. Do I even want to know what SID means?"

"No!" They both yelled at once.

The two men bantered back and forth, evident that they shared a friendship, not just a partnership. Dillon's assignments took her to other agencies or other FBI units that needed her help on cases. She had never worked close enough or long enough with someone to develop any kind of relationship. She caught Damien's eyes as he stared at her in the mirror. He may not like her, but she could tell he definitely had a soft spot for Joe.

"Do you have any family, Agent?" Damien asked.

Dillon bristled. "No." She pursed her lips together. "Well yes, I have a grandmother and grandfather. I mentioned him earlier. They live in Iowa. That's it." She didn't want to answer any more questions. "What about you two—wait, let me guess." She sat still for a moment thinking about her two subjects. She tilted her head to the side and directed her attention towards the handsome Irish cop.

"Joe, you have at least a couple of brothers and sisters. At least one sister is several years younger than you are. Your Mom and Dad are still alive. You see them every Saturday or Sunday morning. Probably Sundays so you can go to Mass with them. You never miss a Sunday football game with your friends. Your mother pesters you for a grandbaby. You tell everyone you're never getting married, when in actuality if you met your perfect woman, you would marry her in a heartbeat. I have a sneaking suspicion you are closer to finding that perfect girl now than before this case." She teased him with a grin and a wink.

Dillon stared at Damien in the mirror. She pushed her disdain for him to the side. She wanted to be as accurate as she could be. "Now Lieutenant Kaine, you also have quite a large family. Several brothers and sisters or at least a lot of cousins and a very loving but strong-willed mother. You're the baby of the family. Your father is traditional in his beliefs. He takes great pride in the fact that you bring criminals to justice. Your parents want grandkids, but they have them from your other brothers and sisters, so they don't harass you as much.

"Your Catholic faith is the cornerstone of who you are. And even though you may not go to Mass every weekend, you would never turn your back on God. You continually turn to Him for strength. You keep women at a distance, not because you're afraid of commitment, but I suspect you had a serious relationship that ended badly. Couple that with you can't seem to find a woman who understands you and doesn't want to try to change you." Dillon gave them a confident grin. Dead silence filled the vehicle. Joe stared at her with his mouth agape. Dillon's chin poked out a tad. She smirked at him knowing she hit the bullseye.

"Holy fuck, I didn't know the FBI hired psychics," Joe said.

Dillon smiled at Joe. "I'm not a psychic," she said. "A little observation can go a long way. Case in point, Joe every time you look at the pictures of the girls on the whiteboard, the vein in your neck pulses a little harder and sticks out a bit. You're in protective mode with Taylor. I pity any fool that dares to hurt your sisters or your future wife. I can only imagine that the boys your sisters dated had to go under the microscope and threats to their well-being were a daily occurrence.

"Now Kaine you're always messing with the St. Michael's medal around your neck. We all know that St. Michael is the patron saint of police officers, but more importantly, he is the Archangel. I find it fascinating you choose to wear that medal. The Archangel acts as the defender of the Church and chief opponent of Satan, but he also assists souls at the time of their death. You two, being homicide detectives, try to do just that. Find the killer and set it right, help those murdered get home—metaphorically."

Joe turned to her. "There has to be something else that helps you see things so clearly. You couldn't have just learned it in Psychology."

She paused for a moment. "Sure I did. Maybe there's some intuition that comes along with knowing the psychology behind certain kinds of behavior. However, profiling isn't really that complicated. You gather the facts you have. You look at the characteristics, behavioral patterns, and you generalize. Then use those generalizations and apply them to current circumstances and surroundings in which those facts are present. If you get lucky, you can use them and predict future criminal behavior." She winked at Joe.

Damien sat stoic in the front seat as he drove. He waged an internal war with himself about Agent McGrath. She had quirky habits. She often forgot her train of thought or just drifted off into her own world. She interrupted, and she asked questions before he or Joe had a chance to. She got along well with Joe, and hell, that just pissed him off.

Yet for all those things, he found her intriguing. She had proven herself as a profiler, and a damn good one at that. Scarily so. She seemed down to earth and didn't have to be the center of attention. Damien felt as if an invisible rubber band had tethered him to Dillon. Every time he pulled away from her and his attraction to her, the rubber band tightened and snapped him back to her.

CHAPTER TWENTY-THREE

Joe filled them in on the information Matt had completed about the hog farm. "Mr. and Mrs. Archetta have owned the farm since the 1960s. They have four kids. Two of them went to school for agriculture, they live on the farm. Both are single. The other two are lawyers, one in corporate law, and one in criminal law. They both live in Chicago. They aren't married either." Joe gave Damien a shit-eating grin as he closed the file that held all the information on the four farms.

Damien pulled into a huge hog farm. He parked the vehicle and glowered at Joe.

"What?" Joe asked innocently.

"I know damn well what you are thinking. Just let it go." Damien had a slight edge to his tone. He cocked his head and shook it. With one eyebrow raised, he gave Joe a glassy stare. Damien didn't understand why it bothered him to have Joe mention Camilla. It wasn't like he wanted to hide anything. He just didn't want Agent McGrath to know anything about him. Or at least not from Joe.

Dillon jumped out of the vehicle first. Joe grabbed Damien's arm before he got out and offered Damien a bemused smile then smacked him on the arm. "Lighten up buddy. You're wound way too tight."

Damien all but glared at his friend. "Why the hell do you have to get along so well with her? You two act like you're best friends or something."

Joe laughed. "That's because I don't want to fuck her very smart brains out of her head."

They all stared at an enormous, colorful farmhouse. The shutters had a pristine coat of pearl white paint making the yellow of the house look as bright as Big Bird's feathers. Four herding dogs who had circled the vehicle as they drove up, now ran in crazy circles around their feet, vying for a scratch behind the ears. A massive staircase led to a large wrap around porch.

An older man and woman and two younger men stood at the top of the steps.

"Hello, Mr. and Mrs. Archetta? I'm Lieutenant Damien Kaine, and this is Detective Joe Hagan and Special Agent Dillon McGrath with the FBI. May we speak with you for a few minutes?"

Mr. Archetta led the way. "Well sure, why don't you all come on in and have something to drink. I can't imagine what you need to speak with us about."

They walked into an immaculate living room. The sofa had several blankets folded up on one end. A massive brick fireplace sat at the far end and family photos covered every square inch, including pictures of the four dogs now laying on beds scattered around the living room floor. The room had an immediate warmth. The whole place begged for visitors to sit, get comfortable, and stay awhile.

Damien watched as Joe licked his lips and inhaled deep breaths through his nose. The smell of bacon and biscuits filled the entire house. "We apologize if we are interrupting your dinner. We need to ask a few questions," Damien said.

Mr. Archetta waved them into the dining room and gestured for them to sit down. "No problem at all. Come this way please."

Mrs. Archetta went into the kitchen and returned with a plate of biscuits, butter, honey, and a pitcher of tea. Damien bit his bottom lip to keep from smiling as he glimpsed Joe. His partner's eyes had glassed over at the sight of the plate of food. "Can you tell us if you use these industrial plastic bags from Tanker's feed store?" He showed them a picture of the bag.

Mr. Archetta took the photo and handed it off to his son after a quick glance. "Oh gosh, Jeffrey are we still using those bags? My son Jeffrey handles all that. He purchases the supplies used on the farm."

Jeffrey took the photo. He stood up and grabbed a fat binder off the nearby shelf. Opening to a page marked with DISCONTINUED and a date. "Here are the purchases we make monthly. We stopped using these bags over a year ago. Their expense outweighed their value. We don't have any on the site anymore. Instead, we now have a huge composting area, and we put back on our land what we would have trucked out to somewhere else. We also sell it to smaller farms or even the local family who wants to garden for themselves."

"How about deliveries, do you deliver to the Decatur or Blue Mound area?" Damien asked.

"Gosh yes," the other son George said. "We deliver our goods to most of the state of Illinois as well as a few of the surrounding states.

We also do a lot of shipping due to our online ordering site which allows us to sell all over."

Mr. Archetta took a bite of his biscuit, studying the three investigators. "Why are you asking us all these questions, have we done something?" The entire family waited for a response.

Joe had a mouthful of biscuits and honey. He raised his eyebrows to Damien. Shaking his head. Damien responded to Mr. Archetta. "We are investigating some evidence found with the body of a young girl. The evidence in question tracks back to a feed store just outside of Springfield. Your farm is one of the customers listed who purchased these bags."

"I see," said Mrs. Archetta. "That's disturbing, for you to think we had anything to do with that crime. This has to do with the discovery of that girl, doesn't it?" She clutched her blouse and grabbed her husband's arm. "Oh, David, they think it's someone from this farm." Mrs. Archetta's brow wrinkled, and she bit her bottom lip. Her knuckles whitened as her grip on her husband's arm tightened.

Damien observed the two sons. There could be no mistaking them for younger men. However, the questions needed asking. "Did any of you have a reason to go to the mall in Springfield this past Saturday?" Damien asked them.

Both sons responded at the same time. "No." George looked around the table. "We had an open house this past weekend. We open our farm up to visitors where they can come see how we process foods as well as the opportunity to sample a lot of our items."

"How about your delivery drivers, do they live on this farm or near here?" Damien asked.

George got up from the table and pulled out another binder from the shelf. He opened it up as he spoke. "I will make you a copy of their information and a copy of each of their delivery routes for the last six months. We keep a sheet that has when, where, and who they delivered to. You can verify where they were." He exited the dining room and walked to a small office off the kitchen area.

"One last question," Damien said. "Do you use propylene glycol or iodine on this farm?"

"No," said Jeffrey. "We used to use iodine for cleaning equipment, but we switched to a chlorine-based solution. We also use a quaternary ammonium compound, cetrimide. I can show you all our records if you need them."

George re-entered and handed the forms to Damien. "I think you'll find that neither our employees nor we could have done these crimes."

"Thank you. As to giving us your records, this should be enough. If we have any more questions, we'll contact you," Damien said. "You have answered all our questions, and we appreciate it. Thank you for your time."

At the door, Joe spun on his heels, grabbed Mrs. Archetta in a bear hug, and kissed her on the cheek. "Mrs. Archetta, if you weren't already a married woman, I'd have to give this gentleman a run for his money. Those biscuits were heavenly. Thank you for your graciousness, and for sharing."

***

In the SUV Joe let out a satisfied, sigh. "I haven't tasted biscuits that good ever. They were fantastic. I could have eaten the whole plate."

Damien turned towards Joe. "Dude, we are trying to solve a serious crime, and all you want to do is eat biscuits and flirt with the man's wife who made them."

Joe laughed. "Come on, the minute we stepped through the doorway we could ascertain they weren't involved. They had nothing to hide, and you could tell."

"Well, if nothing else, we marked one farm off our list. Let's get back to the hotel. Agent McGrath, are you staying at the Holiday Inn?" Damien asked.

"Yes, same as you. If you take me to the lab in the morning, we don't need to get my car tonight."

Joe smiled as he winked at Damien. "That sounds great. I'd like to get back to the hotel ASAP anyway. With all that's going on with Taylor, I want to be there as much as possible." He looked at Damien. "When I realized she looked so much like Beth, I can't explain what I felt. To know the guy she has seen around is more than likely the same guy we're after," he shook his head, "at that moment I felt helpless."

"Listen, now we know what we are up against. She can stay with you at night, she will stay at the lab until either we take her to the hotel or Matt drops her off. If she has to go somewhere, the director will make sure one of the officers from the lab are with her. She won't be alone until we get this guy. Do you want to eat in the restaurant?"

"No, I'm going to go up to the room. Taylor is there now," Joe said.

"Agent, what are your plans? Would you like to grab dinner with me in the hotel restaurant?" Damien asked.

Dillon stiffened in her seat. "Why?"

Damien's forehead wrinkled as he looked at Joe, who shrugged and kept his head down. "What do you mean why? I figured you needed to eat. I need to eat. Why be miserable and eat alone?"

She scowled at him in the mirror. "Do you make it a habit of asking people you don't like to dinner?"

Stunned, Damien bristled. "Hey never mind. I'll just sit at the bar." He couldn't believe it. He knew he hadn't been all that friendly, but he didn't think he had been overly rude or nasty. At least, he won't have to worry about keeping his distance from her, which he wanted all along anyway.

"Now, now kids," Joe said without looking at either of them.

"Listen," Dillon said. "I get the feeling you either don't like me or you just don't like the fact that I'm a Fed. Either way, I'm surprised you want to be alone with me. But my bad. Sure, let's get something to eat. It's just a meal." She stared out the window.

CHAPTER TWENTY-FOUR

During the drive back to the hotel, Joe received several texts he didn't share. By the slight twitch of his mouth, Damien garnered it had to do with Taylor.

Joe unhooked his seatbelt just as the car pulled into the parking lot. "Hey, if you need me, let me know. Otherwise, don't call me." He raised his eyebrows at Damien. "I'll see you in the morning down in the restaurant, about seven-thirty? Try not to kill each other at dinner." He turned to leave but stopped and leaned back in the car. "You know, if you two just fucked and got it out of your system, you'd probably get along better." He smiled at them and closed the door, leaving them stunned.

***

Damien led Dillon through the restaurant. Most patrons had taken seats in the bar area. TVs played various college football and late season baseball games while a few rowdy fans cheered on their favorite team.

Damien sat across from Agent McGrath in silence. She eyed her surroundings and then settled on a college game playing on one of the many TVs throughout the restaurant. Damien finally got a good look at her. Her skin resembled silky cream, and her lips were full and pale pink.

She looked everywhere but at him. The silence grew increasingly uncomfortable. Damien knew he was acting like an ass. He didn't want to push her away. He wanted to grab her and throw her on this table and fuck her senseless. Joe had it right. "Listen, I'm really sorry about the other night in the bar. I wasn't honest with you. But you weren't completely honest with me either."

Dillon turned towards the incredible voice that came out of those poet lips. She raised one eyebrow at him, then smiled. "I guess we both seem to have a problem with honesty." She turned her attention back to the game on TV.

Damien had never tried so hard to be nice to someone, but she had a frigid wall up. He sipped his beer and glanced around the room. When he turned back to her, she stared at him. "What?" He asked.

"You don't like me, do you?"

"I don't know you enough to not like you."

She laughed. "Wow! If that's true, I hate to see how you treat someone when you've had a chance to get to know them."

He sat back against the booth. "If I gave you the impression I don't like you, that's not it at all." He took another sip of his beer. "And it has nothing to do with you being a Fed. I came into this case with some personal shit, and I'm letting it get to me. I apologize." He held out his hand. "Let's start over. Hi, I'm Damien Kaine and sometimes I can be an asshole."

Dillon chuckled almost choking on her beer. She didn't like fighting with him. She reached out and shook his hand. "Hi, I'm Dillon McGrath and sometimes I can be a prissy bitch."

Damien laughed at that. "Nice to meet you, Dillon. So, where do you live?"

"Currently, I live in Virginia right outside Quantico, sort of close to DC," She winked at him over her beer. "I spend most of my time at the Criminal Apprehension Unit."

Damien leaned back against the booth. "Are you going back there after this case, or do you have to go somewhere else?"

Dillon frowned and shrugged her shoulders. "No—well yes and no. Ah hell Kaine, I don't know. The great OZ, Deputy Director Sherman, has informed me that I'm going to be transferred, but they haven't bothered to tell me where or when. I'll still be assigned to the CAU, but they're going to move me to another office, another city, hell for all I know another country."

Damien guzzled his beer. "Okay, first if we are going to start anew in this relationship, you need to call me Damien. You call Joe by his first name."

She tried not to laugh but couldn't help herself. "That bothers you huh?"

Damien stared at her. He looked down at his beer. Without looking up, he responded. "Yeah. It does." He lifted his gaze back to her. "It bothers me more than it should."

She smiled sweetly at him. "Hmm, that is something a headshrinker would like to investigate."

He cocked an eyebrow at her. "Let's move off me and my mental problems. Back to you, do you want to move? You sound like you aren't too excited about it."

She inhaled a deep breath. "I don't mind moving. I don't have any-thing or anyone keeping me at Quantico." She took a sip of her beer and fidgeted with the label. "A change would do me good."

A slight frown pulled at Damien's mouth. He didn't believe her. He drank the last of his beer. "I guess you don't have any pets or a boy-friend," he cocked his head to the side, "or a husband?"

Dillon snorted. "No on the pet. Hell no on the boyfriend. And oh hell no on the husband." She shook her head. "Don't get me wrong, I'm not against any of those. They just aren't for me. I travel so much I haven't exactly gotten to know my neighbors well enough to ask them to watch an animal when I'm gone. It didn't seem fair to a cat or dog. Plus, they'd be stuck in an apartment the size of a large closet.

"As for the boyfriend, well that's a long pathetic story. Husband, well that has to do with the pathetic boyfriend story." Dillon thought about the life she had created. A nice boring life for herself. She reviewed cases and chased killers. Pets, friends, and men had proven to be a dis-traction.

Damien's phone chirped. He let out a muffled laugh.

Dillon pressed her lips flat. "Your girlfriend?" *Why did she care?*

"No." He paused, squinting at her. "I have a cat, named Coach." He caught the expression she shot him. Damien held up the palms of his hands. "Before you judge me, let me explain. I moved into my condominium, and he showed up about a week or two later. I didn't want a cat or any kind of pet, but the fellow kept hanging around. When I travel, I get my neighbor Mrs. C. to take care of him. She's in her sixties and has no family to speak of. She has adopted me as a surrogate grand-son."

Catching the server's attention, Damien raised two fingers and pointed to his beer. "Anyway, whenever she watches him, she likes to send me pictures of Coach and her dog. Usually, she dresses them both up in costumes." He fidgeted with his phone while he continued. "Yes-terday she sent me a picture of Coach dressed in a sailor suit."

He held up his phone with an image of a rather large cat in a sailor suit, a size too small. Dillon almost choked snorting at the picture. Da-mien smirked at her. "Yeah, it's funny. Well, this is the latest fashion statement she has put my cat in." He held up his phone again. Coach wore a fluffy, frilly dress and an oversized floppy sun hat to round out the ensemble.

Dillon covered her mouth. "Poor cat. Does she realize Coach is a boy?" Dillon laughed, snorting as she sucked in air, making herself laugh harder.

"Oh, she knows, she doesn't care, and evidently the cat doesn't either. I'm sure she uses food to make him complacent. He always seems to come back a little heftier every time he's with her." He sighed as he put his phone away. "I don't have the heart to tell her to stop. She's by herself, and I think taking care of Coach gives her a purpose. I also think dressing him up and sending me pictures keeps her happy, I can't take that away from her. Plus, I'd be lying if I said I didn't like getting these photos."

Dillon continued to chuckle even with her efforts not to. "Oh man, I'd love to get those pictures. You have to forward them to me."

Damien stopped midway to his mouth with a fry. "So back to the boyfriend—husband thing. Why aren't you involved with anyone? The men must be falling all over themselves to take you out."

Dillon swallowed the bite of food she had in her mouth. In the throes of a coughing fit, she took several sips of water. Clearing her throat and catching her breath, she wrinkled her brow at Damien. "Umm—okay—to answer your question, I don't have time to get involved with anyone."

He raised one eyebrow at her. "Liar. If you wanted to make the time you could. I'm not buying it. What's the real reason?" He didn't care if she had a relationship with someone. It's not like they had something going on, so why did she lie?

Her eyes widened. She shook her head and wiggled her finger at Damien. "So now you're calling me a liar, again. I thought we were starting over? Maybe you need medication. You aren't that friendly all day. Then you apologize. You even manage to compliment me, then follow it up by calling me a liar, again. Seriously, are you bipolar or something?" A slight smile tugged at the corners of her mouth.

"Haha, no I'm not bipolar, and most women love compliments. Plus, all the more reason we should start out our relationship being honest. Don't you think? Seeing as how we didn't do that from the start." He smiled at her over his beer.

"No. I have answered enough of your questions, now it's your turn. Do you have a girlfriend or a wife? Oooh, maybe you have several. Like Joe."

He made a moue then smiled. "Oh yeah, I have a harem. A different girl for each night of the week." He took a drink of his beer. "About eight months ago I called off an engagement I had with a longtime girlfriend. We'd grown apart. She didn't understand the horrors of the job or my desire to stay in this job. I didn't fit into the mold she wanted once she got a job at a high-profile corporate law firm in Chicago. Plus, Coach didn't like her."

"Ah. That explains the visceral reaction to Joe at the hog farm earlier, and the whole corporate lawyer comment." A broad smile spread across Dillon's face. "Your cat has a say in who you choose to date, huh?"

She had noticed his reaction to Joe earlier. Nothing got past this woman, Damien thought. He frowned, halfway laughing. "No—silly. However, looking back, I can see how he never warmed up to her. Coach likes every one of the detectives in my Unit, and of course, Mrs. C., but he never seemed to like Camilla. I should have paid better attention."

Dillon clamped her lips together and swallowed her laughter. Her eyes smiled at him. "Well, pets are supposed to be a good judge of character."

"Okay, I see you think this is funny. Nevertheless, I'm serious. From now on, I'll give a little more credence to Coach." He took a sip of his drink. "Hey give me one of your cards so I can have your phone number. That way if I need to contact you I can. Plus, I can also forward you pictures of Coach."

She smirked at him and handed a card to him. "Well if I ever get to meet Coach, I hope he likes me."

"I don't think you have anything to worry about."

An odd silence settled over them. It wasn't uncomfortable, just weird. During the last thirty minutes, Damien's perception of her had changed. He wasn't sure if he liked that.

"So How long have you been a Lieutenant?" Dillon asked.

"Just made rank Monday. The ceremony will happen after this case is over."

"Congratulations. What about Joe—will he go for Lieutenant?"

"I don't know. Not for a while is my guess. He doesn't want to do any more paperwork than he has to. I wouldn't have done it if my Captain hadn't encouraged me to do so."

Her eyes got wide, and she placed her fingers over her mouth. "I'm in shock; you don't have designs on making Captain and commanding a division somewhere, ruling the known universe?"

"No, I don't. As it is, I will take a leadership role in this Unit. The detectives I work with are the only ones I would want backing me up. However, that's as far I care to go. Too much politics to mess with as you go higher up the chain. I didn't even know I would be put in charge of the VCU under Captain Mackey."

He popped a fry into his mouth. "The captain informed me before Joe and I came down here. He explained he'd been thinking about putting someone in charge of the detectives, someone he could trust to keep the Unit operating smoothly and handle all the personalities in it. To do that, he needed a Lieutenant. I'm sure that's why he encouraged me to take the test. Plus, if I move up in rank it will put me behind a desk and not in the field. Investigating is what I do best not sitting behind a desk."

"As a Lieutenant, will you and Joe stay partners?"

"Yeah, nothing will change there. In this Unit, we work as partners. There are eight Detectives. Sometimes you get switched up, but most often you stay with your partner."

"You and Joe like to say things in Italian and Irish. What gives? Do you guys use it as your secret code?"

Damien laughed hardily. "I never thought of it like that."

Dillon's eyebrows furrowed, "Your last name is Kaine, doesn't sound very Italian."

"Jesus, I feel like I'm being interrogated."

Dillon laughed. "I guess it sounds like that. I'm just very curious about Captain Mackey's team."

Damien shook his head. "I'm disappointed. I hoped you wanted to get to know me."

She chuckled. "Man, you are so sensitive. Now answer my question. What's up with Kaine?"

Damien smiled. "My family immigrated from Sicily. Our surname is Kainetorri. My father has a well-known security company, knows a lot of people in powerful positions. I shortened it when I went to the academy. I wanted to stand on my own and not have my name get me something I didn't work for." He ate a french fry. "Joe's family came here from Ireland around his eighth-grade year. His family, as well as mine, speak their native tongue more than they speak English. I often speak in English mixed with Italian when I'm around my family. Joe and I are around each other so much we know what the other is saying. We often say something we don't want someone to know in either Italian or Irish, sometimes both at the same time. It drives everyone around us crazy."

Damien lifted his beer to take a drink and stopped midair. "He likes to use words I don't know then he won't tell me what they are. Drives me crazy. He, on the other hand, is so damn smart. He started picking up on my Italian right from the start."

Dillon held up her hand pinching her thumb and forefinger together. "I know a little Irish. Not much. A few key terms and a few slang insults. That's really about it."

"Ahh, that would explain the comment at the table earlier today. Joe will be wondering how much you know and where you learned it," Damien said. He held up his hand and waved it in front of his face. "Don't tell him anything. It will make him batshit crazy trying to figure it out. What prompted you to learn?"

"I did an unusual rotation a few years back. A killer traveled around Ireland. They asked for the FBI's help. I volunteered to go. Needed a break."

"Hmm, I see. Pathetic boyfriend story comes to mind. What about a partner, do you have one?"

She shook her head. "A lot of FBI Agents work in partnerships. As a profiler, I tend to work alone. I go to other field offices or even other departments—police, CIA you name it. I may work—as I am here—with a person or partners, but that's just for the duration of the investigation. So, to answer your question, no I don't have a partner."

"Hmm, I don't think I would like that. Do you like being on your own—I mean no partner?"

Dillon's shoulders sagged a little. "Sometimes. Sometimes I'd like to have what you and Joe have." She took a long gulp of beer. She offered him no more explanation. Dillon wanted the partnership, but mostly she wanted the friendship they shared. She raised her eyebrows at him and leaned a little towards him. "So, what about your family? I know my guess hit close to home. Tell me about them. Do you live near them?"

A huge smile spread across Damien's face. "My family lives outside of Chicago. I see them a couple of times a month. More if my mother has planned one of her elaborate family feasts. My brother and sister live near my Mom and Dad. I love them, but I don't want to be that close to them. Like I said my father owns a security company, both work for him. He handles personal security and computer or home security as well. My Dad has wanted me to come work for him ever since I got out of the police academy."

Damien guffawed. "They like to meddle. They always want to know if I'm dating, who I'm dating or why I'm not dating. Anything and everything they want to know it. Joe is fair game too. They drill him as well. My entire family treats him as if he is blood-related. Hell, our moms are best friends. Come to think of it, sometimes they treat him better than me." Damien frowned. "I'm going to have to fix that."

"Ahh, that's where your lie came from. Is that why you haven't gone to work for your father? Because your family would always be in your business?"

"Hey, we have already established that we both weren't honest with each other. But technically my lie was closer to the truth."

She stared at him with a dumbfounded look. "You are delusional. Your lie wasn't even close to what you do."

Damien held up his hands. "Hey, we had a truce going." He laughed. "Okay, you win, my lie was worse than yours. Back to why I don't work for my Dad, yes that's one reason, they would be in my business nonstop. I also like catching the bad guy. Helping to set things right, you know. For the survivors," he said.

Damien tried to get information about Dillon's family, but every time he asked her about them, she gave vague answers or changed the subject. Damien suspected something had happened, something she didn't feel comfortable sharing. It also seemed no matter how hard he tried Dillon still had a wall up.

He finished his meal and sat back. Damien found himself more and more enamored with Dillon. She didn't pick at her food, or pretend she had no interest in eating. She never hinted to get compliments, or once complained about her weight. Not that she had anything to complain about. Her curves were perfect. He came close to six foot three, and she had to be five foot ten. Damien also became more and more annoyed at himself. He didn't want to be attracted to her. He wanted to push her away, to keep his distance from her.

Damien should just pay the bill and get the hell away from her. He felt like a fifth grader. One minute he wanted to carry her books and the next minute he wanted to pull her pigtails.

CHAPTER TWENTY-FIVE

Pangs of discomfort poked at Dillon's insides. Her grandparents were all she had left of her family. The memories of them stopped when she turned twelve. She held on tight to those memories. They were the barrier between her and the nightmares. Something she still had to deal with years later.

Damien's voice was low and sexy. Dillon had a hard time paying attention and keeping track of the conversation. When he spoke of his family, Mrs. C., and Coach, she noticed the way his eyes smiled. She saw the love for them all over his face.

"I noticed you mentioned your grandfather, did you spend a lot of time with him growing up?"

Dillon sat back in the booth and grinned. "I used to go to their house every summer. Then when I turned thirteen, I went to live with them full-time." Dillon straightened her shoulders to stop them from slumping. "They have a farm in Iowa. I liked it there and didn't move away until I went to college. That's the reason I went to the University of Iowa. I wanted to spend my summers back on the farm. I still try to get there as often as I can. They're young, both in their late sixties. I miss them."

Damien heard the sadness in her voice. "How often do you get to see them now?"

Dillon pouted. "If I have a case that takes me that way, I always detour and stop in. But I haven't had too many of those recently. I think the last time I visited them for any length of time had to be about six months ago."

Damien cringed. "I know I said my family likes to meddle, but I couldn't imagine not seeing them for months at a time."

The waitress walked up and gave the check to Damien. He signaled her to wait as he grabbed money from his wallet.

The waitress hovered close to Damien. She leaned seductively against his side of the booth. "Can I get you anything else?" Her voice sounded soft and breathy. She smiled with her mouth, but her eyes held an open invitation.

Damien smiled at her but didn't encourage her flirtation. "No thanks.

We're finished."

Dillon watched as the waitress flirted with Damien. She pinched her lips together to hide the smile. But she couldn't stop the little giggle that escaped as she watched the waitress handle the quick dismissal from Damien. The waitress had been a little miffed.

Damien's brow furrowed together. "What's so funny? What did I miss?"

Dillon leaned forward on her elbows and fluttered her eyelashes. "Do you ever get tired of being the object of every woman's fantasy?" She teased.

"Is that what happened just now? I figured she enjoyed being friendly and sociable while she did her job." Damien gave her his best smile.

Dillon chuckled. "Sure. I imagine you and Joe have women falling at your feet. Throwing their panties in your path."

Throwing his head back, Damien laughed. "Well, I haven't had any underwear fly in my direction—lately. Are you offering?" He grinned at her.

She scooted towards the edge of the booth leaned across the table and whispered, "I'd like to make the offer, but I can't, seeing as how I'm not wearing any panties." Dillon winked at him and headed out. She turned back to see him sitting with his eyes wide and mouth open. "Well, you coming or not?"

They strolled to the elevators and remained silent up to her floor. He exited with her and walked her to her room.

Holding the door open, she stepped to the side. "You want to come in for a bit?"

A smile spread across his face. "Sure."

She smacked him on the back. "Get your mind out of the gutter. I just want some company for a while longer. Unfortunately for me, besides Joe, you are the only other person I know." Dillon lied. She wanted him naked in her bed screaming her name. She turned on the same college football game from down in the restaurant and pulled her hair out of the ponytail she had worn all day. "I have some beer or soda you want one?"

"Yeah, beer. Thanks." He tilted his head towards the TV. "Have you always liked football?" He tried not to gape at her as she held out the beer to him. Her hair hung loosely around her. In this light, the starburst of bronze around her pupils gave her eyes an iridescent glow.

"Oh yeah, I'm glued to the TV during this time of year if I'm not knee deep in a case. My brothers and I used to watch it regularly, they're the ones who got me hooked on it." She winced and cursed under her breath.

Damien's beer stopped midway to his mouth. He tilted his head to the side. "You said you didn't have any other family other than your grandparents?"

Dillon dropped her head down. Those words flew out of her mouth before she could stop them. She closed her eyes. Trying to slow down her breathing, she took two long deep breaths.

"Hey, it's none of my business. You don't have to tell me anything. Let's talk about something else."

Dillon opened her eyes. She moved towards the sofa and sat down next to him. Her hands shook. She blinked rapidly to stop the tears from falling. Damien offered her a chance to switch topics. So why in the hell did she want to tell him? Him, of all people. Dillon hasn't shared this part of her life with anyone outside the police, the counselor, her grandparents and the FBI. She's never wanted to share it. It isn't the kind of story to give warm and fuzzy feelings.

CHAPTER TWENTY-SIX

Dillon stared him dead in the eye. She took a long breath in and blew it out. "When I was twelve, my mother, father and three brothers were murdered by a man my Mom had an affair with." She paused, took a sip of beer, trying to relieve her parched throat. Her hand shook as she lifted the beer to her mouth.

Damien placed his beer on the coffee table and turned back towards her. He reached over, took the bottle from her. He moved his hand when she grabbed it.

"My room had been at the end of a long hallway kind of set off in a little alcove. A noise like a firecracker woke me up. I figured my brothers were playing a trick or some sort of joke on the family. I peeked out through my doorway, and I saw a man coming out of my brother's room carrying a gun, he didn't see me. I closed my door and got in my closet; in this cubbyhole behind my clothes."

Dillon spoke just above a whisper; the tears came in a steady stream. "I could hear my mother screaming. She kept asking George why and begged him to stop. My father yelled for my Mom to run. George shot him twice in the head. Then he raped and killed my mother. All the time he screamed at her if he couldn't have her, no one else could. I could hear her screams while he raped her."

Dillon squeezed Damien's hand. Her body shook as the fear she had felt that night washed over her. "I could hear him in my room, searching under the bed and moving things around in my closet. At some point, I know the front door opened and closed." She laughed at the memory. She wiped her face with her sleeve. "The door always had this squeak that my Dad could never fix. It became a running joke between us kids. We teased him endlessly about it.

"I recognized the police when they entered the house, but I still stayed in the cubbyhole. I must have fallen asleep or fainted—I'm not sure which. I'm not sure how much time passed before they located me. I'd been there so long I couldn't walk. I couldn't even get out by myself. An officer had to carry me down the stairs to the paramedics.

"I recounted the whole incident to them. Everything that I witnessed and heard. I gave them George's name and that he had a gun. They arrested him, and I testified at the trial. He is currently on death row. That happened sixteen long years ago. It feels like yesterday." When she looked into Damien's eyes, she saw more than just sadness. Something much more than that. Something that made her heart beat faster.

Damien's chest rose and fell with rapid breaths. The pounding of his heart echoed in his ears. He didn't know what to do, what to say. He wanted to protect her from the long ago horror. Damien pulled her into his arms. Her body shuddered with every breath. He stroked her hair and laid his cheek on the top of her head. Dillon wrapped her arms around him and wept.

She stayed wrapped in his arms and the comfort of his body's warmth for a few moments before she pushed away from him. "I blubbered all over your shirt," Dillon said as she sat up wiping her eyes with the heel of her hands. "I never tell that story to anyone. And I sure as hell don't cry about it with a perfect stranger."

Damien pushed her hair back from her face caressing her cheek as he wiped the wetness away. "Hey, I'm not a stranger and don't ever apologize to me. I'm so sorry that happened to you. I'd give anything to take your pain away, Dillon. I don't want to see you hurt, ever."

Damien looked into those wet drink me up whiskey-colored eyes, and he could feel his heart slam against his chest. The pounding of his pulse echoed in his head. Her lips parted, and she leaned into him. Damien shouldn't have done it, but he couldn't stop himself. He reached out, lifted her chin, and placed his lips on hers. Damien moved his tongue along the softest pair of lips he'd ever touched. Dillon's hands moved back around his waist, and she tightened her grip as she sank deeper into the kiss. His hands moved to her cheeks as if to hold her there so she couldn't get away.

Dillon's brain tried to stop her. It screamed in her head—run, you stupid fool! But her body craved the touch of his hands. Her fingers ached and tingled with the need to caress him. The fluttery feelings in the southern half of her body rose towards her chest.

Their lips parted. An immediate longing to kiss him again whispered through her. Damien's eyes darkened making her skin ignite with desire.

Dillon almost leaned into him again when common sense smacked her into reality. She removed herself from his arms and put distance between them.

Damien cursed under his breath. "I'm sorry, Dillon. I didn't mean for that to happen," he closed his eyes. "That's not true. I wanted that to happen since I first noticed you in the bar the other night. I know my behavior earlier doesn't reflect that, but that's only because—it doesn't matter. I just don't want you to think I'm trying to take advantage of you."

Dillon felt breathless. She walked to the bar area. "I don't think that."

Damien followed her. When he had seen her in the bar, he thought she would be a nice fuck. Now that didn't seem like enough. One time, one kiss, would not be enough to satisfy him. "Dillon, look at me." He waited for her to turn towards him. "I don't regret kissing you. As soon as you let me, I'll do it again." He stood at the counter of the little bar area. "I'm willing to give you some space, to wait." He sighed. "You're not the only one who can read people. You're pretty damn good at putting up walls. I just don't want you to build this one so damn fast."

She scowled at him. "Don't pretend like you know anything about me. A few hours ago, you didn't even like me."

His jaw tensed. "Look, I'm not pretending anything. After what happened to you and the work you do, hell I would build myself a little fortress. Just don't be so quick to shut me out." He almost pouted, "You haven't put up any roadblocks with Joe."

Dillon's jaw dropped open. "Are you seriously jealous of my working relationship with Joe?"

"No, damn it! Just the ease with which you fell into it." He saw her expression soften. "Listen, this isn't the time or place to tell you, but there have been some things that have happened in my life that make me question everything about it. I don't even know if I want to stay on the job.

"But right this moment, the one thing I do know, is I want to kiss you again." *I want to do a hell of a lot more than kiss you.* He pinched the bridge of his nose. "You are by far the most frustrating woman I have ever met." He pulled her to him and kissed the top of her head. He felt her body stiffen and then relax as her arms wrapped around him and she held on tight. He placed his mouth right next to her ear and whispered. "*Sei così bello.* You are so beautiful."

He stepped back. Every inch of him craved her. Desire radiated between them. He wondered how long she would hold him at arm's length. It didn't help he had acted like an ass all day. "Meet us for breakfast around seven-thirty? Then we will head to the lab. If you need me tonight, call me." He set his card on the bar. "I mean it, Dillon."

Heat curled down Dillon's spine. She took a deep breath closing her eyes as she exhaled. She walked him to the door. Damien leaned down and gave her a whisper-soft kiss on her lips and left.

Dillon leaned against the door. Her legs too weak to move. He was right. She had become damn good at building walls around herself. She had spent the last few years building her perfect world, devoid of friends, pets, or commitments of any kind. If she gained a friend or lover, she didn't let them get close to her. After one taste of Damien, she knew one thing for sure—she wanted more.

CHAPTER TWENTY-SEVEN

Damien's hands moved up Dillon's curvy waist. He cupped both breasts in his hands. The moisture on her skin from their earlier shower glistened under the moonlight peeking through the sheer curtains in the bedroom. She straddled him. He sat up and took one of her nipples in his mouth. She ran her fingers through his hair and placed her lips on his. Her hips moved in slow rhythmic circles.

Damien heard the noise. He opened one sleepy eye. The sound came from his phone. He checked the clock on the side table, four thirty. He rubbed his face, "What the fuck?" He grabbed his phone "Kaine!"

"Damien, it's Matt. We just got a call, a man who lives out on State Hwy 6B, discovered a body on his property. The local police called it in."

"*Madre Stronzo*! Merda! That fucking son of a bitch," he hissed. Every muscle tensed as anger raged through him. "Send me the damn address." He sat on the side of the bed until the trembling stopped. He called Dillon.

"McGrath."

Damien liked the sleepy throaty sound of her voice. "Hey Dillon, it's Damien. Matt called we got a body. They will hold the CSTs until we get there. Can you be ready in fifteen or twenty?"

"Yeah, I'll meet you in the lobby in fifteen." She hung up before he could answer.

Damien dragged on a pair of gym shorts and walked across the suite. He banged on the connecting door. "Joe, we got a body. We have to get on the road." Within seconds the door opened, Joe stood buck naked. Damien shielded his eyes. "Oh crap, my eyes. Seriously dude, cover yourself. I don't need to see your junk."

"Fuck, give me fifteen." Joe turned away.

Damien started back to his room when he stopped and listened to Joe tell Taylor he had to leave, but he wanted her to be back here tonight.

***

As much as she loved hearing his voice, Dillon knew Damien hadn't called to say hi. She set the coffeemaker to make a cup while she got dressed. A little mascara and a quick brush of her hair, and Dillon pulled it up into a ponytail. In a pair of black jeans, black boots, and a button up white shirt, she threw on her black leather jacket. Dillon grabbed her coffee, badge, gun, and headed out the door. She hated purses. If a woman needed a bag of any size, she carried too much shit.

Dillon waited in the lobby for Joe and Damien. Her heart skittered at the sight of him. He wore dark blue jeans, black t-shirt, and a jacket. His dark hair tousled and sexy. Damn, a man shouldn't be that handsome this early in the morning, she thought. "Hey, got any details?"

Damien unlocked the doors to the SUV. "Matt said someone found a dead body on their property out on State Hwy 6B. He didn't give me any other details." Damien's mouth watered at the sight of her. Dressed in almost all black, she oozed sexy, and she looked like she could kick someone's ass. He stared lasciviously at her as his dream came back to him. "Good morning Agent." He held the door open and waited for her to climb in.

She tilted her head and squinted at his expression. "Morning, Lieutenant." Dillon had the distinct impression she had just been eye fucked.

CHAPTER TWENTY-EIGHT

Damien's GPS rattled off the first series of instructions. The sky was as dark as the coffee in Dillon's cup. The silence in the SUV hung like thick drapery. Within twenty minutes they pulled onto the property, where a Sheriff's Deputy waved a flashlight at them.

Damien rolled down the window. "Lieutenant Kaine, Detective Hagan, and Special Agent McGrath, FBI."

The Deputy stepped back, allowing entry onto the property. "Yes sir, they're expecting you. Pull all the way down the lane you'll see everyone. It's awful sir. I've never seen anything like this."

The CSTs had rigged five enormous floodlights to illuminate the heavily wooded area. Their brightness cast eerie shadows against the darkness of the woods surrounding the property. Many of the CSTs worked at the edge of an enormous pond.

Matt jogged up to them. "I hope none of you have eaten."

Damien exchanged a glance with Joe and Dillon. "Okay give us what you have."

Matt nodded towards an old pickup. "Well, Mr. Powell has a few dogs. They were barking and sprinting up and down his porch. He came out, and the dogs started to race up and down the lane, so he followed them. Back up this way." He pointed towards the CSTs. "This is his pond, and it seems like whoever dumped the body tried to weigh it down, but didn't anticipate the dogs. You can see them there."

Matt pointed to an old man sitting on a tailgate of a truck, with five dogs in the truck bed. "When his dogs discovered an intruder had come on to the property, they bolted off after him. He dumped everything where he stood and took off. We can tell from the tracks he went down the trail. Mr. Powell said it leads off the property out to the highway. He never uses it, but he hasn't blocked it off—until now. He said he would be doing that straight away. Upon preliminary inspection, it's the same plastic bags."

Damien flinched and swallowed hard. "Bags?" He asked as he leaned back on his heels.

"Yeah bags," Matt said. "It appears he cut her up into a lot of pieces. The dogs pawed at one of the bags, and it tore open, allowing them to get at some of the contents. They dragged several pieces out, but the old man got here in time before they managed to drag them all over creation."

Joe took a deep breath. "Son of a bitch." The breath hissed out. He grabbed a pair of gloves Matt held out and cursed again. "How many bloody fucking bags are you talking about?"

Matt rubbed the back of his neck. He took a small step back before he gave them the answer. "Umm—three."

"Oh fuck me," Joe yelled. "I am so cutting this fucker's *clackers* off and making him eat them."

Joe wasn't alone in his feelings. The anger and frustration that dogged Damien since this case started collided together. His emotions exploded with fury. "*Ho intenzione di fare questo stronzo mangiare i suoi occhi!*" Damien stormed off towards the CSTs.

Dillon touched Joe's arm as they walked towards the dumpsite. "What did Kaine say?"

Joe's lips curved up. "He's going to make him eat his eyes. Between that and me making him eat his balls, this guy will have one hell of a meal."

***

Damien walked up as two techs picked up what resembled pieces of meat. "How many pieces do you have there, Doc?"

"Well, there are six pieces here on the ground. We're trying to minimize contamination. By keeping them separate, debris from the ground won't contaminate the remaining pieces in the undisturbed bags. It's one body but in a rather large number of pieces. When we get the bags back to autopsy, I'll be able to get a better idea of what we are dealing with. I'll have something for you ASAP. This is priority number one, and will stay that way until you guys catch him," the ME said.

"Thanks. I appreciate that," Damien said. He saw no reason to harass the Doctor here in the shadow of floodlights. He heard Joe as he muttered curses under his breath. Damien glanced back to see Dillon had stayed behind to speak to the ME. What the hell was she up to now? He turned his focus back to Mr. Powell. "I'm Lieutenant Kaine this is my partner Detective Hagan. Mr. Powell, can you answer a few questions for me?"

Two huge bird dogs flanked Mr. Powell in the back of his truck while three others moved from side to side behind him. "Sure. Ask away."

"Can you tell me what happened tonight? What prompted you to head down your lane?" Damien asked.

"Well, the dogs started going ballistic. Barking and howling as if they were on a coon chase. I figured that's what they were doing, chasing a coon. I didn't think much of it until they started scratching at the door and darting around the porch. That's when I noticed a truck pulling out from this area." He waved his hand around indicating the area where he discovered the body.

"How far from the vehicle were you? Were you already walking towards this area or were you still on your porch?" Damien asked.

"No, I had started down the lane. The dogs were racing around in circles, so they alerted me to something going on down this way. That's why I have Bertha with me." He raised his rifle up.

Joe looked around from the lane and the intersecting trail that led from the property. "Mr. Powell, did you see the vehicle at all?"

"No, I didn't see it. I can't tell you the make and model, but from the sound of the engine, I figure it's a large truck. Those dual cabs have a distinct sound. It tore off down the road as I came up to the pond. Delilah here," he pointed at the biggest dog in the truck, "started wrestling with one of those bags. That's when some pieces came out, and I got the dogs out of there."

Damien sensed Dillon coming up alongside him. He watched her scan the area. Her eyebrows furrowed then released as she turned back to Mr. Powell. Damien began to ask another question when she cut him off.

"Mr. Powell, what are the boundaries of your property?" Dillon asked.

Mr. Powell's eyes shifted between Damien and Dillon. "Hwy 6B, Rogers Road, Forest Road, and Widow's Road. Why do you need to know that?"

Damien frowned at Dillon.

She smiled at Mr. Powell. "Do you know your neighbors?"

His brow wrinkled, as he looked around his property. "Sure I do. You don't live here as long as I have and not know who you live next to."

"Have you ever had any trouble with any of your neighbors?" She asked.

"No, most of these folks lived here for years. The only problems would be from Jake Freestone's dairy farm. Stray cow gets across and ends up in my yard. They seem to end up at my pond. Nothing to worry about, though. I call up David, and he comes and gets them."

"Who's David?" Damien asked him.

"He's the foreman over at the Freestone dairy farm," Mr. Powell said.

Damien handed Mr. Powell one of his cards. "Well thank you for your time. If you remember anything else, please let me know."

Damien walked back towards the SUV. His anger simmered at a low boil. He found himself irritated as hell at Dillon.

"The ME is ready to head back; you mind if we follow?" Dillon asked.

Damien cocked his head then shook it. "No, not at all. You mind filling us in on the direction you're taking, I get the feeling we weren't invited to the damn party." Irritation rattled off with every word out of Damien's mouth. He had no right to be mad. She had every right to ask questions so she could help narrow in on a suspect. But damn if he had to like it.

She raised an eyebrow at him. "Don't get your dick in a knot. I know you're frustrated but don't take it out on me. I'm not the damn villain." She hissed out a long breath. "I asked him those questions for a specific reason."

Glancing at Joe and Damien, she waved towards the pond area. "This area sits back from the house. Tell me something, unless you know the area, how would you know about the back entrance?" Her head swiveled between Joe and Damien. "I think the killer knows this place and he knows how close the house is to the pond. I think he lives near here or has intimate knowledge of Mr. Powell's property, but I don't think he expected the dogs. They surprised him, and that messed up his plans."

Damien tilted his head back and sucked in the crisp cool air. "You know, Joe and I have been detectives for a while. Surprise, I came to the same damn conclusion. It's not as if I didn't pay attention to what Matt said earlier. He said that particular part of the drive exited onto the highway. You might see the entrance driving by, but unless you were familiar with it, you sure as hell wouldn't drive up it with a shit load of garbage bags filled with pieces of a girl you just fucking chopped up. *'Oh hey, there's a road let's see if I can dump this dead girl.'* Fuck Dillon, we aren't stupid bumfuck idiots." He took another deep breath.

Joe watched Dillon's reaction to Damien's rant. Aside from the daggers that flew from her eyes, she had none. She let him get it out of his system. Joe tipped his head towards his partner. "Damien, she never said *I* was stupid." He winked at Dillon. "You, on the other hand, well that's still up for debate. Listen, give her a break, and pull that stick out of your arse."

Damien stomped his way back to the SUV. Joe and Dillon followed at a slower pace. Before they reached the vehicle, she cleared her throat. "There is one more thing you should be aware of." She stood still while Damien and Joe stopped and looked at her. She met their hard stares. "This is going to piss him off. He didn't get to finish what he had planned. He killed Tiffany earlier than we expected; than *he* even expected. Something messed up his plans. Couple it with this botched dumping. He'll take another girl sooner than later."

Damien glared at Dillon. "Well Agent McGrath, there isn't a damn thing we can do about that. Now is there?"

***

Dillon had tried not to smile, but with Joe making faces behind Damien's back she found that hard to do. Joe nodded to Dillon for her to walk beside him. "Don't take Damien's reaction personally. We expected this killer to take another girl. We hoped we'd be closer to figuring out who the hell this shithead is. Mix in now we know Taylor could be in danger—well this is just a horrible case."

He kept his voice low. "Damien is going through something personal right now. This case is adding to that misery. I can't tell you about it, but it is making this case harder to deal with. Not to mention, he has a special attachment to the victims of the crimes we investigate. They get in his head and his heart. Then he tends to lash out. I'm so used to it, as are the other detectives in our Unit. It doesn't even faze us anymore. I wanted to make sure you knew it had nothing to do with you." He chuckled. "Well, it might have something to do with you. You seem to be the object of his wrath or desire. Either one works."

Dillon's mouth opened and closed. She didn't know what to say to that comment. After a moment, she gathered her senses. "When I work a case with detectives or anyone else for that matter, I never take their reactions to me or the circumstances personally. I didn't expect any other type of reaction from him, or you. Frankly, if he hadn't reacted the way he did, I'd be more concerned."

Joe smirked at her. "Yeah, right. You keep telling yourself that." He smiled at her as he continued towards the vehicle.

Dillon started to argue but decided against it. *Damn Irishman.* She glanced in the direction of the ME's van. "I asked the ME if I could be present during the autopsy. This whole thing seems a little off to me. The timing, it seems wrong. He had Tiffany a full day or two, if it is Tiffany. However, I think we all know it's going to be her. Why did he kill her so soon? Something happened, and I'm hoping the autopsy will help me put the pieces together."

Dillon winked and smiled at both men. Settling her gaze on Damien, "Sorry, sick humor. Anyway, while I'm observing the autopsy why don't you two go out to those other farms and see if you can get any information? When you get back, I bet we'll have some answers."

His annoyance and anger dissipated. "Alright. This might give us a break. If the killer does have intimate knowledge of Mr. Powell's place, it might help make a connection to one of the girls, we should be able to start narrowing in on someone." Before Damien got into the SUV, he noticed Matt a few feet away. "Hey, Matt?"

Matt spun around at the sound of his name. "Yeah what do you need?"

"Did you get any info on Jim Goshen?" Damien asked.

"Yeah, I did. I left a folder in the conference room, along with what I could get on the Taylorville farm. Oh, by the way, Jim is a real piece of work."

"What do you mean by that?" Damien asked.

At that moment the ME called for Matt. He walked backward towards the pond area. "My notes will explain. I've got to go." He turned and ran towards the ME.

Damien nodded, but Matt had already walked away. "Thanks."

Standing at the passenger side of the vehicle, Joe looked at his watch. "Crap it's seven. I need something to eat. What about you two?"

Damien opened his door. "Yeah, I'm going to need something." He glanced over his shoulder at Dillon. "Dillon what about you? You have to be hungry?"

"No, I'm all right. Go ahead and drop me off at the lab. My car is there if I need to go get something. Then you two go on, and I'll text you if anything breaks loose at the autopsy."

CHAPTER TWENTY-NINE

Damien pulled up in front of the lab, Joe opened his door and glanced back over his shoulder. "I'll go get the folder. Be right back."

Damien got out and opened Dillon's door. "Hey Dillon, I'm sorry for how I acted at old man Powell's place. You're right; you aren't the bad guy in this. This fucking case and all my personal shit are just messing with my head. I had no business taking my frustrations and anger out on you."

She stared at him, stunned. "I can't believe you. One minute you're telling me not to put up a wall, then the next you're apologizing for the very behavior that makes me want to build a fucking wall." She moved her back to lean against the vehicle.

Damien stepped closer to her. "What the hell do you want from me? I'm doing my best. We just witnessed the ME pick up pieces of a dead girl that look like meat that should be on a fucking grill somewhere. Hell, it didn't even resemble a human. You walk up and ask questions like you're the only fucking person with a brain that works..."

Dillon poked him in the chest. "Do not make what I do out to be some kind of fucking joke. The questions I ask serve a purpose, they aren't just so I can hear myself talk. You seem to..."

Damien stepped towards her. He grabbed her face and kissed her. Hard. His tongue battled for supremacy against hers. He heard her growl then felt her relent. Her hands reached up and grabbed his hair.

He pushed her against the side of the SUV and yanked her shirt out of her pants. He slid his hand up her torso and found one of her breasts, squeezed it. Needing a breath of air, he stopped kissing her and laid his forehead against hers. "Jesus," he said panting. "You drive me fucking crazy. God, what am I going to do with you?"

She had to catch her breath. Dillon didn't care they were in the middle of a parking lot, and his hand was still up her shirt. Her breathing slowed enough to speak. "I make you crazy? What about me? This case is messing with me too, throw you into the mix, and I can't do my job." She looked him in the eyes. His lips were red from their kiss. "You need to pull your hand out from under my shirt. Someone might notice you're holding my boob."

He grunted as he removed his hand and glanced casually around. "Sorry, I—I don't know, Dillon." He tugged her shirt back into place. "I can't help myself."

"I know you think I'm going to shut you out; I don't want to. Outside of my family and the Bureau, you're the only person I've ever told my story to. I hope that counts for something." She interlocked her fingers with his.

He lifted her chin and kissed her tenderly. "You have no idea what that means to me."

"Yeah? Okay—so after we get done tonight, let's eat in the restaurant?" She surprised herself when she pulled him towards her and touched her lips to his. "The next time you eye-fuck me, you should share the details." She kissed him again, the heat from the kiss rocking her back on her heels.

Damien feigned shock. "Huh? I'm not sure what you're talking about."

"Really? That's what you're going with?"

He snorted. "Okay, you got me. I had the most incredible wet dream of my life, thanks to you." He stepped closer, bent down and put his lips next to her ear. "In my dream, you were wet, hot, and oh so delicious. Every inch of you." He stepped back and winked at her.

"Well damn," she said. The heat of his breath still warmed her neck as she headed into the lab.

***

With enough food to feed a small regiment, Damien and Joe started the drive out to Findley. Between bites of his breakfast sandwich, Damien tried to speak. "Let's hit the furthest out first then work back. I know the Waverly farm location isn't too far from Powell's land and that alone has my interest piqued."

Joe pushed the bite of food into his cheek, like a squirrel packing nuts in his mouth. "We also have Jim Goshen from the Taylorville farm, and he was at the diner. Mmm, this is so good. I started to see my life pass before me. If we hadn't stopped for food when we did you would've had to perform CPR." He managed a wicked grin even with a mouthful food. "Taylor and I got room service, but I worked all the food off way before midnight."

Damien put a hand over one ear and chuckled. "No, no, no! I don't want to hear about your sexcapades. It's bad enough I had to see your

Johnson this morning." He took a bite of his sandwich, "speaking of Taylor, how is she doing? How did she get to the lab this morning?"

Joe gave Damien an exasperated look. "She drove herself. She did assure me she had someone walk her to her car and she went straight to the lab. The phone call ended with her mumbling something about not needing a babysitter and that she carried a gun." Joe laughed. "I swear she makes me crazy. She and Matt spoke with the director, and during her lunch hour, an officer will accompany her home so she can check on her cat. She has enough clothes for a couple of days." Joe paused and glanced at Damien. "She's scared. I think it hit her late last night that this guy has stalked her."

"And you, how are you doing?"

Joe frowned at him. "Why?"

"I know you have feelings for her, more than most of the girls you bang."

Joe laughed. "You're just jealous cause you're not banging anyone. I don't have feelings for her. I really like spending time with her." Joe shifted and stared at Damien. He wanted to change the subject fast. "Since we are talking about 'banging,' how many women have you been with since the breakup? I can guarantee it is less than five. That just isn't normal. It goes against the natural order of things. You need to get laid. You're letting this whole break up thing take over. It's time to get over that wench. Quit giving her so much power." Joe squinted and leaned towards Damien. "Is that why you want to leave the force, to get away from her? You're shitting me, right?"

Damien threw the wrapper from his sandwich into the bag. Shit. He needed to just come clean with Joe. "I'm not considering leaving to get away from Camilla. That isn't why I'm thinking about leaving this job."

"Then why? Explain it to me."

Damien sighed. "I didn't tell you everything. About the night when I found out about Camilla." He took several deep breaths and relayed the story to Joe. "I illegally tapped into her accounts to find out who she traveled with. Then at the hotel, I came so close to shooting her and her fuck buddy. Joe, I had my weapon pointed at them. If I can get that close to taking a life, how the hell can I remain a cop?"

Joe sat there quiet for a few moments. "Listen, I have wanted to kill a few people in my life, who hasn't? But you didn't. You left and kicked her ass to the curb. Quit beating yourself up over something that happened in the heat of the moment. You are the best damn detective I've ever had as a partner. You're the youngest detective to make Lieutenant, and the captain wouldn't have put you as the head of the VCU if he didn't believe in you and your abilities."

"It eats at me every damn day, Joe. I drew my weapon, my finger on the trigger. Not to mention I used my equipment at my house to track her financials and those of the guy she had been fucking. I used that information to blackmail him into not reporting my impromptu visit." Damien paused for a moment. "Trust me, I have enough on this guy that I could ruin his entire life. My actions that day made me question everything."

Joe made a grunting noise. He stared at Damien. "You would throw away the best opportunity you've ever had over a stupid bitch? First, using that software to track Camilla and her bed partners, I don't have a problem with that. Second, you got so angry you drew your weapon, big fucking deal. Pull your head out of your arse. You had no intention of shooting her, or you would have done so. That much I know about you."

Joe sighed. "If you want to leave and go to work for your Dad or for yourself, because you're burnt out, or you just don't want to deal with the murdering assholes anymore, fine. I'll back you one hundred percent. But if you're leaving because you drew your weapon wanting to use it on some chick and now you feel like you aren't a good cop, then I'm going to have to kick your arse. Because that is bullshit. And you know it."

Damien sat stunned. He thought Joe would have told him he needed to step away clear his head that this job was getting the best of him. However, he still hasn't told him about all the illegal searches. About anonymously feeding the DA information he had gathered, illegally, to ensure a conviction. And why not just tell him everything? Damien glanced over at Joe. Why not, he thought? Because at the heart of it all, he was a coward.

Joe took another bite of his sandwich. "I don't want another partner. It took me long enough to get your arse trained. I would have to start over, and that would suck." Joe sat staring at Damien. "Well, what are you going to do?"

He frowned. What was he going to do? Quit? He could work for his

Dad. Money wasn't a worry. Damien could start fresh somewhere, any-where, but that seemed like running. He didn't know if he used the events of that night as an excuse or if he really wanted to quit. He smiled at Joe. "I don't know. Hearing you say I need to just get over it makes me realize it wasn't as bad as I thought. As to whether I want to leave the force... I just don't know. I just don't know, Joe. I promise I'll decide by the end of this case."

Damien had to admit to himself he felt better. He should've spoken with Joe a long time ago. A slight smile lifted the corners of his mouth. "Oh, just so you know, I've been laid. Just because I don't tell you all the details, doesn't mean I'm not getting any." Damien laughed. "I'm just more selective than you. I've managed a night with a woman here or there, so I doubt it will fall off."

Joe cocked his head towards Damien and smirked at him. "Yeah well, a few one-night stands a month would do you a little good. Not one here or there."

Damien snorted. "Really? Is that what's going on with you and Tay-lor? A one-night stand each night you're here?"

Joe's hand with the breakfast sandwich stopped halfway to his mouth. "It sure beats sleeping alone."

"You're giving me shit, and here you are falling for one woman." Da-mien laughed.

"First of all, I'm not falling for anyone. Nor am I even considering a serious relationship with one woman. I told Taylor I couldn't give her that. She's okay with what we have going on. We're both adults, and we're just enjoying each other's company. I will admit, I can't get enough of her. She mentioned coming up to see me on weekends. She has no family to hassle with, in the area anyway. No commitment but work. She has a cat that's about it. That's it. Nothing more. I repeat I am not in a relationship with her. I am fucking her." Joe leaned his head back against the seat.

Damien laughed at his friend.

"SHUT. THE. FUCK. UP. You *blithering eejit.*"

That only caused more laughter to erupt from Damien. "You are so full of shit," he said. "I haven't seen you like this over a woman, ever. You can see it every time you're near her."

"Not everyone has to marry a chick because they fuck her, like you do. I'm quite capable of sleeping with someone and enjoying it for what it is. Sex."

"Right." Damien continued to chuckle at his friend.

"Fuck you, Kaine." Joe glared at Damien. His partner was way off the mark here. Way off.

CHAPTER THIRTY

Findlay, IL

Damien pulled into the huge soybean farm. A bright yellow school bus sat ten feet from them. Through the window, he and Joe could see tons of elementary age kids lining up. Damien saw a hint of fear in Joe's eyes. He and Joe took off almost at a sprint and ran into an ancient barn. Both stopped dead in their tracks. Damien's nose crinkled up as he checked the bottom of his shoes.

Joe covered his nose with the sleeve of his jacket. "Oh man, someone or something let out one hell of an air biscuit. Or your sphincter isn't working correctly, and your pants are filling with arse juice."

"Seriously? How old are you?" Damien asked as he stifled a laugh.

The woman behind a long counter glowered at them. She wasn't amused by their topic of conversation.

Damien and Joe held out their IDs. Damien asked to speak to someone in charge.

Her eyes widened as she placed a hand on her chest. "Oh my, let me see if I can get Carol for you." She walked away and in walked a gaggle of little kids.

A woman Damien assumed to be Carol came out from an office behind the solid oak counter, polished smooth from years of love and care. The woman's pinched expression made her look like an old headmistress of a Catholic school. She wore blue jeans, a t-shirt, and work boots. Not to mention a nasty attitude.

She exhaled loudly as she approached them. "May I help you, Detectives?"

"We need to ask you some questions about an ongoing investigation. Do you have a place we can sit down?" Damien gave her one of his best smiles.

Her gaze flicked upward, and she cursed under her breath. "Yes, fine—let's go back to one of the offices. Stacy, can you get the kids set up and ready to go?" She glared at the Detectives, "this won't take too long." She placed her hand on her forehead and rubbed her temples. "Call Roy if you need extra help. Gentlemen, this way please."

She led them down a makeshift hallway. The barn had a vast open interior, and the added walls helped to break it up into sections. She opened the door to a rather large office and gestured towards two chairs. "I can't imagine what you need to speak with me about. Please have a seat."

Joe glanced around. "Do you own the farm or do you manage it?"

"No, I own it. Inherited it from my Dad. One of the few things he left me worth a shit. I had this vision of having it opened up to schools; you know, maybe influence the next great farmer."

Joe bit down on his bottom lip. The corners of his mouth twitched. *The only thing this place had any chance of influencing was a bunch of kids making fart jokes.*

Damien pulled out his notes and asked her if they still used the plastic bags they bought from Tanker's feed store.

She reached behind her and pulled out a rather large three-ring binder off a shelf. "Let me get my supply list, it has all that information in it." Pausing while she flipped through it. "Okay, I know my Dad used those a long time ago. I got him to stop. He liked to use them for trash or recyclables and then take them out for proper disposal.

"Instead, I set up regular pickups of these items; we're still under budget as compared to using those bags." She thumbed through a few pages. "We quit using them last year. We don't even have any left on site. I finished them off as trash bags. A very expensive trash bag, but it got the job done."

"Do you use iodine or propylene glycol at this facility?" Damien asked.

"Gosh no. We use as little as possible in the way of chemicals. I'm not certified organic, but I don't use any extra chemicals if I can help it. As for iodine, the price has skyrocketed. We now use chlorine. Sparingly"

Damien glimpsed Joe. *What the hell?* Joe sniffed his shirt. Several times. Damien had to cough to cover the laughter. "Do you make a lot of deliveries to the surrounding area?" Damien barely got the question out.

Carol rolled her eyes. "Well sure, how can you farm and not make deliveries? I can get you my delivery log." She reached for another binder. "Here. We make the same deliveries weekly for eight to twelve weeks, starting at the beginning of October. Before that, we have deliveries that are more sporadic. Mostly to our customers who order large quantities of our products."

Joe glanced at the log he saw no dates or times that brought them near the areas of disappearances or the dumpsites. He gave Damien a shake of his head.

"We appreciate your time. We know you're busy." Damien shook her hand.

Joe and Damien tried not to tear out of the barn. On the way out the door, one little boy asked who farted. Joe raised his eyebrow at the little kid and giggled to himself, *yeah, nothing but fart jokes.*

"What the hell were you doing when we were sitting in the office?" Damien asked once in the SUV.

Joe sniffed his shirt. "Smelling my shirt. If I smell like that fucking barn, I'm gonna beat the shit out this asshole before I kill him. Man, that place smelled like rotten skunk farts."

"How do you know what rotten skunk farts smell like?"

"Shut up, you know what I mean. How can anyone work in that smell?" Joe pulled out the folder. It contained information on the farm in Taylorville. "Jim Goshen works at the next farm. That's the guy Betty mentioned. He pulled out of the parking lot when Tiffany went missing. Let's see what Matt found out about our boy."

Joe scanned the information. "Well, Jim has been at this farm since the age of twenty-two. He has some college, but he didn't finish. That doesn't line up with Dillon's profile. Seems Jim started as a ranch hand and now he is in the delivery section. This job seems to have agreed with him. He gets regular raises and hasn't had any trouble with the law or work." Joe said.

"He seems to live within his means. Matt says he buys a lot of flowers and lingerie. Jim buys his stuff in towns that coincide with his deliveries." Joe snorted. "Matt thinks he is having an affair. He also thinks it might be with more than one woman, but he definitely thinks he is not buying this stuff for his wife. He's been married for eight years and has two kids. Damn, shoot me if I become this boring."

"Okay, I will shoot you. Maybe something will shake loose from this guy." Damien did what Joe had done earlier; he sniffed his shirt. "Do you think our clothes smell?"

Joe rolled his window down. "I sure hope not. Or else everywhere we go today people will believe we've been rolling in shit. Rotten skunk shit."

Damien rolled down the rest of the windows. "Well damn, I don't want to smell like rotten skunk shit."

CHAPTER THIRTY-ONE

Autopsy of Tiffany Basset

Dillon tied the plastic apron around her waist and grabbed a pair of gloves, preparing for the autopsy. As she dressed, she went over the timeline of the disposal. It didn't fit with the pattern the killer had established. Even if he had sped up his timeline, he should have kept Tiffany for longer than he did. What happened?

The door to the autopsy room opened, and Dr. Langley walked in. He wore a baby blue lab coat and a clear plastic mask that covered his whole face. He walked to the two tables that sat side by side. One held the three bags from the Powell place, the other empty.

Dr. Langley handed her a clear facemask as he moved around the empty table. "Good morning, Agent."

Her eyebrows pinched together as she took the mask from him. "Hello, Dr. Langley. Thank you for letting me be here for this and to observe."

He raised one eyebrow at her. "You are going to do more than observe. You're going to assist me. That's why I gave you a mask."

She had worked with the Medical Examiner at Quantico, but she didn't do it enough to know what to do. She clutched the mask in her hand as she blinked and her eyes darted between the Doc and the table with the bags on it. "I'd been under the impression you had a full-time assistant. A paid assistant?"

He looked up from the table with the bags on it. An inscrutable smile filled his face. "I do, but he had to step out for a while, so you'll take his place. Don't worry; you'll be helping me put the pieces together. Then we'll gather samples for analysis."

"Great," she said. "It's going to be like putting a 3D puzzle together."

They grabbed a bag and heaved it to the empty table. Opening the bag with great care, the Doc reached in and took out the first piece. Instead of cataloging as they went, he wanted to get the pieces on the table and then go from there. Thirty minutes later, the contents of the first bag lay on the table. They had most of the legs and one foot.

The second bag went through the same process. Another thirty minutes later they had the lower pelvic, the thoracic region, and a partial left arm. Dillon and Dr. Langley didn't speak. Words took too much effort. Dillon rolled her shoulders, and the Doc stretched his arms over his head. They each took long slow deep breaths and started on the third bag. Inside the last bag, they retrieved the head and the rest of the arms, and the remaining parts of the legs, including the other foot. The pieces that had fallen out at the dump site sat in a container at the foot of the table.

When all the pieces were on the table, Dillon's body shuddered. She placed her hands on the edge of the table and hung her head. "Wow! This is sick. Really sick. How can someone do this?"

The Doctor peered at her through his clear eyewear. "The good thing, if there is one; all of this hacking took place after he killed her. You can tell from where the axe hit the skin the blood flow had already stopped." He pointed to the edge of one of the pieces. "From what I can see..."

The Doc stopped, grabbed one of the smaller pieces, and held it under a magnifying light. "Hmm, now this is fascinating. I think she'd been dead for some time before the dismemberment took place." He moved the overhead lamp closer to the piece so Dillon could see it. "See how the blood and the skin have this blotchy look, where it joins together, this indicates the body rested in one position for over six hours."

Dillon's eyes narrowed; with the back of her hand, she rubbed the bottom of her chin. "Why would he keep her for so long before cutting her up and getting rid of the body?"

"I can't help you with that, but let's see if we can figure out what killed her." The ME went to the head and thoracic region to see if he could get those answers. He nodded towards the counter. "While I'm doing this, take her hands and get her fingerprints. We need to get the techs going on that."

Dillon frowned at the separated hands on the table. She had taken fingerprints before but nothing like this. Usually, the body still had the hands attached, and most often, she could use the handheld fingerprint scanner. Not today.

She started on the right hand and covered the fingertips with ink. She rolled each finger onto the card in the appropriately labeled box. Dillon repeated the process with the left hand. Although the killer severed the hands, the fingers themselves were in good condition. She placed the DNA samples the Doc had taken and the fingerprint cards on the counter and moved back to the table to observe Doctor Langley. Within a few minutes, a tech came in and retrieved the samples.

"I think I have a preliminary cause of death. Come over here." As Dillon moved closer to the Doctor, he held the tongue in a pair of forceps. "What do you see?" He asked her.

"A lot of swollen tissue."

"That's right," he said. He then released the tongue. The head had been severed just above the shoulders. What little of the throat remained, showed the swelling continued through to the esophageal area. The Y incision had been pulled back to reveal the chest and the opened rib cage.

"You see the swollen tissue and how it continues through here." He traced the trail from the trachea area to the esophagus. He removed the heart and examined it. "It seems as though she went into cardiac arrest." He placed the heart on a weight scale. "I'd say she died from an allergic reaction to something. When I get her stomach contents, we'll see what she ate."

Dillon lifted a single eyebrow. "Are you sure? Wouldn't you know if you were allergic to something that could kill you?"

"Absolutely. Under normal circumstances, I doubt anyone with this kind of allergy would eat it, knowing it could and most likely would kill them."

She shook her head. "Wait a second. She ate whatever he gave her, knowing it would kill her?" Dillon hissed out air. "Shit. She wanted out so badly she figured dying like this seemed a better choice than what he had in mind. Am I correct in assuming death by an allergic reaction this severe would have been very frightening and damn painful?"

The corners of the Doctor's mouth turned down. "You are correct in your assumption. Immune cells see the 'invader' or the allergen, as a threat and assemble forces to attack and destroy it. This young girl would have the sense that something had started to happen before any symptoms showed up. She would've begun to feel dizzy and a tingling in her limbs. She may have had a tightening in her chest. A rapid heart rate would enhance those feelings. With this critical level of allergy, all the symptoms associated with anaphylaxis would occur rapidly."

Dr. Langley paused as he glanced down at the girl before him. "She would have begun to wheeze as her airway constricted. A drop in blood pressure would have occurred, increasing the dizzy sensation. This symptom has to do with the heart and blood vessel function during the reaction. Chemicals flood the bloodstream, causing small blood vessels to widen, ultimately resulting in cardiac arrest. That would've occurred after she felt as if she was suffocating. Her throat and mouth area are extremely swollen. This would have been a horrific way to die."

Dillon reminded herself to breathe as the Doctor described the young girl's death. Her eyebrows lowered and pinched together as she watched the ME move through the rest of the examination. The scene played out in her mind. She observed the Doctor as she spoke. "He delivers her food and water. She sees what he brought and realized she has a way out of her hell."

Dillon paced from one end of the table to the other. "I don't think our killer had any idea this girl had an allergy. I'm damn sure he wasn't there when she ate it. The killer came back, saw her and his rage took over. He dragged her to wherever he hacked her into pieces. He didn't expect to find her dead. She screwed up his plan, and that pissed him off."

Dr. Langley continued the cursory exam of the vaginal area, as he listened to the Agent walk through the scene. The Doctor's hair on his arms stood up. Her clarity of a very plausible scenario caught him off guard. "I can tell you about part of her hell. She suffered severe trauma, enough to cause bruising and tearing outside and inside the vaginal wall. We have his semen so we can get a match to the previous victim. I found a very deep bite mark on her upper torso area. I'll finish this up and get you the report..." He started to say something else when Matt walked in.

Matt's head hung low on droopy shoulders. "Both DNA and fingerprints are a match to Tiffany Basset. I'll let you get ahold of Joe and Damien and you three can decide how to tell the parents."

"Thanks," Dillon said. She turned back to the Doctor, "You guys must have a RapidHIT machine. Quantico has one. They can identify DNA within ninety minutes. It's an amazing piece of technology."

Dr. Langley stretched his back and twisted from side to side. "Yes, we got one about six months ago. After we had taken all the samples from the kids, we loaded up a separate database that just held those samples. That way if we ever had to check we would be able to identify them quicker." He sighed deeply. "When a child is missing, the parents need answers yesterday. Now, as I started to say a minute ago, I will get you the completed report. If anything alters these preliminary findings, I will let you know ASAP."

CHAPTER THIRTY-TWO

Dillon leaned on the basket that held her bloody lab coat. Her wobbly legs barely supporting her weight. She willed each foot in front of the other, each step harder than the last. The walk back to the conference room felt as if she were walking through a tunnel. She squeezed her eyes shut. Starbursts exploded behind her eyelids, sending darts of pain through her head. She leaned against the wall to steady herself.

Shake it off. That's what she said to herself. *Just shake it off.*

Dillon's body slid into one of the conference room chairs. She stared at the phone in her hand. She needed to make the call, but her fingers wouldn't follow her brain's instruction to dial Damien's number. Lucky for her, it rang.

"Agent McGrath."

"Hey, it's Damien. Got any news for us?"

She sat in a chair and rubbed her forehead with her hand. "The Doctor and I finished not ten minutes ago. Put me on speaker." She paused for a moment. "Where are you two?"

"Getting ready to go into the office here at the dairy farm in Taylorville," Damien said.

Dillon reclined in the chair. "Okay, fingerprints and DNA came back as a match with Tiffany. I don't think that surprises any of us." On the other end of the phone, Joe let loose a string of curse words. "I'm aware that expecting a result doesn't make it suck less. However, some surprising and disturbing items came to light during the autopsy." She hissed out a breath.

"Tiffany appears to have had an allergy to something the UNSUB gave her to eat. I mean a severe allergy. We, Doc and I, believe she ate it knowing she would die. That explains why he got rid of her so much sooner than we anticipated. I think when he found her dead, he went into a rage. He hacked her body up with an axe." Her hand shook as she held her phone. No sound came from the other end of the line. "Hello, you still there?" She asked.

"Yeah, we're here. What this poor girl went through and what this monster did to her makes me sick. She would rather die a horrific death at her own hands rather than let that bastard kill her," Joe said.

Dillon spun around in the chair. "Horrific doesn't even come close to what she went through before she died. However, what she went through while she died beats that. This severe of an allergic reaction caused her body to go through a series of transformations that under normal circumstances would require immediate medical intervention. Her suffering would have been horrible. Do you mind if I inform the parents while you two finish up at the dairy farm? If you guys would rather do it, I understand."

"No Dillon, that's fine with us. Are you sure you're up for it?" Damien asked her. "The results of the autopsy may make this one of the hardest notifications you may ever do. It's okay if you want to wait for us to do it."

The corners of her mouth curved up at the concern she heard in his voice. "No, I'll be okay. It's still part of the job. I haven't done as many notifications as you, but I have done my share."

"Call us when you're done, and we'll meet back at the lab and go over everything. Something has to break soon," Damien said.

"Okay, I'll keep you posted. Later." She pulled the sheet with the Basset's information and dialed their number. After making sure they would be there, she studied the board. The four missing girls from years ago and the recently discovered unsolved cases had everything to do with the three most recent cases—Franks, Martin, and Basset.

Dillon rearranged the board. She lined up all the pictures, starting with Beth. Seven girls stared back at her. She placed the girls in the order of their disappearance. She moved Beth Haut's picture and placed it above the other six. Beth held the key to unlocking the identity of the killer. Of that, Dillon had no doubts. Her eyes lingered on Beth's picture. *Talk to me Beth, tell me your secrets.*

CHAPTER THIRTY-THREE

Basset House

An older gentleman wearing a warm fuzzy cardigan opened the door of the Basset house. "Yes? May I—oh you must be Agent McGrath, please come in. We've been waiting for you." He led her to the living room. Trudy, the dog, followed her. Her cold nose nudged Dillon's hand, wanting attention.

Two grandmotherly women flanked either side of Mrs. Basset, who sat squarely in the middle of the sofa. The older man who had opened the door now stood with another older gentleman behind the couch. Mr. Basset had been pacing in front of the fireplace, but now he stood still as a statue.

Glistening eyes filled the room. All of them fixed on Dillon. That last cup of coffee she drank now churned in her stomach. She took a small step forward, acknowledging each person in the room. "Mr. and Mrs. Basset, before we get started, can you tell me if Tiffany had an allergy to anything? Something that would cause an acute reaction if she ate it?"

"Yes," Mrs. Basset spoke up. She tried hard to catch her breath. "Tiffany has an allergy to corn and anything with corn or corn byproducts in it. She needs to carry an Epi-Pen. It took us a while to figure it out. This particular allergy seems to be a very rare one." Mrs. Basset raised her eyebrows with a questioning gaze.

Dillon noticed Mrs. Basset squirmed in her seat while everyone in the room seemed to hold their breath as they waited for further explanation. She hated this part of the job. She had found that the best way to tell such life-changing news was to just rip off the bandage and do it. Dillon took a deep breath. "I'm so sorry to inform you; we recovered your daughter's body early this morning."

An audible gasp erupted. The wails started as a whisper of despair, slowly crescendoing into sobs of raw pain. She glanced around the room at Tiffany's family members who had hoped for different news.

Mr. Basset looked at his wife and then the others in the room. No one spoke. They nodded their heads, and yet no one could maintain eye contact.

Dillon shifted her weight from one foot to the other. "The reason I asked about an allergy—it seems as though she was given something to eat, something she had an allergy to. It appears that Tiffany ingested the food with the understanding that it would kill her."

Mr. Basset hissed out a shaky breath. "You mean he gave her food, and the food must have been something with corn in it. She ate it, knowing she would most likely die?"

Mrs. Basset rocked back and forth. Her gaze became unfocused, and her mouth opened and closed in silence. Dillon's throat ached from the lump that had formed. She watched as Mrs. Basset's spirit broke, right in front of her. Dillon looked Mr. Basset in the eyes. "Yes, sir. That's what we have determined so far."

Mrs. Basset glanced up at Dillon, tracks of tears flowed down her cheeks. "Did he rape her? I must know. Please." She pleaded. Her husband nodded in agreement. Trudy moved from her bed and sat at the feet of Mrs. Basset.

Dillon's stomach twisted into a tight knot. She moved to sit on the sofa table in front of Mrs. Basset. She took one of Mrs. Basset's hands in her own and maintained direct eye contact. "Yes, he did. I'm so sorry." Dillon had to swallow the bile that crept up her throat. She hadn't wanted to answer that question, but she couldn't lie to them either.

Mrs. Basset pulled her hand from Dillon's and wrapped her arms around herself. Her body shivered as she rocked back and forth again. She muttered something that sounded like a prayer. When the older women tried to comfort Mrs. Basset, she twisted away from them and continued to rock.

A canopy of pain and sorrow filled the room. Dillon stood and moved towards Mr. Basset. She reached out placing her hand on his arm. "Mr. Basset, could you join me on the porch for a moment?"

He nodded and followed her out the door. Mr. Basset lowered himself to the top step and hung his head in his hands. He took several deep breaths before he looked up at Dillon. "Thank you for telling us the truth." He said nothing for a few minutes. "I tried to talk her out of asking that question, about Tiffany being raped, but she said she had to know. Just before you showed up, we all decided and agreed with her. But now I think I made a mistake letting you give her the answer. It may have been too much for her right now."

Dillon took a long deep breath. "Since this is an ongoing investigation, I'm sorry I can't give you any more details, but I can tell you that you need to have either a closed casket or cremation." She wanted to tell him more, but she just couldn't. They couldn't risk the details getting out in the news.

Dillon sat down next to him on the stoop. "Mr. Basset, I know you have a strong Catholic faith. You and your family need to lean heavily on that faith now." She touched his arm. "It will be a few days before Tiffany can be released—if you give me the name of the priest and church that you attend, I will contact him for you. He can contact the funeral home for you and make your arrangements."

Mr. Basset's shoulders drooped, and his head hung to his chest. He wrapped his hands behind his neck and wept. His entire body shuddered with every breath of air. He crumbled under the weight of losing his daughter. Mr. Basset lifted his head and stared out across his yard. "Thank you for your offer. We go to St. Marks, here in town. Father Michaels is who you need to speak with." He grabbed her arm. He glared at her with hard eyes. "Promise me when you get him you will make him pay for what he has done. Promise me."

She placed her hand over his. "I swear I will stop him. Whatever it takes, I will stop him." She stood up and gave him her card. "If I can help you in any way, call me. Please. I can give you and your family some names of counselors in this area who specialize in this type of trauma and loss. I'm so sorry for what you are going through."

From inside her car, Dillon watched as an older man came out and sat on the porch with Mr. Basset. He buried his face in the shoulder of the older man. The birds ceased their afternoon songs. The wails of a broken father pierced the quiet neighborhood street.

Dillon's head fell against the steering wheel. Each breath labored out of her tight chest. Unable to stop the flow, tears ran freely down her cheeks. Mr. Basset's sorrow covered her like a sticky film. Dillon pushed the heels of her palms into her eyes to stanch the tears. *Plug the dam and move on.* She told herself.

Her phone hummed in her pocket. "McGrath here."

"Hey Dillon, it's Matt. Someone reported an abduction in Jacksonville. It's got to be the same bastard, and he did it in broad fucking daylight."

She slammed her palm against the steering wheel. "Shit! Shit! Shit! I knew it. I knew he would take a girl. Send me the address and get ahold of Damien and Joe. Tell them to meet me there."

CHAPTER THIRTY-FOUR

Jacksonville, IL

It took Dillon forty minutes to get to the high school football field in Jacksonville. A local Sheriff held up his hand stopping her access to the parking lot. "Miss, this area is restricted. You have to back out."

She held up her FBI credentials.

"Sorry Agent McGrath, I didn't expect you when they said the FBI would be showing up. Please pull up over there. The chief is waiting for you."

"Thank you," Dillon said. "Two Detectives from Division Central should be showing up in the next few minutes, send them over."

A crowd of deputies huddled in a circle. The conversation stopped as all heads turned towards her. Their expressions conveyed their surprise that she'd been allowed onto the property. Dillon ignored their ogles and stood at the side of her car as she studied the area. The UNSUB didn't think this abduction through. He let the incident at Powell's land rattle him.

Dillon walked towards the chief and his men. Several frowned at her until she held out her credentials. "Good afternoon Chief, gentlemen. I'm Special Agent Dillon McGrath. I'm working with Lieutenant Kaine and Detective Hagan from Division Central on these abductions and murders."

The chief shook her hand and nodded towards the victim's car. "Nice to meet you, Agent McGrath. I'm Chief Roberts. I understand you discovered a body this morning. Would that be the missing girl from Chatham?"

A black SUV squealed to a stop. Damien and Joe walked over to the group of deputies. Dillon noticed the one lone woman officer physically react to the sight of the two Detectives. She couldn't blame her. They had a way of making a woman's heart skip a beat.

Damien strode towards them with an unintentional sexy confidence that oozed from every pore of his body. However, Dillon was damn sure he wasn't oblivious to the effect he had on women. The incredible smile he gave the female officer in the group told Dillon she was correct in that assumption.

Damien reached out to shake the chief's hand. "Chief." He nodded to the other deputies in the group, lingering a tad bit longer on the female officer. "I'm Lieutenant Damien Kaine this is my partner Detective Joe Hagan," he nodded to Dillon, "Agent, didn't mean to interrupt."

Dillon gave him a shrug. "No problem Lieutenant. Chief Roberts and I had just started our conversation." She directed her attention back to the chief. "Yes, we discovered Tiffany Basset's body early this morning. I had just finished with the notification when I got the call to come here. Can you tell us what happened?"

The chief nodded to one of his deputies. "Sully, go over the details for Agent McGrath and the Detectives."

The Deputy pulled out a notepad. "Yes, sir. Amy Custer had been here for cheerleading practice. The girls had been at the other end of the field when she came out to her car to get something she forgot." He pointed to her little Honda, and you could see the keys still hung in the door. "From what a couple of the girls reported, a truck pulled up next to her. Driver side to driver side and a man got out. At first, it seemed like Amy may have been familiar with the man.

"The girls started to walk back to their practice. Not a minute or so later, Amy yelled out. When they turned around, they saw the man put Amy in his truck. The two girls said Amy didn't appear to be moving. He jumped in and drove off. Amy's friends couldn't see the license plate or the make of the truck as it left the parking lot. Both girls said the truck sounded like an older model, looked like one too. It had the boxier style not, the sleeker style of the newer models. They agreed it appeared to be dark in color, possibly black or charcoal."

Chief Roberts rubbed his chin. "You think the guy who took Amy also killed those other girls?"

Dillon focused on Roberts. "We do. He botched the dumping of Tiffany Basset, and I think he abducted Amy out of desperation. I'm hoping this will lead to mistakes that help us locate him. Can you tell us what Amy looked like—even a general description?"

The chief nodded to his Deputy again. He flipped through his notes. "Amy is about five foot five, one hundred and twenty-five pounds. She has brown hair and green eyes."

Dillon nodded. "Thank you." She glanced at Damien and Joe but asked no other questions.

Joe pursed his lips together. "Basically, we got a description of the truck, and that's it?"

"It seems that way," a Deputy said.

Damien looked at the chief. "Your town has some kind of festival getting ready to start; can you tell me about that?"

"Yeah," Chief Roberts said. "It's the Fall Festival. We get vendors from the surrounding area that come in and get booths. Over at the Mayor's office, they have all that information."

Damien handed the chief a card, as did Dillon. "Chief, if we get anything, we'll let you know, and if you guys get any more information let us know too, please. And if anyone from the press asks questions, please don't give them any answers. Just direct them to me or Agent McGrath."

Dillon, Damien, and Joe stood at their vehicles. Dillon leaned against Damien's vehicle. "Amy doesn't fit his profile. Her looks are close with the brown hair, height, and weight. The green eyes don't fit with the other girls, but he wouldn't have had a chance to see them before he grabbed her. The fact that she is a cheerleader is very far from the 'innocent, sweet' look he is going for. Remember I believe he is recreating Beth and his time with her. This puts Amy in extreme danger. He may hurt her more because he has to work harder to recreate that time with Beth."

Damien and Joe both cursed under their breaths. Joe had his hands on his hips. His head hung to his chest. "That's also the same description of the truck Taylor has seen following her. It has to be the same fucking guy."

Damien looked at Dillon. "Let's get over to the Mayor's office and get a list of the vendors. No one recognized the truck which tells me he isn't from this area," Damien said. He looked around the football field. "This guy took Amy with other people around. If we don't catch him fast, he may very well start to abduct a new girl every two or three days. And now with your observation, Dillon, he may abduct any type of girl. Fuck! There has been only one other person in my life that I wanted to kill. This guy has become the second."

Dillon's brow furrowed at Damien's comment, but she let it go. "You got a bunch of strangers in town getting ready for a week-long festival that starts Sunday. Our guy has to be in this group, I'm sure of it."

Damien moved towards the SUV. "Dillon, I got the address to City Hall, follow us over there."

***

It took all of ten minutes to get to City Hall. A very curvy young woman stood behind the counter. She glanced at the three and zeroed in on Damien. He glanced over at Dillon and gave her a wink. This time, she rolled her eyes.

Stifling a laugh, Damien moved towards the counter. Reading her nametag, he smiled at her. "Hey, Michelle, I'm Lieutenant Kaine. I'm here with Detective Hagan and FBI Special Agent McGrath. We need to see the Mayor. Can you call him for us?"

She glared at Dillon. "You're really an FBI Agent?"

Dillon glanced around the office with a blasé expression. "Yes, I am. Can you tell the Mayor we need to speak with him?"

Michelle didn't like the dismissal. She feigned a smile, "Sure I'll call back to him." With a quick lick of her lips, she picked up the phone to inform the Mayor he had company.

Dillon leaned into Damien and whispered, "You shouldn't encourage her. You'll only get her hopes up."

Damien raised his eyebrows. "Do I detect a slight bit of jealousy, Agent McGrath?"

Dillon snorted. "Ha, you wish."

A minute later, a short man came out from a closed set of doors. What the Mayor lacked in height, he made up for in charisma and looks. He had a fit and sculpted body. Sandy blond hair worn a little longer than most Mayors should wear. "Good afternoon. I'm Mayor Childress, what can I do for you three?" He reached out his hand and shook each of theirs. The Mayor's eyes locked on Dillon. His lips parted, and he leaned into her. "Do you need something specific from me?"

Dillon's mouth curved slightly upward at the Mayor. But she focused her attention on Damien as her eyes smiled at him with a teasing gleam. "Mayor Childress, we are investigating a series of abductions and murders in this area. We're trying to find who might have been in the area at the time of Amy Custer's abduction over at the football field just a little while ago. We're aware you guys are preparing for your Fall Festival?"

The Mayor nodded. "A Deputy let this office know about Amy's abduction a few hours ago. News travels very fast around here. Amy's parents are beside themselves. Anything this office can do to help, we will. As for your question, yes, we are. We have the vendors set up, and we're getting all the last minute details put together."

"We need a list of those vendors. Can we get that from you?" Dillon asked.

"Well, I guess so. It isn't like its top secret. Most of these are the same vendors every year. Michelle, print me up a list of all this year's vendors, please," he said.

Michelle spoke to the Mayor but continued to ogle Damien. "Sure thing, Mayor Childress."

"Mayor, can you tell me how many vendors have been around today to get their spots?" Joe asked.

"Hmm, we had over fifteen alone today. We're in the middle of handing out spaces, and everyone wants to get here early to get the best ones. Some don't care, they take whatever they're assigned without complaint," the Mayor stated.

"Do you remember who came by today?" Joe took the print out from Michelle.

"Gosh no, they come in and give their name, and then we give them a spot, that's it. Sorry, I can't give you any more information," he said.

Damien shook the Mayor's hand. He may have squeezed a little too hard. "That's okay. Mayor, we appreciate your time."

Walking out behind Joe, Damien leaned closer to Dillon. "I didn't know the FBI taught flirting as a way of getting information."

Dillon snickered. "They teach us to use our talents and resources to get what we need. It's a skill I've honed well over the years," she said.

"I bet," Damien said.

Standing outside, the Mayor's office, Dillon asked Damien and Joe about their trip to Taylorville.

"What an enormous waste of time. Matt had made some notes about Jim in the file he gave us. Jim has been spending a lot of money on *extra* items. Matt believed he's been having an affair and—Matt was right. Jim has proven himself an ass, not a serial killer. That day at the diner, he didn't have a delivery in the area. Fucking pantywaist," Joe hissed. "He had just come from banging his mistress."

Damien smirked at Joe as he spoke of Jim Goshen. He looked over at

Dillon, "Joe got a little riled up at this guy. Jim had started the interview with a cocky attitude. Once he understood, we liked him for the abductions and murders he changed his tune rather quickly. By then Joe had enough of his shit." Damien smiled broadly at Dillon. "Joe hates cheaters, almost as much as I do. It turns out, Jim has been using one of his delivery routes to hook up with his girlfriend. That particular day, he detoured off his last delivery to see her. Jim had been more worried about his boss finding out about his little tryst than about being accused of abductions and murders."

Joe angled his head to the side to spit. "Jim had no regard for his wife. From the notes we got from Matt, he spends a lot of money on lingerie—for his girlfriend. You think the wife would know about that. But hey, since Jimbo had been in an interview with us at the time of Amy's abduction, he has a pretty damn good alibi."

"We asked Jim about what he may have witnessed when he left the parking lot. He didn't remember seeing anything. Jim thinks he might have seen Tiffany walk out to the parking lot, but he didn't see what car she went to, or if she went with someone else. Jim had been sure he noticed a man bent over checking his tires. He almost asked the guy if he needed help. The guy had a delivery truck. Not a large capacity one, but a smaller refrigerated one. Something that would do specialized or smaller quantity deliveries. And before you ask, no he didn't remember seeing any kind of logo," Damien said.

Joe let out a long breath. "As for the bags and iodine, the dairy farm still uses the bags. They had them in use everywhere—they're used for recyclables. Anyway, only one guy has access to them, the owner's son. This guy's somewhere around fifty, and he looks every bit of eighty. He's not our killer. He logs every batch number off every bag. These bags line different bins, located all over the farm. The man has OCD to the fucking tenth degree. The next bag on the roll matched up with his log. They use the iodine too. Here again, this man tracks every fucking ounce. Every ounce," Joe said.

Damien snorted. "I kept waiting for Joe's head to explode."

Joe rubbed his temples. "Bloody bollix, this guy probably counts every square of fucking toilet paper. Damn, my head still hurts."

"I'm relatively confident this farm is not involved in these murders. We got a list of deliveries, dates and times for the last eight months. So far nothing seems to be matching the day Franks went missing." Damien checked the time. "It's almost five. Let's go to the farm in Waverly and then stop for the day. We can go over this information tomorrow." He dragged a hand over his face. "Shit, we've all been up way too long. I'll call Matt and get him to get all the information on Amy Custer from Chief Roberts. Follow us to Waverly." He nodded to Dillon.

***

Twenty-five minutes later they entered the town of Waverly. "Hey, Joe check out that list, do you see any of the farms that we're interested in on there? We know Jim didn't abduct Amy, could there have been any other drivers from Taylorville in that area?" Damien took a long sip of his now warm diet soda.

Joe read over the list. "The only ones on the list are the rotten skunk farm we went to earlier today, and the farm we're on our way to now."

"Okay," Damien said. "Call the rotten skunk farm and find out when they got their spot and who got it for them," Damien called Matt and got his voicemail. He hung up as they pulled into the Freestone Dairy and Cheese Farm.

Joe hung up his call. "Carol from the stinky farm got her spot a week ago. She'd been up this way for some kind of school thing. She picked it up then."

"Crap," Damien said.

CHAPTER THIRTY-FIVE

His hands shook as he grabbed the steering wheel and pulled onto the highway. He shouldn't have done it, but he couldn't resist. He'd been driving by when he noticed her standing next to her car. He swore he saw Beth standing there.

She'd opened her car door when he pulled up next to her. He realized it wasn't Beth. He had to act fast, to take advantage of the opportunity. The girl's curiosity gave him enough time. He grabbed her around the waist and threw her into the truck. Trying to get away, she got out one scream. He didn't want to hit her too hard, but he had to stop her from screaming for help.

Thirty-five minutes later, he pulled into the entrance of the old farm. The sun had set, and he needed to hurry and get over to the dairy farm to let his workers see him. He pulled up at the back of the house. He dragged her over to his side of the truck and threw her over his shoulder. On the way down the stairs, she moaned, but she didn't wake up.

He laid her on the bed and secured the restraints. He left her clothes on. He wanted her awake when he took those off. Her long legs went on for miles. His pulse quickened at the thought of what waited for him at the apex of those legs. Looking back at her from the bottom of the stairs, a slow evil grin spread across his face.

CHAPTER THIRTY-SIX

Waverly Dairy Farm

Several workers milled about despite the late hour. A sign with crisp white letters directed all visitors down a path to the business offices in a newer steel building.

The door chimed as Damien and the team entered. Several men who sat around the large office area glanced up. Partition walls separated the enormous open space into smaller rooms. A hallway ran down the middle of the barn-like structure. It appeared to lead to two massive sliding doors which he assumed hid a larger storage area.

Damien acknowledged everyone in the room. "I'm Lieutenant Kaine, and this is Detective Hagan, we are with Division Central out of Chicago. This is FBI Special Agent McGrath. We're investigating the disappearance and murder of some local girls from this surrounding area. Who happens to be in charge?"

A man behind a desk stood up and came around. "Umm, that would be Jason Freestone. But since he isn't here, it falls to me. I'm David Hessel. What can I do for you guys?"

Damien shook his hand. "I need to ask you a few questions. Can you tell me if you use these bags anymore?" He showed him a picture of the bag.

"No, we don't use those at all. I don't think I've ever seen them before. What are they used for?" David asked.

Joe took the picture from David while Damien continued to speak. "They're heavy duty bags sold by the feed store in Raymond. They can hold a lot of weight."

"No," David said shaking his head. "We don't use those bags."

Joe handed the picture to the other men in the room. One of them recognized the bags.

"Yeah. Jason's Dad used to use those a long time ago. Before you came on to work here, David. He bought them some years ago. Damn, like ten or twelve years ago. He didn't like them." The older man frowned. "Boy, he was mad too. Couldn't return them, so he used them around the farm for garbage bags. I haven't seen them in years."

"Do you use propylene glycol or iodine at all?" Asked Joe.

David sat on the edge of his desk and folded his arms across his chest. "Propylene glycol—we used to a long time ago. But we went away from that when we began to produce cheeses, about six or eight years ago, I think. Just before I came on to work here. As for the iodine, we used that on the cows and on the equipment as a cleaner and disinfectant. However, we switched to a few different disinfectants. Chlorine-based as well as glutaraldehyde, and ammonium compounds."

Damien remained expressionless. "How about your deliveries, what area do you travel to? Do you have a log of where you deliver?"

"Sure, hang on." David went back to his desk and pulled up a file on his computer. He pushed a button and something printed. "This list covers all the areas we deliver to. We have five delivery trucks that cover the area. We travel all over for deliveries." He handed the forms over to the Damien. "I'm not sure what we have to do with your investigation. You said there had been a few girls that went missing?"

Damien checked over the list. "You have some trucks out now. Did you have any deliveries up in Jacksonville?"

"Not today, maybe yesterday I think," David said. Some men nodded in agreement.

"Who owns the farm?" asked Damien.

"Ah, that would be Jason Freestone. He had some new business appointments today. I'm not sure where, but he said he would be gone most of the day. I hoped he would be back by now." He glanced at his watch.

Damien tilted his head to the side. "Do you guys deliver to Macon?"

"Yes, sure we have an arrangement with the Piggly Wiggly store there. They give us a forty-eight-hour window when they need restocking. It isn't a set delivery date and time."

Damien's expression remained unresponsive. Yet, his skin tingled. Something about this farm put him on high alert. He had no real reason for the tingle. He trusted his body, and when things clicked in a case, his body reacted. "It would really help us out if we could get the deliveries you guys made to the Piggly Wiggly over the last eight months. It would help us eliminate this farm from our list. Would it be possible to get that from you?"

David shrugged. He went back to his computer. "No problem, give me a minute to pull up the file."

Dillon smiled at the group of older men and moved a little closer to them. She sat on the corner of the desk. "So how long have you guys been here?"

The man who recognized the bags spoke up. "I've actually been here the longest. I worked with Jason's Dad a long time ago."

Dillon examined the expansive interior of the building. "Well, Jason seems to have done well for himself." Dillon smiled at the older man, who melted into a gooey puddle. "When did Jason take over the farm? Did his Dad retire or something?"

The older man leaned into Dillon. "No. Jason's father died unexpectedly. Jason took over the farm and made some modifications to be a cheese maker. He's done very well for himself. Brought this place back from the brink, he did."

Dillon's tone softened as she leaned into the man. "Was the farm in trouble of going under?"

"Oh yeah. Their profits were being eaten away by the other dairy farms in the area."

David stepped around from behind his desk and handed two papers to Damien. "When Jason took over and switched from just a dairy farm to a specialty cheese farm, this place took off. He seems to have a sixth sense when it comes to business."

Damien shook David's hand when he took the papers. "Well, we appreciate your time. Umm, one more thing, do your cows get out much and cross over Widow's Road?"

David snickered and glanced at the men in the room. The other men laughed as if a private joke passed between them. "Tell me old man Powell didn't call you to complain? The cows got out a week or so ago and ended up over there. For some damn reason, we got three that love that pond over there."

Damien handed him a card. "Well thank you. One last thing, when did you come to work here, and where did you come from?"

David's eyes widened, but he answered the questions. "I came on five years ago. Prior to here, I was on a farm in Michigan. I can get that information for you if you need it."

Damien smiled nodding at David. "I think that should be fine for now. We might have some more questions will you guys be here tomorrow?"

"Sure will. We have the Jacksonville Fall Festival to get ready for. We always sell our cheeses. The festival starts on Sunday, so we are working overtime to get some extra produced."

"Who went up and got the spot for you?" Joe asked him.

"That would be Jason. He went up there sometime this week to get it. Said he wanted to get in early and get a good spot."

Joe also handed him a card. "Do you know when he went up there to get it?"

"No, I sure don't. Jason takes care of all the business stuff," David responded.

"Well, thanks again for your time and cooperation," Damien said.

***

On their way to the parking lot, they almost ran into a ranch hand. He wore a baseball cap and a pair of coveralls. "Hey there," he said as he walked by.

Dillon observed the ranch hand talking to David. The two men stared back at the three before they walked into the building.

Damien checked the delivery log to the Piggly Wiggly. "This record shows they delivered to the Piggly Wiggly the day Jesse went missing." He went to the next page. "Okay, most of these deliveries have who delivered and when, but on the day Jesse went missing, it only has the time." Damien looked up. "I have to wonder if that had been deliberate or if someone simply made a mistake. It seems to have happened on other dates after that, but it still seems suspicious to me. I'll call them in the morning and see what they have. I'll let them know we can get a warrant and maybe that will get them to cooperate. Maybe they have a record of who did the delivery." He stared at the steel building. "Something about this farm I don't like. Something feels out of place."

Dillon glanced at Joe and Damien. "Yeah, I don't like this place either. The hairs on the back of my neck are standing on end. Something feels way off here."

Joe leaned against the SUV. "The workers said the Dad used the PPG, the iodine, and the bags—a long time ago. That would explain the degraded samples."

Damien continued to scan the area surrounding them. "Yeah but who? David? He didn't even know about the bags, and he wasn't here until five years ago. Of course, unless he's lying. He is familiar with Powell's land. The other ranch hands all looked ancient, and I may be a guy, but I didn't see handsome anywhere in that room."

"You're just used to my good looks," Joe said.

Damien snorted. "You wish." He glanced around once more. "As much as I want to catch this guy, I know if we're operating on fumes we won't do anyone any good. It's been a very long day. Let's call it a night and start fresh in the morning."

Dillon's phone buzzed. She looked at the screen and her brow furrowed.

"What is it, Dillon?" Damien asked.

"It's Matt, he said the autopsy results on the stomach contents revealed that Tiffany ate corn chips. That's what caused her allergic reaction." She glanced between Damien and Joe. "That's the oddest thing to feed someone you have captive. Corn chips."

Damien and Joe shared a glance. "Becca had corn chips in her stomach contents as well."

Dillon frowned. "That has to be important to the killer. It represents something of significance to him."

Joe's stomach growled. "Well, speaking of food, I'm starving. I need to eat something."

Damien patted his stomach. "Damn, I'm hungry too. Dillon what about you? You hungry?"

Dillon's forehead wrinkled. She didn't remember when or if she ate. "Sounds good to me." She climbed into her car. "See you at the hotel."

Damien frowned at her. "You didn't eat today, did you?"

She smacked herself on the forehead, "Damn, I knew I forgot to do something." She waved at them as she drove away.

Joe's phone chirped as he got into the vehicle. He smiled as he read the text.

"Let me guess. Your girlfriend?" Damien smiled at Joe.

"Ha ha, you shitbag. And look who's acting like a mother hen. Or as your father always says, mother chicken."

Damien laughed as reached for his soda. "He never can keep that saying straight. Has Taylor asked to come up and see you in Chicago?"

"She's mentioned it. I'm enjoying the moment. Except for the stalker part. But at least it has kept her in my bed this whole week. Which has made this case more tolerable. I wouldn't mind seeing her on a weekend now and then." He paused, "Damien, you know I don't do relationships, too much work. You have to worry about someone else, their feelings," he waved his hand around, "whether or not they remembered to eat. That's just too much for me to deal with. Look at your relationship fiasco. No, man—I like it just fine the way it is." Joe said the words out loud but even he wasn't sure he believed them."

Joe laid his head back on the headrest. "I noticed the way you glowered at Mayor Childress for the way he ogled Dillon." Joe chuckled. "You hated her yesterday, now—well, now it seems you like her more than you're letting on."

"We had a long talk last night. I misjudged her." He glanced over at Joe, who deliberately lowered his head and stared at him. "Nothing else happened, so don't look at me like that. She doesn't have many friends. Her work takes her all over, and she isn't very close to the other agents. I think she could use a friend right now. I intend to be that friend."

Joe raised his eyebrows at him "Are you thinking a friend with benefits?"

Damien squinted at Joe. "No, you idiot. Not a friend with benefits. Well hell, I'd love benefits. There's just something about her, Joe. I can't explain it. Something I don't understand. Am I sexually attracted to her? Hell yeah. You'd have to be dumb, deaf, and blind not to be. But at the same time, she is annoying as hell." After the kiss last night, Damien had been alarmed at the emotion that stirred in his chest. Something he hadn't felt for a long time.

CHAPTER THIRTY-SEVEN

Holiday Inn

Joe and Dillon sat with their heads resting against the back of the booth. Damien sat with his head in his hands. Silenced engulfed the table. The waitress brought their drinks, and they each gulped their beers as if they'd had nothing to drink in weeks. Dillon set her beer on the table. "Oh man, that tastes so good."

Damien set his half-empty beer bottle down. "Damn I needed that. Ever since the pond. I've felt like I'm on a slow train to hell."

Joe's voice strained with emotion. "You're not alone. I'll be damn glad when we shut this case down. This morning was brutal." Joe looked at Dillon. "I can't imagine what you went through having to be present at that autopsy. Then you went to the Basset's house. How did that go by the way?"

Dillon's eyes moistened with tears as she fiddled with her beer. She recounted the visit to a silent table. "Man, I don't want to have to tell another set of parents we found their dead daughter. We need to find Amy before he kills her."

Joe's phone chirped. His eyes wide and glowing as he tapped out his response. His joyful reaction managed to alleviate the fear and frustration that had settled over the table.

"Taylor?" Dillon took a bite of her steak.

Joe's smile filled his face. "Yeah. She should be here shortly. Officer Jenkins is following her here so she can leave her car."

"Did you two know each other before this week?" Dillon asked him.

"No, met her here. Why?"

"I assumed you two had been dating for a while. You seemed like you've known each other for some time."

Joe stared at Dillon. She was stunningly beautiful, with long ass legs and long blonde hair. The most incredible set of fuck me eyes he'd ever seen. Yet he wasn't attracted to her. Maybe it had something to do with the way Damien reacted to her—like he'd marked her as his territory. Or maybe it just had to with Taylor. That thought unsettled him the most. "We're just enjoying the time together." He wiggled his eyebrows.

"It's a nice distraction from the case."

Dillon tilted her head towards him. "Really, that's all it is? A distraction?"

"Yeah. What else could it be?" He asked her.

She shrugged. "I don't know. I got the impression it was more."

Joe sipped his beer. "No. Nothing too serious."

Dillon nodded, disbelieving what Joe said.

Damien's phone pinged. He damn near choked on his food at the picture staring back at him.

"What you got there boy-o?" Joe asked. "Something about the case?"

"Thank the Saints no, it's Mrs. C. She thinks Coach misses me. He seems to be sleeping an awful lot. She wanted to make sure I've been getting enough rest. And she sent me a picture."

This time, poor Coach wore a cowboy costume; complete with a vest and a cowboy hat. And a red bandanna around his neck. He also had a belt with toy guns in it and a Sheriff's badge on the vest. When Damien held his phone out, Joe couldn't stop himself from laughing.

Dillon reached out for Damien's hand and pulled the phone so she could see. "That poor cat." She burst into laughter. Tears spilled over, and at one point no sound came out as she tried to catch her breath.

Joe wiped the corners of his eyes. "No shit. Coach will need therapy when you get back."

"He needs a diet," Dillon said. "No wonder he sleeps all the time. The cat is too fat to do anything else. He'll not only need therapy, but he'll also need to go on a weight loss plan for big ass cats. But Coach will be the best-dressed feline wherever he goes." Dillon and Joe erupted in more laughter.

"Ha-ha-ha," Damien said. "Go ahead and make fun of my cat. Mrs. C. likes having him to take care of. It gives her something important to care for, and Coach hasn't gotten that fat. He may be a little plump, but that's it." Damien chuckled under his breath as he laid his phone down.

Dillon glanced to her side. Her gaze remained on Damien. Warmth spread through her. Their thighs bumped under the table, and with every touch, her body begged for more. "I can't believe a sexy Lieutenant has a soft spot for a fat cat and little old lady."

Damien squinted at her. "You think I'm sexy?"

Dillon saw his gaze go dark as he stared at her as if she was dessert.

"Umm..." she fumbled her words.

"I think you're sexy," Joe said as he winked over the top of his beer.

"Great. I'm locking my bedroom door from now on." Damien said. "Now back to you." He watched as embarrassment scrolled across Dillon's face. The flush of color growing on her cheeks had Damien understanding Joe's love affair with making Taylor blush. He took pity on her and changed the subject.

Damien popped a fry into his mouth. "I'm going to have Matt run the list from the Mayor and see if we can find out if any of these people have a truck matching the one used in Amy Custer's abduction. If we get any hits, we can go do some interviews and see if anything shakes loose. I think our guy will be on this list. Also, we could have Matt do a check on everyone at the Waverly farm and see if we can find a connection to any of the missing girls."

Dillon placed her beer on the table. "I think you're right. Since no one recognized the truck at the football field, I don't think our guy will be from Jacksonville."

Joe studied the file. "The list from the Mayor isn't all that long. Shouldn't be hard for Matt to run the names. I think checking out the employees at Waverly is a good way to go."

"I want to go back there early tomorrow. I'd like to meet Jason in person," Damien said. "It would be nice if we could get an ID on the man at the mall. That would be our best lead." Damien took a sip of his beer. "So far all the farms have admitted to using those trace items found in the bags. However, that doesn't help us much unless we can tie someone from one of the farms to them."

Damien noticed Joe's eyes light up as a broad grin spread across his face. He looked over his shoulder and saw why, Taylor. Every male turned towards her. Her petite structure only added to her striking appearance. Not very tall, but not fairy-like either. Exceptionally built with perfectly placed curves.

"Hey, guys," Taylor said.

Joe scooted over and gave her a sweet kiss on the cheek. "Are you hungry, babe?"

"No, I got something earlier when I checked on my cat."

Joe's voice strained, "you didn't go there by yourself, did you?"

She halfway rolled her eyes. "No. I didn't. Officer Jenkins went with me right after work. He came in with me while I fed Muffin and grabbed some extra clothes, he then followed me here." She smiled at Joe and the others at the table. "Do you have any leads on your case?" Taylor took a fry from Damien's plate. He growled, only encouraging her to take another one.

"No, babe, and it's frustrating as hell." Joe swallowed the last of his beer and left money on the table. "I'll meet you guys for breakfast at seven-thirty. Then we can head over to the lab. Let's go Taylor." He nudged her out of the booth, winked at Dillon, and headed towards the door.

CHAPTER THIRTY-EIGHT

A different waitress than the previous night lingered next to Damien with a very inviting smile on her face. "Can I get you anything else?" She asked.

Damien gave her a pleasant but not interested expression. "No thanks, we're fine. You ready?" He said as he glanced at Dillon.

The waitress gave Damien an incredulous stare as her mouth fell open at the dismissal. Her sweetly inviting smile soured, and she directed her nasty disposition entirely at Dillon.

A playful grin spread across Dillon's face. "Yes. Let's go, before the waitress tries to stab me." She scooted to the end of the booth. He held out his hand for hers. She took it, without hesitation.

Damien had a shit-eating grin on his face. "Now why would she do that?"

"Hmm, let's see. She's been trying to flirt with you all through dinner, and you've ignored her. I get the distinct impression she feels I'm to blame."

"Technically you are," he said. "Why would I need to flirt with someone when I had the most beautiful woman sitting next to me?"

She rolled her eyes at him. "Oh seriously, you are so full of shit," Dillon said as she pressed the button for her floor in the elevator. She faced him. Those killer eyes stared back at her making her weak in the knees. "Come to my room for a bit. Have another beer with me?"

Damien tightened his grip on her hand. "Sure. I'd love to."

***

Damien watched as Dillon pulled off her boots, got two beers from the mini fridge, and joined him on the small sofa. She laid her head back and closed her eyes.

Her chest rose slowly with each breath. Damien's dream from earlier that morning came flooding back. What he wouldn't give to make that a reality. "Are you sleepy?"

She opened her eyes and took a long sip of her beer. "Mmmm, no just comfortable."

His body throbbed with desire. The light reflected off the tiny gold flecks in her eyes, making them sparkle. Damien reached over and took her beer and placed both bottles on the table. He pulled her towards him.

His lips touched hers, and his tongue demanded entrance. He tasted beer and desire. Damien pulled her closer to his chest and placed a hand on her lower back. In one quick move, she straddled him. Wherever Dillon touched him with her fingers, a trail of tingling heat followed.

His hands moved under her shirt and caressed her hips and waist. He ran his hands up her body until they touched her bra. She had full, round breasts, just the right size. His fingertips grazed across the delicate lace. He ran his thumb across her nipple. An electrical current shot from the hard nub right to his groin.

Dillon pulled her lips away and leaned her forehead against his. "I haven't trusted anyone in a long time. I don't let myself get this close to someone." She leaned back still straddling him. "It's been a long time since I've been with someone. I had a relationship with someone a few years back. He happened to be a colleague of mine. We didn't work in the same division but ran in the same circles. We'd been dating for almost a year when I went over to his house and found him in bed with another woman."

She reached out and ran her fingers through Damien's thick hair. "I don't trust too easily anymore. I want to trust you. Things are a mess right now, Damien. I don't know where I'm going, or even when." She paused and let out a soft sigh. "I'm just not ready for something like this." She kissed him. "I want you—around—somehow, some way. I just don't know how much I can give you."

Damien pulled her hair out of her ponytail holder and brushed through it with his fingers. "I'll take whatever you want to give me. We can go as slow as you need to go." He kissed her again.

Dillon pulled back from him. "This kind of intimacy scares me. I'm not sure I'm ready for this." She whispered.

"Dillon, I don't know what the hell may be happening to me or between us, but I don't want to ignore it. I tried to push you away after we met in the bar by being a jerk to you and trying to make you out to be the bad guy." He twirled a strand of her hair around his finger. "I didn't tell you everything last night. Camilla crushed me. She cheated on me. She had an affair with a man she worked with. Actually, she had several affairs with a lot of men."

He took her hands in his. If he wanted a chance at a relationship with her, he needed to be honest about what he had done. "First, I tracked her down in a hotel room with the other guy. My computer equipment is some pretty sophisticated technology, courtesy of my father's security business. I may have pushed the legal boundaries by using it to hack into their financial records. Then using that information, I figured out the guy she was screwing. Only to blackmail him into keeping his mouth shut about my impromptu visit to the hotel.

"I stood there in that room, with Camilla in a robe, and she tried to tell me it wasn't what it looked like. I held my gun in my hand, pointed at her and her lover. I'd been inches from shooting her." He expected to see judgment or even fear in her expression. Instead, he saw understanding, caring and something deeper in her eyes. "It got ugly for a while. I didn't tell anyone about it except for my father. Joe only found out all the details this week."

His hands moved to her waist. "You don't know how hard it has been for me to rectify what I did. The man I was that night in the hotel goes against everything I stand for. I haven't wanted another woman in my life, in my house, or let alone in my bed since I broke it off with her. I can't explain what I feel for you, but these feelings are so strong I can't turn away from them. I'll never hurt you like your old boyfriend did. I'll never do to you what he did or what Camilla did to me.

"I can't guarantee I won't piss you off, but I'll never intentionally hurt you." He pushed her hair out of her face. "The whole thing has caused me to question whether I want to even be a cop. I don't trust myself. It scared me, wanting to shoot her. Coming that close to pulling the trigger. Breaking the law, I'm supposed to uphold. So I have no idea what's going to happen to me either. But I want you in my life, somehow."

Dillon sighed and brushed her lips against his. "Don't question yourself about your ability to do your job. You were in the heat of a passionate moment, and you chose to walk away. As for the illegal searches, I didn't hear that. I heard you gathered facts and investigated. Those actions have no bearing on your ability to be a detective.

"The FBI vetted you and the other members of your Unit. Don't question yourself. Plus, Camilla sounds like a bitch. And I'm so glad you left her." She leaned in and kissed him again. "Stay with me tonight. I don't want to be alone. I don't think I'm ready to have sex, but I want you here with me."

He grabbed her face. "No place I'd rather be." He kissed her.

She got off his lap and reached out for his hand. "C'mon we need to shower."

"I need to call down to the front desk and see if they have a toothbrush, I don't feel like going up to my room," Damien said.

"You can use mine after your shower," Dillon said.

His eyebrows squinted together. "Really?"

"Yes, silly. We just played throat hockey with our tongues, you think letting you use my toothbrush will gross me out?" She stepped close enough where he could feel her breath on him. "Weren't you the one to have a very erotic dream and didn't you tell me I tasted delicious in that dream? I think if you said I'm delicious then you would have had to put your mouth on me. Surely using my toothbrush won't make you queasy?" She smiled at him. "Now go take a super-hot steaming shower, it will help you sleep." She kissed him. "I'll take one after you."

He wiggled his eyebrows. "Are you sure you wouldn't want to take one with me? You know that was part of my dream?"

She focused on those blue eyes and felt that jolt deep in her belly. She almost said yes. "One day, yes. That I can promise you."

"Well, I guess I'll have to wait." He grabbed her around the waist and pulled her to him. "Trust me, Dillon, I will wait." He kissed her and went to take his shower.

Dillon stood in the center of her bedroom. Why didn't she want to be intimate with this man? He promised he wouldn't hurt her, and deep down she believed him. The one thing that stopped her—fear.

***

Damien laid on the bed in his boxers. He didn't sleep in clothes, but he didn't want to make Dillon uncomfortable by sleeping naked. The room had a soft glow from the outside lights. He had just drifted off when the door to the bathroom opened. His heart stopped. She wore a simple Iowa Hawkeyes t-shirt that reached mid-thigh. He watched those long legs stroll over to the bed. A groan escaped his lips. "Come next to me." He reached for her.

Dillon snuggled up next to his chest and wrapped her arm around him. Her hair smelled like vanilla with a hint of citrus. Her body, still warm from the shower, melded to his. He kissed the top of her head. "I set my alarm for six forty-five, so I can grab some fresh clothes before we go to breakfast."

It took all of ten minutes for her to fall asleep. He felt her heartbeat against him and soon followed.

CHAPTER THIRTY-NINE

Soft whimpers wove in and out of Damien's subconscious trying to nudge him awake. He drifted in and out of a deep sleep. The whimpers became increasingly louder. *Dillon.* Damien sat up to find her curled up into a ball. He could hear her as she mumbled about past traumas that morphed into present-day horrors.

Dillon covered her ears as she cried out. "No oh no, please no." The words were barely audible.

She cried out a guttural sound that tore his heart to shreds. He shook her. "Dillon baby, I'm here. Wake up. You're okay." Damien wrapped an arm around her and rolled Dillon into his chest.

Dillon thrashed and pushed against him. "Stop, let me go. Let me go, you bastard."

She struggled against Damien's hold as he continued to soothe her. "Sweet Jesus, wake up Dillon!" He knew she wasn't talking to him, yet the venom that spewed out with her words rocked him to his core.

The cloudy remnants of the dream faded away. Dillon realized Damien held her and not the nasty man from her dreams. She breathed in deep and slow. Just the scent of him brought her comfort. "I'm okay. I'm good."

Damien caressed her back with his hand. "Can you tell me about it?"

Dillon sat up, pressed the heels of her hands to her eyes, and pulled her knees to her chest. She sat rocking for a few minutes before she answered. "My mother screamed for George to stop, but as I ran through the door, it wasn't my Mom, it was Tiffany being raped. Becca sat on the floor next to the bed. She tried to get up, but her limbs wouldn't work. Her mouth moved, but nothing came out. Tiffany couldn't scream, her throat bulged from the swelling, and the man kept raping her." Dillon's body shook as she continued to whisper. "All the other girls sat at some sort of table. They kept asking me how long it would be before I found them. Beth kept screaming at me. She kept saying 'he took me first; he kept me the longest. She repeated it over and over."

Damien reached over and pulled her to him. She held on tight and buried her face in his chest. He assumed she had gone back to sleep, but she spoke so softly he almost missed it.

"The autopsy had to be the most horrific thing I've ever had to do. I can't begin to explain to you the amount of damage done to her. We pulled over twenty pieces out of those bags today. Piece by piece we reconstructed her body. This bastard hurt her so badly; she had significant tearing and bruising on the inside. He used her for whatever demented pleasure he could think of."

She took a deep breath and blew it out. "Rape isn't about the sex; it's about the power. Except with this bastard. He loves the sex. He loves taking what he wants, how he wants it. Satisfying his sick desires. Yes, power gives him a rush. He has them, and they can't leave or defend themselves, but it's more than that.

"He feels entitled to the sex. That desire motivates him. His cruelty adds to his excitement, and this makes him a sadistic bastard. He enjoys killing the girls as much as the sex. It's as if the murder is the final climax.

"It's the first time in a case that I feel as if a hole to Hell has opened up under my feet and the demons have a hold of each leg." Her grip on him tightened.

Damien kissed the top of her head. "Next time, Dillon—you need to talk to me. You can't carry this kind of stuff inside and not let it out. Even if you can only call me, do you understand? You're the toughest women I've ever met. You can deal with a lot more than most men, but you have to talk about it. There is only so much your mind can process."

She sighed. "Yeah, I understand. I'll be okay if you stay with me. Don't leave me. Damien, just stay with me." She draped her long leg over him. She kissed him. The kiss deepened with a searing passion. His hand slid up underneath her shirt. Dillon's breath hitched. Her body reacted so strongly to Damien. It was as if it waited for just his touch; like her body had lain dormant all these years. His hand cupped her breast, and he pinched her hard nipple. His mouth swallowed her moan.

Damien pulled her t-shirt over her head. His hand slid up and down her back. He pulled back from the kiss. His hand caressed her cheek. Damien stared at her. "Are you sure? I can wait Dillon; I'm not going anywhere."

Her fingers weaved through his hair. She brushed her lips across his. "I don't want to live in fear of what might happen. I want to enjoy what *is* happening. I've never been more certain of anything else."

Damien's lips blazed a trail along her neck. His tongue made its way down to each breast. He circled each nipple and sucked it into his mouth. He traveled down her abdomen to her thighs stopping at the top of her simple cotton panties and teased her with his tongue. Slipping it under the upper part of the soft fabric. He heard the moan as she whispered his name. It was the most incredible sound he'd ever heard. Dillon writhed underneath him, arching, and begging.

Damien's mouth continued down her thigh, avoiding the one spot she begged him to touch. He moved to the other leg and slowly made his way back up. He slid her soaked panties down her legs. The moisture glistened on her sex. He had to taste her. His tongue teased her, moving between the soft folds of skin. The taste and smell of her caused his erection to harden painfully. Dillon grabbed his hair in a vice-like grip. He took both her hands and held them at her side as he continued to torture her with his tongue. He brought her almost to climax before he stopped, only to start again.

Dillon tried to get her hands away from his grip. She had to touch him. She pleaded for more and begged for mercy. She couldn't take the incredible torture any longer and pulled him towards her. "Now. Damien, I need you inside me now."

Damien shed his boxers and positioned himself between her legs. The amber color of her eyes darkened with desire, lust, and something much more. He entered her. Velvet heat sheathed him. Her muscles tightened around him pulling him in deeper. Dillon wrapped her legs around his waist opening herself to him. She met him thrust for thrust, their bodies slick and sliding together. She called his name and mumbled something he couldn't understand.

Dillon's body trembled as her climax began. With each thrust from Damien, he felt her muscles tighten. The orgasm ripped through her. Damien muttered in Italian.

Her walls tightened around him. He had never felt something so luscious. Damien cried out her name as the rush of hot moisture surrounded him. He never wanted her to be in this position with another man. He never wanted to share her with anyone. "*Il mio,*" Damien whispered. "*Solo mio.* Only mine." Her nails dug into his back as a second orgasm took over, and Dillon's body shuddered underneath him.

His hips thrust faster and faster. His own climax erupted with a violent force, and he emptied everything into her. No longer able to support his own weight he lowered himself onto her, his head resting on the nape of her neck. "My God, I can't move." He remained inside her.

A howling wind roared in Dillon's ears. She didn't know if her hearing would ever return to normal. Her heart pounded against her chest. Damien still rested his head against her neck. "That's okay, I can't feel my limbs. Are they still attached to my body?"

A soft laugh escaped Damien's mouth. He pushed himself up on one arm and rolled off her. "I think so. I can't get my eyes to focus yet. Give me a minute, and as soon as I can see, I'll check." He stayed on his back for a few minutes. Turning on his side, he pulled her towards him.

Dillon snuggled up against him and let out a little hum relaxing in his arms. A few minutes later, she fell asleep. He listened to her breathing as it slowed and evened out. Damien wasn't sure about his job whether he would stay or not. But he knew without a doubt he wanted Dillon in his life. He may have to decide at some point how far he would go to accomplish that, but he felt damn sure he would do whatever it took.

CHAPTER FORTY

Amy woke up. She moved her head and flinched as a severe pain radiated from her jaw. Lifting her head, she moved her hand to touch her face. She felt resistance. A strap bound her hands and legs to the bed. She still had her clothes on. She fell back on the mattress and blinked away tears.

Her body shivered. Glancing around, she figured she had been left in a cellar, which explained the bone-chilling dampness surrounding her. A small bulb hung near the stairs, casting eerie shadows across the room. Once her eyes adjusted to the light, she took in her surroundings. The room seemed long but not skinny. She could just make out what she assumed to be tools at the far end. They hung on the wall, but she couldn't quite tell what kind they were. Something else hung from the ceiling at that same end of the room, but she couldn't see it clearly. She blinked her eyes and squinted, but the bulb just didn't offer enough light to make it out.

A sour smell assaulted her and caused her to breathe through her mouth so she wouldn't vomit. The air had a putrid odor of rotten meat and a thick metallic taste coated the back of her throat. Amy's pulse raced. "OH MY GOD," she whispered.

She had become all too familiar with that metallic taste, from hanging out on her grandparent's farm. Blood. Whenever they killed a pig or a goat, the same metallic taste would coat her throat.

Amy jumped at the sound of a screen door slamming shut. Footsteps moved above and became louder as they got closer to her. A door at the top of the basement stairs opened. Heavy boots stomped their way down. She prepared herself to see a monster, but the man that came down the stairs resembled an ordinary, even handsome man.

He carried a black bag as he moved towards her. Amy watched him drop the bag on the floor near the head of the bed. He reached out and pushed a lock of hair out of her face. She cringed at his touch. He bent down and pulled a large pair of shears from the bag.

She yanked against her restraints. "Let me go, you can't do this, you fucking monster, let me go!"

His eyes widened as he stepped back. Most girls whimpered and pleaded. He pulled the straps a little tighter. He didn't want her to impale herself on the scissors. "Oh, Beth, this will be so much fun."

Amy's eyes narrowed as her eyebrows squished together. "Beth? Who the hell is Beth? My name is Amy."

He ignored her as he methodically cut all her clothing off. Naked on the bed, Amy's pulse raced. The sound of her heartbeat thrashed in her ears. "Please, please stop. Don't do this." Amy's pleading turned into sobs.

His eyes darkened and constricted into beady little marbles as he continued to leer at her. He rubbed his groin and Amy could see the bulge through his jeans. He reached down and traced her stomach with the tip of his calloused finger, advancing it towards her entrance.

"Beth," he whispered.

She squeezed her eyes shut and pleaded with him. "I'm not Beth. I'm Amy. Please stop. My name is Amy."

He sneered at her as he continued to trace her stomach and breasts with his finger. Her lips and chin trembled. Amy's eyes widened, and her breathing became raspy as she watched him unbutton his jeans. "Oh, dear God, please help me. Please help me," she whispered her mantra.

He moved towards her feet and messed with the straps around her ankles when his phone rang.

He glowered at her. "Well, fuck." He yanked it out of his pocket. He stepped closer to her and put his hand over her mouth. "Yeah? What the fuck, I thought those had been sealed up. All right. Fucking shit...Meet me out there. I'm on my way."

He removed his hand from her, and she breathed in a few deep breaths then held it as he moved towards the foot of the bed. Her eyes darted between him and the straps that held her secure. He reached over, loosened the straps a little, and threw an old blanket on her. He started up the stairs. Before he disappeared, he turned and smiled at her.

Amy's lungs burned from the breath she held. He had been moments away from raping her. Amy's whole body trembled. Her breath exploded in and out of her chest. Her eyes filled with tears. Amy struggled against the straps. She didn't want to die like this. She didn't want him to rape her. She wanted to go home.

Amy pleaded and begged to an empty room. "Please God, help me. Just let me live through this, oh please God, please."

CHAPTER FORTY-ONE

Joe glanced at the clock on the nightstand, four thirty. "Crap I'm never going back to sleep," he whispered to himself. Taylor stirred next to him. He stared at her for a few moments. Her hair fell around her face. Her full lips were parted as she slept half on her back, half on her side facing him. He loved watching her sleep. A few times the last couple of nights he had woken up unable to get back to sleep and just laid there watching her.

Joe leaned over and kissed her on the cheek. "I'm going down to the gym for some exercise. I'll be back in time to wake you for a shower and breakfast."

"Mmm, okay," she moaned and rolled over and went back to sleep.

He had to clear his head. The gym was the one place he could get away for some time alone. He headed downstairs and entered an empty room. His legs fought the first mile of the run, protesting every step. By the third mile, his legs had their rhythm. His thoughts drifted to Taylor. Never had Joe gotten involved with someone associated with a case. In all fairness and a good rationalization, he didn't know Taylor had any association with the case until after he had been intimate with her. Hell, she didn't even know she was involved in the case.

Joe had broken his own first rule. Never get involved with someone in the business. He doesn't like to mix his work and his sex life together. It makes for a messy work environment.

To make matters worse, their conversation last night had revealed all about Taylor's family. She had a falling out with her parents, and their relationship had become strained. Although she spoke with them, they just weren't that close any longer.

Knowing all this personal stuff about her complicated things. It made it hard for Joe to separate out his feelings. Joe shook his head as he thought about what he was doing. In all his other relationships, he never wanted the details of their lives. He just wanted light and uncomplicated. Details complicated things.

"Joe, what the hell are you doing?" He asked himself as he hit mile five of his run. "You know you don't want a relationship." He felt something for Taylor he hadn't felt for another woman. At least not since college. Ever since that summer before his senior year, when Lisa died, he just couldn't allow himself to get that attached to a woman. He just wasn't ready for that level of commitment. Joe didn't know if he ever would be again. Only one person outside his family knows about what happened. He's never shared the story with Damien and he sure as hell wouldn't do it now. He pounded out the last few miles to Metallica.

Taylor's strong independent personality set her apart from most women. Hell, most women who found out they were being tracked by a serial killer would freak out, cry constantly, or cling to you. Not Taylor. After the initial shock, she insisted on doing her job. Director Jones wanted her to think about going to a safe house, she flat out said no. She had a life and a cat, and she would not quit living because of a deranged killer. Plus, she told him she had a gun and knew how to use it.

Joe wondered how much of this was just a distraction from the case, or if he cared for Taylor. What if it was just the sex? He feared for her safety, so maybe he just wanted to be her hero, her knight in shining armor. Isn't that every man's dream fantasy—to rescue the girl from danger and be the hero? All that happily ever after crap.

By mile eight he slowed his pace. The clock on the wall read five forty-five. He slowed his run to a jog. Joe knew he would have to decide how far he wanted to take this relationship. He'd already let it get farther than he should've. Whatever they had going on between them, could never be just a fling.

CHAPTER FORTY-TWO

Forensic Lab

Damien sat and studied the board. "Matt, have you found anything on the video from the mall?"

Matt frowned at Damien. "Yes and no. The girls gave me a timeline as best they can remember. I spotted them a few times on the cameras. But every time I get Becca in the frame you can see a guy from the back, and he maneuvers her to either block him, or he pulls her just out of the camera's view."

Damien frowned. "So, you can see him, but only from the back?"

Matt winced. "Not really. In every single frame that I found Becca, you see part of him. I can't see what he is wearing, except for a piece of a dark jacket. He has a hat on, but you only see part of it from the side, and you can't see any of his face. I watched it several times, and I'd swear he knew where all the cameras were. He purposely maneuvers away from them. It's the damnedest thing I've ever seen."

"Well shit. I really hate this fucker," Joe said.

Damien sighed. "Matt, can you start pulling all the auto registrations on the list of people for the Fall Festival?"

Taylor reached across the table. "Matt, I'll take the bottom half of the list. We will get through them faster."

"Thanks, Taylor. I appreciate it," he responded.

Damien moved to the board. "Matt, start with the Waverly farm first. See if any of their registered vehicles match the one seen at Amy's abduction." On the map, he placed a red pin on the Waverly farmland. "I know this farm is involved. I have no evidence, but Freestone has some connection to these abductions."

Damien sat back down at the table. "Joe, what do we have in the Waverly file? Anything of interest?"

Joe pulled the file on the Freestone farm. "No. He's listed as the owner. Except, okay—there is one thing. Matt pulled the records on his ownership, and it seems to start with the date he incorporated the cheese and dairy farm. Yesterday in the office, that old guy said he had been around since Jason's father had owned it. But there aren't any records prior to Jason taking control of the farm. I'll dig more into it." He worked on another laptop.

Damien leaned back and closed his eyes. He thought about where Tiffany had been dumped and what Dillon had said about the killer knowing that property. "Hey, Matt can you pull up the school records on Jason Freestone? See what high school he went to."

Matt glanced up from his computer. "Sure. Give me a few minutes to find what they have online."

"Thanks," Damien said. He watched Dillon as she studied the picture of Beth. She seemed oblivious to anyone else in the room. "Dillon, what are you thinking?"

Dillon leaned on the edge of the table. She didn't answer him for a few minutes. She stood up and paced back and forth.

Damien whistled. "Dillon, hello?"

She frowned as she turned towards him. "Why did he pick Beth? She doesn't fit. There had to be something special about her. He chose her specifically. She wasn't a random choice. This abduction had happened before he decided to take young girls." She muttered to herself as she studied the board.

By now all movement in the room had stopped. No one said a word. Everyone in the room watched as Dillon paced and talked to herself. She moved in front of the board. "He picked her. He didn't choose her on a whim. She had special meaning to him."

Dillon rearranged all the pictures of the girls. "These girls, he picked them because he wanted young and innocent. Or what he perceived them to be. I believe he chose these girls because he wanted to relive a time in his life. What they represent is tied to Beth." She pointed to Beth. "She was different—older. The killer and Beth had to be close to the same age at the time of Beth's disappearance. We've established the killer's age within a certain range, due to his appeal to young girls."

She stood at the end of the table. Dillon rubbed her temples as she paced. "The girls all resembled Beth. She had to be special. How do you become special to someone? You have to see them... you have to see them...." Dillon paused and stood still for a few moments. She spun around and faced everyone at the table. "Oh shit, shit, shit. I can't believe it took me so long. I focused so much on the little things I didn't see it. He knew her. Holy shit. The son of a bitch took Beth because he had been personally acquainted with her. He saw her every day. You covet what you see."

Damien hissed. "He had to know her from school. If the assumption is they were the same age, or close to it, they had to go to school together. Matt, get all the school information on Freestone and Haut. Focus on one grade above and a grade below Beth, and see if they went to the same school and if they did, if they were in the same class. We will start with Freestone if he has no connection to Beth we can move on."

Matt's fingers flew across the keyboard. "Okay, the school doesn't have a lot of information online. It looks like they don't have any way to search for former students. Hang on I have an idea."

Dillon reached for Damien's open can of diet soda and took a drink. She winked at him. The slight gleam in his eyes reminded her of their night together. She had no idea what he wanted from this relationship. Dillon hoped she'd be able to see him after this case. She needed to see him. "One of us could go out and interview Beth's parents. Ask them some questions about Jason," Dillon said.

Damien raised an eyebrow at her and took back his soda. "Yeah, that's the next stop."

"Okay, here we go," Matt said. "Waverly and Pawnee both feed into the same school district. They both would have attended the same high school."

Damien made a note on the board. "It isn't much of a stretch to think he and Beth had some kind of history together. What that entails, we can't be sure. Now we have to prove the link. Dillon, you should go out and speak with the Hauts."

Joe noticed Dillon stood still and quiet. "Dillon, what's the matter?"

Damien noticed Dillon's color had paled just a little. "Dillon, what's wrong?"

"If I had seen the connection earlier. If I had paid more attention to what my brain had been trying to tell me all this time, we could have stopped him before he took Amy. I can't..."

Damien walked over to her and placed his hands on her shoulders. Her eyes were moist from tears that floated near the surface. "Listen, don't even go down that road. If you'd recognized the connection earlier, we still might not have figured out Jason had been involved until now. This is not your fault. You didn't cause this asshole to abduct Amy. We had to wait for things to fall into place.

"You can't beat yourself up over this. I won't let you. Everything you came up with so far in the profile has been right on the money. You are one hell of a profiler." He pulled her into his chest. He leaned down placing his mouth right next to her ear. "If I have to smack that beautiful ass of yours all over this building, I will. Do I make myself clear?"

She gazed up at him, with a thin smile on her face. "Yeah, thanks. I think I needed to hear that."

Damien sat back down at the computer. "Damn skippy on that."

The room buzzed with activity. They all worked on laptops or phones, trying to gather information about Jason Freestone and his cheese farm. That all stopped when Damien's phone rang. "Lieutenant Kaine... Yes, I remember you, Mr. Watkins. How are the girls doing? Well, it will get easier as more time goes by... It will take a lot more to get better... Oh okay, yes hang on."

Damien reached for a pen and paper then continued. "Yes, I remember the girls said they had an idea that he seemed familiar but they couldn't place him," he paused, "hmm no, okay, yeah go on. Are you sure? Okay, the commercial aired last night. No, I can find that... No, I understand. This is great... Yes. If we need to get in touch will you be around? I got it. Thank you so much, tell the girls this will help us. I'm sure it will help them too. Thank you." Damien hung up, and everyone in the room stared at him.

Joe leaned back in his chair. "What the hell was that about?"

"Jamie Watkins father said Jamie and Melissa had been hanging out last night and watched a commercial for the farm in Waverly. The girls are positive the man in the commercial is the same man that they saw Becca talking to at the mall."

Damien pulled up the browser one of the computers. He searched for ads for the Freestone farm. "They don't know his name; they just recognized him from the TV commercial. Someone pull up a picture of Jason Freestone." Damien found the commercial in question and froze the screen on the only man in the commercial.

Joe handed his phone to Damien. "I got the latest picture of Jason Freestone."

Damien's eyes bulged. He did a double take between the image on the phone and the computer. "Mary Mother of God, it's him. Sweet Jesus, it's Jason Freestone."

Taylor peered over Damien's shoulder at the phone that held Freestone's picture. She squinted at it. She closed her eyes and remembered where she had seen his face. Taylor had been walking to her car at the mall and noticed the truck had made several circles around the parking lot. She reached out and took the phone from him. She zoomed in on his picture.

Joe watched her, "Taylor? What is it?"

When she looked back up her eyes were filled with tears. "I'm sure this is the guy I saw in the parking lot of the mall. He drove around in a gray truck, older model. I can't believe he got so close to me. He could've taken me."

Joe took her in his arms. "Hey, it's okay. We know who he is, now we will get him. Stay here with Matt. We'll be back." He kissed her softly on the lips, oblivious to anyone else in the room.

Dillon, Joe, and Damien put on their jackets and headed towards the door.

"Fucking *mutts nutts*," Joe said as he winked at Taylor.

Damien touched Matt on the shoulder. "Matt, can you connect Freestone to Haut? That may be what gets us our warrant to get on the property. Right now, all we have puts Jason at the mall talking to Becca, but that alone won't get us a search warrant. Get us everything you can about the farm. Parents, grandparents, cousins, fucking cats and dogs, I don't care just get everything."

Damien, Joe, and Dillon ran down the hall. They barely had the doors to the SUV closed when Damien peeled out of the lot. He flipped a switch under the dash that activated sirens and lights on the mirrors and the rear window.

Fifteen minutes later Joe's phone beeped. "Matt sent us a file. He compiled some of what I found with some new stuff. Jason Freestone took ownership of the farm about eight years ago. At seventeen, his mother died. He worked with his father and then took over the farm when his Dad died. His Dad had an accident in the field one afternoon and died from his injuries. Ouch, the accident involved a combine. Man, that had to hurt." Joe cringed. "That guy from Jason's farm yesterday said the father died unexpectedly. I wonder if Jason had anything to do with that accident."

"Tell me Jason's age?" asked Dillon.

"Twenty-eight. Right in the range you profiled. His Dad passed away three years after his mother, making Jason twenty when he gained control of the farm. The exact age as Beth when she disappeared. Right again Special Agent." Joe closed his eyes for a moment. "What the hell could this girl have done to him that would cause him to kill her?"

Dillon smirked at him. "That's easy. She rejected him."

Joe rubbed his chin. "Why would that cause him to react that way?"

Dillon folded her hands in her lap. "Again, that's easy. First, I bet when we speak with Beth's parents, they'll tell us Beth and Jason had some kind of scuffle. It doesn't matter what caused it, or how it ended. He perceived it to be a slap in the face. By her rejecting him, she embarrassed him. Remember, women are for his pleasure and satisfaction, they don't have the right to reject him."

Joe turned back to his phone to read the file Matt had sent him. "This guy has some serious issues. Anyway, let me finish going over this information for us. Not too long after his Dad died, he transformed the farm and made it a specialty dairy farm. The change saved the farm. It would have been bankrupt within the year if he hadn't made some drastic changes. Follows what that rancher said yesterday. None of the trucks registered to the Freestone farm match the vehicle seen at Amy's abduction. None of the other registrants for the Fall Festival match up either."

Damien flipped off the siren and lights off just before pulling into the farm. "So," Damien said as he cut the engine. "I think we should hit him with an informal interview approach. We need some more information for our records. That kind of thing. Let's not give anything we know away. Let's see what we can get him to tell us. I don't think we should let him know we have a witness that places him near Becca. That may put Amy in jeopardy." Joe and Dillon nodded. "Dillon, you take the lead. Having it seem as if the FBI has taken over the investigation may make him sweat. Not to mention you're a girl. That should piss him off and get him off his game." Damien's lip twitched with amusement.

Dillon folded her arms across her chest. "Wait a second, wait for just a second," she said. "*Seem* like the FBI has taken over the investigation? Baby, I *have* taken over the investigation. The FBI usually has to take over just to ensure the job gets done correctly."

Joe chuckled and smacked Damien across the chest. "Oh man, you are so screwed. She will eat your *clackers* for lunch."

CHAPTER FORTY-THREE

An older woman sat behind a desk. "Well, hi there. Can I help you all with something?"

Dillon moved to stand in front of her. "Yes, I'm FBI Special Agent McGrath; this is Lieutenant Kaine and Detective Hagan from Chicago. Would Jason Freestone be around?"

The woman at the desk raised her eyebrow at them. "Sure, let me call him." She reached over and grabbed a small handheld from its cradle. "Jason, there are some Detectives and an FBI Agent here waiting to speak with you."

"Okay Mary, tell them I will be there shortly. I'm out in the field." Jason responded.

Mary smiled at them. "We had a few cows get out last night, and they have been shoring up the fence where it happened. He'll be right with you."

Dillon watched Mary for a few minutes. "Mary? How long have you worked for Jason?"

"Oh my, I worked for his Dad for about three years before Jason took over. I had come on board after his mother passed. After his Dad's accident, I couldn't see bailing on him. He'd been trying to get the farm rearranged, and he needed all the help he could get."

Dillon waited. She gave a quick glance to the guys to keep quiet. A few moments later Mary continued her story.

"Jason had wanted to modify the production line before his Dad died, but Jason's Dad had been a traditional farmer. He didn't want any part of the new ideas. Today teenagers would call him 'old school.' Jason's ideas ended up being the best thing for this farm. Now we are the premier cheesemaker in the state." A smile beamed on her face. A moment later, Jason walked through the door.

Dillon had seen his picture, so she didn't expect a rugged farmer aged from seasons in the sun. However, she didn't expect the man that stood before her. Damn good looking, lean muscles and smooth buttery tanned skin from years spent working outdoors. He wasn't tall, barely six foot, but lanky, so he seemed taller.

Jason stuck out his hand and introduced himself. When he took Dillon's hand, his eye color changed from gray-blue to a steel gray.

The hair on the back of her neck stood up. "Thanks for taking the time to speak with us. We have a few questions to clear up. Can we step outside?"

Jason pushed open the door and held it for them. "Sure."

As Dillon and Damien followed him out, Dillon glanced over her shoulder and noted that Joe stayed behind. "Mr. Freestone, can you tell us if you had any reason to be at the Decatur Mall last Saturday?"

He leaned against the wall of the building. "Sure I did. I delivered an order of cheese to a boutique shop there, The Barn. I make regular Saturday deliveries to them. It's small enough, so I don't have to take the huge refrigerated truck. Our smaller one does the job."

"Can you tell me what trucks you have here?" Asked Dillon.

"Let's see, we have two large capacity delivery trucks and three smaller ones. I have one dual-cab Ford truck and one Ford F150. Why?" Jason asked her.

She ignored his question. "Can you tell me what color the Ford trucks are?"

He eyeballed Dillon. "Sure, they're both red."

Dillon noticed the twitch in his upper lip. She asked about the Fall Festival and Jacksonville.

A sneer crossed his face. He gave Dillon a dismissive nod and addressed Damien when he answered the question. "Let's see, I started doing the Fall Festival a short time after I modified the production line of the farm. I figured I had nothing to lose and it might turn out to be an excellent way to get the word out about my cheese. It ended up being the best business decision I've ever made."

"When did you last go to Jacksonville?" Dillon asked

He again focused on Damien. "I think about two days ago. Could've been three. I wanted to get my spot early. I hoped to get a better one than last year."

Damien glimpsed Joe coming out of the office and heading towards them. "You were pretty young when your father died. I imagine that caused a lot of difficulty in taking over an operation like this."

"My Dad had just died, and I had to figure out a way to guide this farm back from the brink of ruin. Yeah, difficult just barely scratches the surface of how hard that time had been," Jason said.

"Are you familiar with the Powell land, on the other side of the state highway?" asked Dillon.

Jason shifted his weight from one foot to the other. "Sure. Old man Powell used to let us go swimming in his pond back in the day. That stopped a long time ago. We had a bad storm come through and tear down a bunch of trees. Most fell into the pond. Made it too dangerous to swim. Man, that had to be ten maybe eleven years ago." Jason rubbed the back of his neck.

"What time does the Fall Festival start on Sunday?" Dillon asked him.

He removed his hat and ran his fingers through his hair. "Early. We have to be there by seven to set up. It will wrap up on Sunday around seven p.m., and then it goes all week with various activities. It's a great festival."

Dillon studied Jason. The sheer beauty of his face drew you in, but something about the way he stared through her had her subconsciously touching her weapon. She had the distinct impression she would be nothing but prey to him. "Tell me about your farm. Where does the farmhouse sit on the property? You can't see it from the entrance at all."

He pointed to an old dirt road just off the back of the parking area. "That road takes you up to my farmhouse. All my ranch hands live in the surrounding area."

Dillon glanced around the property. "Did you live there with your parents?"

"Yes. I've been renovating it. You know updating it, so it still has the old charm of a farmhouse, but modern amenities." He smiled.

Dillon noticed that as Jason spoke, he stared past her shoulder. Instinctively she spun around and gazed at the same area. Nothing but pasture and cows. *What do you see Jason?* She thought as she smiled at him. "Just a couple more questions. A few evenings ago, did you eat at Toni's Café up on Route 104?"

His eyes narrowed; he angled his body away from her. "Yes. I finished up a delivery and stopped for dinner. I think I had the steak. I've eaten there regularly over the last few years."

She nodded at him. "By chance did you see anyone harassing a young girl? Maybe forcing her into a delivery truck or large vehicle?"

He rubbed his chin. "No, not at all. It seemed to be a quiet night. I don't remember it being very busy."

"Mr. Freestone, do you know anyone by the name of Beth Haut?" Dillon asked him. For a nanosecond, his eyes told her he recognized the name. He recovered fast.

A slight frown pulled his eyebrows together; Jason shook his head. "No. That name doesn't sound familiar."

Dillon studied him. He had lied on almost every question. He volunteered extra information that no one asked for. She smiled at him. "Well Mr. Freestone, we may have some other questions for you. I hope you'll be around." She didn't offer her hand.

"Sure, I'll be here all day. Then off and on during the week, with the festival and all. Mary will know how to reach me."

She nodded at him as she headed for the vehicle. "Thanks for your time." Dillon followed Joe and Damien as they all headed towards the SUV. She glanced over her shoulder to find Jason watching her. Their gazes met. A cold chill ran down her spine when he smiled at her.

Damien beamed with satisfaction. "I think those last two questions frazzled him a little. Jason flat out lied when he answered he didn't know Beth and he lied about Toni's."

Dillon stared at Damien in the rearview. She remembered that devilish tongue and mouth and what it did to her body. She had to close her eyes to regain her focus. "He exhibited classic signs of deception. Moreover, he seemed annoyed that he had to answer questions from me. Did you notice he directed several of his responses towards you?"

"Oh yeah, he did not like having to answer to you." Damien turned to Joe. "I guess Mary had lots to say?"

Joe smiled at him and Dillon. "That, my friend, is an understatement."

CHAPTER FORTY-FOUR

Forensic Lab

The delicious aroma of food greeted them as they entered the conference room. Joe leaned down and gave Taylor a kiss on the cheek. He then grabbed a plate and loaded it up with different slices of pizza, pasta, and salad. "I'm so hungry."

Matt took a bite of pasta. "Taylor and I have been trying to gather as much information as possible on the Freestones and their farm."

Damien sat with a plate loaded with food. "Alright, by his own admission, Jason had been at the mall on Saturday when Becca Martin went missing. Her friends swear Becca talked to him. He also admitted to being at Toni's Café the same night Tiffany went missing. Joe, what information did you get from Mary?"

"Well, Mary likes to talk. I asked her about Jason's parents. Seemed his Mom got sick and died from her illness. The illness went on for quite some time, but she never got a diagnosis as to what made her sick. The mother didn't like to go to doctors."

Joe paused for a minute. "A short time later, Jason graduated from high school and began helping his Dad around the farm. But it wasn't the loving father and son bond you would think would happen after the loss of a mother." He took a sip of his soda. "It seems as though the son really wanted to make changes to the farm."

"Mary said she heard them argue about the amount of money they were losing to other dairy farms in the area. Jason's Dad became more and more frustrated with Jason's nagging about changing the farm into a cheese production farm. He let Jason make minor modifications, which appeared to keep Jason quiet for a while.

"Oh, I asked about the Piggly Wiggly delivery. She pulled it up on the computer. Get this—so we know from the list from David that it showed a record of the delivery, but not who or time. I didn't mention we got a delivery list from David. I wanted to see if the report David printed out would match what she said. Mary explained every delivery driver filled out the log with the date, driver's initials, and time of delivery.

"She said that Jason kept impeccable records and he didn't like it when the drivers skipped over procedure. Since this delivery happened six months ago, they wouldn't know who did the delivery for sure. She did say it seemed unusual not to have a record of who made the delivery. If nothing else, the driver should have initialed the log. As she read through the delivery records for the month afterward, she noticed there were a few other deliveries that weren't initialed.

"She seemed puzzled by that. She stated that normally the workers would have had an earful from Jason about keeping sloppy records. So far as she remembers, Jason hasn't complained about the deliveries. I think Jason made the later deliveries and conveniently forgot to fill in the log. That way the one on the night Franks went missing wouldn't stand out so much." Joe reached for his drink. "I got the feeling she had more to tell me, but the phone rang, and she had to deal with a customer. I told her I might need to call her later and get some more information from her."

Dillon's gaze shifted from Joe to Damien. "Going back to the father and son relationship, it seems as though they weren't close at all. You would expect them to lean on each other after the death of the mother, not the opposite. I have to question what would make a father push his only child away. There is usually a deep bond between father and son."

Joe shrugged. "I got the impression from Mary that something had happened between the two, but either she didn't know all the details or she didn't want to tell me."

Damien nodded towards Joe. "Call Mary up, see if you can get any more background, also ask about any conflicts with girls, or if he got into any trouble in high school. We need to have something more than just going to the same school as Beth. Since Mary had been with the business before Jason got out of high school, she may know something more. The fact that Jason went to high school with Beth doesn't mean he killed her years later. We need a little more to get a warrant. Matt, what other information have you gotten so far?" Damien took another bite of pizza.

Matt set his slice of pepperoni pie down and pulled out a sheet of paper. "From the records I could find, the mother's illness matches up to what Mary said. The local doctor, your average small-town general practitioner, assumed she had complications due to pneumonia. Nobody had reason to question it. Small town older woman gets a cold/flu then gets sicker. That's even what the death certificate says, natural causes due to illness. Their local paper did a small story on her death. The wife happened to be from this area."

Damien tapped his fingers on the table. "These symptoms lead me to think this could have been ethylene glycol poisoning. You can poison at such a slow rate that unless you test for it or the signs are overtly present, you wouldn't see it. I could see an old-time doctor thinking it had been due to natural causes. Her death didn't raise any red flags nor did it have any unusual circumstances associated with it—so no investigation had been needed." Damien said. "Matt, have you found anything regarding a burial?"

Matt scanned through his notes. "I don't see anything listed for burial services. I haven't been able to find any records concerning a funeral home on record either."

Dillon glanced around the table. "That means we can't find the body to do any testing on. Which leads me to think he had her cremated. Not that we have the warrant to get on that farm and search. That's just it. We don't have any tangible evidence to get on that farm. He had a plausible reason for being at the mall, the diner, and the Piggly Wiggly."

Damien took a gulp of his soda. "Joe when you talk to Mary, see if she knows anything about the mother and the father's funeral. I'm going to go call that store, The Barn and make sure Jason did a delivery last Saturday. If someone from the store can give us a description of what Jason wore that day, we might be able to show a connection to the man on the tape we see with Becca. Be right back." He took his phone and his notes and stepped out of the room.

Taking a bite of pizza, Joe picked up his phone. "I'm going to call Mary again."

***

Dillon continued to eat and make notes as Taylor and Matt worked. "Matt, there has to be some other information. What about the farm itself? What do you have on that?"

Matt responded as Joe and Damien both came back into the room at the same time. They stared at each other.

Joe bowed towards Damien. "Go first, Lieutenant."

Damien frowned at him. "Yes, Jason had been at the mall on that Saturday. He does a regular delivery every Saturday. The girl said that he sometimes walks around the mall. Occasionally, she would see him when she took her break. She explained how the deliveries work at the mall. The delivery drivers park their vehicles at the back and enter through a separate entrance. That entrance is unseen by people in the mall. They come in, go through hallways, and then go out into the central area of the mall to make their deliveries.

"The girl from The Barn didn't notice when he left." Damien paused for a drink, "most deliveries happen during the week, so on the weekends that hallway area is pretty deserted. You could be in the hall for hours and not see anyone. The clerk couldn't remember what he wore either. Matt, check those security tapes. Pay close attention to the delivery entrances and video of everyone going in and out of that area. Let's see if we can see Jason going in or out. If we're lucky, maybe we see Becca at some point leaving the mall." Damien sat back in his chair. "I also called Piggly Wiggly. The manager is searching for his delivery receipt for the day Jesse Franks disappeared. He said he was having a hard time finding records for the day in question. He will call me as soon as he finds it."

Dillon glanced at everyone in the room. "So, if he did take Becca, Jason got her to leave with him voluntarily or got her to go to the hallway, then took her by force. Perfect getaway since it's deserted on weekends. I'd be willing to bet he has hunted at the mall before."

Joe spoke up. "I have some information from Mary that will make him even more of a prime suspect. Mary said after the mother died, the father didn't have a funeral. She doesn't know about the exact arrangements, but she said the father never had a public ceremony. After her death, the Dad became more and more distant. You could find him doing the fieldwork while Jason would work on anything else. The father never wanted to be alone with the kid. Ever.

"Two years before the Dad's accident, he began to get sick. The symptoms were similar to the mother's, but the father wasn't sick all the time. The illness came and went. The Dad spent a lot of his time out in the barn—which happens to be where the combine accident took place."

Joe gulped down half of his soda while he held his finger in the air. "Now according to Mary, sometime in high school, Jason had some kind of incident with a young girl. She said she wasn't sure what happened, but nothing came of it. Mary said she remembered it taking place at a summer party. She told me she would call me back; Mary thinks she knows where it happened. She didn't know the girl's name, but I'm betting it has to be Beth."

As soon as Joe finished Matt jumped in. "Even though the farm is considered small for a farm, they've always made a profit. There's nothing in the financial records to indicate foul play. Without a warrant, I can't dive too far into them.

"When the father died and Jason inherited the property, it wasn't much. Of course, that included all the land. The odd thing, we know the farm has been in Jason's family for a while, but I can't find any record of this farm before Jason's Dad. There isn't anything listed under the father's family. The financials are under the father, but that's it. The records aren't adding up. I'm still trying to track back the records, but they aren't all online. Makes it slow going trying to locate all the information."

Damien spoke up. "The missing girls disappeared starting the year the Dad died. He had to have somewhere on the property that Jason could bring the girls. If not on the property, a cabin or another building somewhere. Matt, did you find any other assets listed under Jason's Dad or under Jason's name?"

Matt leaned back in his chair. "No, I can't find any other assets listed. That's just it—I'm not finding anything but the farm and the farmhouse that Jason listed under his name. Everything that he inherited. When Jason incorporated the new cheese farm, he moved everything to his name. But there is nothing on record before that except in the father's financials."

Damien frowned. "What about under the mother's maiden name? Have you checked under that?"

Matt flipped through his notepad. "Yeah, as a matter-of-fact—I figured that might be a line to tug. However, I couldn't find anything under the mother's maiden name. I'm sure it has to do with the records not being online. Come Monday, if we have no answers, I can get them from the records department at City Hall.

"On the open market, the value of the farm would be more than several million dollars, not including its yearly profit. Jason brought the farm into the black with all the changes he accomplished. It seems Jason has quite the knack for cheese making and he has proven himself a very savvy businessman," Matt paused. "His Dad didn't have much in the way of life insurance either. A one hundred and fifty-thousand-dollar policy, which alone doesn't seem like a huge motive."

Damien ran his fingers through his hair. "Sure, by itself it isn't a huge motive. But I think it goes to the bigger picture. I think he wanted control of the entire farm. In short order after his Dad's death, Jason reinvented the farm." He leaned on the table with his elbows. "The disturbing part of this is how patient this asshole is. Starting around sixteen or seventeen, Jason began poisoning his Mom. Enough that it would kill her, but not arouse any suspicion. Then a couple years later he makes his Dad sick. Slower than the process he used on his mother. He didn't want to alert the authorities, or they may backtrack on the mother's death. He plans the murder to look like an accident and gains possession of the farm. Then he waits two years before he starts abducting and killing girls."

Matt sat hunched over a computer, muttering to himself before addressing the group. "Hey, I'm examining this security footage of the delivery area. The camera picks up a guy going in, but he keeps himself angled from the camera. I can't get a picture of anything but the back of him. I have yet to find anything with Becca coming out this entrance. There has to be another way out that isn't monitored."

Joe's phone rang. The room fell silent. "Hagan... Yes, Mary, thanks for calling me back. No, I promise he won't know you gave me the information... Oh, Mary thank you so much... Yes, and you can call me if you need anything, anything at all. Thank you." He jumped up. "We got him. She didn't know the name of the girl, but she lived in Pawnee County. And get this, it happened at Powell's pond."

Dillon pulled her phone from her pocket. "Alright, we have him on record lying that he didn't know Beth. He could say he didn't remember her, but it does go to the overall picture. I'm going to reach out to the Hauts, see if I can speak with them," Dillon said as she tapped out a text to her Deputy Director and left the room.

Damien stared at the board of pictures. "There's no way we can get a warrant with what we have."

Dillon walked back into the room. "The Hauts are expecting me. I told them I would be there within the hour." Her phone beeped, "my Director said if we could get something tangible on Jason's relationship with Beth, he could get us a warrant."

Damien gathered his jacket. "Hey, how about we split up? Dillon, you go to the Haut's place, and Joe and I will go to the Sheriff over in Waverly. Hopefully, he will have something on the property chain, Amy can't wait until Monday."

CHAPTER FORTY-FIVE

Waverly Sheriff's Department

Joe called the Sheriff in Waverly on the way out of the lab parking lot. "It's a go for Sheriff Winsley. He said he'll pull all the information he has about the farm and the family."

Twenty–five minutes later Damien pulled up outside the Sheriff's office.

Joe raised his eyebrows as he turned towards Damien. "Oh hey, I meant to ask where you slept last night?" Joe had a glint of amusement in his eyes.

Damien gave Joe a shit-eating grin. "I stayed in Dillon's room last night."

Joe snickered. "Hmm, did you now?" Joe studied Damien. The revelation that his friend spent the night in the Agent's room explained a lot. All morning he noticed that even though Damien and Dillon kept their distance from each other, they struggled at it. Joe's smile broadened. "I knew that something seemed different about you today. You haven't had sex for so long it had to have been like getting your cherry popped again, huh? I want details. I deserve details after having to spend the last nine months with your sourpuss arse."

"Well, you're a pig. I wouldn't expect anything less."

Joe oinked as they walked through the door of the Sheriff's office. No one sat at the front desk. "Hello, anyone home?" Boomed Joe.

An older man in his late fifties came out of an office down the hall. "Hey come on down this way. You two must be Lieutenant Kaine and Detective Hagan?" He gestured towards two oversized chairs in his office. "Have a seat. I'm Sheriff Winsley. You're interested in Jason Freestone. This about the missing and dead girls, isn't it?" He asked as he opened a file on his desk.

"Yes sir," Damien responded. "We don't have any evidence linking him directly to the girls, but there are a few coincidences that have moved him to the top of the list. We need to see if we can get anything that will tie him to Amy, the latest girl that has been abducted or quite possibly one from eight years ago."

Joe waited as the Sheriff read over the file. "Can you tell us anything about the death of his mother and father?"

"Well, the mother had been sick off and on and the local doctor, he isn't alive anymore, diagnosed her as having had pneumonia. When she died, we didn't have any need to request an autopsy. The son pushed the father to have her cremated. Now when the father died, it appeared he'd been drinking, not stone cold drunk, but enough to make him lose his balance. He fell onto the front of his combine while he worked on it."

"What made you think he'd been drinking?" Damien asked.

"The workers said he seemed intoxicated earlier that day. He seemed to have a lack of coordination, dizzy like symptoms." As he said this, the Sheriff pulled out a photo. "I have a picture taken at the scene. The father pulled over a heavy-duty tool chest to work on some of the cutters from the combine. The photos from the scene allude to him tripping as he moved towards it. He impaled himself on one of the cutters.

"No sign of foul play, he'd been working alone when it happened. Jason had been out in the field repairing a fence when he came in and discovered his Dad. The officers at the scene said Jason seemed extremely upset. Paramedics had trouble getting the kid to calm down." He handed the report to Joe. "At the time, old Doc Withers gave him a sedative, and some of the ranch hands stayed with him through the night."

Damien read the sheet. "Did you guys do an autopsy and test for an elevated blood alcohol level?"

The Sheriff looked embarrassed as he sighed. "No. The Doctor didn't think anything seemed out of place, and the previous Sheriff felt he had no reason to investigate." He sat back in his chair. "We've evolved a lot in the years since then. If this accident happened today, there would be a full-blown investigation."

Damien nodded in agreement. "Do you know if he buried the father or had him cremated?"

Sheriff Winsley took a drink of his root beer. "Cremated, same as his mother. Jason said he had a small area he sprinkled her ashes in and planned to do the same with the father."

"What about the farm itself—can you tell us anything about it, anything at all?"

Winsley frowned as he reclined in his chair. "Nothing too exciting to tell. They built the current farmhouse when Jason turned ten. That's the one he currently lives in and is remodeling. Other than that, there's not much else."

Joe and Damien had to pick their jaws up off the floor. "What do you mean built the farmhouse? Where did they live before moving to the current house?" Damien asked.

The Sheriff rubbed his chin. "The farm has been around for some time. The family lived in the original house for years. I know the Freestones wanted another child, and the original house would have been too small for a bigger family, so they built the new one up on the far side of the property."

Damien cocked his head to the side. "You're telling us that another house exists on Jason's property?"

"Well, sure." Sheriff Winsley gave both Joe and Damien an incredulous stare. "You guys didn't know about the original house? It's in the records."

Damien's eyes widened as he opened his mouth then closed it. He let out a heavy breath. "No Sheriff we haven't located any information under the current farm property records, either under Jason, his Dad, or even under the mother's maiden name. It seems the online records we have access to go back in a limited capacity."

Winsley let out a loud hoot and slapped the side of his leg. "Aw hell, I forget the records in this area, as well as all the other areas around here, don't necessarily match up the way they're supposed to. Back in the old days, you didn't necessarily change the name on the land or property when you married." He held up his finger and spun his chair around. He rifled through an old file cabinet.

"Here we go." The Sheriff pulled a large file out of the drawer. When Winsley spun back around, he chuckled at the Detective's expressions. "I had some questions about Freestone's father's death after I took over as Commander. I pulled as much as I could on the family." The Sheriff sighed. "I didn't necessarily think that Jason killed his father, I just had some questions about the way the former Commander handled some of his cases. The Freestone case happened to be the most recent one he worked on before his death. So that's where I started."

Winsley opened the file. "Mabel Freestone, Jason's mother, her maiden name was Roundtree. The original property was listed under her grandfather, Wilbur Roundtree," he paused as he read the papers. "Actually—my bad—the original deed goes back to Wilbur's mother, Freda Schneider." The Sheriff chuckled as he glanced at Damien and Joe. "Well hell, no wonder you couldn't find any records. You need a damn flow chart to follow this one. The online records wouldn't go that far back; they haven't been updated yet. You would need to know what to look for.

"When Roundtree died, Mabel inherited the property. Royce, Mabel's father, died about a year before Mabel married Jason's Dad." He gave the paper over to Damien. "You know; Jason would have had all this information. He would've needed it when he incorporated it under the new name, Freestone Cheese and Dairy. Going forward from that point, all vehicles and property associated with the farm, even the old property would be under the new corporation. It should've come up under Jason's name when you pulled his file."

Damien cursed under his breath. "Not if he wanted to keep that whole aspect of his life a secret. When Jason incorporated, he listed the newer farmhouse and the dairy business, which included only the vehicles he wanted recognized. He didn't carry over the old property or any vehicles under his parents or anyone else for that matter. Every year when he renews any vehicle registration, under the old farm, he just renews the tags."

Damien and Joe shook the Sheriff's hand. "When we get a search warrant, we'll notify you. We'll need your help in executing it."

"No problem, fellows. Whatever you need, just let me know."

"We would appreciate it if you didn't mention this to anyone. Not even any of your deputies. We aren't sure we have anything, but we sure don't want Jason to find out we are looking at him."

"You got it. I'll wait to see if you come up with anything." Sheriff Winsley handed them a card. "Call me at that number anytime. The entrance to the old farmhouse is located off Scotts Road. If you turn off Hwy 18, also known as Nortonville Blacktop road, there will be an off street, called Ford's Lane. It dead-ends at the old farmhouse. You will want to list the entire boundary of the property for your search warrant."

He raised his hand and snapped his fingers. "Hey—I got something else you should know. Not that it means anything. After the Freestones had moved into the new house, Jason's mother got pregnant. She had an accident and tripped down the stairs. The poor woman lost the baby; it took her a long time to recover. She never seemed to be the same."

Winsley glanced down at his desk then back up with a sullen face. "Jason's parents were good people. If he ends up being responsible for these abductions and murders, it won't be because of the parents."

***

Damien and Joe sprinted to the vehicle. Joe called Matt to give him the information on the names and the other house on the property. "Matt is checking the names we now have," Joe said.

Damien once again hit the lights and sped out of Waverly, back to the lab. Damien considered what the Sheriff Winsley said about Jason's mother and losing the baby. The implications were staggering. Jason may have started his killing spree at the ripe old age of twelve.

CHAPTER FORTY-SIX

The Haut's Residence

A twenty-minute ride to Pawnee gave Dillon enough time to clear her head. She pulled into the driveway of a quaint little cottage style home. She took slow deep breaths and readied herself to meet the parents. Before she even got out of her car, the front door flew open. A middle-aged woman stood there in an apron, wringing the life out of a poor hand towel.

"You must be Agent McGrath, oh please come in. I'm Beverly. Let me get my husband." She ushered her into a larger than average living room and ran to the kitchen.

Dillon's chest tightened as if she wore a bra one size too small. A picture of Beth covered almost every surface of the living room. The pictures spanned Beth's short life. Dillon had seen this type of obsession before in other families. She understood the loss of a child had a profound effect on the parents left behind. It affected people differently, but for Beth's parents, it's as if they had become visitors in a shrine built for their dead daughter.

Mrs. Haut came back into the room. "David, David she's here. Come on now, get in here!" The husband followed his wife. Mrs. Haut gestured towards the sofa offering the Agent a seat. "Please tell us you have information about our daughter." She sat across from Dillon and waited for her to answer.

"Mr. and Mrs. Haut, I don't have any information at this time about your daughter's whereabouts. We are investigating the disappearance and murders of some other girls, and we believe your daughter's disappearance may be connected." Dillon paused a moment. "I want to ask you some background questions. First, did your daughter have an altercation with Jason Freestone back in high school?"

Both parents' eyes widened. Mrs. Haut covered her cheeks with both hands, and the father opened his mouth to say something then shut it again. Their eyes darted to each other and then back to Agent McGrath. "Yes, she did," the father said.

Bingo. "Can you tell me anything you remember about the incident?"

The mother began first. "The kids went to old man Powell's place to have an end of school summer party. All the teenagers from around these parts attended. They had beer and fireworks. Beth was a responsible girl, so we weren't worried about her drinking. We had given her permission to stay until eleven and then head home. We wanted her home before midnight." Beverly took a deep breath.

David Haut took his wife's hand in his as she continued. "Beth ended up coming back home around nine. She explained that Jason had tried to kiss her while she sat on the back of a truck. When she pushed him away, he became angry, and another boy had to settle him down. She decided the best thing would be for her to leave. Beth didn't want to be around when he returned to the bonfire."

The father took over. "I called up Jason's Dad and let him know what happened. We weren't going to press charges or anything, it didn't warrant that. I wanted him to know his son got a little carried away, and next time it happened we would call the police. We gave Jason some slack on his behavior due to the loss of his mother not too long before this incident. His Dad apologized and said he would talk to Jason. I know that Powell learned about what happened and he didn't let Jason come back to the swimming hole anymore."

"Did anything else happen between the two of them after that incident?"

The parents exchanged glances. "Go on honey, tell her," Mr. Haut, said.

"I don't know if it is even important. After the party and we had talked to Jason's father, things seem to settle down. Then a few months later, Jason started showing up at places Beth would be. If she was hanging with other kids, Jason would show up with a few of his friends. He never made advances to her. I think I remember Beth saying he even apologized for his behavior that night at the pond. Jason never called her. Or asked her out. He just seemed to show up."

"We never thought anything about it because it seemed harmless. I mean, it's a rural area, all these kids grow up together and go to the same school. They were bound to run into each other," Mr. Haut said.

"How long after the pond incident did Beth go missing?" Dillon asked them.

Mrs. Haut glanced at her husband and then spoke. "I think she disappeared about two years later. Beth had a job up in Springfield at a local hotel. She took classes at the college in Hospitality. She wanted to have a bed-and-breakfast on a real working farm." Mrs. Haut's lower lip trembled.

"It was over the two years prior to her disappearance that Jason began randomly showing up where Beth was?" Dillon asked.

"Yes. Is that important?"

Dillon softened her expression. "I'm not sure yet. Can you tell me about her disappearance?"

The father hung his head, when he met Dillon's stare, he had a hangdog expression. "Before you hit I55 to go into Springfield there used to be an old gas station. Beth's friends used to hang out there, so it wasn't unusual for her to stop there and see them. Between her classes and work, she didn't have much time to spend with her friends."

Beth's father paused, he let out a sharp breath. "It shut down about five years ago; the gas station. Anyway, she stopped there one night on her way home. Beth always filled her tank in the evening, so if she ran late she didn't have to worry about stopping on her way into work. She probably figured some of her friends would be there, so it didn't seem out of the ordinary to us. She had called us from the hotel before she left to head home."

He paused again and pinched the bridge of his nose, trying to stop the tears from spilling over. "I'm sorry. It never gets easier. I don't know if it ever will. When Beth failed to get home by nine p.m., I called the gas station and spoke with one of the employees. They said she had left over an hour ago. I asked them if Beth left with anyone or if they noticed someone talking to her. The young girl said no. I couldn't get any more information over the phone.

"I left immediately, drove the route over there hoping to find her car on the side of the road. When I got to the gas station, I located her car parked well behind it. Kind of off in a ditch that ran along the back of the property. I called the Sheriff, and a Deputy showed up."

"What did the Deputy do?" Dillon asked him.

The father frowned shrugging. "Not much. They searched her car, didn't find the car keys or her purse. Nothing seemed disturbed or out of place. They put her information into the computer. We organized searches and put up fliers all over this area and all the surrounding areas.

We put her picture out there as much as we could. No one ever reported seeing her."

"One last question and it will sound odd, but did Beth have a favorite snack?"

Mrs. Haut's eyes widened, "Oh my gosh yes; corn chips. It was just about the only thing she ever wanted to eat. I told her she should try something else, but she just loved corn chips."

Dillon stood up to leave, knowing she would more than likely be back with the closure these parents needed, but not the outcome they hoped for. "Thank you for meeting with me. I believe the information you have given me will help in the current investigation and hopefully give you some answers."

"Agent McGrath," Daniel said. "Do you think you will find our daughter?"

Dillon gazed at the father. "Within a few days, I hope that I will have some kind of information for you. I can't give you any more than that right now. I know how hard not knowing what happened to your daughter has been on you. I promise I will contact you in the next few days with any information I can give you. I would appreciate it if you could keep this conversation just between us. I can see myself out."

As she stepped out, Dillon heard Beth's parents crying. The kind of cry that left your face puffy, your nose stuffed up, and your head and heart aching.

CHAPTER FORTY-SEVEN

Forensic Lab

Dillon watched as Damien pulled into the lab parking lot and skidded to a stop in front of the building. She felt her pulse stammer. The air crackled as his long muscular legs closed the gap between them. "I'm gathering you two are in a rush to share your information. Either that or you think you can park where ever the hell you want."

"Maybe I wanted to get back to see you, and parking in a spot way over there would be too far away." He fluttered his eyelashes at her.

"Well, that makes perfect sense. I have that effect on so many men."

"Funny." He leaned into her and whispered, "I hope there will be no more men other than me." He smiled. He saw a flash of surprise pass over her face. "As to your assumption, oh hell yes we got some great information. We called Matt to get him working on it, so hopefully, he will have something for us," Damien said.

Joe fell into stride with them as they entered the building. "Did the parents confirm Mary's information?"

"They sure did. Beth argued with Jason while they both attended a party at old man Powell's swimming hole. It also seems as though Jason stalked Beth for a couple of years before he abducted her. Her parents said he would show up where Beth was hanging out with her friends."

"That sheds some light on his stalking of Taylor. I wonder if he may have stalked some of the other girls as well," Joe said.

"I don't know. But I think it's safe to assume he has. I think this will go a long way towards his pattern of abduction. I'll wait to see what else we have from Matt and Taylor, but this might be enough to get a search warrant. On a side note, Beth's favorite snack—corn chips." Dillon said.

They walked down the hallway to the conference room. They heard Matt and Taylor shrieking and laughing.

"What's with the happy dance? Did Notre Dame win their football game?" asked Joe.

Startled they stopped their victory dance. "Oh man," Matt said. "Way better than that. We did a search using the information you obtained from Winsley. We tracked down Mabel's mother. Her name is Fordham, she had a dark gray double cab truck. Mabel never switched the registration over. Jason could walk into any tag agency—pay the fee, show proof of insurance, and renew the tags under the old dairy farm's registration. If anyone ever questioned it, all Jason had to do then would be to show ownership of the property. He would have had no problems.

"When Jason registered the new house as a listing under the new farm operations, for tax purposes, he never incorporated the old farm or property. He kept two separate worlds, his cheese farm, and the old farm and farmhouse. That explains why nothing came up under the Freestone name. The original farmhouse had been listed under Wilbur's family name. Jason kept the truck registration under Mabel's mother. No wonder we couldn't find anything."

"Holy shit, I'm calling my boss, that should be enough to get us on the farm and search the premises." Dillon walked out of the room.

Damien's gaze followed Dillon's ass as it left the room. His smile faded when Joe's steely stare caught his. "What?"

Smiling Joe pointed at him, "Nothing. I'm not saying a word."

Papers that laid undisturbed on the table scattered in all directions as Dillon blew through the door. "Got the warrant. It should be coming through in the next five minutes or so."

"WTF! How did he get it so fast?" Joe asked.

Dillon's face lit up with a smile. "After I texted him earlier, my boss had the ball rolling. He happened to be playing golf with a federal judge. The judge told him if we got anything tangible, he'd get the warrant. I guess it pays to play golf."

"I'll call Sheriff Winsley in Waverly, ask him to meet us at his station. We need to get them to help us with the execution of the warrant. I'm going to have him round up some other groups of deputies too. We should have some of the deputies go through the new house, the barn, and the milking area. We'll also need some help at the old farmhouse." Damien grabbed his phone and headed out into the hallway.

Joe stared at Dillon. "I can't imagine we could get the warrant that damn fast. Division Central operates a little slower than the Feds."

Dillon spun around in her chair. "Well, not everyone can be the boss. There have to be worker bees." Her eyes gleamed with amusement.

He snorted, and even Taylor giggled. "Hey, whose side are on you on anyway?" Joe glared at Taylor with a very sexy version of the evil eye.

"Hers, of course," Taylor said. "She has way more power than you."

"Smart woman," Dillon said as she and Taylor exchanged some kind of girls only look.

Joe grabbed Taylor and nuzzled her neck. "Hmm, you shall be punished later for that, *tú cailín droch.*"

Dillon rolled her eyes. "Oh brother, threaten your bad girl on your own time. And lay off the kissy smoochie shit. Try to have some professionalism, please."

Joe stared at her. "You never did explain how you know Irish."

She gave him a wicked grin. "Didn't I?"

Joe gave her a dirty look. "No, and I think I deserve an explanation."

Dillon laughed. "Well thinking you deserve something and actually getting it are two different things."

Damien walked back into the room. "Okay, the chief can have everyone there within forty-five minutes. I also notified Captain Mackey. He's probably on the phone as we speak with your boss, Dillon."

"Did it come through?" Dillon asked Matt.

"Yup, printing it now." He reached behind him and grabbed the warrant. He printed two copies and handed them to Dillon.

Dillon took the search warrants and read them over. She smiled and chuckled. "Leave it to Deputy Director Sherman."

Joe squinted at her, "What did your Director do?"

"He made sure the warrants cover every piece of equipment, every building, every vehicle on the property at the time of the raid, and every animal if need be."

Joe laughed. "I sure as hell hope we don't have to test the validity of that warrant."

CHAPTER FORTY-EIGHT

Road to Waverly

Damien put on the lights and the siren. He accelerated to seventy and took his half of the road out of the middle. He screeched to a stop in front of the station. The deputies milling around outside gawked at the three of them as they bolted for the front doors.

The sheer number of law enforcement gathered at the small station made Damien smile. The Sheriff had come through. His determined stride parted the deputies. He extended his hand towards Sheriff Winsley. "Thanks for gathering, everyone. We have a lot of ground to cover over at the farm. We need everyone here." He held out his arm in Dillon's direction. "This is Special Agent Dillon McGrath. The FBI procured the search warrant."

Dillon handed Sheriff Winsley one copy of the warrant. "Thank you for your help in this matter, it is greatly appreciated." She laughed inwardly at the raised eyebrows Sheriff Winsley gave her.

Damien addressed everyone. "Thank you for getting here as fast as you did. We have a warrant that covers all vehicles, all buildings, and all areas of the property known as Freestone Cheese and Dairy farm. It also includes the original farmhouse located on the land that sits adjacent to Scott Road. Some of you will be heading to the central farm and the new farmhouse."

Damien paused as a murmur of disbelief weaved through the crowd of deputies. "A group of you will be assisting Detective Hagan, Special Agent McGrath, and myself at the old farmhouse. We've not been able to get a layout of the house, except that it has a cellar and one main floor. We have reason to believe Jason Freestone abducted the girl, Amy Custer, from Jacksonville. We also believe he abducted and murdered Tiffany Basset and Becca Martin. New information has led us to believe that Jason kidnapped five girls spanning the last eight years."

Dillon stepped up and waited a few moments while the deputies whispered amongst themselves before she took over the briefing. A ghost of a smile crept across her face when Damien winked at her. "Good afternoon, I'm Special Agent Dillon McGrath. I understand some of you may have a hard time accepting Jason Freestone as a murderer.

"We believe Amy Custer is being held at the old farmhouse. The crime lab will be sending a couple of CSTs to help collect evidence. If you think you've located something that could be evidence, mark it. If you aren't sure, mark it. We have tons of markers in the back of our vehicle. Grab some before we head out. Wear gloves while searching. I don't want any technicalities getting this asshole off."

Dillon addressed Winsley. "If you could divide up your men, I would appreciate it. We need about ten to help us cover the old farmhouse. Sheriff, take the rest of the men with you along with your copy of the warrant and head to the main farm. I need you to oversee that entire area."

She nodded at him as she addressed the crowd of deputies. "Do not let anyone make any phone calls. We don't think Jason is working with anyone, but we don't know for sure. The deputies assigned to us, some can ride with us, and others follow in another vehicle. When we get to the original farmhouse, we go stealth. We think he will be there and we don't want to spook him. We fully believe he has Amy. He could kill her if he hears us. If you have any questions or concerns, let's hear them now." She paused giving anyone a chance to speak up. She noticed a Deputy raise his hand. "Yes, Deputy?"

The young Deputy glanced around. "I've known Jason since we were in high school together. I don't mean to question you, and I mean no disrespect, but are you absolutely sure you have the right guy?"

All the men stared at her. They wanted an explanation, and she understood that, but they didn't have time. Amy didn't have time for explanations. "I appreciate your concern, and I understand it is hard reconciling the fact that someone you know is likely a kidnapper, rapist, and murderer. Right now, we have a small window to get to Amy Custer before he kills her. So, I don't have time to go over the evidence we've gathered, to convince you that we are making the right move. If you are uncomfortable performing the duties of your position, please remain behind.

"Now some of you may know Lieutenant Kaine and Detective Hagan from Division Central's Vicious Crimes Unit. They have been working this case from the beginning. We are all aware the FBI likes to come in at the end and take all the glory, well this time will be no different." Muffled laughter wafted through the deputies. "In all seriousness, this has been a joint effort and again without your help today, this would be harder to do. So, thank you."

Turning her attention to Damien, she continued. "Lieutenant, do you have anything else you need to touch on?" Both Damien and Joe responded no. Dillon adjusted her weapon. "Alright then, the Sheriff will divide you up, ten of you will come with us. Let's roll."

CHAPTER FORTY-NINE

Freestone farm

Jason needed to buy time. "Hey, David. I'm going to check the perimeter and make sure the rest of the fence has no security issues, then head into town and grab a few things for us for dinner tonight. I'd planned on getting some steaks and beer for this evening."

"Sure Jason, that sounds great. We'll finish up here in a few hours so, about the time you're getting back, we should be done," David said.

It seemed the list of things to do before heading to the festival got longer and longer each year. Therefore, to cut back on time, it had become a tradition for the ranch hands to stay at his house, play poker, and drink beer the night before the festival. It made the morning routine easier and more efficient.

Jason had other things he would much rather do than sit around with his workers. The same old men who had been with his Dad back in the day. He hated having to sit there and listen year after year about how great a man his father had been. He hated having to listen to how much they loved his father. It made him sick to his stomach. His father had been a stupid man. Stupid and careless.

However, if he varied the plans now, the men would become suspicious. Jason could not afford to become more appealing to the FBI and those Detectives. They buzzed around like gnats. They didn't have half his brain. Those three would be chasing their tails for years to come.

He'd been curious what brought them to his farm. The question the FBI Agent asked him about Beth and dinner at Toni's Café rattled him for a split second. There could be no way they had any information on Beth. They couldn't connect him to Tiffany, either. No one observed him speaking to her in the parking lot. He had covered his tracks well. He figured they had to question all the farms in the area.

Jason noticed the FBI Agent had a rocking body. How could you not? If he got her alone, he had a few things he would like to do to her. His hand would've fit nicely wrapped around that long blonde hair of hers. If you strip her of that badge and gun, she was still just a woman.

His father never learned that the place for a woman was under a man.

His Dad let Mom govern the house and make decisions. She should've had no choices. He and his father should've been the only ones making the decisions. The last straw, the final act that showed Jason his father had lost his ability to command the family and the farm? His father let his mother get pregnant. No chance in hell Jason would've let another kid come in and ruin everything.

Jason checked his watch and cursed. He had about an hour to fill with a little fun before he had to get food and beer for the evening. Jason glanced at the supplies he brought with him. A few bottles of water and two apples. He didn't think she had an allergy to apples, but he wouldn't make the same mistake twice. Seriously, Jason thought, who the hell had a corn allergy? The fucking world just about ran on corn or corn byproducts.

He would miss serving Beth's favorite snack, though. She used to eat those fucking corn chips like they were her last meal, every damn day for lunch at school. Jason laughed out loud. He would never forget the look on her face when he made her eat bag after bag. She was such a bitch.

If he wanted his new guest to have strength for Sunday night, he had to give her something to eat and drink. Jason had been thinking about keeping her longer than planned, but to do so, he needed to make different arrangements. He cursed under his breath. He wanted to stay longer than an hour. Jason spent the last day thinking about those long legs and an hour just wasn't long enough.

He pulled up by the back door of the old farmhouse. His heavy boots announced his arrival. Coming down the stairs into the basement he stopped abruptly. For a quick moment, he saw Beth on the mattress. His pulse quickened as the blood and rage surged throughout his body. After all these years, Beth's presence still lingered as if she were still in his basement. Jason moved towards her. He paused, tilting his head to the side. It wasn't Beth. That's all right, he thought. He had Beth's bitchy face burned into his memory. "I regret that I won't be able to stay as long as I'd like, but the real fun will happen tomorrow." A malicious grin spread across his face.

Jason placed a bowl that held the water and apples down on the table. He held a bottle of water when he turned towards Amy. He noticed she licked her lips as her eyes locked on the bottle. He loosened one of the straps allowing one of her arms more movement. "I'm sure you're thirsty. Here, take a few sips." Jason handed her the bottle and watched as she readily gulped it down.

He reached over and grabbed it. "Listen, you don't want to drink it that fast. You could throw it right back up, and that would be a mess." He took the water and placed it back in the bowl.

Jason removed the blanket that covered her. He moved to the foot of the bed and adjusted the leather straps. Once he had her on all fours, he re-tightened them. Now she could go nowhere. He positioned himself on the bed.

All the hair on Amy's arms stood on end. She tried to prepare mentally for what he planned to do to her. She took a deep breath. She decided she would not beg nor give him the satisfaction of her tears. That's what Amy tried to do. "Go to fucking hell you monster!" Amy yelled at him. Even though she told herself not to cry, the tears flowed.

"What a mouth you have on you. Maybe tomorrow I should gag you."

Amy screamed.

CHAPTER FIFTY

Road to the Freestone Farm

Sheriff Winsley and his team of deputies peeled off from the caravan and headed to the main entrance of the Freestone farm while Damien continued to the original Freestone house. They pulled off Scott Road through an open gate onto a long drive that led them to the house. He slowed the SUV to a crawl stopping well short of the residence.

The occupants of both vehicles convened at the back of the SUV. Joe pointed at a rough drawing of the house. He spoke just above a whisper. "When we reach this front corner of the house we need to split off." He pointed to the largest Deputy in the group. "What's your name?"

"Mills."

"Okay Mills, you take half the men and go to the left. Stay low and quiet. Do not venture onto the porch. We don't know what kind of setup we will be walking into. Wait until we get around to the back. You will hear this," Joe produced a very soft bird sound. "Only when I do it, it will be deafening. When you hear it, give us two minutes to get in and then position yourself at the front door. When you hear the bird sound again, break the door down—just don't shoot us," Joe said.

Damien gave Joe a subtle nod then took over the briefing. "We know this house has a cellar. We think that's where he'll be. Check the volume on your radios. Don't use them until after we secure Jason and Amy is safe, unless it's an emergency. Let's try to take this asshole alive. Team one let's go. Team two, follow Mills."

They started up the old road. At the front of the house, they split up. Half going to the left the other going around the back. When the team led by Joe and Damien reached the back of the house, Joe slowed the progress to a crawl as he neared the back door. Joe crouched down as he stepped up onto the stairs. Damien tapped his shoulder and pointed towards an old lean-to. Parked underneath—a dark double cab truck.

Joe reached for the doorknob; he made his bird sound, and he pulled the door open. The group followed Joe and Damien single file through the kitchen door. Blood-curdling screams echoed off the walls. Joe crept his way through the kitchen; the door leading down to the basement was ajar. He stopped at the edge, using his left hand, he signaled that four stairs led down to the cellar. Joe crouched down. From his angle, he could see the legs of a bed on the far side of the basement. The screams sounded like a wounded cat caught in a trap. Adrenaline rushed through his body. He wanted to hurt this asshole.

Joe signaled to Damien. He acknowledged Joe's signal and glanced over his shoulder at Dillon. She waved to the deputies behind her. Using her fingers, Dillon started the countdown. When she held up two fingers, Joe generated the bird sound. Dillon went from one to zero, at the same time the front door flew open. Joe and Damien had already disappeared down the stairs.

Three long strides carried Joe to within striking distance of Jason. He grabbed Jason by the neck and yanked him off the bed. "Vicious Crimes Unit asshole, you're under fucking arrest dick-brain." Joe had one hand wrapped around the back of Jason's neck, holding him six inches off the ground. Time seemed to stand still. Joe's hand almost engulfed Jason's entire neck. He squeezed with so much force that Jason struggled to breathe.

Damien yelled Joe's name several times before breaking the enraged trance he had been in. Joe threw Jason to the floor. He hit the concrete with a bone-crunching thud and crumpled at Joe's feet. Bending down, Joe cuffed Jason's hands behind his back before checking him for a pulse.

"The fucker is still breathing," Joe said.

Damien stepped towards the girl. He fought back the tears that moistened his eyes. Blood ran down her thighs. She peered over her shoulder and screamed even louder at the sight of him. She yanked and pulled on the straps that held her secured to the bed. He tried talking to her. Damien tried to tell her they were the police and she was safe now, but the sight of another man coming towards her proved to be too much. Amy's screams increased.

Dillon pushed Damien to the side. She grabbed the blanket and covered the young girl. Dillon noticed the blood, and the look on Damien's face said he saw it too. She caught the terrified eyes of one of the deputies in the basement.

"Call for paramedics. Now." Dillon said. The Deputy stood with his mouth wide open and his eyes bulging. Dillon spun around. "Hey, Deputy! Call for the damn paramedics. Now!" She squatted down and whispered in Amy's ear. "Sshh, Amy we are here to help." She ran her hand over the top of Amy's head. "I need you to calm down. Can you do that for me? Come on, look at me, Amy."

Amy peered through wet sticky strands of hair that hung in her face. She gulped in air as she tried to breathe through the sobs. She reached out towards Dillon, but the straps were bound too tight and kept her from doing so. "Untie me, please," Amy whispered in a trembling voice.

Dillon reached up and removed the straps from the head and foot of the bed. Dillon didn't have time to untie them from Amy's wrists and ankles before Amy clawed at the straps.

Amy yanked and pulled at them. "Get these fucking things off me. Please, please." Amy held out her hands while her eyes pleaded with Dillon. Her voice cracked as she screamed at Dillon. "Get these damn things off me, now!" She continued to claw at her wrists even as Dillon untied the straps. Once removed, Amy calmed down and tried to sit on the edge of the bed. She shifted trying to find a comfortable position. The color drained from her face as she sucked in air through her clenched teeth. "This hurts too much," she whispered to Dillon.

"Here, let me help you lay on your side." Dillon guided her down on the mattress.

Amy grabbed Dillon's hand. Tears gushed from her eyes, "I didn't think anyone would find me." She squeezed hard and pulled Dillon's hand towards her chest. "Oh God, thank you. I didn't think anyone would find me." She kept repeating the phrase over and over.

***

Joe and Damien stood in the middle of the basement which spanned the length of the house. A wall at the far end resembled a set out of a horror movie. Various cutting tools hung on hooks. A thick chain hung on a ring from the ceiling above a five-inch drain.

Blood and tissue covered the walls and ceilings. Pieces of flesh dangled from links in the chain. Within a few minutes of being down there, a metallic taste coated the back of their throats. A pungent sour smell permeated the room. The rotten smell assaulted the senses with every inhale. Underneath a long table near the wall of tools, a container held a roll of black bags. On top of the table, antique bottles sat in a straight line against the wall.

Damien noticed Joe rested his hand on the butt of his holstered weapon. Anger simmered in his partner's eyes. Not wanting to have to do the paperwork that went with shooting a restrained suspect, Damien reached out and touched his best friend's shoulder. "We got him, Joe. We got him," Damien said.

Joe took a deep breath and nodded as he gazed around the room. "This is where he dismembered Tiffany and Becca. Jason kept them here. He raped them. Then he killed them. He kept them like caged animals. He didn't even clean the area. He brought all the girls here." Joe turned towards the bed. "He raped all of them there on that shitty mattress. It's a fucking torture chamber."

Joe rubbed his hands over his face. He squeezed his eyes together. The moisture receded. "Can you imagine what the girls went through as they laid on that bed? I haven't been down here thirty minutes and the odor and metallic taste coating the back of my throat are almost unbearable. How fucking bad do you think it was to be down here for days or months? The girls had to have known what surrounded them. To realize what this bastard had in store for them at any given moment had to be horrifying. What bloody fucking hell did they go through?"

Damien's shoulders sagged. "I can't even begin to imagine what the girls went through. Now we get every piece of skin, every drop of blood, and every hair and fiber we can find in this shit hole, and we nail this asshole to the wall." Damien regarded Dillon as she sat on the bed with Amy. "As long as I'm alive I don't think I'll ever forget what I witnessed when we came down those stairs. However, that girl over there? She survived, she's alive. At least, we got him before he killed her."

Joe turned towards a loud sound at the stairs. The paramedics had arrived. He watched as they gave Amy a mild sedative, to keep her calm as they prepared her for transport—pain medicine wouldn't come until later. The sedative would, at least, take the edge off. He had noticed that Dillon had remained at Amy's side and now she helped the paramedics guide Amy towards the EMS chair that would carry her up the stairs.

Joe watched as they wrapped Amy in a clean blanket. He wondered how she would get past this. He knew her physical wounds would eventually heal, but Joe knew from years on this job, that the emotional wounds could take much longer.

Joe moved towards the end of the basement when a heard a strange sound. He looked back over his shoulder, Amy's breath hissed in and out, as she moved free of Dillon and the paramedic's support. She glared down at the still unconscious Jason on the floor. Her hands shook as she held the blanket around her. "I hope you rot in fucking Hell you son of a bitch!" She lifted her right foot and reared back. The kick landed on the side of his stomach. She kept kicking. Each landed with a resounding thud. "I. Hate. You!"

Joe scanned the room, all movement in the basement had ceased. Everyone gawked in stunned silence. Amy grunted as each kick landed on its target. By the time she finished, she panted, and her skin had a light sheen of sweat.

Joe stood next to Damien. He looked at his partner, not sure of what he saw on his face—a confused look of admiration and sadness. Dillon reached for Amy and eased her into the EMS chair.

Joe started to turn away, unable to witness the gut-wrenching display of raw emotion from such a young girl, when Amy glared at him and Damien. Tears streamed down her cheeks as her bottom lip trembled. "He's a monster, and he deserves worse. I hope someone kills him. After they rape him." Amy held eye contact with Joe. "Someone needs to hurt him like he hurt me." Joe's stare followed the paramedics as they carried her up the stairs.

After the paramedics left with Amy, everyone collectively released the breath they held. Joe took several long strides towards the lump of crap on the floor. He reached down and jerked Jason to his feet. The man staggered as he tried to steady himself. A large welt on the side of his jaw had turned a nasty shade of dark red where his face had hit the floor. Blood trickled out the corner of his mouth. Jason leaned heavily towards the side where Amy kicked the shit out him. His dick hung out of his pants. Joe looked at Damien and snorted.

Damien stepped back, waving his hand at Joe. "No, no, no! No way in hell I'm touching that fucker's dick. He'll have to walk around with it hanging out." Damien pointed at Joe. "You can take care of it if you want to, but I'm not touching his pecker." Several deputies in the basement chuckled at the exchange.

An evil smile spread across Joe's face. He grabbed Jason's pants by the belt loop and yanked them up. Jason hissed as the zipper scraped against the sensitive skin. Joe pushed Jason back down to his knees. "In case you didn't hear me earlier, I'm going to reread your Miranda Rights." When Joe finished Mirandizing Jason, he waited for a reply. "I said, 'Do you understand these rights?'"

Jason's dark, cold eyes glared at Dillon. He refused to respond or engage. Without taking his eyes off Dillon, he turned his head to the side and spat out a mouthful of blood.

Joe yanked on Jason's hands. "Listen asshole, if you don't answer using your mouth, I'll be forced to repeat this Miranda over and over until you do."

Jason smirked at Dillon. Blood outlined his teeth. "Yes. I understand."

A Waverly Deputy called over to Dillon. "Hey, Agent McGrath? A Deputy has arrived with a patrol car. Where do you want us to take him?"

Dillon glanced over at the Deputy. "Take him to your station. We'll keep him there until the State or the FBI decides where to hold him until the trial." Joe lifted Jason up to hand him over to the officer. Dillon stepped in front of Freestone. Damien and Joe flanked him on either side. They gave each other a curious look.

Dillon placed herself inches from his face. "You are nothing but a sick fuck. You had your time, now you'll spend the rest of your life rotting in a cage. I'll make sure you spend what's left of your pathetic life in the worst prison possible. All those things you did to those girls will pale in comparison to the things that are in store for you. And when your new buddies are introducing you to some very nasty sexual positions, you'll be able to thank me, a woman, for putting your ass in there." She stepped back and winked at him. "Go ahead Deputy, take this asshole away."

CHAPTER FIFTY-ONE

Damien, Joe, and Dillon stood on the porch of the farmhouse breathing in fresh air. Inside, deputies swarmed, searching every nook and cranny. CSTs were in the process of going over the basement. Mills moved to a built-in bookcase, methodically tapping the back side of the shelves. As he tapped the back of one shelf, it had a different sound than the others. Mills removed his knife and used it to wedge between the edges of the wood. It took minimal effort, to slide the back of the shelf to the side. A little nook hid behind it. Inside he found several leather-bound journals. He reached in with his gloved hand and pulled out a book. His pulse raced echoing in his head as he read the first few pages. "Agent, Detectives, I think you need to come over here!" He glanced over his shoulder towards the open front door.

Dillon walked in first. "What do you have?"

Mills pointed to the nook area and then handed her the book. "It seems our guy kept a record of everything he did. It appears they go back twelve years."

Joe and Damien stood next to Dillon. Damien leaned in so he could inhale her scent. He wanted to reach out and hold her. Just for a few moments. Just long enough to push the horror of what he saw in the basement into the dark corners of his mind.

The image of Jason hurting Amy would forever be etched in his memory. The way Amy had glared at him as if he intended to hurt her, ripped him up inside. His heart ached for the girl. He didn't want to see this brutality anymore. Damien didn't think the punishment for Jason would be severe enough, and if no one else had been around, he would have shot him and made it look like he struggled against his arrest. How could he be a cop if he so easily wanted to take someone's life?

Dillon thumbed through the book and spot read. She handed the book to Damien then went to the nook. She pulled out all the books and read the first few pages of each one. Dillon opened one and thumbed through it. Her eyes widened as she scrolled through the pages.

"What do you have Dillon?" Joe asked.

"Call Matt. Tell him we will need someone to bring a ground-penetrating radar. He buried our five missing girls here on the property. We have to find those bodies."

Joe rubbed his eyes. "Shit the bed. This is going to be a cluster fuck." He went out to the porch. "Hey," he yelled at the deputies, "don't walk around this damn property. We have bodies buried, and we don't want to trample any evidence. Set up a perimeter, wide out to the tree line." Immediate movement halted. Each person retraced their steps and backed out into the driveway.

Damien nodded to Joe as he walked back into the house. "He wrote about his mother and father too. He's been killing since the age of seventeen. I wonder if we'll find anything about his mother's pregnancy in these journals." Damien continued to thumb through the writings.

"CSTs will be here tomorrow with the radar. Some CSTs are on the way now with a bunch of lights to rig up. I made sure to let Matt know to notify Director Jones, FBI Deputy Director Sherman, and our Captain. The press will shit themselves when they hear what we have here. We need to keep some of the deputies here at the house, to keep the idiots off the property." Joe pointed at Mills. "You have permission to shoot anyone who comes on this property."

"Excellent." Mills held up the journal he'd been reading. "This guy is a sick bastard." He handed the book off to Damien and headed outside. He paused at the door and turned back to the group. "I'll coordinate with Sheriff Winsley about setting up around the clock watches. I can't believe this guy has been part of our community. He had us all fooled."

A CST came up from the basement. Damien gathered up the journals. He had the tech put them in evidence bags and mark them. He planned to take them back to the lab so they could read them and narrow the search area to find the girls.

CHAPTER FIFTY-TWO

Forensic Lab

Damien, Joe, and Dillon stopped just inside the doorway of the con-ference room. "Hey guys," they said at the same time.

Taylor beamed a full-face smile at Joe. "We figured you'd be hungry and that you guys would need to start going over those journals. Matt and I decided we could put in some time and help you. Then we can all head home to sleep for at least a few hours," Taylor said.

They sat filling their plates with food.

Matt sheepishly looked around the table. "How's Amy? Will she be okay?"

Dillon swallowed her bite. She struggled to keep the emotion out of her voice. "Well, she's alive. That's the best thing." Dillon pushed her salad around her plate. "What we caught that bastard doing to her when we got in the basement—fucking sick." She took a deep breath. "He hurt her so badly, that she couldn't sit up on the bed. She had to lay on her side." Dillon smiled at Joe. Her face softened. When Dillon spoke, her voice quivered with emotion. "Joe damn near broke the guy's neck after almost choking him to death, when he yanked him away from her."

Joe grunted. "I may have thrown him to the ground a little harder than necessary." Joe lifted his chin and sat straighter in his chair. "On the way to the EMS chair, Amy kicked him in the stomach." A smile spread across his face. "She kicked him several times screaming at him. She's going to be okay. It'll be hard, but Amy will be okay." Joe said the words, but deep inside, he didn't know if she would ever heal from the time spent in that basement.

The room fell silent. Everyone sat still, no longer eating. Joe ad-dressed everyone. "Now we find those other girls and get them to their parents. Shit, the parents. When are we contacting them?" Joe asked.

Damien set his can of soda on the table. "The Sheriff's office called Amy's parents they were going to meet her at the hospital. After we find and locate the five remaining girls, then we'll make the notifications. We started this; we will finish it."

Three hours later, after reading through the journals, they had the location of Beth Haut and the other four girls. Damien and the others didn't speak about the descriptions of torture they had read in Jason's handwriting. He had taken joy in torturing the girls sexually and physically, his journals detailed the various instruments of pain he had used. The description of what he did to Beth was exceptionally heinous.

He held her for two months before he tortured her to death. He described in detail the rapes she endured. Damien had to fight the tears as he read the description of those last two months of her life. The team decided to tell her parents. They were sure this information would come out in the trial.

There were pages of vague entries about other girls in the journals. Entries with no names, no details on where or when they had been abducted, only mentions of the torture they had endured at Jason's hands.

Damien's gut told him the unknown girls were runaways like the four unsolved cases they had discovered early on, he also thought Jason had abducted them from way outside his hunting area. Damien's body tingled uncomfortably as he read those journals. Jason had been at this for a long time, and Damien had no doubt that tomorrow the farm would reveal more horrors.

CHAPTER FIFTY-THREE

Once in the elevator, Joe watched as Damien whispered in Dillon's ear. The blush on her cheeks and subtle nod showed her agreement with their private conversation. Dillon got off the elevator and Damien continued with him and Taylor. Joe had his arm around Taylor. "Aren't you staying with Dillon tonight?"

Damien nodded. "I just want to get a few things, so I don't have to come back up here in the morning."

Joe unlocked the door, and all three went in. He glanced over at Damien. "What time you want to meet in the restaurant?"

Damien rubbed his hands through his hair. "Let's meet at seven-thirty. The techs with the radar will be there by nine. That should give us a decent night's rest." He walked into his bedroom and closed the door.

Joe looked down at Taylor. "I need to shower, and I think you do, too."

"Oh, you do?" Taylor teased. "After the shower, you'll need to sleep. It's going to be a hell of a day tomorrow."

"Don't remind me." Joe dragged her into his room.

Between kisses, Joe disrobed Taylor. Leaving a trail of clothes on the way to the bathroom. In the shower, Taylor's eyes swept over every inch of him. Joe's emerald green eyes darkened. There wasn't an ounce of fat on him. Joe's waist tapered in giving him that V shape so many men worked out endlessly to achieve. The thin line of hair that started below his navel pulled her gaze downward leaving her breathless.

"Hey babe, your thinking is deafening. Want to tell me about it?" Joe had built up a rich, creamy lather of shampoo in Taylor's hair as he waited for her to respond.

She tilted her head back. Tears mixed with the water. "I hate that you'll be leaving to go back to Chicago in a couple of days. I don't want to be so far away from you. I know it shouldn't be this intense in such a short time, but I can't help my attachment to you." Taylor wiped her face of the soap that had dripped down from her hair. "I just can't imagine not having you in my bed at night."

Joe spun Taylor under the water. The soapy suds ran down her chest between her full round breasts. "You know you can come up and visit me. It's only a few hours away."

Taylor pouted. "I know."

She switched positions so he could be under the water.

The disappointment in her eyes just about crushed him. But Joe had decided he just wasn't ready to give up his lifestyle. Or let go of his past. He took her face in his hands and kissed her. A hot, needy kiss. "You can come up whenever you want. Stay the weekend with me." He needed to distract her from this conversation. Reaching down between her legs, he teased her. Taylor's slick wet heat coated his fingers. Her moan rumbled in her chest. Joe brought her legs up around his waist and rubbed himself against her. Slowly he slid into her. He pulled back and pushed back in—harder.

He braced himself with one hand and held her with the other. She clenched down around him. Her moans of pleasure pulled him closer to the edge. Wet flesh slapped at a furious pace. The sound echoed off the tile walls. A tremor rolled through her body as Joe continued to thrust harder and harder. Taylor held onto him. He tightened his grip around her waist. Joe took everything she gave him. Then he took more. She cried out his name. He buried his face into her neck.

Joe stayed buried within her. Her legs were still wrapped around him. He kissed her temple, placed his cheek on her head. "Did I hurt you?"

"No," Taylor whispered. She clung to his neck. "You could never hurt me."

Joe felt an instant pang of guilt. He knew he would hurt her when she realized he wouldn't be able to give her the relationship she wanted from him.

In bed, Joe pulled Taylor close to him. "You're thinking again, Taylor."

She started to say something but thought better of it. "I'm just tired. I'll come up whenever you want me to." She knew going into this that he didn't want a relationship. At first, spending these last few nights with him was worth the risk. Now she wasn't so sure.

He grabbed her chin to turn her face to look at him. "Taylor, I do want to see you again. I'm not just going to leave and never talk to you. I promise you that."

Taylor's eyes were wet with tears. She blinked hoping they would recede. She kissed him and laid her head on his chest. "I'll come up whenever you want me to." She whispered.

Joe sighed and held her tighter. He knew she wanted more from him. He wanted to give it to her. He just couldn't. Joe wasn't sure he'd ever be able to give his heart fully to another woman again.

CHAPTER FIFTY-FOUR

Damien's eyes traveled up and down Dillon's body. She answered her door in a t-shirt that stopped mid-thigh. Her hair dripped water down the front of her shirt, making it stick to her skin. He licked his lips at the sight of that shirt as it clung to her body. No one ever intended a ratty old t-shirt to be the sexiest garment a woman wore.

The heat in Damien's eyes made Dillon's pulse quicken. She stepped aside allowing him entry. "I had to shower. I had to get the smell from the basement out of my hair."

Damien faced her as she closed the door. Dillon turned around, and he took one step towards her, pushing her back against the door. He placed a hand on each side of her head, boxing her in. Damien lowered his mouth to within inches of hers. He could hear the soft pants of her breath. He placed his lips on hers. Her mouth parted allowing his tongue access. Their tongues dueled for control. Damien pulled his lips away from hers, and he heard a soft moan of disappointment. "I don't want to touch you till after I shower, but I waited all day to kiss you." He strolled towards her bathroom with his bag in tow.

Dillon set the alarm for six forty-five. Plenty of time to get down and eat at seven-thirty. Her body melted into the mattress when Damien stepped out of the bathroom. He wore a towel wrapped around his waist. Her eyes followed the outline of his rippling abdomen muscles, only to be stopped abruptly by the top of the towel. Dillon watched him as he moved to the other side of the bed. He dropped the towel, allowing her to glimpse his chiseled body, a body created for pleasure and enjoyment. Dillon had never desired any man as much as she wanted Damien. It was more than just physical attraction, and that scared her.

They faced each other in the bed. He smelled like an Oregon forest in the fall; woodsy masculine and delicious. Dillon's eyes narrowed. "What are you smiling at?"

Damien scooted a little closer to her. He reached over and pushed a few strands of hair behind her ear. "I'm smiling cause all day, every time I looked at you, I fantasized about being right here."

"So now you're fantasizing about me during the day, not just in your dreams? Do you think you might have a concentration problem?"

He laughed. "Absolutely. If you're near me or not, I can't seem to keep you out of my mind. I'd say that's your fault."

Dillon reached out and touched his chest with her hand. "I found myself thinking about you during the day as well. Knowing you were on the property with me made dealing with the basement of horror that much easier."

Damien smiled. "Yeah, well watching you work is an unbelievable turn on. You're the one to blame for my fantasies." He moved closer to her. "You are authoritative without being a bitch. You had those deputies eating out of your hand, and you are the sexiest FBI Agent on the planet." He kissed her mouth and moved to her neck. "I'm naked, and you're not. Why is that?"

Dillon laughed. "Umm, I didn't want to seem that easy?"

Damien moved closer. Sliding his hand up her t-shirt. "Hmm, I like easy."

Dillon could feel his erection against her, and she reached down and wrapped her fingers around his length. Hard and yet silky soft. She pushed him onto his back and dragged her tongue down the length of his torso. She sat on her knees long enough to remove her t-shirt.

Dillon bent down and took the length of him in her mouth. She slid her hand up and down, squeezing with the right amount of pressure. Her tongue teased the tip, coaxing the first drops of moisture. She felt his moan as it rumbled from the depths of his chest. His fingers grabbed her hair and guided her head up and down.

"Oh sweet Jesus, Dillon. If you keep doing that, this will be over before it gets started." He pulled her up the length of his body. Her lips were swollen and pink. Her eyes were molten pools of amber. The want and desire on her face almost made him come. He pulled her close to his chest and rolled her over, flipping her onto her back.

"Now it's my turn," Damien whispered as he suckled each breast. He scraped each nipple with his teeth. He kissed his way down to her abdomen. He hooked his thumbs under the band of her lace panties and slid them down her legs. Damien dragged his tongue from her knee up the inside of her thigh. When he reached her mound of soft curls, he sucked her hard nub into his mouth. Dillon bucked under him. Her knees fell farther apart as she opened herself up to him.

The onslaught of pleasure became too much for Dillon. She heard the rushing of blood in her ears. It sounded like the roar of a freight train. His fingers were inside her, teasing her but not filling her. She needed more. She needed him. Inside her. "Damien." She moaned emphasizing each syllable. "Oh God Damien please." She pulled him by his hair. Crushed her lips to his. She tasted the sweet musky taste of herself.

Damien slid into her. He buried himself deep within her walls. Her muscles tightened around his entire length. He tried to say something but growled instead. His heart pounded in his ears. Dillon screamed his name. He felt her orgasm as it tore through her. His hips rammed into her at a frantic rate. He climaxed with such power it felt as if a jolt of electricity shot through his body.

For a moment, he couldn't breathe. His brain told his lungs to work, but his body was in shock. He rolled onto his back and pulled her into the crook of his arm. Dillon fit perfectly against his body. She molded to him as if God had created her just for him. She reached her arm across his chest and caressed him.

"My God, we are going to kill each other. I'm pretty sure my heart wasn't meant to beat this fast," Dillon said. Her breath came out in pants.

"A hell of a way to die. I'm damn sure I have a smile on my face, even though I can't feel my face."

Dillon rose on her elbow. "Yep, you have a smile on your face. Glad I make you happy."

Damien stared at her. Her eyes had a glow as if the gold flecks had been ignited with fire. His throat swelled. He wanted to tell her she made him feel alive, awakened. He wanted to scream he couldn't live without her. "You make me more than happy," he said.

Dillon snuggled against him and let out a satisfied sigh. He listened as her breathing slowed and evened out. Something had happened. He couldn't let her go now. She had gotten under his skin. No way could he go back to this life without her. Now he had to convince her she needed him as much as he needed her.

CHAPTER FIFTY-FIVE

Freestone Farm

News vans from every news agency lined the street in front of Jason's property. Reporters gave live updates with the house and property as their backdrop. Several reporters stood in front of the barrier the Waverly Sheriff's Department had erected. The deputies worked hard to stay ahead of the overzealous reporters trying to get through.

Joe whistled as he saw all the vans. "Look at this circus. I told you this would happen. These fuckers are so bloodthirsty. They'll give Jason all the press he has ever wanted."

The Deputy at the barrier studied their IDs and waved them through. Damien pulled in front of the farmhouse. All three stayed in the car for a few minutes, none too eager to start the day.

Damien smiled at Dillon in the rearview. "Hey, boss! You're in charge of this show, Dillon. I guess that's the perk of being an FBI Agent."

She glared at him. "Har—dee—har—har." Because she was FBI, and it was the Fed's warrant, she had to be in charge. Dillon would've gladly given that distinction to anyone else. She became a profiler to stay on the fringe. However, knowing she had procured the warrant, she prepared for this and had spoken with the head CST earlier that morning before breakfast. Dillon gave him a rough layout of where to start their searches.

Now as she watched the CSTs work, the head tech had proved himself efficient, if nothing else. He had his crews coordinating a grid search using three ground penetrating radars. She had also stressed to him the importance of the basement. All the samples they got would help tie each girl to that property and put another lock on Jason's cage door. "Well, since I'm in charge, why don't you two lug heads check on the perimeter and see what the ground search has come up with so far. I'll start in the house."

Dillon stepped down into the basement. The stench rocked her back on her heels. She covered her nose with her hand. Slowly she took in the gruesome scene in front of her. The techs had brought in some lighting so that no evidence would be overlooked. The bright lights showed every drop of blood, every piece of skin, and every other horror. The walls had more space covered with blood than without. Pieces of flesh and bone draped almost every surface. Knowing Amy survived seemed of little comfort to Dillon. She had to wonder how long it would be before this room quit showing up in Amy's nightmares. *Hell, how long before it didn't show up in hers?* Dillon knew they would never go away; Amy must learn to live with them.

A CST crouched over the drain. He had removed the chain and placed it in a box for transfer to the lab. He had the drain cover off, and he used a long squiggly instrument with a claw at the end and retrieved anything still caught in the upper portion of the pipe. The other CSTs collected samples of blood and tissue from the walls, cutting tools, and any other surfaces. They logged, tagged, and bagged everything. The CSTs also recorded every square inch of the basement on video before the evidence had been collected. Dillon stared at the clump of hair mixed with bone, tissue, and a bunch of other disgusting crap. "I'm glad I have a strong stomach. That shit looks nasty."

The tech peered at her over his mask. "Yeah, well the odor is way worse. It has to be the most revolting smell I've ever come across. I have so much damn Vick's VapoRub under my nose, I may never smell normally again." The tech placed the clump in a plastic container.

Dillon glanced around at the other techs. "Please make sure to take all the items that can be carried out of this room with you. I want everything from down here. I want to make sure this asshole never sees the light of day."

He smiled at her. "We will, Agent. I can promise you that."

Back up in the kitchen, Dillon breathed deeply. She sniffed her clothes and hoped like hell that smell was only in her nostrils. She wandered into the living area. CSTs covered every room. She had no reason to impede their process.

Dillon stepped out onto the porch. She watched the news vans on the street. She hated reporters. She understood they had a job to do, but some seemed to take great joy and delight in the destruction of lives. Dillon had learned about the media after her family's murder. Being a minor had afforded her some protection from the reporters.

Occasionally a news reporter had tried to bring up her past to push their stories to the front. She spoke with her Director that morning about the press conference and how she should handle it. She had prepared herself for the onslaught of questions about her family. Her boss said to take them in stride and just steer it back to the case at hand.

She closed her eyes and took a deep breath of the fresh, crisp air—with no odor of dried blood or rotten flesh. Heavy, determined footsteps lumbered up the front stairs. Dillon opened her eyes to find Sheriff Winsley stood before her. She smiled at him and extended her hand. "Morning Sheriff. Thank you for your help with keeping the news crews and others off this farm and the main one as well."

Sheriff Winsley smiled at her. "That's part of my job, Agent." He glanced around at all the work going on. "Listen, I know you have a ton of stuff on your plate. However, we need to go over a few things. Jason isn't talking. He hasn't asked for a lawyer, either. Hell, the man just sits in the cell whistling. What are your plans for him?"

Dillon stuck her hands in her pockets and rocked on her heels. "The FBI will be sending down a team in the next day or so. They'll take him into custody and transport him up to Springfield. You'll have him as a guest until then."

Winsley nodded. "Okay, that gives me some kind of time frame. Next, I'm getting phone calls from all the news channels, local and national. I've given them the standard response; *information will be forthcoming soon.*"

"Sheriff, I have the authority to hold a press conference. I need to gather some more information before I inform them of the time and place. I'd appreciate having you and some of your men, especially Mills, present during the conference. Will that be okay with you?"

Winsley's eyes widened, and he opened his mouth to speak then shut it. He hadn't expected the Agent to include him in the process. He'd never had an FBI Agent in command of any investigation ask him for his opinion. "Sure, Agent McGrath. I'm available anytime you're ready. Would you like to hold it in front of the farmhouse or in front of our station?"

"Your station will work fine. I'll let you know as soon as I'm aware of when. I'm going to check on the CST's progress concerning the searches." She glanced at her watch. "Give me thirty or forty minutes, and I will have a time for you." She walked off the porch, leaving the Sheriff stunned.

CHAPTER FIFTY-SIX

Damien and Joe stood by the techs operating the ground-penetrating radar. The tech had located four bodies already. Jason had buried them in shallow graves. However, the excavation needed to move slowly and with skilled care.

Damien called out to Dillon and waved her over. "Hey Dillon, come over here a minute."

"What is it, guys?" Dillon asked.

Damien pointed to a bunch of flags. "The techs have discovered four bodies so far. These are in the area described in the journals where Jason buried our first five girls, starting with Beth. We should have the fifth one pretty quick." Damien said.

Dillon spun around at the sound of a very excited tech calling for her. "Okay boys let's go see what we have over there." As they got closer to the tech, they could tell what had him so excited. The odor hit them at the edge of the roped off area.

"We have two bodies here. I can't give you a time line, but since this is a shaded area and our nights have been cool, the low temperatures have kept these from decomposing as rapidly as some of the others. These have a lot more flesh on them," he said.

Dillon raised an eyebrow. "Or Jason buried them more recently." That idea made her shudder. She kept her eyes on the Detectives. "Do you two think these could be two of the four that he mentioned in the journals?"

Damien rubbed the back of his neck. "Crap, Dillon, I sure as hell hope so. If there are more girls buried out here—we're going to have a nightmare when it comes to this news conference."

Another tech called to them from the far side of the search grid. He stood over a rather large area. "Agent, Detectives we need you over here."

Dillon's head snapped around. "Well shit, what the hell could this be?"

Carefully walking towards the tech, needing to walk around various markers, they trudged to the far side of the property.

Damien approached first. "What do you have?"

"We have what looks like three more bodies. Do you have any information about the number of bodies we're going to find?" The tech asked.

Dillon shook her head. No digging had begun in this area yet. "You mean just in this area," Dillon pointed, "you have three more bodies?"

The tech nodded his head. "Yeah, we're going to enlarge this search area. We have marked each body with a set of different markers." He pointed to the colored flags that littered the area. "A new color flag represents a new body."

Joe clenched his fist, and his entire body went rigid. "Oh, bloody hell. You've got to be kidding me." Joe exclaimed. "This bastard has been collecting girls for donkey's years. No wonder we had such gaps in time. He's filled those gaps with all these other ones." He waved his arm around the search areas. "How many bloody fucking girls are we going to find?"

Dillon steadied herself. This new development would turn their news conference into a ten-ring circus for sure. She placed her hands on her hips. "Alright. At this moment, we have five extra bodies. Maybe we have located those four referenced in the journals, the ones with no names or details, and now we have just one extra girl unaccounted for. Let's hope to God we don't have anymore." She pinched the bridge of her nose. "Will you do a quick preliminary scan of this entire area?"

The tech set up the grid search and went to work using the radar on this new area. Dillon watched as each body showed up on the scanner's screen. Each one of these girls frozen in whatever position they landed when Jason dropped them in the ground. The acid in her stomach churned. Dillon's voice cracked with raw pain and emotion. "The FBI uses Dr. Henrietta Mars, better known as the Bone Doctor. She's our leading forensic anthropologist. She will put faces to all these bones and get us their identities. Then we can get them home."

The preliminary scan revealed five more bodies. The techs set to work marking all of them and then started the process of removing them. Fifteen total. They were all in various stages of decomposition, some were nothing but bones. It would take several more days before the property would give up all its dead.

"Based on the journals and the DNA, we should be able to identify Beth Haut, Tracy Ford, Jill Macon, Wendy Bettis, and Jesse Franks straight off," Damien said. He continued to watch the techs work on the bodies. "It will take a few weeks for the rest of the evidence to get

sorted, and who knows how long it will take to get the other girls identified. We will have those five unsolved cases revisited as well."

Joe interlocked his fingers above his head. "Did you tell Dillon the
other exciting news?" Joe glanced at Damien, who shook his head.
"Well, our boss wants us to speak at the press conference. He wants the
Vicious Crimes Unit to stand as one united front with the local police
and the FBI. Won't this be fun?" Joe clapped his hands together like a
little kid.

Dillon's shoulder sagged. "Damn. I'm going to go speak with all the
techs and get updates on where everything for the investigation stands.
Then I'm going to talk to the Sheriff and the deputies concerning Jason
Freestone. I'll be back in a few."

CHAPTER FIFTY-SEVEN

Damien watched Dillon walk away. He glanced over at his partner. "What are you going to do about Taylor? Have you decided what you want?"

"Yeah, I told her she could come up and visit me whenever she wanted to." Joe saw the look on Damien's face. "What?"

"I can't believe you. You're scared. You know you want more from her."

"No—I don't. I'm happy with seeing her when she comes up. Plus, I'm not ready for a committed relationship. C'mon, you know me. And why the fuck do you care so much? Not everyone is a hopeless romantic like you."

Damien shook his head. "I'm not a hopeless romantic. And I don't care. If you want to fuck every girl in the damn state of Illinois, go ahead."

"If you didn't care, you wouldn't lecture me. Jesus, you're worse than my fucking mother. Just let it go." Joe glanced around then settled back on Damien. He knew he meant well, but he didn't want to discuss it anymore. "What about you and Special Agent McGrath? You going to marry her tomorrow? I'm guessing you'll be picking out china any day now."

Damien's eyes found Dillon on the other side of the property. He caught the stare from Joe, with a shit-eating grin on his face. Damien smiled at him. "You are such a fucker," Damien said with half of a laugh. "No, I'm not going to marry her. At least I'm not a *pollo*. I'm not going to shy away from whatever we may be trying to start. She's up for a transfer, but she doesn't know where or when. All I know is I wouldn't mind having her in my life."

Joe raised an eyebrow at him. "What about your position? Have you decided if you are going to stay on the force?"

Damien didn't look at Joe. He didn't want to face him. He lied. "I haven't made up my mind yet. I'm going to have to finish out this case and then talk to the captain." His thought trailed off. He hoped that satisfied Joe at least until he figured out how to tell him he planned on following Dillon where ever she went. Hell, he hadn't even told Dillon.

***

Dillon called out from the porch and motioned for them to follow her. When they were secluded far enough away where no one could eavesdrop on their conversation Dillon spoke. "First, the press conference is at four in front of the Sheriff's office. Winsley offered to inform the news crews." She motioned towards the street. "That's why they resemble a colony of ants scattering to collect supplies for the winter." Damien and Joe watched the commotion.

Dillon stared at the news crews as she continued. "We have enough time to speak with each of the parents of the five local girls. I want to let them know everything that the news conference will cover. I don't want them to find out the details from the media. They have to deal with the realization their daughters are not coming home. The last of their hopes crushed, they don't need to hear the horrific details from a red-lipped stranger on the five o'clock news."

***

Several hours later, the parents of the five missing girls knew how their daughters died. They took DNA samples from the parents for comparison. Damien told the parents that based on preliminary findings, he believed Jason buried their daughters on his property. He watched these parents crumble knowing what their daughters went through.

Initially, Damien had felt the parents needed to know everything so they could move forward in their healing. However, now he second-guessed himself. Even though the parents all wanted to know the details of what had happened, they weren't prepared for the reality of the horrors their child suffered.

Damien had been awestruck by Dillon. She didn't shy away from their pain. She held them, cried with them, and prepared them for the onslaught of media attention they were about to receive. Dillon gave each family names of counselors in their area that could help them through what was about to unfold for them over the next few months.

She gave each set of parents her phone number and told them to contact her if they needed any help. Anything at all. Damien worried that she took too much of their pain on and left a small piece of herself at each home.

***

Silence filled the SUV on the way back to Waverly. Joe's head rested against the back of the seat and Damien drove the vehicle as if he was on autopilot. Dillon sat and stared out the window. She wiped the moisture from her cheek and hoped that her eyes would dry before they reached the news conference.

Dillon glimpsed Damien's gorgeous face in the mirror, a face she wanted to see every day. She bristled at the thought of those lips touching someone else. Yet, the timing couldn't be worse. *I can't start a relationship. Who the hell am I kidding?*

She took a deep breath, wiping the last of the tears away. "Hey guys, I wanted to go over how the news conference will work. I'll start it off by filling them in on how the investigation started and that will introduce you two. After I give them some other information, I'll then pass off to you two. You can decide between the two of you who will answer questions. Then I'll say a few more things and hand it over to Sheriff Winsley. After some time for him to respond to the questions, I'll close it out."

Dillon sat up and stared out the window as they neared the station. "Be prepared for all kinds of questions. By now, they know who you two are. They've already done some research on you. Be prepared for personal questions. Understand that nothing is off limits to them. If they ask you a question about your personal life, you can answer if you want or you can steer them back to Jason and his farm. I have found that if you answer one or two of their personal questions, they tend to move on. If you don't know the response to a question defer to 'those answers will come later' or look at me, and I'll jump in."

Joe spun around in the seat. "They've already researched us? Why?" Joe asked.

Dillon turned from the window and saw a hint of fear in his eyes. "That's what the news does, Joe. They'll want to know all about you two. It'll help drive their story. If they can get a fresh angle to use to keep their story at the forefront, they will." A wisp of a smile crossed her face. "Don't worry. They'll concentrate on Jason. I just didn't want you thrown for a loop when they ask you something about your personal life."

Damien pulled in front of the Sheriff's office. They all sat quietly as they watched the chaos outside. Joe glanced at Dillon then Damien. "Ready? Let's do this."

CHAPTER FIFTY-EIGHT

Forensic Lab

Three hours later Damien, Joe, and Dillon sagged in the conference room chairs. No one said a word. The stillness and quiet that surrounded them came as a welcome relief after the chaos of the news conference. Damien and Joe had fielded questions about this case and the Vicious Crimes Unit.

At one point, the reporters had seemed very interested in the three investigators. Several times Damien and Joe deflected personal questions and steered them back to the dead girls and their killer. Damien gave lots of credit to the Waverly Sheriff's Department and Deputy Mills, as well as all the Sheriff's departments that had assisted them since they started investigating this case.

Matt smiled as he walked into the room. "Hey guys, the whole lab watched your press conference. You three were totally dope. Agent McGrath, you had them eating out of your hand. Quite impressive."

"Hey what about us?" asked Joe.

"You and Damien were okay," Matt said with a grin. "All three of you seemed like you did this kind of thing in your sleep. The camera loves you. They keep showing all three of your pictures on the news as they talk about the story as well as each of you. You guys are major vid stars now." Matt winked at Dillon.

Damien's head sagged. "Great, my Mom will be calling any minute." His phone rang. "Madre. What did I tell you?" He answered, "Hey Mom, what's up? *Sì, che era Joe e io.* No, we're fine. *Mi dispiace sì lo so che eri preoccupato.* No mamma..." Damien's voice trailed off as he went down the hallway.

Joe laughed for several minutes. "His Mom will bug the living shit out of him for like a week now." Joe's phone rang. "Well crap, just shoot me in the head now." As he answered, Dillon and Matt stifled their laughs. He gave each a hard glare that would stop most in their tracks. Unfortunately, for Joe, it added to their hysterics.

"Hey *mam*, yes go *raibh mé agus* Damien. I know sorry but, well I've been a little busy ma..." Joe slinked down the hall as he talked to his mother. Dillon and Matt could no longer contain themselves.

Damien came back into the room to Matt and Dillon's hysterical laughter. "Where's Joe?" Damien plopped in the chair, running his hands through his hair. He scowled as their laughter erupted with a new vengeance.

Regaining some composure, Matt managed a squeaky answer. "His Mom called. He wasn't happy and didn't like us laughing at him." Matt wiped away tears. "What happens now, guys? How long do you stay?"

Damien spun around in his chair. "Joe and I will head back tomorrow. We're having a news conference with our Captain in the afternoon. We'll be back for the trial or any preliminary hearings. We'll take care of most things from Chicago."

"How about you Dillon, where do you go," Matt asked.

"Hmm—what?" Dillon smiled at Matt and Damien. "Sorry—what do you need?"

Matt cocked an eyebrow at her. "Where do you go next, and when do you go?"

Her eyes fixed on Damien. "Oh, I'm waiting to find out. My boss just sent me a message, said to expect his call in a few minutes." She pulled down the evidence from the boards when her phone rang. She winked at Damien as she walked out the door.

Joe strolled back into the conference room. He glared at Matt, causing him to let out a muffled snort. "Matt we're all going to the bar tonight. Why don't you come, bring your girlfriend, and hang with us awhile? We'll get a shitload of food, eat, drink and try to get back to normal." Joe finished putting the evidence in the box.

An enormous smile spread across Matt's face. "That sounds like a plan. She gets off from her shift at nine. I can have her meet me there if I can ride over with you guys?"

"No problem," responded Damien.

Matt grabbed the evidence box to put in storage. "I'll be right back."

Damien sat waiting for Dillon and Matt to get back to the room. Joe fiddled with his phone, no doubt sexting with Taylor. Damien's phone chirped. He cursed at the screen. "That's it."

"What's up?" Joe asked.

"Mrs. C. has gone too far. I have got to rescue Coach from her."

"Come on, what did she do now? Can't be that bad." Joe asked disbelieving that Mrs. C. could do something that would rile Damien up that much.

"Yes, it is. It's bad." Damien held up the phone for Joe to see.

Joe nearly fell out of his chair. "Okay, I agree with you on this. She can't put him in that. It's sacrilegious." He continued to laugh.

Matt entered. "What's so funny? What did I miss?"

Joe nodded in Damien's direction. "He got another picture of Coach."

Excited Matt grabbed the phone from Damien before he could protest. "Yeah, let me see." Coach, who looked very plump, wore a Dallas Cowboys uniform, complete with helmet and a little toy football attached to his paw. "She needs to be stopped." Giggling, Matt held out the phone. "You know; you need to give her my number. I'd like to get those pictures. They would make my day a hell of a lot better."

Damien snatched his phone back and texted Mrs. C. He told her he would be home Sunday evening. She told him she watched him on the news and that she was proud of him. *How could he ever be mad at that woman?*

Joe noticed the expression on Dillon's face when she came back into the room. He gave a quick glance to Damien and nodded his head as he looked in her direction.

Dillon addressed the room. "Okay. They'll be sending several FBI Agents from the Springfield office to take over tomorrow. Matt, Director Jones already knows this, but you need to know it too. I spoke with my Deputy Director Sherman; these FBI Agents will not come in and trample over everyone. I explained we worked well with Sheriff Winsley, and they need to remain in the loop. If you have any problems or hear of any, tell Jones or call me and I'll get on it."

Matt nodded in agreement. "No problem. I'll keep in contact with the Sheriff Winsley to make sure your boys are playing nice."

Dillon grabbed her jacket. "Hey, Damien will you ride with me to the hotel?"

Damien glanced at her and then Joe. "Sure." He threw the keys to Joe. "We'll meet up in the bar. Get a large table or better yet, put a bunch together. Some of the deputies from Waverly are going to show up."

CHAPTER FIFTY-NINE

Just before Dillon reached the car, she threw her keys to Damien. "You drive."

"Okay." He snatched the keys from the air. He waited for her to get in the car. "Dillon, I know there must be something wrong. Are you going to tell me what it is?"

She wrung her hands and kept her head down. "Just drive, will you?" She said nothing for a few moments. "Deputy Director Sherman told me where my new assignment will be; effective immediately. They'll be announcing it later tonight or tomorrow when I get to the CAU. I'll be packing up my stuff up, and the movers will be moving me on Thursday. They've already lined up an apartment, and I'll be reporting next Monday for work." She didn't plan this. She had no idea this was even in the works. Dillon just hoped Damien didn't think this was the plan all along.

"Don't keep me in suspense. Where did they send you?"

She took a deep breath and let it out slowly. "Well, it seems Sherman thinks I handled the press conference like a seasoned agent, his words." She had to pause before she continued. Her pulse beat so fast she wondered if her heart wouldn't just explode. "His boss thinks that because of the way I handled this entire case, with Division Central, that I should be the FBI Liaison for—Division Central." She gave him a sideways glance and chance to say something. He sat stone-faced and quiet. "I'll be working with you, your Captain, and your other detectives. Your boss and my boss have concluded that we worked well together.

"They spoke with Sheriff Winsley, who told them how much I impressed him. Winsley let both our bosses know how the whole thing played out. The FBI has had a hard time deciding which profiler should work with Division Central. They needed someone who could work well with various police officials and divisions. After the way this case went down, they decided I seemed to be the logical choice. I'll be working out of the Chicago FBI office, but I'll be a regular at your division."

Damien showed no emotion while she spoke. He shifted in his seat, trying to get comfortable. He pulled the car into a parking spot and cut the engine. Damien had taken his time before he responded to Dillon. He turned towards her, and her expression shocked him. "Hey, what's wrong?"

"I didn't plan this. I had no idea they were even looking to assign a profiler to Division Central. You're not saying anything, so I can only imagine you think I had something to do with this. I promise I didn't ask for this."

Damien sat stunned. "Why would I think you planned this?"

Dillon's whole body tensed. "I don't know. You're just sitting there not saying anything." She breathed out a long hiss of air. "This is why I build walls around myself. I don't like putting myself in situations like this. Complicated situations. In no way will I let our personal life interfere with your work." She sucked in a breath of air. "Just because we slept together doesn't mean I expect anything from you." *Liar.*

Damien reached for her hand and pulled it to his mouth. He kissed her knuckles. "Are you kidding me? I damn well expect a hell of a lot from you. I'm not like Joe. Don't get me wrong. I love the guy and wouldn't ask for another partner or best friend, but I don't want the same type of superficial relationships he has. Whenever he starts to get close to a woman, he bolts the other way. But that just isn't me.

"I've had my share of one-night stands. And as much as I enjoy sex, I don't like just banging a different chick every weekend. I want the relationship that goes with it. This is the best news I could've gotten. I told you I wasn't avoiding whatever was happening between us. After all that shit that went down with Camilla, I haven't thought of having a serious relationship."

Dillon let out a huge breath. She faced him and wrapped her arms around his neck. She whispered against his skin. "I don't like feeling like this. I don't like depending on anyone, or feeling like I need someone."

Damien laughed. "You're going to have to get used to it. I'd already decided, Dillon, that if you got sent somewhere far away from Chicago and me, I'd figure out a way to be with you. I told you I didn't know if I wanted to stay in this job or not, but I would've followed you, wherever you went."

Dillon sat back, stunned. "What exactly are we doing here? What do you want from me—from us?"

Damien saw just the whisper of fear in her eyes. A silly grin spread across Damien's face. He chuckled. "Something happened this week. I don't understand when or what, but I know I want you in my life." His voice stammered. "I tried desperately not to like you. I tried to let all your annoying habits bug me. Instead, I found myself enjoying all those quirky habits."

Dillon stared at him. She couldn't get her tongue to work. She shook her head. "Do not even think of telling me you love me. I'm not buying that. It's not love. I mean seriously, we only just met. The sex is great, but it's not love."

Damien laughed. "Why does that scare you so much? The thought that someone could love you?" He grabbed her and kissed her hard. A kiss full of passion, desire, and joy. "Dillon, I don't know what the hell it is. Love or lust or both combined. I don't know. All I do know is I want to spend time with you. All my time with you, no other woman. And I sure as hell don't want you letting another man put his hands on you." He rested his forehead against hers. "Whether I stay in this job or work for my Dad, that doesn't matter to me. I want you. I need you, Dillon."

Dillon's heart fluttered. "I don't know Damien. After what happened to me, I don't trust easily. Letting myself trust this, trust you, it scares me." Silence filled the car. "If you think you have any feelings left for Camilla, I can't do this. We shouldn't even be doing this anyway. The complications of our working together and sleeping together will warrant some serious explanation to our superiors."

"First, you never have to worry about Camilla or any other woman. It's just you; it will always be just you. Second, there are no rules about us dating. Our superiors can't stop us. I think we are both capable of working together and sleeping together." *Plus, if it becomes a problem I'll just leave the VCU.* He said to himself.

CHAPTER SIXTY

One week later
Chicago

Over the top of his laptop, Damien watched Joe and Taylor as they sat on his couch. Joe sat on one side of Taylor and Coach sprawled on the other. Every once in a while, Taylor would stop rubbing Coach only to have him head butt her to make her start again. Coach laid on his back as Taylor caressed his fat furry belly. All four of his legs splayed out, giving her access to the most surface area.

Damien eyeballed Coach. Ever since Joe and Taylor had walked through his door, Coach had stuck his fat ass next to Taylor. Why wouldn't he? She hadn't quit rubbing some part of his fat little body since she got there.

Taylor had come up for a four-day weekend. Joe kept saying he just wanted to date and see her when she could come up to Chicago, but Damien didn't believe him. He figured Joe would realize he wanted more before too long. From many conversations with Joe, Damien witnessed the transformation slowly taking place. Taylor had woven her way into Joe's heart. Joe just hadn't realized it yet.

"Joe?" Damien said.

"Yeah?"

"The DNA evidence against Freestone has come back to the five missing girls. His DNA matched to the semen recovered from Becca Martin and Tiffany Basset. They identified two of the unknown girls as well." Damien read the update.

"Jason abducted them from a couple of towns located about a hundred and fifty miles away. Jason didn't write in his journals how he came to abduct the girls, and he still isn't talking. It looks like during a search of the farm the FBI found several barrels used for burning waste. They retrieved several belongings of the girls from the barrels."

"Was anything recovered that will lead to the identity of some of the girls?" Joe asked.

"I'm not sure. This is just a quick update from Matt. He says he will let me know more later in the week."

"Hey, I forgot to tell you guys," Taylor said. She now held Coach in her arms as if he were a baby. "I learned that Amy Custer stayed in the hospital for three days. She had a lot of physical injuries, internal." Taylor cringed at her own comment.

"That ass-kicking she laid on Jason in the basement tells me she will be strong enough to face that bastard," Joe said.

"Shit." Damien finished his beer. "I still hear Amy's screams in my head." He had regular nightmares about what he witnessed in the basement. Plus, Becca showed up now and then as well.

Joe kissed the top of Taylor's head. He looked at Coach as he slept in Taylor's arms. "That's not my baby," he said as he scratched Coach's exposed belly. "I have nightmares about Becca almost every night."

Damien frowned at Coach. "Taylor, you're spoiling my cat. I refuse to carry that lard ass around like he's a baby."

She smiled at him. "He is the sweetest kitty ever. I love him." She snuggled him closer to her. "How did everyone treat you guys after you got back to Central? Especially after the news conference," Taylor asked.

Damien got up to get another beer. A mirthless chuckle came out. "Everyone gave us a hard time about it at first. The worst part is the captain and the political machine that controls Division Central. They all seem to think Joe and I make the perfect poster kids for the Vicious Crimes Unit."

Dairy King turned serial killer had been the topic of choice for TV crime reporters and newspapers. If they didn't center on that, they focused on Damien, Joe, or Dillon. They all wanted to know about the beautiful FBI Agent. The FBI milked that for all it's worth. Dillon had given several news conferences herself from Quantico.

Joe took the beer from Damien's outstretched hand. "Hey, what about Camilla, has she continued to call you?"

Damien scoffed. "Not since I told her I had become involved with someone." Damien sighed. "The first call came right after we got back." He addressed Taylor. "Camilla asked to have drinks and hang out. I told her no and hung up. I hoped that would be the end of it, but she called back after that interview concerning the whole Unit. She begged, I mean begged, me to give her another chance. She kept saying how good we would be together." Damien drank his beer. "See before, as a lowly detective, I wasn't good enough for her status. Now that I'm a Lieutenant, and all over the damn news, I would do wonders for her career."

Joe patted Taylor's leg. "That interview has brought all kinds of old girlfriends out of the shadows. Good thing for me I didn't have any girlfriends."

Taylor snorted. "I can imagine how many of your prior bedfellows have come out to try to get a piece of your fine ass." She kissed him and continued to scratch Coach.

Joe's smile beamed at Taylor. "So back to Camilla. She told Damien that now they could help each other's careers take off. How much she missed him and loved him. Blah, blah, blah."

"Are you kidding me?" Taylor asked, surprised.

"Nope," Damien said. "She just wants what she thinks I can do for her. I would never go back to her, with or without Dillon. I told Camilla I wasn't interested and that I had become involved with someone else." He smiled a wicked grin. "I told her not to call me anymore and hung up on her. Hopefully, she gets the message."

Taylor wrinkled her brow at Damien. "What has Dillon had to say about Camilla calling you and wanting to get back together?"

A smile spread from ear to ear on Damien's face. "She reminded me that she carries a gun."

"I for one like Dillon so much more. Camilla was and is a bitch." Joe took a swig of beer and a smack in the arm from Taylor. "What?" He said. "If you ever meet her, you'll think the same thing."

"When will Dillon get here anyway?" Taylor asked.

Joe patted his stomach. "Yeah buddy, we're starving, we need to go eat."

"You're always starving. Try to relax, she'll be here soon. She said the movers had left and she finished putting her bed together so she wouldn't have to worry about it later tonight."

Joe snorted, and Damien had a twisted grin on his face. "You know she isn't sleeping at her apartment. I guess *she* just needs to realize she isn't sleeping at her apartment. I just want to go eat something, so I don't care where the hell she sleeps."

Taylor smiled at Damien. "Are you nervous about her being the FBI Liaison, Damien?"

"No, not at all. Joe and I talked about this."

Joe nodded. "She is the best liaison we could've gotten. Way better than some rigid asshole. The detectives in the VCU have already made many comments about her appearance. Stuff like 'if all FBI Agents were as pretty as her, more police personnel would be willing to work with them.'" Joe smiled at Damien.

Damien scowled at Joe. "Fuck you, Hagan. You aren't going to rile me up. They'll figure out she is mine soon enough."

Taylor chuckled. "Trust me, they'll know the minute you two are in the same room. I could tell you two had it bad for each other the first time I saw you together."

The doorbell rang, and when Damien answered it, so did Coach. He picked up the cat just as he opened the door. "Hey, gorgeous."

"Hey, yourself." Dillon reached out and scratched Coach on the head. "Is this Coach?"

"Yeah, Coach meet Dillon." Before he could stop the cat, he leapt from his arms into Dillon's. She caught him just before his fat ass hit the ground.

Coach rubbed his face against hers and purred. She looked at Damien. "I think he likes me."

Damien pulled her to him and kissed her passionately. "Someone once told me pets were a good judge of character."

THE END

Other books by Victoria M. Patton
Damien Kaine Series
Innocence Taken
Confession of Sin
Fatal Dominion
Web of Malice
Blind Vengeance
Series bundle books 1-3

Derek Reed Thrillers
The Box

Short Stories
Deadfall

If you enjoyed this book, please leave a review wherever you purchased the book.

ABOUT THE AUTHOR

Victoria M. Patton is forced to share her home with a husband, two teenagers, three dogs, and a cat. If she isn't plotting her escape, she uses her Search and Rescue/Law Enforcement skills from the Coast Guard and her BS in Forensic Chemistry to figure out the best way to hide all the bodies and write amazing stories about the murders. If she has any free time, she drinks copious amounts of whiskey and binge watches Netflix. Check out her blog **www.whiskeyandwriting.com** where she tries to help new authors navigate the indie publishing world. Contact her at **victoria@victoriampatton.com**. She is on most social media outlets, type in her name, you'll find her.